HOW COULD SOMETHING SO LIFE AFFIRMING TURN OUT TO BE SO DEADLY?

Why would Dr. Kate Martin suspect something was wrong with the miracle drug Genelife when the U.S. government gave it its blessing?

Why would she doubt the word of corporate head Michael Nolan when he had more than kept all his irresistible promises to her when she took the job he offered?

Why would she want to question Tucker Boone, the missing scientist who had discovered the secret of Genelife, and who was now declared mad?

Why would Kate worry about what Genelife could do to those who used it when she only had to look into a mirror to see how wonderful it made her look?

But behind the glowing lies about Genelife are the dark truths . . . behind everything Kate Martin wants is everything she fears . . . behind the miraculous mask of youth is the horror of death. . . .

SIDE EFFECTS

SIDE EFFECTS

Nancy Fisher

A SIGNET BOOK

SIGNET
Published by the Penguin Group
Penguin Books USA Inc., 375 Hudson Street,
New York, New York 10014, U.S.A.
Penguin Books Ltd, 27 Wrights Lane,
London W8 5TZ, England
Penguin Books Australia Ltd, Ringwood,
Victoria, Australia
Penguin Books Canada Ltd, 10 Alcorn Avenue,
Toronto, Ontario, Canada M4V 3B2
Penguin Books (N.Z.) Ltd, 182–190 Wairau Road,
Auckland 10, New Zealand

Penguin Books Ltd, Registered Offices:
Harmondsworth, Middlesex, England

First published by Signet,
an imprint of Dutton Signet,
a division of Penguin Books USA Inc.

First Printing, August, 1994
10 9 8 7 6 5 4 3

Copyright © Nancy Fisher, 1994
All rights reserved

 REGISTERED TRADEMARK—MARCA REGISTRADA

Printed in the United States of America

PUBLISHER'S NOTE
This is a work of fiction. Names, characters, places, and incidents either are the product of the author's imagination or are used fictitiously, and any resemblance to actual persons, living or dead, events, or locales is entirely coincidental.

To the loving memory of my father,
Seymour S. Fisher

"By wisdom a house is built,
and by understanding, it is established;
by knowledge the rooms are filled . . ."
—Proverbs

ACKNOWLEDGMENTS

A great big thank you to my agent, Robert Diforio, for his continuing guidance and support, and to my editor, Hilary Ross, for her perceptive insights.

I'm also grateful to my brother Dr. Robert Fisher for assistance with medical procedure. Any factual errors are mine, not his.

And hugs and kisses to my mother, Tema, and my daughter, Sarah, prime sources of strength and encouragement.

PART ONE
1982–1983

Chapter 1

It began with a low, deep rumble like distant artillery fire, and a far-off hissing. In the trees, howler monkeys whined and roared their displeasure. The rumble and the hiss grew louder; so did the monkeys.

Then the water hit the canopy foliage like bullets, and a shrieking wind tore violently at the treetops. Torrents of rain sheeted down, like a dam suddenly breached.

Tree limbs crashed to the ground; vines, torn from tree and earth, whipped around like frenzied snakes. Now trees themselves were falling, rending the air with thundering crashes as they dragged myriad vines and smaller trees down with them. Violent stabs of lightning cast a brief eerie fire over the carnage.

"Having a good time so far?" said Steve dryly.

Tucker Boone huddled under an umbrella-sized elephant ear leaf, protected from the actual downpour but drenched by the wind-whipped spray. "Where's Atalpa?" he asked tensely, pushing back the wet blond hair that dripped water down his forehead and into his eyes. The locals who had found them their Indian guide had assured them Atalpa was reliable, but who knew what might happen so far out in the bush?

Steve Kavett shrugged, but his brown eyes were worried. Atalpa often wandered off on his own to reconnoiter, and both men were always relieved when he returned. This anthropological adventure was turning out to be more than either of them had bargained for.

Whippet-thin, Tucker shivered in his torn and dirty clothes; before he'd come to Brazil's Amazona Selva, he'd never realized tropical rain could be so cold. They had pulled their packs under cover when they'd heard sounds of the approaching storm. Now he rooted through his gear

for a long-sleeved shirt, a scowl contorting his
features.

Their first rain forest storm had been exciting; was
three weeks ago? Exhilarated by the primal energy,
danced and cavorted under the trees, drenched to th
These days they simply squatted, damp and bored,
for the rain to stop and hoping nothing would fall on

An hour passed. Storms at this time of year we
pected, but the frequency and violence they'd encou
were unusual. Just four days ago, a huge tree had
down not twenty feet from them, jolting the groun
the force of its fall. Too close for comfort.

Suddenly Atalpa appeared through a curtain of
water streaming off his nearly naked body. He si
urgently to them with a raised hand; the rain incr
and he disappeared from sight.

Steve stared after him with a growing sense of di
Then he turned in the direction Atalpa had seemed to
cate, toward the bank of the narrow river where their
was tethered. A tide of thick brown water was ru
along the forest floor toward them. What the . . . ?

"Atalpa!" Steve leapt out from under cover, grabb
pack. "Tuck! Come on! Move!" The wind tore his
from his mouth, flung them up into the trees.

Tucker scrambled out into the storm, shoulderi
pack.

"The river!" Steve shouted. "It's flooding!"

They ran for the bank, slipping on wet vegetation
across the forest floor. The water was ankle deep and
Tucker headed for the canoe and began to untie th
that held it, straining, to a tree.

"Cut it!" Steve yelled hoarsely, and Tucker grabb
machete at his belt and sliced through the rope in a
blow, hanging on to it as he struggled to free the big
from the tree. "Atalpa!" Steve shouted again, but
was no response.

Around them the forest boomed and shrieked; the
was midcalf now, mud-brown and roiling. The cano
began to slip through Tucker's strong, slim fingers as
dark and bearlike, struggled through the water to
grabbing a handhold and pulling against the river cu
They stood for a moment, breathing hard. Steve co

Chapter 1

It began with a low, deep rumble like distant artillery fire, and a far-off hissing. In the trees, howler monkeys whined and roared their displeasure. The rumble and the hiss grew louder; so did the monkeys.

Then the water hit the canopy foliage like bullets, and a shrieking wind tore violently at the treetops. Torrents of rain sheeted down, like a dam suddenly breached.

Tree limbs crashed to the ground; vines, torn from tree and earth, whipped around like frenzied snakes. Now trees themselves were falling, rending the air with thundering crashes as they dragged myriad vines and smaller trees down with them. Violent stabs of lightning cast a brief eerie fire over the carnage.

"Having a good time so far?" said Steve dryly.

Tucker Boone huddled under an umbrella-sized elephant ear leaf, protected from the actual downpour but drenched by the wind-whipped spray. "Where's Atalpa?" he asked tensely, pushing back the wet blond hair that dripped water down his forehead and into his eyes. The locals who had found them their Indian guide had assured them Atalpa was reliable, but who knew what might happen so far out in the bush?

Steve Kavett shrugged, but his brown eyes were worried. Atalpa often wandered off on his own to reconnoiter, and both men were always relieved when he returned. This anthropological adventure was turning out to be more than either of them had bargained for.

Whippet-thin, Tucker shivered in his torn and dirty clothes; before he'd come to Brazil's Amazona Selva, he'd never realized tropical rain could be so cold. They had pulled their packs under cover when they'd heard sounds of the approaching storm. Now he rooted through his gear for a long-sleeved shirt, a scowl contorting his chiseled features.

Their first rain forest storm had been exciting; was it only three weeks ago? Exhilarated by the primal energy, they'd danced and cavorted under the trees, drenched to the skin. These days they simply squatted, damp and bored, waiting for the rain to stop and hoping nothing would fall on them.

An hour passed. Storms at this time of year were expected, but the frequency and violence they'd encountered were unusual. Just four days ago, a huge tree had crashed down not twenty feet from them, jolting the ground with the force of its fall. Too close for comfort.

Suddenly Atalpa appeared through a curtain of spray, water streaming off his nearly naked body. He signaled urgently to them with a raised hand; the rain increased, and he disappeared from sight.

Steve stared after him with a growing sense of disquiet. Then he turned in the direction Atalpa had seemed to indicate, toward the bank of the narrow river where their canoe was tethered. A tide of thick brown water was running along the forest floor toward them. What the . . . ?

"Atalpa!" Steve leapt out from under cover, grabbing his pack. "Tuck! Come on! Move!" The wind tore his words from his mouth, flung them up into the trees.

Tucker scrambled out into the storm, shouldering his pack.

"The river!" Steve shouted. "It's flooding!"

They ran for the bank, slipping on wet vegetation strewn across the forest floor. The water was ankle deep and rising; Tucker headed for the canoe and began to untie the rope that held it, straining, to a tree.

"Cut it!" Steve yelled hoarsely, and Tucker grabbed the machete at his belt and sliced through the rope in a single blow, hanging on to it as he struggled to free the big knife from the tree. "Atalpa!" Steve shouted again, but there was no response.

Around them the forest boomed and shrieked; the water was midcalf now, mud-brown and roiling. The canoe rope began to slip through Tucker's strong, slim fingers as Steve, dark and bearlike, struggled through the water to him, grabbing a handhold and pulling against the river current.

They stood for a moment, breathing hard. Steve couldn't

PART ONE
1982–1983

ACKNOWLEDGMENTS

A great big thank you to my agent, Robert Diforio, for his continuing guidance and support, and to my editor, Hilary Ross, for her perceptive insights.

I'm also grateful to my brother Dr. Robert Fisher for assistance with medical procedure. Any factual errors are mine, not his.

And hugs and kisses to my mother, Tema, and my daughter, Sarah, prime sources of strength and encouragement.

believe how fast the water was rising. The filthy swirl was nearly to his knees, and the current was incredibly strong.

"We can't hold her!" Tucker shouted.

"We've got to!" Steve replied. "Rations ... medicines ..." Survival.

"Can we unload it, carry it?" Each word was a struggle, a battle against wind and water.

With great difficulty the two men wrestled the canoe into a wedged position between two violently shaking trees and peeled back the tarp. Quickly they jammed the extra packs with essentials and strapped them across their chests.

"I think we should stay with the canoe," Tucker shouted above the wind. "Refloat her. We can't walk out of this."

Steve felt the water lap his waist; Jesus! "You're right," he said. "But keep the packs strapped on. In case the canoe capsizes ..." Can we swim with all this weight, if we have to? he wondered. And where would we swim to? "Okay, let's pull her loose!" Together the men refloated the canoe and managed to clamber in. The current immediately caught them, banged them against a tree, and flung them into the growing maelstrom.

"Where the hell's Atalpa?" said Tucker. "Atalpa!"

"Gone," Steve said.

"Gone?"

"Or dead."

"Shit!"

The canoe floated on the rushing flood waters like the Ark, constantly banged around by trees and floating debris. The men half sat, half lay, protecting their heads from low-hanging branches as they bailed furiously, Tucker with an aluminum cooking pot, Steve with a bowl. As the hours passed, more and more animals and insects appeared in the water beside them, swimming and floating, some living, some dead. A small monkey called to them from the top of a tree surrounded by water. Some distance away, a tapir crashed through the flooded underbrush. A caiman raised its head to stare at the canoe as it went by.

"Looks like we've got some passengers," Steve called to Tucker. A jewel-green frog and an assortment of insects and spiders had taken up residence on the gunwales and along the curved bottom.

"Fucking Noah," Tucker muttered. Two capybaras, large

swimming rodents, approached the fragile craft and he swiped at them with a canoe paddle.

"Leave them alone," Steve told him. "They're just curious."

"Sure they are," said Tucker morosely. Several minutes passed in silence. Suddenly he stopped paddling. "How about *him*?" he asked Steve nervously. "You want to let him have a look at us, too?"

Hearing the barely controlled hysteria in Tucker's voice, Steve looked anxiously through the rain in the falling light. Some way ahead, a large tubular shape undulated through the water toward them.

"Just sit still," Steve said as calmly as he could manage. "It'll probably pass alongside."

Both men watched tensely as the huge anaconda came closer. Nearly as thick around as a man's waist, it looked powerful and mean, but it bobbed languidly past the canoe without incident, its twenty-foot length distended and swollen around the midsection. The flood waters had caught it at dinner.

Still the rain fell and the water rose.

"This can't go on much longer, can it?" Tucker asked. Wearily, he scooped up yet another potful of water and emptied it over the side. They were afloat, but just barely.

"Who knows?" Steve told him. "Down here, rivers can rise as much as forty feet in a few hours. Franklin said when he was in Costa Rica six years ago, he had to swim over submerged bridges to get back to the research station at Finca la Selva." Franklin was a popular professor at B.U., and had supplied many of the contacts through which Steve had designed their trip.

"That's reassuring," drawled Tucker glumly. He looked around; wherever they were didn't look a whole hell of a lot different from wherever they'd been. The rain, which had tapered off a little, suddenly intensified.

"Where are we headed?" he called, bailing furiously. "You're the anthropologist. Any ideas?"

"I don't know," Steve shouted back over the scatter-shot sound of pelting rain. "I think maybe the river's reversed its course. They do that sometimes, down here. According to the compass, we're going sort of southwest." He paused. "I'm not sure we're even *on* the river anymore."

For a while both men continued to bail in silence. Finally Tucker spoke.

"What's southwest of where we were?" he asked.

"Nothing," said Steve.

Tucker Boone and Steve Kavett had been buddies for five years. Thrown together as lab partners in an undergraduate anthropology course at Boston University, the two men eyed each other warily at first. Steve knew Tucker mostly by reputation: brilliant, moody, reckless; a shooting star. "And don't let the 'shucks, Ah'm jest a country boy' stuff fool you," a female friend warned him. "That guy is sharp."

For his part, Tucker was envious at first of Steve's greater experience and sophistication, but he soon came to admire his lab partner's powers of concentration, his cheerful optimism, his coolness under stress.

As they worked together, they found that despite their differing personalities and backgrounds—Tucker's scattered Southern family traced its ancestry back to Daniel Boone, a fact Tucker played for maximum effect; Steve's Armenian grandfather had changed "Kevorkian" to "Kavett" when he'd arrived in America some sixty years earlier—they had a number of important things in common: a love of adventure both physical and intellectual, the ability to use humor to shield pain, and a keen sense of the ridiculous. By the end of the winter term, they were fast friends.

They also shared a certain inner strength, born of familial trauma. Steve's parents were killed in an automobile accident when he was fifteen. He moved in with his uncle Avram, a theatrical producer, and finished the last two years of high school in New York. Avram urged him not to return to Boston for college, but Steve insisted; the return was emotionally stressful.

Tucker barely remembered his father, who left his embittered mother and three other children when Tucker was six. Raised in poverty and unhappiness, Tucker found escape both in books and the Kentucky wilderness. By fourteen, he was living in a shack he'd built in the woods. A sympathetic teacher tracked him down, lured him with books, tutored and encouraged him. Now he was attending Boston University on a full scholarship, with a chip on his shoulder and a deep, hidden vulnerability.

Female classmates found them an interesting contrast. The dark-haired, romantic-looking Steve was a cultured, amusing companion, cuddly and emotionally accessible. He was sexy but safe. Tucker, on the other hand, carried about him a sense of concealed danger that many young women found quite heady. His lean blond good looks, down-home charm, and academic brilliance, coupled with a certain remoteness and a sardonic wit, offered a sexual challenge.

Together the two men aced the course and fieldwork of a shared major in anthropology. During school breaks, Tucker took Steve on wilderness camping trips, and Steve introduced Tucker to Avram and the world of New York theater. They worked hard and played harder, partying, drinking, and womanizing, until the winter weekend during their junior year when Steve introduced Tucker to his sister Marianne. The partying continued but the womanizing ceased; Tucker was in love.

Steve was dismayed. Tucker was his best friend. But he knew Tucker's mercurial, obsessive side, and he didn't want his sister hurt. He tried to dissuade Marianne, but she was furious with him, and reluctantly Steve backed off. Marianne was two years older; he had to agree that at nearly twenty-three, she had the right to make her own decisions. He watched their blossoming romance with unease. But much to his surprise, Tucker and Marianne remained committed to each other. And to his relief, Marianne never told Tucker of his original opposition to the match.

At the start of their senior year, Tucker had abruptly forsaken anthropology for biochemistry. After graduation, he'd enrolled at MIT and had recently been awarded his doctorate. Though unwilling to commit to one of the numerous job offers he received, he and Marianne were planning to marry soon.

Steve remained loyal to his original choice of major, and was now teaching at Boston University while pursuing his own doctorate. It was in search of a subject worthy of his dissertation that Steve decided to come to the Brazilian rain forest for several months, planning to contact some of the lesser-studied Indian tribes.

When Tucker offered to accompany him, Steve was surprised but delighted. "You sure you're up for this?" he warned Tucker, thinking not only of the hardships of the expedition itself but of Tucker's mood swings.

"It's just what I need," Tucker assured him. "I've been hitting the books too hard lately. I can use a little R & R ... give me a chance to think about what I want to do next."

"What about Marianne?" Steve heard himself ask.

"She won't mind," Tucker assured him. "Probably be glad to get rid of me for a while." He paused. "I've been kinda restless lately."

"Well, I'd be happy to have you along," Steve admitted. "But this really won't be an easy trip ..."

"Hell, I come from pioneer stock," Tucker interrupted with an infectious grin. "Remember those camping trips back in college? We'll have a blast!"

How many days had passed since the flood waters had receded, stranding them, starving and feverish, somewhere in the Amazona Selva? They'd lost count. The air was dank and thick, the humidity oppressive, the tiny black flies voracious.

Food was all around them, they knew, yet neither man was willing to bet his life on his ability to tell the edible from the poisonous. The symptoms of intestinal parasites had drained and dehydrated them; they took what medicines they had and hoped for the best. Flies tormented them; insect bites itched and festered.

They had no way of knowing how far they'd drifted, or where the nearest settlement might be. The region they were in was thick with vegetation and crisscrossed with swampland. The Amazon River was far to the northeast, but how far? They'd traveled some four hundred miles before the flood had caught them; how much farther might the waters have taken them?

When Tucker suggested they try to walk out by heading in the direction of the Amazon, Steve smiled bleakly. With a guide, their chances were slim; without one, there was no way they'd make it. Still, using Steve's compass, they trekked northeast. There was nothing else to do.

When darkness came they retreated under the thin nylon camping tarp, surrounded by the flickering green glow of fluorescent insects and the cries, shrieks, barks, rasps, and twitters of nocturnal creatures.

"What are the chances there are people around here?" Tucker asked one night.

Steve shrugged. "Who knows?"

"But there might be. There might be Indians."

"Sure, there might be. But you'd never find them. Not if they don't want to be found."

Tucker scratched at a sore on his arm, drawing blood. "Wasn't that why we came to this damn place? To find undiscovered Indians?"

Steve shook his head. "Not undiscovered. We were looking for tribes like the Mayoruna, the Guaja ... remote but occasionally accessible. Tribes whose locations we more or less know ..."

"Well, somebody had to discover the Guavas ..."

"Guaja."

"Whatever."

"There might not be any Indians within two hundred miles of us."

"Or they might be a hundred feet away from us right now."

They fell silent; the thought was both reassuring and chilling.

"That little trail we saw today," Steve said at last. "We thought it was an animal track. Maybe we were wrong."

"Maybe."

Steve's head was muzzy with fever. The track had led into the swamp. There were flat high areas in the swamp. What had he read about such dry, flat areas? "Remember that expedition in Surinam, back in the sixties? The one where they discovered the Akuriyo?"

Tucker shrugged; his college anthropology courses seemed a long time ago.

"The Akuriyo camped in the swamp," said Steve. "On the dry, flat areas."

The men fell silent.

"We could bait the trail," Steve said at last.

"Damn right we could," Tucker agreed.

Next morning, they hung their battered aluminum pot from a looped vine at chest height along the faint, narrow track. It was still there when they checked the trail at nightfall. And it winked at them in the thin shards of early morning sun that stabbed through the canopy of trees the following day.

"Someone's been along here," Tucker said, stooping to

examine the trail. "Someone or something. Why didn't they take it?"

"Maybe they don't know what it is," Steve said, "Pour some water in it."

By dusk on the second day, the pot was gone. In its place was a small roughly woven basket containing three purple fruit.

The rhythmic drumming that had abruptly ceased while the young chief and his wife took deep draughts from the ceremonial calabash now began again as the brew was handed to the outer circle of Indians. Each man in turn put the calabash to his lips, then passed it along to his left.

Tucker shuddered at the calabash's slow but inexorable approach. He and Steve had lived among these primitive hunters and gatherers for nearly three months, during which time he'd learned to survive on such delicacies as mashed caterpillar larvae. But he didn't think he'd be able to bring himself to drink the thick, glutinous stuff in the calabash. It smelled incredibly foul, even at this distance.

Two teenage boys, selected with much fanfare earlier in the ceremony, now took up positions just behind the chief. Apparently they had not been invited to partake of the odoriferous brew. Lucky them, thought Tucker. Although their parents don't seem to think so.

Now the Indian on Tucker's right received the calabash, holding it reverently in both hands. The smell was nearly overpowering, and Tucker looked away, eyes watering. A sharp jab in the ribs swung him back toward the Indian, who gave Tucker a meaningful stare and shook his head violently, pressing his fingers against his mouth. Then he lifted the calabash to his lips, held it there, and lowered it. Again he looked sternly at Tucker and shook his head, hitting his mouth several times with the flat of his hand.

"Don't drink!" Steve hissed at him from across the circle. "He's telling you not to drink!"

Tucker shot him an ugly stare. "I know what he's telling me!" he hissed back.

Steve looked at the scene around him, trying to memorize every detail. The children's frightened screams when he and Tucker had first entered the Indian camp had convinced him these people had never seen a white man before. Since then he'd realized they'd never had contact with

other Indians, either. They were completely isolated, and
had been for centuries, perhaps forever. Short of stature
and constantly dirty from wading through swamp water to
their campsites, they were essentially a stone-age people.
They'd even lost the art of making fire, if indeed they'd
ever possessed it; they carried smoldering embers wrapped
in leaves as they moved from place to place. Their bodies
smelled like the smoked meat that formed the mainstay
of their diet. They believed they were the only people in
the world.

The tribe, about a hundred strong, was constantly on the
move in what seemed to be a predetermined cycle of travel
through the rain forest; this place they were now camped
in was obviously a sacred spot to which they returned at
some regular interval. The compass had gone missing weeks
ago, but Tucker's innate sense of direction, developed during his country childhood, helped the men keep a rough
record of the tribe's progress. Steve's carefully dried notebooks were filling with observations. What a story he'd
have to tell! What a dissertation he'd write.

The calabash was coming around to his side of the circle,
and he repeated the gesture the Indian had made to
Tucker, indicating to the man on his right that he would
not drink. The man nodded gravely and passed the calabash. As Steve lifted the gourd to his closed lips, he wondered what it contained. Nothing the tribe had eaten or
drunk had smelled like this, not even the medicinal paste
they'd plastered on Tucker's festering insect bites.

As he passed the calabash along, he glanced around the
circle, noticing yet again the contrast between the strong
young chief, resplendent in his white egret-feather head-
dress, and the other members of the tribe, most of whom
seemed older and more careworn. His eyes fell upon the
two sturdy youngsters squatting behind the chief. They'd
obviously been chosen for some honor, but what could it
be? Increasingly, Steve was troubled by the impossibility of
accurately interpreting his observations. He and Tucker had
managed to learn only a very little of the Indians' primitive
language; it bore no relation to the Indian languages he'd
studied in graduate school.

He still marveled at the ease with which these people
had enfolded them into the tribe. The gifts of gear to the
chief and the two shamans, coupled with an intense curios-

ity on the part of the tribal members, had certainly had something to do with it. But remembering how the Indians hadn't thought to hide the trail that had originally brought them together, Steve had decided his and Tucker's welcome probably had more to do with the Indians' lack of contact with other peoples and hence their lack of enemies.

Steve glanced across the circle at Tucker, dirty, under-nourished, exhausted. He knew he himself looked no better, but still he experienced a familiar stab of guilt. He was responsible for his friend's condition. Whenever Tucker struck out at him verbally, as he had just now, Steve felt it was no more than he deserved. Adding to his guilt was the realization that when—if—they were ever able to rejoin the world they'd come from, this experience would be of major importance to his career. But of what use would it be to Tucker? Recently, Tucker had begun talking about running away into the jungle, trekking back to the Amazon alone. Crazy talk; despite Tucker's backwoods adventures in Kentucky, he must realize how impossible that would be.

The drums continued beating as the calabash was passed to the teenagers who covered it reverently with leaves and tied it with vines. Then they carried it between them to the chief's makeshift shelter and disappeared inside. As they vanished within, a thin, sharp wail of anguish echoed through the trees. Turning quickly, Steve saw the mother of one of the youths being roughly restrained by her husband. He frowned; why was the woman upset? There was so much he didn't understand.

The drums had stopped and the tribe was dispersing. Steve levered himself upright, knees creaking, and approached Tucker, offering his hand. Tucker glowered at him, rose slowly, and tottered off after one of the Indians with whom he seemed to be developing a friendship.

Steve looked after him, his thin, dark face creased with worry. During the months they'd been with the tribe, three people had been left to die along the trail. Two had been delirious with fever, the third mortally wounded during a hunt. No one had been surprised, no one had protested. A group constantly on the move in search of food could not afford to burden itself with the sick or the hobbled.

Apathetically he swatted at a cloud of tiny mosquitoes. They'd run out of quinine pills weeks ago, and the antibiotics were fast disappearing. He hoped he and Tucker would stay healthy enough to keep up.

Chapter 2

The steel blade slashed through leaves and vines, clearing a hip-wide path through the overgrown bush. The narrow file of men moved quickly and silently along the tiny, twisting trail. The chief grinned as he wielded the large knife. Such a wonder! The two teenagers, chosen in the sacred place, strode behind the chief in positions of honor. Exhausted by constant physical testing, they pushed themselves to keep pace with their chief. Just after them marched the two shamans in their conical leaf hats.

Steve and Tucker lagged behind this first group, passed at times by more vigorous members of the tribe. Six months had gone by since the calabash ceremony, and they were still hanging on, filthy, haggard, and undernourished, yet toughened by their ordeal. They'd discarded most of their clothing piece by piece as the material ripped, then shredded, then rotted away. Tucker wore ragged shorts and a cotton shirt from which he'd hacked the sleeves and collar. Steve was bare-chested. Their arms, torsos, and legs were scratched and bitten and scarred. Tucker's long blond mane hung lankly about his face and shoulders; Steve's dark hair curled around his head like a large dirty halo. Periodically they sliced at each other's hair and beards with a pocketknife and lied to each other about how well they looked.

According to Tucker's reckoning, roughly diagrammed in one of Steve's tattered notebooks, their track had recently brought them closer to the Amazon than at any time during the past nine months; now they'd begun circling back toward what he and Steve thought of as the sacred place, although no deity had been invoked during the ceremony they'd witnessed there.

Lately Tucker had again begun insisting that they head off on their own in the direction of the river; they might never get a better chance. Steve vacillated. After so many months in the jungle, he had to concede that discovery by outsiders seemed unlikely. But what if Tucker's dead reckoning was off? What if he went rogue once they were on their own? Stress and the trials of deprivation had exacerbated Tucker's mood swings and erratic behavior. There were times when Steve wondered whether the man was completely rational.

His thoughts drifted to Marianne and her intended marriage. His original qualms about the union of his sister and his friend had returned. He'd have to tell her—

He forced his thoughts away from home; it was simply too painful, and too remote. This tribe was his family now, the rain forest his home. It was the only way to survive.

Up ahead the chief had increased his pace, the w-shaped scar on his cheek a livid purple. He seemed excited. Behind Steve, men began to murmur. A small light gap appeared among the trees where a giant tree had recently fallen, clearing an opening in the canopy above. The chief stopped, his nude body radiant in the sudden sunlight. Aside from the shamans' headgear, penis sheaths and genital aprons made of fiber and leaves were the Indians' only garments. Steve smiled as he remembered the gasps of horror when he'd first peeled off his shirt; they'd thought the cloth was part of his skin.

Tribal members flooded up the trail past Steve and seethed around their leader.

"What's up?" Tucker asked, but Steve could only shrug as they moved forward along the trail.

When everyone had entered the light gap, the chief held up both his hands in a ritualized gesture, and the tribe quieted. Then he turned slowly in a circle, half chanting, half singing. Steve watched, fascinated; this was something new. When the chief had finished, the two shamans stood and chanted a response. Then they disappeared purposefully into the brush. Once they had gone, three others began to erect a shelter of sticks and leaves.

Steve stood riveted, and even Tucker seemed to perk up and take notice. Counting the makeshift lean-to in the sacred place, this was only the second structure the tribe had built in all the months they'd been with them.

Tension thick as mist held the rest of the little group quiet and unmoving. Tucker slumped against a tree, chin in hands, apparently deep in thought.

What's happening? Steve wondered. And why here? He looked around; the rain forest looked no different from what they'd been walking through for months ... or did it?

Gradually the people began to move, to talk, to relax. Yet the feeling of expectancy lingered.

Steve's curiosity was piqued. What had the men been sent to find? It couldn't be game; the chief hadn't sent hunters. It couldn't be food; everyone would have been told to gather.

Half an hour passed. Tucker, his mood improved by both the unexpected rest and this new ritual, came over and plopped himself down beside Steve. Around them, neon-blue butterflies dipped and soared, and large furry bees, emerald and ruby, investigated a deeply perfumed flower.

"Weird bees," Tucker said. "Kinda weird place."

"You think so?"

"Sure," said Tucker. "Doesn't it feel weird?"

"Not really."

"That's because you're not really looking."

"How do you mean?"

Tucker grinned. "I was born in the woods, remember? Just like ole Daniel. 'Raised in the woods so he knew every tree ...'"

"Not *these* woods," Steve told him. "And that was 'The Ballad of Davy Crockett.'"

"Fuck you," said Tucker pleasantly. "Now maybe you haven't noticed, but in most of the rain forest we've been through, the trees are all sort of mixed up. Some of them look alike, but they're scattered, they don't grow in a grove, like spruce or maple back home."

Steve nodded.

"Well, look around you."

Steve did so, then turned back to Tucker. "So?"

Tucker shook his head in disgust. "They're the same trees."

"No, they're not."

"Not all of them, but a lot of them. Some are skinny and some are thick, and some have different color lichens growing on them, but a lot of them are the same."

Steve studied the trees more closely. Yes, he could sort of see it now.

"And I'll tell you something else, city boy," Tucker

drawled. "All these trees that are the same? They're unique."

"How do you mean, unique?"

"I mean we haven't seen them before. Not anywhere in the rain forest we've been through."

"Are you sure?"

Tucker nodded.

"So what does that mean? Were they planted? Cultivated? By whom? Our guys don't go in for agriculture." Steve paused. "Is that why we've stopped here? Does the ritual have to do with the trees?"

"Beats the shit out of me," said Tucker laconically. "I gotta take a leak." He rose and sauntered off into the bush.

Steve gazed at the trees with curiosity, but he was no botanist. Whatever mystery they held would have to reveal itself through the tribe's actions when the shamans returned. Despite himself, he dozed.

A chorus of high-pitched whistles brought him suddenly awake some twenty minutes later. The Indians believed that whistling calmed the spirits of forest and the clouds, and the spirits of the dead. Thunderstorms brought on a veritable symphony of whistling, as did the rare sighting of an airplane through a break in the high canopy of trees. Rising quickly, he saw the two shamans standing at the edge of the small clearing. They were carrying large bundles of leaves bound with vines.

At the chief's gesture, the whistling stopped. As the shamans stepped into the circle of sunlight, the tribe drew back. Looking at the face of a woman near him, Steve realized it was not fear she felt, but reverence.

Slowly the shamans made their way to the rough shelter and gently placed the leaf bundles inside, out of sight. Then the chief's wife came forward. She'd unstrapped the sacred calabash she'd carried on her back throughout the long trek, and now she held it aloft. Then she returned to her place in the crowd, taking the dried gourd container with her.

Steve reached for his notebook and began to write.

The tribe remained in the clearing for three days. Apparently the presentation of the calabash by the chief's wife had marked the end of the ritual, for the people had immediately gone about the business of food gathering and making camp, completely ignoring the leaf bundles and the shelter. For several days, not even the shamans went near it.

"What do you think it means, Mr. Anthropologist?" Tucker asked one night as they sat beside the tiny tribal fire, tearing strips of smoked meat from half-cooked agouti and howler monkey carcasses. "You think the leaves are a sacrifice of some kind? You think they'll just leave them there when we move on?"

Steve chewed thoughtfully on a monkey paw. He hated when Tucker referred to him this way, taunting him for his lack of knowledge and experience, for getting them trapped in this impossible situation, for not understanding everything. Yet he'd been asking himself the same questions.

"No, I don't think it's a sacrifice," he said. "It's obviously part of whatever's in that calabash they passed around in the sacred place."

"So why don't they hold the ceremony here?"

Steve shrugged. "This is the collection place, that's all. You said these trees were unique. Maybe this is the only place they can get the leaves."

Tucker shrugged. "Maybe. So what?"

"Come on, Tuck. You obviously have some idea—"

But Tucker was silent.

"Well, we do know it's connected to the calabash ceremony," Steve said.

"I guess so," Tucker said, reaching for more meat. "But . . ."

"But what?"

"Nothing. Forget it."

Steve seethed. If Tucker had a theory, why didn't he share it? He pulled a last strip of flesh off one of the barely cooked animals and got up. The night was humid and fragrant. Still chewing, he walked to the edge of the clearing and looked back at the primitive scene around the fire. He felt a rush of affection, a protectiveness. His confidence returned. Yes, he thought. I *am* the anthropologist. These were simple people; how complex could this practice be? With time and patience, all would be revealed.

Around them, a number of tribesmen slumbered fitfully; others ate or chatted. A woman played with her baby. Steve had been amused to learn, early on, that the Indians treated nighttime rather casually, sleeping for a few hours, rising to eat or relieve themselves, joining an ongoing conversation, eating again, sleeping again . . . There was always activity within the encampment during the night.

He was rising to sling his hammock when a flash of movement caught his eye. As he watched, the shamans, carrying the hollowed shell of a large gourd, emerged silently from the jungle and disappeared into the shelter.

"Tuck!" he called softly, but Tucker was staring intently at the dark jungle beyond the dim circle of firelight. Resettling himself against a tree trunk, Steve watched until sleep overtook him, but the shamans did not emerge.

For most of the following day, while women gathered giant nut pods in the nearby forest and hunters shouldered their longbows in search of game, the shamans remained sequestered.

By late afternoon, the women were grinding the nuts and roasting the meal, then mixing it with water and baking it in the fire. Men sharpened the tips of their arrows with the agoutis' jawbones. Tucker had disappeared along the barely defined trail that led to a small nearby river. A feeling of restlessness pervaded the clearing. The air was thick and still.

Although no one had approached the shelter all day, Steve wondered whether his presence would be tolerated there. In the past he'd unwittingly broken several taboos and the tribespeople had been unusually patient with him. Early in their relationship, he'd tried to communicate that he wanted to learn from them, and he'd discovered that as long as he was respectful, they'd seemed flattered by his interest.

As he was debating the pros and cons of attempting such an investigation, he was surprised to see Tucker emerge silently from the forest and approach the shelter.

Tucker ambled toward the lean-to at a leisurely pace. He'd hoped his progress would go unnoticed, or at least ignored, but he could feel the stares of the tribespeople who looked up as he passed. He hesitated a moment at the narrow entrance as an acrid smell filled his nostrils. Then he ducked his head and stepped silently inside, blinking in the near-darkness. As his eyes adjusted, details of the scene before him became clearer.

Against the far wall of the shelter sat the two shamans in their conical hats, the hollowed-out gourd between them.

Into this one man threw a handful of shredded leaves, and the other mashed them into a glutinous paste with a short wooden staff, its end rounded and stained a deep reddish-brown. As they worked, they softly chanted a single sing-song phrase over and over, trancelike. If they knew he was there, they made no sign. Tucker was puzzled; when the women made the primitive intoxicant the tribe occasionally enjoyed, they spit chewed manioc paste and saliva into large gourds and allowed it to ferment. But the men weren't chewing, they were grinding. Why?

Now one man reached into the gloom and brought back a dipperful of brown river water that he poured into the mixture. More leaves were added, and the paddle was again applied.

Tucker's eyes were tearing from the acrid fumes; his throat felt dry and scratchy. Instinctively, he coughed. The shamans started, then leapt up, surprised and angry; the man with the paddle waved it threateningly. Tucker drew back, shocked. Yes, he was trespassing, but he'd seen Steve do so before without invoking anger, much less violence. These were a peaceable people; never had he seen even the threat of physical violence among them. Whatever he'd just witnessed was obviously far more sacred, more secret than anything he and Steve had observed—a fact which, despite his fear, Tucker found extremely interesting.

He backed quickly out of the entrance as the shamans hissed venomously at him, only to find his way blocked by a crowd of whistling tribespeople.

Beyond them stood the chief, a scowl on his youthful face.

The hostile crowd ebbed and flowed around him as he backed away from the shelter, unsure of what to do next. He looked around for Steve; if they attacked him, they'd probably attack Steve, too.

But Tucker was surprised to see that Steve didn't seem particularly concerned. He was looking around at the angry tribespeople, a friendly grin on his face.

In fact, Steve was both frightened and puzzled. It was obvious that whatever was going on inside the shelter was tied to the ceremony months ago, when he and Tucker had been welcomed into the calabash circle. So why this sudden, ritualistic secrecy? As an anthropologist, he knew better than to try to explain the behavior according to his own sense of logic; his reasoning was not theirs. But he deeply regretted Tucker's venturing into the lean-to and angering these people, on whom their survival depended.

Reassured by Steve's calm expression, Tucker approached the chief, his hands open at his sides, palms up; reassuring body language. He spoke rapidly in English, mixing in some of the Indian concept-words he'd managed to learn: friend, regret, respect.

"He doesn't believe you!" Steve called out, continuing to smile innocently at the crowd. "You've broken some taboo, and he's extremely pissed!"

"But I—"

"Shut up," Steve said pleasantly. Still grinning, he shot Tucker a warning glance as he shuffled slowly through the crowd toward the chief. As the people made way for him, he began to speak. Although they'd both found the Indians' language extremely difficult, Steve hoped he'd be able to get some vestige of meaning across. To his relief, as he spoke and gestured, the people began to laugh, and even the chief smiled.

"What are you telling him?" Tucker asked.

"Smile at the nice people!" said Steve, grinning widely. "Try to look like an idiot. I said you were looking for food. You thought they were cooking special food in there. You were hungry."

Tucker opened his arms in a wide shrug and smiled apologetically at the amused crowd. One woman brought him a piece of one of the hot half-baked nutmeal cakes.

"Eat it," Steve told him. "Make a big thing about it."

But Tucker didn't need to be told; he was already entertaining them, pretending to burn his fingers and tongue in his eagerness to eat.

"Thanks for saving my bacon, Steve."

"Anytime, Tuck. What would I do without you?"

"No need to get sarcastic."

"I mean that."

Night had fallen. The tribe had polished off a feast of agouti and nut cakes, and Steve and Tucker now sat on the ground a little away from the others, crushing the roasted bones and sucking out the marrow.

"I know I'm a real pain in the ass sometimes," Tucker said softly. "And I needle you with that 'Mr. Anthropologist' stuff. But you really are good at all this; better than I am. And you're a good buddy."

Steve put a hand on his friend's shoulder awkwardly. "You, too," he said.

Tucker sighed. "Sometimes I think you're all that keeps me sane. You and the thought of Marianne."

For a while they sat silently, side by side, thinking about home. At last Steve spoke.

"So what were they doing in there?"

Tucker shrugged. "Making a mash from the leaves. The calabash drink."

"The shamans were doing the chewing? That's unusual."

Tucker stared into the gloom and said nothing.

"Well, the good thing is, they've forgiven us."

"Yeah," said Tucker. "For now."

Just before dusk, the tribe had filled the giant calabash with the fresh mash and reenacted the sacred ceremony Tucker and Steve had witnessed six months before. The Americans had hung back, but members of the tribe had encouraged them to take up positions in the circle around the chief and his wife, as they had done the last time. The drumming, the ritual passing of the filled gourd, all was as before.

"We'll have to be more careful from now on," Steve said. "I've never seen them so riled up. I really thought we'd had it." He fell silent, thinking yet again of the precariousness of their situation. "Maybe you're right about heading out on our own," he said at last. "That small river . . . we could trace it back to something bigger . . ." He tossed away the remains of his bone and rubbed the grease on his feet. "We've learned a lot from these guys. We have our own bows and arrows. Maybe we *can* make it."

Tucker stared thoughtfully into the darkness.

"How about it?" Steve asked. Tucker had perked up considerably since they'd arrived at the light gap. For the first time in many months, Steve felt he might be able to depend on his friend again. "How about it?" he repeated.

"I don't think so," Tucker said finally. "You were right when you said we wouldn't stand much of a chance without a guide."

Steve looked over in surprise. "That's a new tune."

"Yeah, I know. But . . . look, I saw something in the jungle today when we were hunting. They saw it, too."

Tucker gestured with his chin in the direction of a small group of hunters busy picking lice out of each other's hair beside the dying fire. "Somebody's out there."

For a moment Steve was deeply angry. Why hadn't Tucker told him before? Then the implications of the statement overwhelmed him. "You actually saw someone?" he asked excitedly.

"No, but I saw their track. Scraped bark. A cleanly cut vine."

"A large animal, maybe?"

"Do large animals use knives to cut vines to get a drink? No, there are people out there."

"Indians?"

"Could be. Maybe friendly Indians, maybe not. I don't want to go out there on my own and run into something that might be a lot worse than these little guys."

"I agree," Steve said. "Who did the hunters think it was?"

"Our fellas? They were scared. They said something about spirits. Dead spirits, bad spirits . . . I can't understand a quarter of what they say."

"I know. A couple of weeks ago, Kuna and I were talking—I use the term loosely—and I asked him why the tribe had chosen such a young man to be their chief. I mean, why not choose one of the shamans? He thought the question was a laugh riot. He and that other young stud that was chosen with him at the calabash ceremony, they giggled like anything. And then Kuna said—at least, I think he said—that the chief was old. He said the chief was the oldest man in the tribe."

Tucker swung round to stare at Steve. "He said the chief was old?"

"Maybe he said 'wisc.' I'm not sure."

"He must have meant 'wise,' " said Tucker. "The chief's not a hell of a lot older than we are."

"Right. That's what's so frustrating about the language. Meanings seem to keep shifting, you know?"

Tucker nodded. "Same thing happened when I tried to talk to Akua about those kids. Kuna and the other one. First I asked if the chief had adopted them. I used their word for 'keep' or 'have,' at least I think I did, I don't know."

"What did he say?"

"Nothing. It didn't seem to make sense to him. So then I tried to say 'Why do they make the boys do all that stuff,' or words to that effect."

"Did he understand?" Steve asked.

"Probably not. He told me they do it to see which one is the youngest."

"Youngest?"

"Or strongest, maybe."

"Well, 'strongest' makes sense."

"Yeah, as much as anything does in this goddamn language." Tucker yawned and massaged his shoulders. "Better get some sleep," he said. "Back on the trail tomorrow." He shivered slightly. "I won't be sorry to leave this place. Like I said before, it's weird."

"So somebody's out there ..." Steve mused as they strung their hammocks among the trees at the edge of the small clearing. He felt a thrill of excitement. Was somebody looking for them? Or maybe just looking around? Would they increase their chances of being found if they stayed with the group or struck out alone?

Tucker dug his fingers into the tattered side pocket of his rotting shorts. "Yeah, somebody's out there, all right," he said softly. "And the poor fella's got a rip in his shirt." Carefully he withdrew a small piece of blue cotton denim and handed it to Steve, who stared at it, wide-eyed. "I wonder if he knows the way home?"

Chapter 3

"Nine *months*?" The gangly American missionary shook his head in disbelief. He'd been called to his small, remote mission nearly six years before, and he'd seen what the rain forest could do to a man. In his experience, the survival of these two was nearly miraculous.

Steve nodded slowly. A day and a night had passed since Father Jim Hensley and his mapping party had surprised the tribe in the light gap as they were preparing to break camp in the early dawn, yet Steve still found it hard to believe that he and Tucker had been rescued.

Father Jim glanced again at the deep slash, barely healed, along Steve's forearm where an inexpert hand had gouged out—what?

"Screw worms," Steve said, and Jim's eyes slid away in disgust. "I opened the swelling with a penknife and almost passed out when I saw the thing. There were more on my back. The shamans sucked them out."

"You're lucky," Jim said roughly. "I've seen those maggots kill cattle in under a week." Again he studied the man before him: filthy, rank, and painfully thin, his skin loose and sallow and his eyes dull, his body covered with bites and cuts and inflammations. And his friend there was no better, possibly worse, with that twisted ankle.

Across the clearing, Tucker was hunkered down next to Kuna, doling out globs of the honey they'd found in the forest that afternoon. Their arms and necks were pocked with bee bites, but they smiled broadly; honey was rare.

"We've had hints that these people existed," Jim enthused as he and Steve watched the tribe devour the honey. "Other Indians in the area, people we have contact with, have a tradition that there are wild, bad Indians who travel through this region from time to time. They keep out of the way. They're frightened."

"Frightened of *these* guys?" Steve asked in some surprise. He looked around at the chief licking happily at the dollop of honey in his palm.

Initially the tribe had melted into the forest at the arrival of the mapping party, leaving Tucker and Steve speechless with emotion as they faced their rescuers. But even as Jim was embracing the two stunned and ragged Americans, others in his expedition were unpacking multicolored bracelets and small, sharp axes, shiny scissors, and bright red wool, scattering them on the ground and hanging them in the trees along the perimeter of the clearing. Curious, the Indians had peeped through the leaves. Then, unable to resist the trade goods, they'd drifted back one by one, drawn by the booty and reassured by Steve's and Tucker's presence. Within hours, all was as it had been before.

And as it would never be again.

Steve sighed, gratitude and relief mixed with uneasiness. He had an innate distrust of missionary zeal. And this middle-aged man with the baby face seemed so eager.

"You won't ... do anything to them, will you?" he asked tentatively.

" 'Do'? You mean, drag them back to the mission and forcibly convert them?" Jim smiled and shook his head. "We'd like to bring them in, of course. There's a small dirt airstrip not too far away; that's how we got here. We could fly them back. It's been done before, as you must know."

Steve nodded. He'd read a number of articles about "rescued" tribes. The thought sickened him.

"They'd get proper medical care, a balanced diet ... I can see you don't like the idea. Well, never mind. It's not up to us, it's up to them. And despite the attraction of bracelets and tools, I don't think they're planning to leave the jungle just yet."

"But mapping means development. What happens to them then?"

"Maybe nothing. If this area *is* developed, and that's by no means a sure thing, your friends might simply avoid it, go somewhere else."

"This place is special to them," Steve said. "It's ..."

"Holy?"

"Something like that."

Jim dismissed such primitive religious feeling with a wave

of his hand. "Sooner or later they'll come in to trade," he said. "Most Indians do. And after that . . ."

"Trade? That's ridiculous!" But Steve remembered the basket of three purple fruit that had been left in exchange for their pot of water.

Jim put an arm around Steve's shoulder. "Nothing stays the same," he said kindly. "Nothing."

"I'm not going back!"

"The hell you aren't!"

The two companions faced off angrily. Around them, the active night life of the encampment ebbed and flowed. Tomorrow the tribe would move on, along the pathways they'd followed for centuries, and Jim would fly the Americans to his mission. That had been the plan. Now Tucker had other ideas.

"Please, Tuck!" Steve implored his friend. "You're weak, sick, nearly starving. You can't walk far on that ankle. You'll die here."

"Kuna will give me hunting powder for the pain," Tucker said calmly. "I want to see the calabash ceremony again."

He's mad, Steve thought. What we've been through's enough to send any man nearly round the bend. And now the shock of being rescued has driven him over the edge. "You can't," he said firmly. "You'd never make it."

But Tucker shrugged and turned away. Steve grabbed his shoulder and spun him around. "This is crazy!" he shouted. "How will anyone find you, five, six months from now? This is the only place Jim can be sure of locating again, and the tribe won't come back here for a year."

"So I'll stay a year."

"You'll be dead in a *month*! Besides, there could be other places where they gather leaves. They might *never* come back here."

But Tucker was silent.

Steve sighed deeply. It wasn't the ceremony that was keeping Tucker here. After all, Tuck was no anthropologist. No, the man had finally cracked. He had to get through to him, to save him from himself.

"Listen, Tuck. As you keep reminding me, I'm the anthropologist. And of course I want to know more about that calabash ceremony, too. But not this time. We just can't stay any longer." He put a hand on his friend's arm, but Tucker shrugged him away, then turned and limped toward a group of Indians squatting by the dying fire. Steve followed.

"We'll mount a new expedition," he promised. "We'll come back. But we have to go home and get well first."

Tucker lowered himself painfully to the ground, his ankle throbbing, and stared into the embers. "I'm just not ready to go home," he said flatly.

Steve clenched his fists in frustration. Suddenly the accumulated strain and fear of the past nine months came flooding out in a burst of rage. "Tucker, you sonofabitch!" he shouted. The Indians looked up curiously. "You selfish bastard! What about Marianne? You claim you love my sister, that thoughts of her kept you sane. Oh, right! Sure! *Look* at me, Tuck!" But Tucker had turned his face away.

Steve stood over Tucker, breathing deeply in an attempt to control his anger. "Can you imagine how she's been suffering these past months?" he continued more gently. "Hoping we're alive but believing we're dead? Are you really willing to put her through another year of that kind of torture? Are you willing to put *me* through it?"

Minutes passed. At last Tucker looked up at Steve, his gaunt face a mask of suffering. "All right," he said softly. "I'll come with you."

As a cool mist swirled through the campsite early the next morning, Steve rose from his hammock in time to see the last of the Indians disappear into the rain forest. Kuna, usually near the front of the file, hung back, but finally he too melted into the bush. Steve swung his legs onto the ground and experienced a sudden panic as he realized Tucker's hammock was empty, but soon his friend emerged from the forest, buttoning the fly of the khaki shorts Father Jim had given him. Both his ankle and his spirits seemed much improved. The cocainelike tree bark derivative called hunting powder?

The missionary and his small team distributed a breakfast of biscuits and Cokes, then shouldered their packs. Home. They were going home. For just a moment Steve's elation was laced with an ineffable sadness, and he understood Tucker's reluctance of the day before, but then he thought: Home!

Jim checked his watch, then studied the tiny pieces of

sky visible between the treetops. "Let's move out!" he called, and the small knot of people unwound behind him and filed into the jungle. With an air of forced cheerfulness, Tucker stepped out after Jim, but a short while later, he dropped back and began peering with furtive eyes into the dense foliage around him.

Steve discovered that despite a certain sententiousness, Jim was good company. Trekking beside him along a widening trail that played hide and seek with the bank of a small tributary, sharing stories and experiences, Steve began the process of cultural return.

Now taciturn and glum, Tucker lagged behind, stripping berries off bushes and popping them in his mouth as though savoring the last taste of primitive living. Several times the little group was forced to stop until he caught up.

"Another hour or so, and we'll be at the airstrip," Jim announced at last. He glanced up at the tree-fringed patch of sky above the river; under the canopy, it was impossible to tell whether it was cloudy or sunny. "Hope the weather holds," he said. "The flight's an adventure even on a good day. Hungry? Have some chocolate." He handed a bar to Steve, then turned and called back down the winding trail.

"Hey, Tucker! Chocolate?"

Behind them, the track was empty.

They waited ten minutes, hoping he'd appear. When he didn't, they retraced their steps for nearly a mile, calling and searching, with no result except the loss of ninety valuable minutes of travel time. Jim was furious; Steve's eyes were wet with tears of frustration and loss. Finally they turned back onto the trail in silence.

They arrived at the primitive airstrip in a violent rain shower and took shelter within the plane; water drummed on the thin metal shell and cascaded down the Plexiglas windows in thick translucent sheets. Steve thought of Tucker and Kuna, crouching together somewhere along the trail beneath their elephant ear umbrellas, and of the Indian children who would be cavorting among the drops as he and Tucker had done so many months ago.

Eventually the storm moved on, and the small plane rose from the soggy ground. Its nose turned precipitously skyward, it lurched and yawed in the turbulent air currents. Below them, the canopy was a solid green; what lay beneath it, a continuing mystery.

PART TWO
TODAY

Chapter 4

"Code call, Three North. Code call, Three North."

Dr. Kate Martin was just coming off a long shift in the ER when the code came over the PA system. She'd been looking forward to a hot bath, some food, a little sleep. The scrubs she wore on duty in the Emergency Room were splashed with the blood of the last case she'd seen, a gunshot wound in the stomach, but there was no time to worry about it. A code call meant cardiac arrest. If you were anywhere nearby, you got moving, and fast. You did not pass go; you did not collect two hundred dollars.

She took the stairs two at a time—the nearby elevator would take too long—and almost ran into the crash cart as she banged through the stairwell door into the third-floor corridor.

A woman lay stretched on the linoleum tiles just beyond the nurses station. Four nurses crowded around her; one felt for a pulse; a second had raised an eyelid and was checking pupil dilation. Now a third nurse yanked aside the hospital gown, exposing the woman's chest as Greg, the senior resident, dropped to the floor and began doing chest compressions. Another resident Kate didn't recognize—Paul, according to his ID badge—was already bagging the patient, pumping air and oxygen into her lungs through a squeeze bag. Other members of the team were busy pulling equipment off the crash cart. They all looked up at Kate with relief; emergency medicine was her specialty, and she had a reputation for keeping her cool under stress.

Kate evaluated the situation in a heartbeat, as she pushed a strand of red hair out of her eyes. "Anything?" she asked urgently of Greg. He shook his head.

A member of the crash team was attaching an electrocardiogram machine; another had pulled the defibrillation monitor from the cart and was applying the self-adhesive electrodes. "Is she hooked up yet?" Kate asked.

"One sec."

Kate turned to a short blond resident named Ruthie. "Is she perfusing?" Ruthie slipped a hand beneath the woman's hospital gown. "Yes, I can feel a femoral pulse."

"Good. Let's tube her." The nurse-anesthesiologist, a vital part of the crash team, began inserting the endotracheal breathing tube. "Ruthie, run a new line," she told the resident; a fast look at the small IV already in place had told her it wouldn't be big enough. Ruthie immediately began swabbing the patient's arm with alcohol as she looked for a vein. "Anyone know this patient?"

"I do," Ruthie said immediately. "Maude O'Brien. Sixty-five. Diabetic. Admitted yesterday for amputation of a toe." She described the patient's history and status briskly without looking up, her hands busy attaching the IV tubing. A nurse pulled a bag of saline and glucose from the cart and hung it on the metal IV stand. Ruthie opened the tube stop and liquid began running into the patient's vein.

"Monitor's up."

"Good." Kate looked toward Greg. "Stop CPR. Any pulse?"

"No."

"How's the tracing look?"

"She's in ventricular fibrillation."

"Okay," Kate said. "Let's shock." She grabbed the paddles from the crash cart. "Clear!" she called, and everyone backed up fast. Checking carefully to be sure no one was touching the patient, Kate applied the paddles, one over the woman's heart and the other as far around the side of the chest as she could reach.

The patient's chest heaved upward as the electric shock surged through her body. Kate withdrew the paddles and looked at the monitor inquiringly.

"Nothing."

"Clear!"

Again, the chest heaved.

"Anything?"

"Nothing."

"Shit! Resume CPR."

Greg immediately restarted his chest compressions. The nurse-anesthesiologist was still squeezing a mixture of air and oxygen into the woman's lungs. "Give her an amp of bicarb," Kate ordered. Someone swabbed the rubber IV port with alcohol; someone else took a filled syringe from the cart and injected the solution into the IV line. A nurse handed Kate an electrocardiogram printout.

"Let's try intracardial epi," Kate directed. "Then we'll turn up the juice."

Again, the IV port was swabbed and the epinephrine was injected. The moment the syringe was withdrawn, Kate tweaked the dial to increase the voltage and grabbed the paddles again.

"Clear!"

Again the woman's chest heaved up, and the monitor suddenly came to life.

"Heartbeat has resumed!" Ruthie called, but Kate had already seen the pulse on the monitor.

"Is it perfusing?"

"Yes!"

"What's the rate?"

"Up to sixty beats a minute and stable."

"Yes! Paul, we'll need blood gases."

The young resident leaned in and begun pulsating the woman's wrist for an artery he could tap into. He looked scared. Drawing the arterial blood needed for measuring oxygen and carbon dioxide was harder than performing a venal puncture.

"Someone call transportation to the CCU," Kate called. "How's she holding, Ruthie?"

"Still sixty."

"Good. Got that arterial, Paul?" Blood welled from the patient's wrist; the young resident had already had several misses. He looked terrified, and his hands shook, but he gamely reached for the other wrist.

"Try the femoral," Kate told him. "It's bigger." She tried to keep the urgency out of her voice; the more nervous he got, the harder it would be for him to act effectively. A nurse lifted the hospital gown and Kate guided Paul to the large artery in the woman's groin. He got the needle in on the first try and his face registered profound relief as the dark arterial blood welled up into the syringe.

"Good work," she told Paul. "Run it to the lab." He stuffed the blood-filled syringe into a cup of ice and took off, moving fast.

Again, she checked the monitor; the heartbeat was up a little, and steady. The woman was coming back.

Transportation to the cardiac care unit arrived, and the woman, pale, unconscious, but alive, was loaded onto a gurney.

"Thank you, everyone," Kate said, beaming. "Strong work."

Later, showered, fed, and rested by a few hours of sleep in the hospital's on-call room, Kate stood before the staff-room mirror and applied her lipstick carefully. Then she stepped back and studied herself critically in the full-length mirror. Her long red hair now looked sleek and neat, pulled back and gathered into a black velvet ribbon. but she wondered whether the short turquoise dress looked a trifle too young.

Kate had started medical school at twenty-six, after completing a master's degree in biochemistry at Columbia and a year of study abroad. This had made her a good five years older than her peers, and a brief, failed marriage to a successful bond trader had made her older still, in terms of life experience. Now thirty-four and an emergency room doctor at New York General Hospital—at least for four more days—she was still somewhat self-conscious about the differences, age and otherwise, which separated her from her younger colleagues. Well, her age wouldn't be an issue in the private sector.

"Hey, Kate, you look great!"

Kate turned to smile at Rebecca Klein, an acquaintance from medical school who was now a pediatric attending. "So you're really leaving us," Rebecca said, rummaging in her locker and extracting a pair of black high-heeled shoes.

Kate nodded, wanting to make conversation with this friendly woman, but unsure of what to say. "You're coming to the party?" she murmured at last. Of course she's coming, dummy. Why else is she changing her shoes?

"Wouldn't miss it!" Rebecca chirped. "At the Stanhope, no less! But then, you're classier than the rest of us."

Meaning "different," Kate thought. "Oh, that's not true!" she protested. "It's just ... I wanted to make it special."

"Special it will be!" Rebecca agreed. "A real treat!" She hesitated, about to suggest she and Kate share a cab downtown. But Kate had always been rather reserved, even back in school. Never snobby; just sort of . . . separate. Rebecca decided not to intrude. "See you later!" she said brightly, and scampered off.

As a battered yellow taxi carried Kate through the rush-hour traffic toward the Stanhope Hotel, she thought about the new world she would enter the following week, and what it would mean. As corporate medical consultant to a small but growing pharmaceutical company, she'd have the chance to combine medical training with pure science. Being based in an office rather than a hospital meant no on-call nights; she'd have plenty of time to indulge her passion for the theater and the ballet. She'd buy a new wardrobe; green scrubs obviously wouldn't be appropriate at Randall Webber. It would be a whole new beginning.

Her decision to abandon the hands-on practice of medicine had not been taken lightly. And in fact, when the executive recruiter had called her, she'd turned him down flat. But she hadn't been happy at the hospital for several years, and she knew it wasn't the hospital's fault. Correctly or not, she had always felt somewhat of an outsider.

For some time now, her life outside the hospital had not been particularly rewarding either, and a typically heavy workload left her little time to attempt to improve it. She felt stale, bored, at a standstill. Life was passing her by.

A job in the private sector might be just what she needed to put her work and her life in perspective. And as the recruiter had pointed out when she'd called him back, she could always return to medicine at any time. In fact, the retiring medical consultant she'd be replacing had always maintained an office and a small practice, even while working for Randall Webber. She could do the same if she wished.

Traffic was heavy, and it was nearly six-twenty when she jammed a five-dollar bill into the small plastic slot in the bulletproof plastic panel separating her from the driver, and hurriedly pushed open the door of the cab.

"Doctor Kate!"

Kate turned. A second taxi had drawn up behind hers and deposited a small, gray-haired, impish-looking man on the sidewalk.

"Harold! I'm so glad you could come!" she said, smiling with genuine joy.

Dr. Harold Gould was one of her great favorites at New York General. Professor of a brutally difficult gross anatomy class Kate had taken as a medical student, he'd become both her clinical tutor and an encouraging and empathic mentor. It was he who'd suggested she do her residency at General, and later urged her to accept the staff position the hospital had offered her. She felt more comfortable with him than anyone else she'd worked with.

Together they pushed through the brass doors and headed for the large paneled room that housed the Stanhope Bar.

"It wouldn't be a celebration without you," she told him.

"I'm not sure that losing you is something I want to celebrate, exactly," he said with a smile. "But I appreciate the sentiment."

Part of the room had been set aside for Kate's party, and they headed that way, settling themselves in the leather chairs and ordering drinks.

"So you start on Monday," Gould said. "Excited?"

"Of course! But I'm a little scared, too. It's going to be so ... different."

"Isn't that part of what you like about it?" he asked gently.

"Well, yes," Kate admitted. She paused. "You don't think I'm abandoning ship, do you? A lot of people seem to feel that way."

Gould shrugged. "A few people, maybe. We ivory tower types automatically look down on the corporate world, even though we're happy to accept all the free drug samples they care to send us. Don't let it bother you. Besides," he added, "I think it'll be good for you. You're not happy here."

"It shows?"

"Only to me." He smiled reassuringly. "And as I said when you first told me about the job at Randall Webber, I think you can make a significant contribution. What's that new product you're going to be working with?"

"It's ... confidential," Kate told him, blushing. "Frankly, even I don't know much about it, yet. But it's a sort of prescription cosmetic. Does that sound horribly trivial?"

Ignoring the question, Gould pretended to scan the room for newcomers. It did sound trivial, but he hardly liked to say so. Kate deserved her chance. "What does your father say?" he asked at last.

A retired dermatologist, Kate's father had decamped to Florida with her vibrant, socially active mother eight years before.

"Strangely enough, he's all for it," Kate replied. "I've bounced around so much over the past ten years, I was sure he'd want me to stay put. But he thought it was a great idea. I think he was a little surprised they actually wanted to hire me. I'm not exactly the most experienced person they could have chosen. I think he was impressed."

"So was I," Gould told her. A background that combined science and medicine seemed ideal for a company such as Randall Webber, yet Kate was relatively junior; he too had been surprised that she'd been offered the job.

He signaled to the waiter for refills. "Now you stay in touch," he ordered her over his shoulder. "You're a fine doctor. Don't disappear on me. Hey, there's Rebecca Klein. and Ken Stone . . . who's that with him? Lisa Braun? She sure looks different out of whites. Well, let the festivities begin!"

Her eyes alight with happiness and anticipation, Kate rose and went to greet her guests.

Forty blocks away at the Harvard Club, another party was in full swing.

Michael Nolan, recently appointed CEO of Randall Webber, was hosting a retirement celebration for Dr. Nicholas Butler, the man Kate would replace.

"More champagne, sir?"

Nolan gave the waiter a regal nod; he was having a wonderful time and he felt he deserved to. First there had been the recent approval of Genelife by the FDA, then the extremely favorable article about him in today's *Wall Street Journal,* and now a congratulatory telegram from Bettina Hollis at Omni International's Chicago headquarters.

His only regret was the absence of Hollis herself. A mover and shaker in the world of mergers and acquisitions, she'd been instrumental in the acquisition of Randall Webber Pharmaceuticals by the giant Japanese-owned conglomerate she worked for, thereby thrusting the old family-owned company into the twentieth century.

And by forcing the retirement of Clark Randall, she'd thrust Nolan into a position of visibility and power.

It was after seven; time to say a few words about Butler and present him with the Cartier wristwatch Nolan had personally chosen, a neat and very expensive parody of the "gold watch for long service" tradition. Well, Butler had earned it.

Nolan strode to the front of the room and held up his hand for silence. A forceful, driven man of forty-five, he was determined to steer what was now his ship with an iron hand. As the crowd slowly quieted, Nolan's thin lips smiled warmly, but his ice-blue eyes mercilessly raked the sea of faces turning toward him. Some of them would have to go, of course. Dead wood. Old Clark Randall had been far too softhearted. Well, Randall had had a large trust fund to fall back on; he could afford to be Mr. Nice Guy. Things were different now.

As Randall's second-in-command for the past ten years, Nolan had often disagreed with the man's overly cautious attitude toward change, and had watched with a jaundiced eye the repackaging of the same old cough syrups, the same old analgesics. But Randall had been nearly sixty when he'd hired Nolan, and Nolan had hung on, knowing his chance would come. When Randall, bowing to family pressure, had taken the company public in the late 1980s, Nolan had solidified his stock ownership position. But the company still failed to launch any significant new products, and the stock had lain dormant. Nolan was determined to change all that—and become rich in the process.

"Thank you all for coming . . ." He spoke forcefully, pitching his voice slightly lower than normal, the way he'd learned at the expensive Executive Presentation Skills Workshop he'd attended, on company money, the previous year. As he spoke, his eyes roamed the crowd; Butler stood modestly off to one side, a tall, stocky man with a shock of salt-and-pepper hair. The company had done well by Butler, and the generous pension Nolan had arranged for him, coupled with a permanent seat on the board, would guarantee his loyalty in the future. And he was pleased to see Butler's eyes widen in surprise and delight when he was presented with the Cartier wristwatch. Yes, Nolan could count on him.

As he finished his remarks to hearty applause, he realized

he hadn't noticed Jerry Lim, his recently promoted chief of research. Not for the first time he wondered whether he'd acted wisely there; Jerry was awfully young. Still, he'd been with Randall Research and Development ever since he'd graduated with honors from Stanford. No one knew more about Genelife than Jerry.

People crowded around Butler to congratulate him and admire the watch, and Nolan angled his way toward the drinks table. A believer in clean living and rigorous exercise, he was suddenly feeling the effects of his two glasses of champagne. Perhaps some mineral water would help.

Jerry Lim stood to one side of the bar, downing a Scotch on the rocks. Nolan didn't think it was his first. Lim's broad pale face shone with a thin film of sweat, and his eyes were slightly unfocused as he extended his glass toward the barman for a refill.

"No more for him," Nolan instructed the barman, intercepting the glass and setting it down out of reach. He put a hand on Lim's thin shoulder and guided him firmly toward the high narrow door that opened into a paneled hallway and somewhat cooler air.

"What the hell's the matter with you, Jerry?" Nolan said.

"Celebrating," Lim told him fuzzily.

"Well, stop. I need you bright-eyed and bushy-tailed." He'd never realized Lim was a drinker.

"Right," Lim agreed. "No more for me." He giggled.

"Go home, Jerry," Nolan told him. "Drink some coffee, get some sleep. And if I ever find you like this again on company time, you can kiss your new title and overinflated salary good-bye."

Lim stopped giggling. "Yes, sir," he said. "Sorry, Mr. Nolan." He looks scared, Nolan thought. Good.

"Don't worry, Mr. Nolan," Lim said, weaving slightly. "I'm not usually like this. It's just, I don't know, I guess I'm a little nervous about being in charge of Genelife, you know?"

"Job too big for you, Jerry?"

"Oh, no! No!" Lim leaned on the doorjamb for support. "I can handle it all right!"

"I know you can," Nolan told him. "Thanks for coming, Ron ... Dave ..." He stepped aside to let several staff members pass through the door; people were beginning to drift off home. "Well, Jerry, why don't you—"

"When does Dr. Butler's replacement start?" Lim interrupted, striving desperately to prolong the conversation in the hope of convincing Nolan he wasn't as drunk as they both knew he was.

"Monday," said Nolan, bored. He'd made his point. Now he wanted some dinner. "Didn't you read the memo?" He scanned the room; Butler was still entertaining his admirers.

"Sure. I just forgot. Uh, I'm looking forward to working with her, showing her the ropes, you know? I mean, she's never worked in the pharmaceutical field before, has she? In fact, I was kind of surprised you hired her. She's not really experienced . . ."

Nolan smiled; he recalled that Butler too had expressed surprise at the selection of Kate Martin. Together he and Butler had interviewed a large number of older, more qualified candidates. But Nolan had insisted he'd wanted someone who could grow with the company, someone who had no preconceived ideas about how things should be done.

"Well, she won't be spending much time in R&D," Nolan said casually.

Lim's eyes widened in surprise. "She won't?"

"Not really. That's your area. I've got other things for her to do. Promotion, publicity. Liaison with the advertising agency, when we choose one."

"But she's a scientist," Lim protested.

"And a damn good one. That's why she's the perfect person to be our interface with the public. Now go home, boy."

Lim tottered out into the hallway and Nolan turned back to the party. The crowd around Butler had diminished. He'd better get Nick moving; their dinner reservation was for eight o'clock.

So Lim also questioned his selection of Dr. Martin. So what? As far as he, Nolan, was concerned, Kate Martin was precisely what he was looking for.

Chapter 5

"It needs to come up a little on your side, Pat ... No, that's too much. Drop it a couple inches ... Whoa! Too much! Tommy, bring your end down a little ..."

"Jeez, you guys still at it?" the receptionist complained as she emerged from the elevator. She tossed her shoulder bag onto a beige leather sofa. "I already gave you half an hour!"

Plaster dust covered her desk. Behind it, two workmen perched on their ladders, holding the heavy metal "MacAllister Agency" sign against the wall, while the foreman studied its position from below. "Boys, I think we've got it," he announced.

"Heaven be praised," the receptionist muttered.

"Almost. Pat, raise it up a little on your side ... whoa! Too much! Now, Tommy—"

"Damn!" exclaimed the receptionist, flinging a copy of *AdWeek* across the room.

"A good job takes time," Tommy told her.

"How would *you* know?" she retorted.

"Now, children, children ..." Todd MacAllister breezed into the reception area. Elegantly slim, blond of hair and green of eye, and blessed with rugged good looks, Mac-Allister—"Mac" to his friends—had often been taken for a male model in one of his company's ads, rather than a partner in a successful medium-sized advertising agency. This illusion of passive beauty was immediately shattered, however, as soon as he opened his mouth. Two years past his thirtieth birthday, he was already something of a legend in the advertising business.

He'd come up through the creative ranks, unusual for an agency president; account management, with its heavy client contact, was the more usual route. Because of his background, he had great affection for and trust in his creative staff, the people who wrote and produced the advertising campaigns that sold the clients' products. This enlightened attitude at the executive level produced a loyal, hardworking staff as well as industry awards that impressed new clients and kept the current ones happy.

"Logo looks great right where it is, fellas," Mac told the workmen firmly. "Get it stuck on that wall and let my favorite receptionist get back to work." Together they watched as the sign was finally, firmly, attached to the rear wall of the MacAllister Agency reception area.

The tall bronze letters shone brightly in the sunlight that streamed through large windows framing a spectacular view of midtown Manhattan. To Mac, the letters would have looked equally good sideways, upside down, or hanging from the ceiling. He'd just bought out his partner Bob Lee; replacing the old "MacAllister & Lee" sign represented freedom, excitement, control.

Of course, it also represented debt, worry, and responsibility for the livelihood of his four hundred employees, especially since his erstwhile partner had taken a certain amount of business with him when he'd left. But with any luck, today's meeting would be a big step toward dealing with the down side of running his own business.

Mac checked his watch: nearly ten. The drive to Connecticut would take at least forty minutes, and the briefing was scheduled to begin at eleven.

"Find Art and Dave," he told the receptionist. Arthur Haines was the agency's ranking account director, Dave Randazzo, the creative director. Both were to attend the briefing with him. "Tell them the car'll be out front and I'll be in it."

He walked quickly across the maroon carpet and punched the elevator button. Behind him, Tommy and Pat were clearing away ladders and debris. The receptionist sneezed her way down the hall. The phone began to ring again. He heard Lou say, "Hey, Pat, you missed a whole pile of shit over there. No, there, on your left. No, your other left."

It may be chaos back there, Mac thought happily, but at least it's *my* chaos. The elevator door slid open, and whistling the theme music from the agency's new dog food commercial, he stepped inside.

*   *   *

A winding asphalt road led back through acres of woods and meadowland. Along the way, rustic wooden signs directed visitors toward the research lab, the executive offices, and, surprisingly, a gym. They passed two men in suits, driving a golf cart; the Randall Webber logo was stenciled on the front.

"I wonder how much a two-bedroom with a terrace goes for?" Dave mused.

And indeed, the Connecticut headquarters of Randall Webber Pharmaceuticals did look more like an expensive condominium than an office complex. The offices themselves were housed in a series of low, modern interconnected buildings sporting lots of glass and redwood. Bright flower beds, neatly maintained, bordered each building.

The Lincoln Town Car deposited them in front of a double-height glass atrium entrance, then slid quietly off in search of a parking spot.

The three men looked around at the buildings, the rolling lawns, the extensive parking areas, as though their surroundings might give them a clue to the mind of the prospective client, and hence an advantage in winning the account.

"Hey, isn't that Scott O'Neill?" said Arthur. "I didn't know Imagemakers was in on this, too."

Mac and Dave turned. Two figures, briefcases in hand, approached from a nearby parking area.

"Who's that with him?" asked Dave, more familiar with the faces of creative directors like O'Neill than with the competition's other executives.

"Richard Day. Account guy," Mac told him.

"Imagemakers have been doing very well lately," Arthur said. "They picked up a piece of Toyota last month. And I hear they're short-listed for Canada Dry."

"They give great presentation," Dave said scathingly, "but their creative sucks. They'll never hold on to Toyota."

Mac looked over at his creative director. Dave's graying hair was pulled back in a ponytail that hung over the collar of his trendy cream-colored Italian suit; a small gold earring dangled discreetly from one ear. In some creative people, this would have been an affectation, an attempt to cover a mundane mind with a creative look. Not Dave, Mac reflected; Dave was brilliant. O'Neill, Dave's counterpart at

Imagemakers, both looked and thought like an accountant.
Maybe the prospect of a wild and crazy creative team
would appeal to Nolan, give him something to lunch out
on. Clients could be like that sometimes.

"Any idea who else will be here?" Dave asked.

"The third agency is Riding & Levy," Arthur told him.
"They're good, but small; too small to handle something
like this. And Benson Hughes will be here, of course."
Benson Hughes currently handled Randall Webber's analgesic advertising. "Nolan had to include them, but they
don't have a prayer. What do *you* think of the competition, Mac?"

"Screw 'em all," Mac said firmly. "Let's go in."

"Good morning, gentlemen, ladies . . ."

Michael Nolan smiled at the circle of top-level advertising executives assembled around the huge rosewood and
silver conference table. Decanters of water and pots of coffee flanked by milk and sugar had been set out along its
polished surface at regular intervals. On the table in front
of each chair were a yellow pad, two sharpened pencils, a
delicate porcelain cup and saucer, and a water glass. On
top of each pad was a one-page nondisclosure agreement.

Imagemakers or MacAllister? That's what it would probably come down to, Nolan reflected. Riding & Levy was a
dark horse; they did interesting work, but probably weren't
big enough to handle an account of this size. And from the
bored expression on the face of the president of Benson
Hughes, he obviously realized that his agency had been
included merely as a courtesy.

"Thank you all for coming. Before we begin, I'd like
you to read the agreement in front of you. It's a standard
nondisclosure form, which I'm sure you've all signed many
times before."

A rustle of paper ensued. Nolan gave them time to look
over the agreement before he continued. "Anyone have a
problem with it? No? Good. Then please sign them now
and pass them down this way."

A secretary stationed behind Nolan's chair went forward
to collect the agreements. Nolan stood silently by as she
checked that each was signed, and counted them twice.
Then she nodded to him and left, taking the forms with her.

"I realize it's a little unusual to brief all four competing agencies at the same time," Nolan told them once the conference-room door was closed. "But due to the unique nature of our new product, and the absolute necessity for secrecy, I thought it best that you all hear about it together."

The agency people nodded. Arthur Haines leaned forward in his typical new-client attitude of worshipful attention. Gloria Riding, president of Riding & Levy, poured coffee for her partner Andrea Levy and herself. Ignoring the sharpened pencils, Scott O'Neill produced a thin silver pen and wrote "UNIQUE NATURE ... ABSOLUTE SECRECY" in large block letters on his yellow pad. Mac, seated across from him, read the upside-down writing and smiled to himself.

"I'd like to start by introducing two of our key people in this endeavor. This is Jerry Lim, group director of Research and Development. He's been involved in the development of the product for a number of years."

Mac watched the young Chinese man in the white lab coat rise from his chair on Nolan's right and smile diffidently at the group. An attractive woman with copper-colored hair was seated to Nolan's left. Beige silk suit. No lab coat. Probably marketing, he thought.

"We usually keep Jerry locked away in R&D," Nolan explained with a chuckle. "Reachable only by golf cart. That's how we get around this place, by the way. Of course Jerry's mighty busy these days. So if you have any questions about the product as you work on your sample ads, don't call him!" The group around the table laughed dutifully.

"Thank you, Jerry," Nolan said. Jerry sat down. Gloria Riding poured more coffee. Arthur gazed at Nolan as if at the Second Coming. Scott O'Neill retrieved his silver pen and wrote "JERRY LIM. R&D. DON'T CALL HIM."

"And this is Dr. Kate Martin, our medical consultant," Nolan announced. "Until recently—last week, in fact—she was on staff at New York General Hospital. In addition to an MD, she has a degree in biochemistry."

Kate smiled at the group around the table but remained seated.

An MD, not an MBA, Mac thought in surprise. So who's running their marketing show?

"Dr. Martin will be liaising with Jerry Lim on the medical aspects of our product. She'll also be your contact. Any

questions you have about how the product works, and what
you can say about it, she's the one to call."

Kate scanned the faces that had turned toward her with
interest. There were several good-looking men of appropriate age among them. The blond wasn't wearing a wedding ring, but she couldn't see the ring finger of the other
man—Day, was it?—who had caught her eye. She mentally
chided herself for thinking such thoughts in the middle of
her first important presentation for Randall Webber, then
shrugged. Part of the reason she'd taken this job was to
broaden her life, social life included.

"Once an agency has been selected," Nolan continued,
"Dr. Martin will work closely with you to make sure your
ads are medically correct. We don't want to run afoul of
the FDA."

"Who do we talk to about marketing strategy?" Mac
asked

"I'll be in charge of the marketing effort," Nolan said.
"Dr. Martin will be involved to some extent, too. But we're
looking to you for real marketing expertise."

A physician and a CEO running the marketing of a
breakthrough product? Obviously Nolan was counting on
his chosen agency to do the company's job as well as their
own, Mac reflected.

Everyone around the table nodded and smiled as though
this were perfectly normal, while inwardly they toted up
the cost of hiring additional marketing personnel. No
agency would be willing to cut their commission on this
assignment.

"I know Jerry's anxious to get back to the lab," Nolan
said, nodding at Jerry who rose and scurried out of the
room.

Nolan stood too, and walked to a large easel set in front
of the curtained windows behind him. The easel was covered with a sheet of blank presentation paper.

"Genelife is the answer to everybody's deepest wish,"
Nolan announced. "The look of eternal youth."

Gloria Rider stifled a yawn; all this fuss over yet another
gimmicky cosmetic.

"The look of eternal youth," Nolan repeated. "We've all
heard it before. But this time it's the real thing."

Sure, Gloria thought. Like Coca-Cola.

"Gentlemen . . . ladies . . . I give you Genelife!" With a

flourish, he ripped off the paper, balled it up, and tossed it aside. On the easel was a blown-up color photograph of a package; next to the package was something small, round, and beige.

The group stared at the photograph. The packaging was beautifully designed. That was a good start.

"Genelife," Nolan repeated. "Truly a breakthrough product. Even the delivery system is unique in this market. A patch."

Now people leaned forward, curious. a patch? Scott O'Neill wrote "PATCH" on his yellow pad, and underlined it twice.

"Genelife will be available only by prescription. It's an extremely effective age retardant. It produces a dramatic, ongoing cosmetic effect."

"What exactly do you mean by an age retardant?" Gloria Rider asked. Some years ago she'd worked on a cosmetic lotion that was absorbed into the skin around the eyes. The added moisture plumped up the surface tissue, thereby softening and reducing wrinkles. Was this something similar?

"It's not like Lotion Ondine," Nolan told her, reading her mind. "With Genelife, your skin actually becomes younger."

" '*Becomes* younger'? Can we really say that?"

"We can," Nolan replied. He flipped the product picture back over the top of the easel, revealing side-by-side photographs of two faces. "The same woman," he said. "Before and after."

"No retouching?" Dave asked.

"Absolutely not," Nolan assured him.

The room buzzed with excitement.

"How long does it take to work?"

"How long does it last?"

"Why do you need a prescription for it?"

"How will you sell it?"

"What's in it?"

"I think it's time I turned you over to Dr. Martin," Nolan told them. He nodded toward Kate, who rose and waited for the room to quiet.

"I'm not a very formal person," she began, "so for starters, I'd like you to call me Kate. Now, Jerry Lim can tell you a lot more about this product than I can ..." From the corner of her eye, she saw Nolan give her a warning little headshake. "But I've taken a crash course in Genelife over the past few days, so I'll leap in and try to explain it all in laymen's terms."

Confidently she moved to the easel, her skirt clinging softly to her body. She'd chosen her outfit with care, from the selection of new clothes she'd bought with her first two paychecks. She was enjoying the life-style changes that came with corporate life, including the unique experience of wearing clothes that wouldn't be covered with a white coat all day. She flipped back the side-by-side photo. Beneath was a blank page. Picking up a large blue marker from the easel ledge, she wrote two words on the paper.

"Superoxide dismutase," she told them. "S.O.D. for short. It's an enzyme that breaks down free radicals."

Everyone was writing, now.

"Free radicals are . . . well, they speed up the breakdown of normal cells in the body. Get rid of the free radicals, and your normal cells function better. Genelife uses a newly discovered superactive form of S.O.D. called SOD-2000."

"Those photographs . . ." The man Arthur Haines had identified as Richard Day of Imagemakers interrupted. "It looked like age reversal, not just retardant."

Others in the room were nodding.

"Yes. Yes, it did," Kate agreed. "It's rather complicated, but it seems that when you retard a cell's breakdown process this way, the cell gets . . . healthier, somehow. That is, it becomes optimized. It reverts to its optimum state. The cosmetic effect is the manifestation of that. That's why the woman looked younger after taking Genelife."

"So Genelife consists of this new S.O.D.?"

"Not entirely," Kate replied. "You see, normal cellular breakdown is partly the result of the body's built-in genetic suppression of S.O.D. Genelife combines a synthesized form of this unique S.O.D. with something that inhibits that suppression to some extent."

Silence greeted her words, as her audience worked through the information she'd just given them.

"I don't get it," Mac said at last. "Did the woman in the picture actually become younger?"

"Well, no, I'm afraid not." Kate smiled. "It's purely a cosmetic effect."

"Too bad," Mac said in a rueful tone. Everybody laughed, and even Nolan smiled.

"Genelife is delivered via this transdermal patch . . ." Kate continued, flipping back the page with "superoxide dismutase" written on it. Beneath was an enlarged photograph of what looked like a small circular Band-Aid; next to it was an artist's rendering of its various layers.

"This drawing tells you more than you need to know," she apologized. "Basically, the patch is multilayered and adhesive. It's worn against the skin of the torso, anywhere from shoulder to waist. After one week it's discarded. A new patch is then applied one week after the first patch has been taken off. In other words, the patch is meant to be worn only two weeks out of every four."

"Why?"

"Because that's all that's needed to produce the desired effect," said Kate. "Why take more of anything than you need?"

Mac nodded in agreement; he himself hated taking so much as an aspirin.

"We've done . . . that is, Randall Webber has conducted extensive testing, of course. Some people have experienced certain side effects. Nothing major, of course. And the package will carry a warning."

"What kind of side effects, exactly?" Mac asked.

"The primary one is delayed reproduction. Women on the patch find it harder to conceive a child. There's also some diminution of appetite and a lowering of libido. Research indicates these effects are reversible once the drug has been discontinued."

"Sort of a conflict of interest here," Richard Day joked. "You become more attractive to men, but less interested in doing anything about it."

"Or more attractive to women," Audrey Levy said pointedly. "I mean, men can take it too, right?"

"Absolutely," said Kate. "In fact, we plan to encourage them. Michael?"

Nolan stood and joined her front and center. "As Dr. Mar—Kate's told you, Genelife is only available by prescription. And of course our medical agency is already preparing a trade campaign aimed at doctors around the country. We'll want you to mount a national campaign to generate consumer interest."

"What sort of budget are we talking about?"

"We're talking print and television, right?"

"How soon do you plan to launch?"

During the last few minutes, Nolan's secretary had entered and placed four thick booklets on the conference table. Now Nolan began distributing them. "I believe these packets will answer all your questions," he told them. "Take them back and study them. Anything you don't understand, or need more information about, call us."

"I'm still concerned about the side effects," Gloria Riding said. "How bad are they, Kate? How widespread?"

"From the research I've seen," Kate answered, "they're relatively rare. Of course it's impossible to make a drug, any drug, which absolutely no one will have a reaction to. But remember, the FDA wouldn't have approved Genelife if there had been any question about the side effects."

Gloria looked doubtful; a friend of a friend had recently become a victim of the silicone gel breast implants debacle.

Kate smiled at her. "Don't worry," she said. She hesitated for a moment, then thought what the hell, and began to undo the top button of her blouse. Someone gasped. She undid the second button, then slid the neck of the silk shirt to one side. A small beige circle was affixed to the smooth skin just below her clavicle.

"Feel better?" she asked.

On that rather dramatic note, Nolan ended the formal part of the briefing and suggested a tour of the facilities. Collecting their booklets and notes, the group followed him out of the conference room and down the long carpeted hallway toward the atrium. But he stopped short of the entrance through which they had all entered an hour before, and led them instead through a small side door that opened behind the building. A dozen battery-powered, four-seater golf carts were parked beneath a sheltering cement overhang.

Despite Richard Day's jockeying as they'd all left the conference room, Mac had managed to position himself alongside Kate, expressing enthusiasm for Genelife and complimenting her on her presentation skills. Now it seemed natural for them to share a cart. He immediately seated himself on the passenger side and Kate slid into the driver's seat. But just as she was turning the key in the ignition, Richard Day hopped into the seat behind her. Disappointed, Mac reminded himself that the Genelife account would be won with advertising ideas, not chitchat.

Nolan led the procession of carts along the narrow asphalt paths, pointing out various buildings: research and development, cafeteria, gym. Everything looked clean and well cared for. Nolan did not suggest that they get out of their carts and go inside.

The tour lasted some twenty minutes; afterward they returned to the rear of the atrium building and reparked their carts beneath the overhang. Nolan thanked them graciously for attending the briefing and wished them good luck with their speculative campaigns.

"As you know, presentation dates will be arranged for the first week in August," he reminded them as they headed back through the building to the atrium entrance. "Not long, I know, but better for security. Less time for leaks to develop." He looked around at the group sternly. "I can't say this strongly enough: what you've heard today is extremely confidential."

Gloria Rider raised a cynical eyebrow. Come on, fella, she thought. It's still just a cosmetic.

The guests said their good-byes, and Nolan walked Kate back along the corridor toward her office.

"I think that went very well," he told her.

"Yes," Kate agreed. "They all seemed very enthusiastic."

"Were you nervous?"

"A little, at first," Kate admitted. "Then I started to enjoy myself." She grinned at him. "It was fun."

"You're a natural!" He studied her. She looked prettier and more relaxed than she'd been when he'd first interviewed her for the job. "Trading medicine for a corporate career seems to suit you."

"Well, I hardly like to think I've done that," Kate told him.

"No, of course not," he said quickly. "And the way you defused the side effects issue was masterful."

Defused? Kate thought. A strange word to use. "I only repeated what your research says," she said. "I mean, it *is* a nonissue, according to the material you gave me."

"Yes, of course," Nolan agreed. "That's what I meant."

Chapter 6

Kate sipped her tea as she studied the marketing plan Nolan had dropped on her desk earlier that morning. Some of the language was hard to follow. She sighed and leaned back in her large leather swivel chair, gazing out at the summer rain spattering against the windows. There was a low rumble of thunder.

I suppose I should be flattered that Michael wants to involve me in so many aspects of the project, she thought. But it does seem rather removed from what I thought I was hired to do.

In contrast to the dull gray of the storm outside, her office was bright and cozy. Decorated in tones of pale peach and warm brown, it was both comfortable and efficient. A leather sofa stretched along the wall across from her wide mahogany desk. The two side chairs were upholstered in a pale peach-and-white print. Matching drapes had been looped back to frame a view of woods and lawn.

The rain was beginning to taper off as she finished the report and pushed it to one side, uncertain what to do next. People in the other offices on the floor—the marketing and sales people for Randall Webber's other products—seemed busy and productive. But Kate felt underworked. Nolan had told her the pace would quicken once they'd selected an agency.

"Use this time to get acclimated," he'd told her. "It'll never be this quiet again."

Taking her coffee mug, a gift from Dr. Gould that read "Trust me. I'm a doctor," she wandered out of her office and past the secretaries' area to the ladies' room, where she washed and dried the mug and reapplied her lipstick. At the hospital she used to dream of having long lunches at nice restaurants; now that she actually had the time to do so, she had no one to lunch with. Even her nonmedical friends led busy lives; who could drive all the way up from New York in the middle of the day?

Back in her office, she placed the mug carefully on the built-in bookshelves behind her desk, then straightened the two pencils and three ballpoint pens beside the desk blotter. Outside, the rain had stopped but the clouds were still thick and dark.

Get acclimated, Michael had told her. Well, now that she'd slogged through the marketing report, maybe she'd wander over to Research and Development. Since her office was in the executive building, she hadn't met any of the R&D staff except for Jerry Lim. And even Jerry hadn't had any time to really talk to her. Maybe they could have a working lunch.

Grabbing her shoulder bag and slicker, she went purposefully out of her office and down the corridor to the little side door that led to the golf carts. From the solid roof of each cart, rolls of clear plastic sheeting had been let down to keep driver and passengers dry. Kate pushed the sheeting aside and climbed in. All the carts had the same ignition lock; each employee was issued a universal key with which to drive whatever cart was handy. She started up the electric motor and eased the cart out onto the wet asphalt.

The R&D building was partially hidden within a thick patch of woods. Though quite near the executive offices, it was six or seven minutes away by cart since the road had been designed more for beauty than efficiency. Winding through stands of majestic trees and around low hillocks, Kate felt her hair frizz up and her clothes grow clammy in the wet and humid air.

A young man in a gray mechanic's overall ran up as she arrived, and waved her over to a neat wooden shack beside the rear parking area. Pulling aside the curtain of plastic, he extended his hand to help her disembark.

"Got to check the batteries on all the carts," he explained. "Some guy got caught out in the storm when his cart went dead." He looked up at the lowering sky. "Make sure you take one from over this side when you go back. That's where I'll put the good ones."

Her slicker over her arm, she hurried around to the front entrance of the building, arriving just as the rain began again, and pushed quickly through the unlocked outer door into a stark, empty anteroom. Two steel doors set at opposite sides of the small room appeared to lead into the interior. A card-operated lock plate was set into each door about halfway down. There was no doorknob. Kate tried each door in turn, but both were securely locked.

Puzzled that she'd been given no entry card to an area she considered key to her involvement with Randall Webber, she was wondering whether she'd have to drive all the way back to her office and call Jerry from there when one of the doors opened and a man in a white lab coat hurried out.

Kate lunged for the quickly closing door as the man turned back to stare at her. "Thanks!" she said, flashing him a brilliant smile. "I'm Dr. Martin."

"You can't—"

"It's okay," she said quickly as she slid past him. "I work here. I'm new."

The door slammed shut in his surprised face and Kate looked around her. She was in a long, low corridor. Walls and ceiling were painted an unremitting white, and the floor was covered with pale vinyl tiles. Fluorescent tubes threw a cold blue glare over everything.

At the end of the corridor was a windowed door that opened onto a cinder-block stairway. As Kate climbed the rough, worn stairs, she wondered why she should be feeling as nervous as she did. She was an executive with the company, she reminded herself. If someone had forgotten to give her a pass to this building, they were at fault, not she. She'd have to talk to Michael about it.

The stairway was short and stopped at a small landing where another door opened onto a corridor similar to the one below, but wider. Doors opened off the hallway that ended in what appeared to be a wide common area divided into small work cubicles.

Sounds of activity greeted her as she walked slowly down the corridor. She heard voices, the chatter of a computer, a soft electric hum. Several doors had neat labels affixed to them: Lab 2 . . . Conference Room A . . . Tabulation . . .

As she neared the last door before the cubicle area, she heard a voice she recognized.

"It's too late for that kind of thinking," Nolan was saying angrily.

The door stood partly open; on it was stenciled "Director," and below that in fresher paint, "Dr. Jerry Lim."

"I'm just saying you ought to consider postponing the launch," Jerry insisted. Both men sounded upset.

Kate drew back, uncertain what she should do.

"We've been through this before, Jerry," she heard Nolan say. "We're going ahead."

Could they be talking about Genelife? Kate wondered.

"You're awfully young to have this job," Nolan continued in a slightly threatening tone. "And I know you don't want to lose it."

"No sir!" Jerry said. "It's just . . ."

"Just what?" But Jerry was silent. "Just *what,* Jerry? The trials were good, we have FDA approval. I don't see what the problem is."

"Yeah, I guess . . ."

Kate looked back down the hallway. What if someone came along and found her eavesdropping outside Jerry's office? I should leave, she thought. But if it really is Genelife . . .

"You're going to have to trust me on this," she heard Nolan say. "There are big bucks riding on it, and plenty of glory to go around. If you want to be a part of all that, you've got to be a team player. Are you a team player, Jerry?"

"Sure. Sure I am, Mr. Nolan."

"That's what I thought when I promoted you." Nolan's voice became avuncular. "So don't let me down, fella. Don't follow in the footsteps of your predecessor."

"I won't, Mr. Nolan."

"Good."

A chair squeaked; Nolan was getting up. Feeling very foolish, Kate raced back down the corridor to the stairwell. She was just pushing through the door into the hallway again when Nolan emerged from Jerry's office. He saw her and drew back in surprise and dismay.

"Kate?" Recovering quickly, he smiled broadly. "What are you doing way over here? And in a rainstorm, too?"

Kate smiled back. "Just getting acclimated, as you advised. Thought I'd see how the other half lives." My half, she thought. "Is Jerry in his office?"

"Yes, I just came from there. Anything I can help you

with? He's awfully busy. By the way, how did you get in here?"

"Without a key, you mean? Someone was going out. I meant to talk to you about that. Who do I get an entry card from?"

Nolan frowned. "Entry card? You won't need one. Just call Jerry anytime you want to come over; he'll have you met and escorted in."

"But, Michael, I'm your medical consultant. R&D is central to what I do."

"Not really, Kate," Nolan said soothingly. "Genelife's already out of development. All the ongoing research is handled by an outside lab. The action's in 'Exec' now; that's why your office is there. But if you want an entry card," he added, seeing her expression, "of course you can have one. I'll arrange for it this afternoon."

"Thank you," Kate said rather stiffly.

"And since you're here, let's go on in and say hi to Jerry, maybe give you the grand tour?"

"Fine."

Nolan walked her back to Jerry's office and knocked twice on the glass panel before swinging the door wide. Jerry looked up in surprise, then smiled with pleasure when he saw Kate.

"Come on in," he said. "Take a pew."

Jerry's office was smaller than hers, Kate noted, and papers, memos, and stacks of computer printouts were piled everywhere: on the metal desk, on the floor, on the low cabinet, even on the nubby green sofa. Kate perched on the sofa's arm. "See you later," she told Nolan, but to her surprise, he seated himself in the one unencumbered side chair.

"So what did you want with Jerry?" Nolan asked her in a helpful tone of voice.

"Oh, I just wanted to get acquainted," Kate replied. "And I wanted to chat a little about Genelife." To Jerry she said, "You must be very proud."

"Proud?" Jerry squeaked, glancing at Nolan.

"Well, sure. It's quite a drug—er, product. You must have been working on it for years. Did you start at Stanford?"

"Not really. My boss . . ."

"Our former director of research actually developed

Genelife," Nolan said smoothly. "Of course Jerry worked closely with him in the synthetization process and the clinical testing."

"Former director?" Kate asked. There seem to have been a lot of changes at Randall Webber recently, she thought. I replace Dr. Butler, Jerry replaces his boss ... "How long ago did he retire?"

"Oh, he didn't exactly retire."

"How about that tour?" Nolan offered. He rose and walked to the door. "Coming, Kate?"

"Just a minute," Kate told Nolan firmly, then turned back to Jerry. "You were saying?"

Jerry was silent for a moment. "He was brilliant, but he was sick," he said at last. "I heard he went into a rehabilitation program."

"You mean he drank?" Kate asked.

"Something like that," said Nolan. "Frankly, it's painful to talk about. Now Jerry's got a load of work to get through today, so let's leave him to it."

"That's right, yes." Jerry nodded several times. "Nice to see you."

"Nice to see you, too," Kate said. "Maybe we can have lunch sometime."

"Okay," Jerry said.

"How about tomorrow?"

"No, not tomorrow. Er, I'll call you, okay?"

"Sure," said Kate lightly.

She followed Nolan out into the hallway. He was already heading toward the cubicle area in which six or seven people were working at computers.

"These are our number-crunchers," he told her over his shoulder. "Here is where we—"

"Michael, hold it a minute."

Nolan swung around, and she took a few steps toward him, then stopped.

"I know I'm new here, and new to the whole corporate arena. And I didn't ask a lot of questions about the job or the company when you hired me. It all seemed pretty straightforward."

"It is."

"Good. So what's all the mystery about Jerry's boss? Why did you stop Jerry from talking about him? I'm bound to find out sooner or later, so you might as well tell me now."

Nolan shook his head in a tired yet amused manner. "There's no mystery," he said. "The man had an emotional problem. He left. Jerry replaced him."

He paused and looked back toward Jerry's office door, still partly open. "It hit Jerry hard," he continued, his voice low and confidential. "You have to understand that Jerry sort of hero-worshiped him. Also, I think he feels a little guilty about stepping into his shoes. As for why I stopped Jerry from talking about him ... well, Jerry's important to us, especially now, and I don't like to get him upset."

Kate nodded; what Nolan said made sense. "I understand," she said. "I'm sorry if I ..."

"That's okay."

Together they began walking toward the cubicle area again. Nolan smiled reassuringly at her. "You're important to us, too, Kate," he said. "And I don't like to see *you* upset, either. I'm glad you aired your feelings just now. I hope you always will."

Kate smiled back. "Count on it," she said.

The rain had stopped and the clouds were clearing when Kate arrived back at her office after the brief uneventful tour. On her desk was a pink phone message slip. Grateful for any sign of business activity, she threw her slicker on a side chair and picked up the square of paper.

Richard Day. Imagemakers. A phone number.

As she dialed, she tried to remember which one he was ... the cute dark-haired one, wasn't he? The one who'd made that joke about Genelife making women more attractive to men and less eager to do anything about it. Good face, bad sense of humor.

Day's secretary answered and she told the woman her name; he came on the line right away.

"Thanks so much for returning my call, Dr. Martin ... Kate, that's right. Look, I had a few questions about the material in the booklet you guys gave us ... no, not anything specific, more of an overall kind of thing. I was wondering whether we could have lunch together sometime soon. Ever been to Côte Basque?"

A lunch date! "I'd love to," she said, then hesitated. "Only ..."

"Or I could come up there," Richard said, misunderstanding her reluctance.

"It's not that ..." Damn, Kate thought. He *is* the cute dark one, I'm sure of it. But would it be fair to talk to him about Genelife without giving the other agencies equal time?

"How's tomorrow? Or would early next week be better for you?"

"Look, Richard, please don't misunderstand. I'd really like to have lunch with you. But I don't think it would be ethical to give your agency extra discussion time."

"I'll never tell." Kate could hear the smile in his voice.

"That's not the point. I just can't."

Richard was silent for a moment. "I understand," he said. "I'm disappointed, but I understand."

"Good," Kate said. "But thanks for the invitation. Maybe ..." The unfinished thought hung in the air between them.

"Maybe after the pitch is over," Richard finished her sentence. "I'll call you, win or lose. I hope it's win, though."

"Yes, well ... Good luck, Richard."

"Appreciate it. See you soon."

"What?"

"At the agency presentation."

"Yes, of course. Well, good-bye."

"Bye."

Kate recradled the receiver slowly. Lunch with Richard might have been fun.

She rose and retrieved her shoulder bag; the navy bean soup in the cafeteria wasn't too bad.

"Dr. Martin?" A perky, slightly chunky woman in a serious suit stood in the doorway. "I'm Freda Pershing from Sales. A bunch of us are going out to lunch. Nothing fancy, just soup and salad at Bonjour ... been there yet? It's not bad. Well, I figured you probably haven't had time to meet anybody around here, and God knows we've been busy as one-armed wallpaper hangers ... Want to come along and meet some of the gang?"

Kate smiled and gathered up her slicker. "Call me Kate," she said. "And you're playing my song."

Chapter 7

July 21

The field telephone in the makeshift office shrilled seven times before Andreas, picking his way through mountains of gear, managed to grab the handset and shout "M'bulu Research Station!" into its unreliable transmitter.

The ramshackle single-story building served as headquarters for most of the scientific expeditions that came through the area, and therefore as depository for any valuable equipment that could not be trusted to tent storage. As district director, Andreas was in charge of the small semipermanent staff that manned the research station, as well as the care and feeding of visiting scientists.

He listened for a moment, then shouted "Hold on!" Setting the receiver carefully on a wooden crate, he went and stuck his head out of a nearby window.

"Kavett! Hey, Kavett! Telephone!"

Steve Kavett looked up from the impressive jumble of equipment that lay on large tarps spread under a baobab tree, his tanned face lined with exhaustion. He wiped the sweat from his forehead with the back of his hand and stood, knees creaking. Having just completed the first half of a three-month field trip in Central Africa, he was attempting to separate the things he could now send home from the gear he'd need to keep with him for the rest of the trip.

The years had been kind to Steve. Keeping physically fit was important for a man who spent a good part of each year in primitive conditions, and he'd been strict about keeping in shape. Equally important to survival both in the field and back at the anthropology department at Boston University had been his keen sense of the ridiculous.

The scar tissue on his forearm and shirtless back gleamed pinkly; despite the passage of the years, he still bore the physical marks of his experience in the Amazona Selva. But he didn't regret them; the trip had indeed proved a boon to his career. He was now a full professor at B.U., his books and articles well respected, his expeditions fully funded, and his lectures playing to standing room only. Uncle Avram was still going strong, and Steve managed the occasional trip to New York and New Haven to see his stage productions. Steve hadn't married; it seemed that the peripatetic life he led wasn't conducive to long-term relationships. But his dark, weathered good looks and zest for living guaranteed him more than enough romance, one way or another.

He stretched his cramped limbs and headed for the phone with a certain amount of trepidation. Who could be calling him out here?

"Kavett here."

The connection was not good, but then who could expect it to be? Cupping a hand over his free ear, Steve listened intently.

"What? She what? When did this happen?" he exclaimed. He shook his head in disbelief. Shit! "Any idea where? Well, is she all right? Does she need any money?"

Again he listened, his lips compressed and his face tight.

"Tell her I'll be back early in September. I'll come see her as soon as I get in. Meanwhile, make sure she has anything she needs, will you? Thanks a lot. And, well, just tell her I'm sorry."

He disconnected, then stood there, a distinct feeling of déjà vu flooding over him.

Nodding to Andreas, he wandered, unseeing, out of the office and back to the clearing where his gear was laid out. He stood there for a moment, then made his way toward the small river. Andreas looked after him with concern.

Steve sat on the grassy bank and stared at the brown water. So many years since he'd walked out of the rain forest alone ... So many years since the shock of Marianne's phone call some six months later. And now this.

He remembered being nearly overcome by a feeling of light-headedness as she'd told him, all those years ago; of course he'd still been on medication. Neither he nor Marianne had dared to let themselves hope; they'd tried to resign themselves to the loss. And then after months of hoping against hope came the staggering news that Tucker had survived.

He'd blundered into a logging camp about a hundred miles from where he'd left Steve and Father Jim some six months earlier, half dead and starving. They'd flown him out to the nearest town with medical facilities, and soon afterward, back home to Boston. The first phone call came from one of the doctors who was treating him, the second from Tucker himself. Would Marianne come and see him in the hospital? She would. Would she forgive him, marry him? She would indeed.

Steve was less ecstatic. Over the past six months his feelings of resentment and betrayal had been tempered by guilt: Should he have foreseen what his friend was planning? Could he have prevented it?

But once Tucker returned, so did Steve's bitterness. He refused to attend the hospital wedding, then berated himself for causing his sister still more pain.

Weeks passed. At last Marianne came to see him, pleading with him to make peace with her husband. "He's applied for a research grant with a foundation in New York," she told Steve. "And it looks like he'll get it."

"You'll move to New York?"

"Yes, and soon. Please come. I know he wants to see you."

Steve remained silent. He longed to see Tucker, to hear what had happened to him, and what he had learned during his additional months with the tribe. Yet Tucker had hurt him deeply.

"I've forgiven him," Marianne said. "Why can't you?"

"Okay," Steve told her. "I'll try."

Steve got up and walked along the track beside the river, his hands shoved in his pockets. It was nearly three o'clock; he had to get the gear sorted and under cover before nightfall. But his memories were too strong. For the first time in years, he replayed in his mind that first meeting with Tucker after his return from the rain forest.

Their reunion was deeply emotional; the two men wept, and Tucker apologized profusely for abandoning Steve along the trail. But the evening soon degenerated. Tucker's early elation and openness soon turned moody and sour.

"He's still not well," Marianne apologized. "He barely eats. The medication ..."

Steve nodded. "I understand," he said. "He's had a rough time." At Marianne's urging, he began to talk about the dissertation he was writing, and the excitement it had already generated.

But Tucker smiled scornfully. "That's nothing," he said. "I could tell you—"

"What?"

Tucker shrugged and shook his head.

"It's hard for him to talk about those months," Marianne explained, but Steve, looking at Tucker's stubborn visage, knew it was something else.

"Don't do this, Tuck," Steve told him angrily. "We went in there as partners. I'm not trying to steal your thunder. But anything you've learned concerns me, too." He paused. "You stayed because you had an idea about the calabash ceremony. What did you find out?"

"About the ceremony? Nothing we didn't already know. About what was *in* the calabash? That's something else again."

Tucker's eyes gleamed; they looked enormous in his thin face. He stood and began to pace excitedly, his depression suddenly replaced by a hectic elation.

"It is just possible that I have made the discovery of the century," he announced.

Steve stood too. "Tell me!" he said.

"The discovery of the century," Tucker repeated. He was keyed up, energized. "But not in your line of work, old buddy. In mine."

"That's great!" Steve told him, and meant it. He glanced at Marianne; this was apparently news to her, too.

"Tucker, you never told me," she said in surprise.

"Well, I'm not a hundred percent sure," he explained. "That's why I need the grant."

"You mean the grant is connected to—"

"You bet! This thing needs research, a lot more research. but if I'm right—"

"This is so exciting!" Marianne exclaimed. "What's it all about?"

But Tucker, suddenly secretive, shook his head. "Not till I'm sure," he said, and refused to be drawn.

The roast lamb was succulent, the potatoes crisp and hot.

As a self-catering bachelor, Steve hadn't had such a meal for longer than he cared to remember, and he devoured it with relish.

"My compliments to the chef," he told Marianne afterward as he helped her bus the plates into the small kitchen.

"It's nice to see somebody eat my food," Marianne said lightly as she scraped Tucker's uneaten meat and potatoes into the trash.

"His loss." Steve smiled.

Afterward they all sipped the brandy Marianne poured, and the men reminisced. Although Tucker was still reluctant to pursue the subject of his research grant, he spoke freely about the additional time he'd spent with the tribe: the hunts he'd participated in, the progress he'd made in communicating with the tribe, the injuries he'd sustained, and how Kuna had helped him find the lumber camp where he'd been rescued.

Without doubt it had been a grueling and hazardous experience, and Tucker admitted there had been times he'd berated himself for his stupidity in not having left the jungle with Steve. But ultimately, his desperate gamble had paid off, he exclaimed, and he expected his research, funded by the foundation grant, to fully vindicate his decision.

Steve and Marianne looked at each other; how reliable was Tucker's judgment in his current state of mind?

It was late now, and Tucker seemed suddenly weary. He lolled back against the sofa cushions and closed his eyes. "Sorry I can't add much in the anthropological line," he said after a while. "We didn't do anything you and I didn't do a hundred times, out there."

"I should go," Steve told Marianne. "It's nearly midnight."

"There is one thing you might be interested in, though," Tucker added sleepily. "I'm pretty sure I know what the chief was doing with those two young men."

Steve leaned forward eagerly. "Yes?"

"He was choosing a successor."

"But the chief was so young," Steve said. "It doesn't make sense."

Tucker's eyes remained closed. For a moment he didn't respond. "No," he agreed at last, with a slightly puzzled air. "It doesn't, does it?"

Smiling fondly, Marianne covered him with a knitted afghan.

The scolding of monkeys in the trees across the river interrupted Steve's reverie. He checked his watch: three-fifteen. He turned and walked purposefully back toward the research station.

As soon as he got home in September, he'd go to see Marianne in New York, and offer what comfort he could. But he couldn't help feeling that what had happened might actually be for the best.

Over the intervening years, he and Tucker had been unable to pick up the pieces of their strained friendship. And what little remained had worsened as he'd seen Tucker's increasingly erratic behavior and pathological secretiveness intensify, and his sister's marriage deteriorate as a result. But Marianne had hung on, God knew why.

He'd found himself avoiding Tucker on his trips to New York, meeting Marianne at a restaurant, or keeping in touch by phone. Tucker had become so involved in his work, he hadn't seemed to notice or to care.

Back at the research station, Steve surveyed his scattered equipment with a professional eye, then knelt and began separating items for crating and shipping.

His thoughts drifted to Marianne. He hoped she was okay. The B.U. colleague he'd just spoken with on the field telephone had been relaying a message Marianne had left with the department six weeks ago. He'd been unable to contact Steve at the time, since he and his small team had been deep in the bush.

Well, there was little he could do from here. And after all, it had been nearly two months since Tucker had disappeared. Surely the police would have come up with a lead by now.

Chapter 8

Mac MacAllister threw another dart across the room. It hit the edge of the dart board and fell onto the sofa, there to join two other darts that already lay among the seat cushions, and a fourth that was embedded in the Victorian sofa's rigidly upholstered back.

Sighing, he got up, retrieved the darts, and went back to his desk. Setting the darts in a careful row on the cluttered Lucite desktop, he settled himself into his Eames chair, picked up a dart, and, sighting carefully along its shaft, let fly. The dart bonked into the wall to the left of the target and clattered onto a small end table.

Dave's face appeared cautiously around the edge of the half-open door. "Any news?" he asked.

Mac shook his head and threw another dart. Dave ducked behind the door as the dart soared across the office and hit the target, scoring a ten before falling off and landing behind the sofa.

"When do you think they'll call?" Dave asked, edging around the door and into the office.

Mac shrugged. "Nolan said they'd make their decision today. Could mean five minutes from now, could mean six o'clock tonight." He reached for a dart, then put it down again. "Christ, I can't concentrate on anything," he complained.

Dave nodded. "Me neither. I just want them to decide."

Both men were exhausted, yet keyed up. They'd made their speculative presentation to Randall Webber three days before, and now waited in a limbo of expectation.

"So what do you think our chances are?" Dave asked Mac for the hundredth time since the pitch.

But Mac just shook his head. "I think we did well, very

well. The creative work was great, Dave. But . . . I just can't call this one."

Dave seated himself on the sofa. "I got about a million things to do," he told Mac, "but I just can't seem to get moving." Mac nodded. He raised a dart, realized Dave was sitting beneath the target, and put it down.

The phone rang; both men looked urgently toward the large multiline instrument. Outside Mac's office, his secretary Beth took the call; Mac watched the blinking light go solid red, then begin blinking again as the caller was put on hold. He and Dave looked at each other: was this The Call?

The intercom buzzed. "Victoria's on line two." Beth's voice announced.

Both men visibly sagged; Victoria was Mac's girlfriend.

Mac punched the line two button and lifted the receiver. "Hi, babe," he said. He smiled as Victoria's voice, with its upper-class British accent mellowed by a hint of West Indian lilt, flowed down the phone line to him. "No, no word yet," he told her. "Sure, I'll call you if we win. You and *Advertising Age* and the *New York Times* . . . "

On the wall at right angles to his desk hung a large colorful abstract painting, pulsing with life and energy, yet controlled and disciplined. Not for the first time, Mac marveled at Victoria's ability to invest her work with her very essence. "Yeah, me, too," he told her fondly.

He recradled the phone and sank back into his chair. Tipping back, he studied the acoustical tiled ceiling, then reached for a sharpened pencil and hurled it sharply upward. It stuck point-first in the tile. He threw another that also stuck.

"Wanna try a few?" he asked Dave.

"Sure."

Mac pressed his intercom button. "Hey, Beth," he said, "could you get me a couple of boxes of yellow pencils, please? Nice and sharp, okay? Dave and I are working on a project in here."

Beth got up and went to the low cabinet in which she kept Mac's private stash of stationery supplies. As she got out the boxes of pencils and began feeding them, one by one, into the electric sharpener, she made a mental note to call building services at the end of the day to ask them to bring a ladder and pull the pencils off the ceiling again.

*   *   *

"Who would you choose?"

Kate and Michael Nolan were sitting in the small, elegant private conference room that opened off Nolan's office. On the polished table in front of them were the remains of a sandwich lunch. Tacked onto the walls around them were sample ads presented by the various competing agencies, as well as summaries of their marketing strategies and approaches.

Kate took a sip of her iced tea and looked around at the materials on the walls. "Frankly, I don't think I'm qualified to judge," she said. "Who would *you* choose?"

Ignoring the question, Nolan stood and walked to one group of ads. "Riding & Levy did some interesting work, don't you agree?"

"It's interesting, yes," Kate said slowly. "But it's a little . . . cerebral. I mean, the advertising makes a lot of sense, but it's not very emotional. I think Genelife is an emotional product." Nolan nodded encouragingly. "Wanting to look good isn't a logical decision," she continued. "It's an emotional one."

"Good for you!" Nolan told her, a little surprised. "You're absolutely right. I don't think they understand the emotional side. Or maybe they don't want to. Also, they're a little small to handle this account. So let's say no to R&L."

'And Benson Hughes withdrew . . ."

'That was a smart decision," Nolan said. "They knew they'd never win. So why waste time and money on a presentation?"

"Why wouldn't they win? Aren't they any good?"

"Sure they're good. They handle Dentricreme and Anabasic analgesic for us. But they're kind of middle of the road. Genelife needs fresh, contemporary creative thinking."

"So that leaves MacAllister and Imagemakers."

"Right. Don't you like that sandwich?"

"It's fine," Kate told him, looking down at her partly eaten turkey club. "It's just awfully big." She smiled and took another sip of iced tea.

"Imagemakers showed some excellent strategic work," Nolan said. "They're big enough to handle the account, small enough for us not to get lost. And O'Neill seems very businesslike." He ate a pickle and looked at Kate.

"O'Neill seems very boring," Kate said. She scanned the advertising on the walls. "The work is very finished-looking. The way the ads are designed ... the colors ... the placement of the words on the page ..."

Nolan smiled. "The layouts are very well designed," he agreed. "The art direction is first-rate."

"But once you get past that and look at what the ads are actually saying," Kate continued, "Genelife doesn't come across as being nearly as exciting as the ads themselves. Does that make sense?"

"It does indeed. The ads are all sizzle, no steak. And that's too bad, because in this case, we definitely have the steak."

He wiped his hands on the linen napkin that Jenny, his longtime secretary, had placed beside his china plate, and poured himself another cup of coffee. "We could work on that with them," he said thoughtfully. "This is only the first go-round, after all."

Kate nodded, feeling somewhat out of her depth.

"If Imagemakers and Riding & Levy were the only agencies we'd seen," Nolan said, "I'd go with Imagemakers. I think we can get what we need from them."

"So you've selected Imagemakers?"

"I said 'if.' In fact, we do have another choice. What did you think of MacAllister?"

"Mac seemed very intelligent, very receptive," Kate said.

"Yeah, Mr. Charm. My secretary's already in love with him." Nolan laughed. "But I hear he's got a gorgeous British girlfriend. So don't let any romantic ideas influence your opinion."

Kate blushed. "I wouldn't do that," she said, and meant it.

"So?"

"So ... the ads look good, and they're certainly emotional. I loved Dave's presentation. He got so excited, jumping around and pulling out ad after ad. He did everything but dance on the conference table!"

Nolan laughed. "He is enthusiastic, isn't he?" He stood and began to pace. "MacAllister's a little smaller than Imagemakers, but they're still a pretty good size for us. Their marketing department is strong; Haines has an excellent reputation. Of course MacAllister himself is something of a wunderkind. And the guy with the ponytail—"

"Dave."

"Yeah, Dave. He's off the wall, but he's good. He's very good."

He studied the group of MacAllister ads. They were unconventional; they'd definitely cut through the clutter. And they were emotional, appealing, and motivating. The more he looked at them, the better they got.

"MacAllister just bought out his partner," Nolan said. "He's cash-poor, and he needs this account. I think they'll work their tails off for us." He turned back to Kate. "I'm giving the account to MacAllister. You comfortable with that?"

"Sure. I liked their presentation. And I think they'll be easy to work with."

Kate rose and began clearing away the remains of her lunch, but Nolan waved her away. "Jenny'll do that," he said. "Look, do me a favor and call Imagemakers and Riding, tell them thanks but no thanks? Oh, and you'd better set up a meeting for us over at MacAllister so we can get them started. I'll brief you tomorrow morning after I've put my thoughts down on paper. All this"—he gestured toward the MacAllister grouping—"is a good start, but we have a long way to go before the January launch."

"And this is the bullpen." Dave led Kate between the cramped drawing tables and computer equipment. Artists were manipulating computer images on glowing screens, or rendering storyboard panels and print ads in paint and markers. "This is where we put together the presentations of our work for various agency clients," Dave explained. "That's Roger, that's Barbara, this is Gil . . ."

"Hi," Kate said.

People turned, smiled, and waved. Their workstations were small, but efficient. Giant pads of paper were stacked in open cabinets against the walls. Paints and brushes, rubber cement, cans of Spray Mount adhesive, and carousels of colored markers stood everywhere.

"Over here's the paste-up area," Dave told her. Across from the artists, a young woman was picking up strips of printed copy with a tweezer and placing them carefully into position beneath a photograph.

Kate nodded, trying to appear knowledgeable. Nearly a week had passed since MacAllister had invited her to their celebration of the assignment of Genelife, and encouraged by Nolan, Kate had spent a fair amount of time in meetings at the executive level of agency life. Today she was being given a look at the workaday world in which the advertising was created.

A young woman with the delicate face of an angel rushed past them into the bullpen. "Who's got the frames for Puppy Life?" she called testily. "Meeting's in half an hour!"

"Not ready yet," the man Dave had identified as Roger told her laconically.

"Why the fuck not?" the angel demanded angrily.

"Only got them late yesterday."

"Liar! I brought them down myself yesterday morning!"

Roger shrugged.

"How far have you gotten with them?"

"Four out of six." Roger gestured to a small stack of individual storyboard frames beside his computer terminal. "Help yourself."

The woman grabbed the finished frames. "I'll be back in fifteen minutes!" she threatened, and left at a run, cursing under her breath.

"Just another morning with the folks," Dave said with a smile. "Careful! That paint looks wet."

He guided Kate out of the art department and along a short corridor in the direction of the reception area. "Let's head upstairs and I'll show you where the suits live."

Kate smiled. She was enjoying the informality of agency life. MacAllister felt like a happy place to work. Although people were serious about what they did, they seemed to be having a very good time doing it. The copywriters and art directors, some of whom she'd already worked with at creative briefings the week before, were an interesting mix of people with an often irreverent attitude that Kate found refreshing. And Mac, Dave, and Arthur Haines had all made her feel like one of the family, a member of the agency team rather than The Client.

A raucous barking echoed along the corridor, rising in volume as they approached the reception area.

"Pooch audition," Dave said. "We're shooting a new commercial for Chow-Down dog food."

And indeed four large, hairy animals and their respective trainers waited more or less patiently for their chance to strut their stuff. The fifth dog, somewhat smaller but quite vocal, was voicing a strong protest at the delay. Kate's eyes lit up at the sight of him; he looked so much like her own dog, Cheerio.

The receptionist turned a distraught face toward Dave. "They promised they'd keep them all in the casting room," she complained. "But I can't find Laura anywhere." Laura was one of the agency's casting directors.

Kate went over to talk to the yelping dog, who quieted down and regarded her with deep curiosity.

"May I pet him?" she asked the trainer, who nodded.

"It's his first audition," the man explained. "He's a little nervous."

Kate grinned. "You'll be just fine, boy," she told the dog. "A handsome fella like you! They'll love you!" She ruffled the dog's shaggy head and he licked her hand enthusiastically. "What's his name?"

"Winston the First."

"Winston the First . . . ?" Kate repeated in some amusement. "Hey, Winnie One, I have a dog just like you at home!"

"Really?" The trainer leaned forward, interested. "What breeder did you get him from?"

"Actually it's a her," Kate said. "I got her from the pound."

The trainer stiffened. "You got a Wheatley terrier from the pound?"

"A Wheatley terrier, is that what this guy is?" Kate looked thoughtful. "I never asked the pound what breed my dog was. I mean, I didn't really care. I just fell in love with her."

"She probably isn't really a Wheatley," the trainer said starchily. "There are lots of mutts . . . uh, mixed breeds that look like Wheatleys."

Kate shrugged. "Oh, it really doesn't matter. Cheerio's a great dog."

"Cheerio?" The trainer regarded her with horror. "You call your dog Cheerio?"

"It's her favorite snack food," she explained. "That and pizza." The trainer looked deeply pained.

"Laura! You're here! Thank goodness!" Behind Kate, the receptionist greeted the arrival of the casting director with relief. "Okay, people, follow me!" Laura announced.

The trainers began herding their dogs toward the casting room, and Kate gave Winston's head an extra pat for luck.

"I can't get over how much he looks like Cheerio!" she told Dave as they started up the white industrial-style spiral staircase that led from the reception area to the floor above. The MacAllister Agency occupied three floors in the large, modern office building, and these interior staircases were far more convenient than waiting for the elevators that served the top twelve floors.

" 'You got a Wheatley terrier from the pound?' " Dave did a wicked imitation of the horrified trainer and they both laughed, but then Kate grew serious. "I hate that superior attitude some people have toward dog and cat shelters. They have some wonderful animals there."

Dave nodded. "Yeah, I know. I've got an old stray tomcat at home. Hey, you want some Chow-Down? The client sends us tons of the stuff every time we shoot a commercial. You live in the city, right? I'll send some over to your apartment."

"Well, great, but are you sure it's okay to do that?"

"Of course it is. The client doesn't want it back. We'll call it a 'taste test'. Let me know how Cheerio likes it."

"I'll get you a doggie testimonial," Kate promised. "Thanks."

"Up here is media, market research, and account handling," Dave explained as they climbed the last few steps to the thirty-seventh floor. "Like I said, the suits." Dave was wearing distressed blue jeans and a loose-weave collarless cotton shirt.

The decibel level was appreciably lower on the floor above, and even the receptionist was more formal-looking. Everyone was dressed conservatively and spoke in low voices. "This floor is a lot less fun than ours," Dave told her. "Their expense accounts are bigger up here, but our conversation is more stimulating. Remember that when Arthur asks you to lunch."

"He already has. We went to La Reserve."

"Exactly. No one there under fifty, right? Now, I know a great Mexican place down on West Twenty-first Street . . ."

He led her in a large semicircle through the various departments and back out through a door at the opposite end of the reception area. Mac was standing at the bank of elevators, pushing the call button impatiently. Next to him stood a tall and very beautiful black woman.

"Hey! Victoria!"

The woman turned and, recognizing Dave, smiled broadly. "My favorite creative director!" she announced.

"I thought *I* was your favorite creative director," Mac told her. "Hiya, Kate."

"You went and got promoted," she told him. "You'll have to settle for being my favorite agency president." She grinned at Kate. "Hello. I'm Victoria Ward."

"I'm—"

"Kate Martin," Mac finished for her. "Dr. Martin, actually. She's our new Genelife client. She's going to keep us out of trouble with the FDA."

"Glad to hear it," Victoria said. "Look, we're just going round the corner to Mumtaz for a curry. Want to join us?"

"Actually, I was going to take her downtown to Sol y Sombra," Dave said.

"Then I have probably saved your life," Victoria told Kate.

"Come on, Victoria, you've eaten there," Dave protested.

"Once," Victoria said. "Once was enough."

"Why don't you both come with us?" Mac suggested. "We can talk about the new tag line."

"God save me from another business lunch!" Victoria exclaimed. "Can't we all just have a meal together like real people? You know, 'How do like you this weather?' 'I love what you've done to your hair!' 'Did you catch the new show at the Met?' "

" 'What's in this curry?' " said Dave. Victoria stuck her tongue out at him.

Kate laughed. "I'd love to come," she said. Dave nodded reluctantly. "But I ought to check in with my office. Can I meet you there?"

"Sure," said Mac. "Dave'll wait for you, right?" Dave nodded. The elevator arrived, and Mac held its door open with his foot. "Want to use my office, Kate?"

"Thanks, but the phone in reception will be fine."

Victoria waved as the elevator door closed. Kate turned toward the reception area where the guest phone stood on a side table.

"I'll meet you back here in five minutes," Dave told her.

"Lunch with the boss means a jacket." He disappeared down the stairway to the creative floor.

Among the messages her secretary gave her was one from Richard Day. She hadn't spoken with him since she'd broken the news that his agency had not gotten the Genelife account. She'd chosen her words carefully, but he'd been cold and curt. Why could he be calling her now? Curious yet slightly nervous, she dialed the number he'd left.

His secretary was extremely pleasant and passed her along to Richard immediately.

"Thanks for returning my call so quickly," he told her warmly. "Listen, I just wanted you to know there are no hard feelings."

"I'm glad to hear that," she said gratefully.

"Business is business, right? So how's my competition doing?"

"Fine," Kate said a bit stiffly. What an inappropriate thing to say, she thought.

"Sorry," he said, hearing her tone. "Just making conversation. The reason I called was to renew my lunch invitation. Now that you've assigned the account, there's no reason we can't get together as people, is there?"

Kate smiled; hadn't Victoria just used a similar phrase? "Of course there isn't," she said. "No reason at all."

"Good. Then how about Wednesday?"

Kate thought for a moment. "Actually, I have meetings at Randall Webber all day Wednesday, but I'll be in New York on Thursday. Will that work for you?"

"Thursday will be fine. I'll have my secretary call you with the time and place, okay?"

"Great."

Richard paused. "Kate," he said, "I'm really looking forward to seeing you again."

"Uh, thanks, Richard," she replied, feeling a little awkward. "It'll be nice to see you again, too."

She hung up the phone and turned around. Dave, a black cotton blazer slung over his shoulder, stood just beyond the seating area, trying not to eavesdrop. Kate felt her face flush. Why did it feel somehow traitorous to be having lunch with the competition when the account had already been assigned? She shrugged, deciding she was just being silly. Her personal life was her own, after all.

Making light conversation as they walked the few steamy

blocks to the small restaurant, Kate asked Dave about Victoria Ward.

"She and Mac have been together for eons," Dave said. "Well, six years. Madly in love with each other, but she refuses to live with him. Says she needs her own space."

"Is she a model?"

"God, no! Everybody thinks so, and it drives her nuts. She's an artist, a painter. You know that big abstract canvas in Mac's office? That's one of hers."

"I remember noticing it," Kate said. "It's very good."

"Some of her stuff's in the permanent collections of a couple of museums. And she shows a lot in some of the galleries down in SoHo."

"She's British, isn't she?"

"Actually, she was born in Antigua and moved to London back in the early seventies, when things were cheap. She loved it for a while, made a pile in real estate, then decided she hated what the economic recession was doing to England. So she sold up, came here, bought a gorgeous brownstone in Chelsea, met Mac, lived happily ever after. Nice lady."

The Indian lunch was a great success. The company was well matched, the food was delicious, and everyone laughed a lot. Soon Kate and Victoria were chatting away as though they'd known each other for years. Kate found herself talking about her stay in London, her return to New York and medical school, and her foundering marriage.

"There were faults on both sides," she said. "It's hard being married to a medical student."

"I should think it would be hard being married to an investment banker, too," Victoria told her.

Seeing Kate's surprise, she explained. "I've always had a problem with people who didn't actually produce something. You know, create a work of art, or teach, or cure people, or manufacture breakfast cereal or grommets, or cook a decent meal. Most of us make things and do things that are ... real, that we can feel proud of. Money's important, too, of course. But to most of us, money's just a tool. Now the financial guys like your bond trader don't actually make anything *except* money. Money's the product. I've always thought that diminished people."

"An interesting theory,'" Kate said with a smile. "Bert wouldn't agree. But I think I would."

"Bert the bond trader ..." Victoria smiled. "So why did you give up a promising career as a ... what is your specialty, by the way?"

"Emergency medicine," Kate said.

"... a promising career in emergency medicine, to join Randall Webber?"

"It's kind of complicated, actually," Kate told her. "Partly, I was starting to suffer from burnout. And partly ... well, I've always felt rather like an outsider at New York General. I started medical school so much later than everyone else, and did my residency under doctors my own age ... Also, while I was married, we lived in a fabulous apartment, and we had a maid ... And Bert would whip me off to these great parties and skiing weekends and stuff—that is, when I could steal the time from studying. That was another bone of contention. Anyhow, I didn't know any other medical students or residents who lived like that, and I guess I felt sort of guilty about it, and ... different. I mean, they'd be having these potluck dinners all the time, and I'd be off with Bert at Aureole. I felt guilty, but also I was jealous." Kate sighed. "I'd have preferred the potlucks and the camaraderie, you know?"

Victoria nodded. "Still, it sounds like it was fun."

"Oh, it was, for a while. And then, when the marriage ended, and I was back to living on my resident's salary—"

"No alimony?"

"Didn't want any. Anyway, when I was a poor second-year resident instead of a rich, glamorous one, I felt sort of self-conscious about it."

"For heaven's sake, why?"

Kate sipped her tea thoughtfully. "Well, I'd been more a part of Bert's world than my own, so I didn't have any really close friends among the people I worked with. And it felt awkward to suddenly reach out to the hospital staff. I thought they might pity me. Or think I was slumming."

"And then along came Randall Webber and offered you a way out."

"Not exactly. Randall Webber offered me a chance to build a world of my own, from scratch. Without the ghost of Bert or my previous social failures." Kate smiled self-deprecatingly.

"And do you miss the actual practice of medicine?"

Kate shrugged. "I'm not really sure," she said. "The cor-

porate life is still so new and different. And it's great not
to be on call every third night. But sometimes I do miss
the hectic energy of the hospital. I like action!"

Victoria smiled and patted her hand. "You just wait till
launch time," she said. "You'll get all the action you want."

Mac, deep in conversation with Dave about the new tag
line, glanced in their direction and nodded approvingly. Out
of the corner of her eye, Victoria noticed his look with
amusement. She whispered to Kate, "He thinks I'm chatting you up because you're the client. But I really like you.
Come to dinner on Friday?"

"I'd enjoy that."

"Great. Bring a date if you like."

"Actually, I'm not seeing anyone right now," Kate said.
God, how long had it been since she'd been out with a man
she wanted to see again!

"Then come alone. I don't believe in dinner parties
where everyone's coupled off. Too boring!" Victoria scribbled the address on a napkin. "Around seven-thirty,
okay?"

Soon afterward, Kate and Dave returned to the office to
review some copy, and Mac and Victoria lingered over
coffee.

"I've invited Kate to the dinner party," Victoria told
him.

"My client? Then I'll be there," he said.

"You're *always* there." She laughed.

"Well, if you won't live with me, I guess I have to live
with you." He studied her fondly. "You're not usually so
ready to invite my clients to your house," he said. "Why
this one?"

Victoria looked thoughtful. "I like her," she said. "She's
direct and honest, and she doesn't play the client act, like
some of them do. And did you know she lived in London
for a couple of years? She had some sort of study grant,
and her ex-husband was doing something with the London
School of Economics. She found the Brits very amusing
and rather silly, so we have that in common." Victoria
sipped her coffee thoughtfully. "It's odd," she said, "but I
feel rather protective toward her."

"Why should you need to protect her?" Mac asked curiously. Kate had struck him as being a confident woman in
control of her life.

"I'm not sure," Victoria answered. "But there's a certain vulnerability about her. This is her first corporate job, did you know that?"

Mac shook his head.

"Well, anyway, I just like her. Now, shall we be wicked and have some dessert?"

Chapter 9

O'Hare Airport was ringed with thunderstorms, and Nolan's flight had landed over half an hour late. He'd called
Bettina's secretary from the arrivals lounge, but still he felt
uneasy. As he stripped off his soaking trench coat and hung
it in the closet that ran flush along one side of Omni International's executive reception area, he found he was shivering, a combination of the strong air-conditioning and his
jangly nerves. Hell, it wasn't his fault the plane was late.

Omni International was situated at the top of one of
Chicago's highest and most famous buildings, as befitted
the huge conglomerate's status and wealth. From the cus-
tom-made leather furniture, to the original works of art
that lined the walls, to the two elegant multilingual recep-
tionists, the carefully designed environment spoke of big
money, spent to impress. Nolan knew this, yet each time
he came here, he was suitably awed.

The blond receptionist finished speaking into her sleek
white telephone, stood up, and straightened her skirt. Then
she turned and walked carefully toward the sofa beneath
the high picture window where Nolan had seated himself.
She had to walk carefully; a woman in high heels could
break an ankle in carpeting that deep.

"Mrs. Hollis will be free in about twenty minutes, Mr.
Nolan," she told him pleasantly. "Would you care for some
coffee while you wait?" She glanced outside at the rain
bucketing down, and felt cozy and protected. The presence
of big money affected most people that way.

"Thanks, I'd love some," Nolan said. "Uh, do you have
any decaf?"

"Of course," she said. "Or perhaps tea? Earl Grey?
Ceylon?"

"Earl Grey would be nice," he said. "Thank you."

He'd only read a few pages of the latest *Fortune* when she returned with a small tray on which stood a bone china tea service, complete with a small round dish of biscuits. It had been after his first visit to Omni that he'd sent his own secretary out to buy similar chinaware for use at Randall Webber. Smiling his thanks to the attractive blonde, he sipped the fragrant brew and began to relax a little.

Ever since Nolan had first approached Bettina Hollis over a year ago with the idea of Omni acquiring Randall Webber, both she and Omni had become Nolan's corporate role models in style and attitude. Bettina's ruthlessness had evoked an echo in his own soul, but he'd realized immediately that she did it with a lot more class. Nolan was determined to learn from her.

She had vision and courage; she'd recognized Genelife's potential immediately, and with the information Nolan had secretly supplied from within, she'd pushed through the takeover rapidly, and at an advantageous price. Throughout the process Nolan had done what he could to undermine Clark Randall, but he hadn't had to push too hard; Clark wasn't to Bettina's taste at all. Once Omni had taken over, with Bettina responsible for the Randall Webber subsidiary, Clark had been ousted and Nolan promoted.

He bit into a biscuit, pale and lemony. Delicious. He turned back to his magazine, but couldn't concentrate. He was anxious to tell Bettina about his progress with Genelife since their last project update, and to show her the new profit projections he'd done. Pushing the tea tray to one side, he placed his attaché case on the marble coffee table and snapped it open. Two light blue folders with the Randall Webber insignia lay neatly on top. Nolan allowed himself a small self-satisfied smile as he took up a folder and leafed through it. Very impressive. Genelife was going to make Omni a bundle. After that, Nolan could write his own ticket.

He looked around at the expressions of wealth and taste. He could get used to living like this.

A slim, conservatively dressed young man with a perky expression appeared at the edge of the reception area and took a few steps toward him. 'Mr. Nolan? I'm William, Mrs. Hollis's new administrative assistant. Mrs. Hollis will see you now."

Nolan gathered up his folders and followed William

down the hall, wondering not for the first time why Bettina insisted on retaining the "Mrs." before her name when she'd been divorced for years.

The woman *Forbes* magazine had dubbed "Bottom Line Betty" studied herself before the ornate antique mirror that hung above the carved sideboard that ran along one side of her richly appointed office. The furnishings had been Omni's idea; she'd never cared about such things. A desk of some sort, a phone, a few chairs, her computer and printer, a good assistant outside the door; that was all anyone really needed. Still, people were impressed by the way Omni had decorated her office, so it was useful in that way, she supposed. Just as the "Mrs." in front of her name made the men she worked with feel more comfortable.

She brushed a minute white speck from the right lapel of her conservatively tailored dark red designer suit, and smoothed back her hair, wavy blond and cut fashionably short. It framed a severe yet striking face with high cheekbones and a long elegant nose. She wore little makeup, but needed none. At thirty-seven, only a few faint lines around mouth and nose marred the perfection of her pale skin.

Her assistant's discreet knock on the partly closed door interrupted her inspection. "Come in," she called, noting the time on her gold Rolex.

She greeted Nolan with a warm smile and a firm handshake, but her blue eyes were steely with intelligence and determination. She appeared taller than her five feet nine inches, her height accentuated by her pencil slimness. "Sorry you had to wait," she said with no note of apology as she gestured him toward the empire sofa upholstered in Chinese silk. "I understand your flight was late," she added, thus making him feel as though the delayed arrival of his airline was somehow his fault, and that his time in the waiting room had been a sort of punishment.

"Terrible weather," he said by way of excuse.

"Is it?" Bettina glanced at the window as though she hadn't noticed.

Bitch, Nolan thought. But he admired the way she'd put him in his place.

Bettina settled herself in a wing chair to one side of the sofa and smiled brightly. "So. How are we doing with Genelife?"

"Very well," Nolan told her. "You got my memo about

the advertising agency we chose." Bettina nodded. "They're doing some great stuff, just great. Will you want to review it prior to launch?"

"Of course. And please keep cautioning them about overpromise. We don't want any problems with the FDA."

"Absolutely,' Nolan agreed. "Actually, Kate ... uh, Dr. Martin's being quite helpful there."

"Yes, how *is* Dr. Butler's replacement doing?" Bettina asked. "You know my feelings about her inexperience, but of course you're the one who has to work with her."

Meaning it's my ass if she screws up, Nolan thought. Well, I'll see that she doesn't. "She's the best person we could want in that spot," he replied. "She's great on detail work, the agency guys love her, and she's the perfect person to front the public relations campaign once we launch."

"I still don't understand why you're not the one to go on TV and be quoted in the newspapers. You're the chairman, Michael. Why leave it to a little girl?"

Nolan allowed one eyebrow to rise slightly. "Dr. Martin is nearly thirty-four, not exactly a girl. Although she does look a lot younger," he added maliciously. "But the point is, she can give Genelife contemporary medical respectability. I mean, everybody trusts a doctor."

"And not a corporation chairman?" she asked tartly.

"I'll be involved as well, of course," Nolan assured her. "But with a product like this, medical trust is paramount. And to our target audience, Dr. Martin symbolizes the endorsement of the entire medical community."

"If you say so. I assume you'll involve her in the long-term tracking study, starting in January."

"Yes, to some degree, although it's not our first priority. After all, the FDA won't be expecting the study for several years. And of course Chemstra will be handling the whole thing, just as they did the original clinical testing."

"Chemstra, yes ... Are you sure you want to stay with them? They're awfully small, and not terribly well known in the industry." Implication: If Omni and I had become involved before you started the trials, we'd never have allowed you to use them.

"They've been doing an excellent job for us," Nolan said firmly, "and I have every reason to believe they will continue to do so." Including a reason best kept from you, he thought. "It'll all be routine."

"Let's hope so." Bettina glanced at her watch. "So, what else do you have for me?"

Nolan reached for his attaché case. "Preliminary market research with physicians has just begun, but the results are very impressive." He snapped open his case and handed her a blue folder. "I think you'll like the new projections."

Bettina's eyes widened as she scanned the figures. "You sure about this?" she said softly.

"Yes, indeed. In fact, these estimates may even be conservative."

Bettina's mind whirled. If the information in the folder proved correct, Randall Webber would be a prime candidate to be spun off by Omni into a public offering, down the road. And not that far down the road either, if these figures were anywhere near accurate. Nolan was a toady and a weasel, she reflected, but he certainly delivered the goods. And she was prepared to back him to the hilt, for just as long as he continued to make her look good.

"Can you stay for lunch, or are you rushing back to New York?" she asked, all smiles now.

For a moment Nolan toyed with one-upping her by claiming a prior engagement, but decided that would be a dangerous game. "I'm at your disposal, Bettina," he said graciously.

Damn right you are, she thought.

Kate sat at her desk at Randall Webber, toying with a pencil. The advertising campaign was progressing, she'd checked over all the Genelife research she'd been given access to, and Nolan was out of town. Although her desk was littered with reports and papers, she felt at a loss for something substantive to do.

She was also feeling a little guilty. Two months had passed since she'd left New York General, and she hadn't been back even once. I really ought to call Harold Gould at least, she thought. She checked her watch: nearly three o'clock. He'd probably be in his office for another half hour. For a moment she felt a stab of regret, of loss. Could she actually be missing the chaotic hospital routine? No, of course not, she told herself. She was merely tired of paperwork.

She reached for the phone, but a knock at her open

office door interrupted her. Freda Pershing was leaning
against the jamb, looking more than usually harried.

"I need a break!" Freda announced. "You busy?"

Kate shook her head. "Come on in."

Since Freda had invited Kate to join a group of cowork-
ers for lunch soon after she'd arrived, the two had become
office friends. But Freda was married and lived in Darien,
and the friendship seemed to stop at Randall Webber's
front door.

Freda collapsed onto the sofa. "Chaos, pure chaos," she
exclaimed. "Your office is an island of calm."

"That's what worries me," Kate laughed. "What am I
doing wrong?"

"Don't worry. Your turn will come! Probably on I-95
going home. Doesn't that commute make you crazy?"

"Not really," Kate answered. "It's a reverse commute—
most of the traffic's going the other way. As long as I leave
around five-thirty or so, it's not too bad."

"Well, you're young and resilient." Freda winked at her.
"And you're smart to leave your other car at home. Why
put commuter miles on the Mercedes, right?"

"Mercedes?" Kate looked at Freda in surprise. "You've
seen my Toyota in the parking lot."

"Yeah, but I always figured you had a better car at home.
All you doctors drive fancy cars."

"Not this doctor," Kate assured her. "To me, a car is
simply transportation."

Freda shrugged. "Whatever works for you. So ... what
do you young swinging singles do after work these days?"
Having been whisked away to Connecticut as a newlywed
thirty years ago, Freda had never lost her conviction that
New York City was nonstop excitement. "Got a
boyfriend?"

"Not exactly. I mean, there's a guy I go out with now
and then. But it's not love."

"You never know," Freda said. "Love can grow."

Kate sighed. Freda sounded just like her mother. Her
occasional dates with Richard Day were fun, but Kate was
quite certain that love would not grow. In fact, she'd
quickly discovered she had no romantic feelings for Richard
at all, despite his good looks. And Richard had never
pushed, which was just as well.

Freda pulled a crumpled Winston pack from her jacket

pocket and slid out a cigarette. "I'm dying for a smoke," she said. "You mind?"

"Actually, I do," Kate told her as nicely as she could. "Sorry."

Freda shoved the cigarette back into the pack with a self-deprecating smile. "I forgot you're a doctor," she said.

"Doctors aren't the only people who don't approve of smoking," Kate said lightly.

"You're right, you're right. My kids are always trying to get me to stop. But I've been smoking too long." Freda stood and straightened her skirt. "Think I'll go for a little walk. Why waste all that sunshine?" She gave a little wave as she left.

Several minutes later, Kate saw her amble down the path toward the gym, drawing deeply on a cigarette.

Freda's "doctor" remark had reminded Kate of her interrupted call to Harold Gould. Now she reached again for the phone and dialed his private number. Soon she was apologizing for not calling sooner, and he was forgiving her.

"But only if you'll come and see me soon. Are they keeping you very busy?"

"It varies from day to day," Kate told him. "actually, I've been spending a lot more time in New York than I'd imagined."

"Do they have a New York facility?"

"No, I ... I've been working with the advertising agency."

For a moment there was silence. Then Harold coughed softly. "Yes, I see. But you're happy, right? That's what matters."

"Actually, I am," Kate told him somewhat defensively. "I know it's not really medicine. Development of Genelife was finished before I got here, and all the ongoing research and tracking studies are being handled by an outside lab. Is that normal procedure, by the way?"

"It's often done by smaller companies, I understand. More economical."

"I just wondered. Anyway, I wander around the research labs sometimes, kibitz with the biochemists and technicians working on the cough medicines and analgesics ... Sometimes I feel kind of underused. But it's all new, and the marketing side's quite interesting. And you can't beat the life-style!"

In fact, despite her temporary boredom with the paperwork on her desk, she was very much enjoying her foray into the corporate world. She felt excited, revitalized, part of something bigger than day-to-day patient care. Away from the small, rather inbred hospital environment, and welcomed as an attractive and respected equal, she felt herself blossoming.

"I'm happy for you," Harold was saying. "And the drug you're working on . . . Genelife, you said? Is it any good?"

"You bet! I've been using it myself for a few months. It takes a little while to get started, but it really works."

"What's in it?"

"Now, Harold, you know I can't tell you that. But we launch in January, and then it'll be public knowledge."

"I'm not sure I like the idea of your taking a drug that's not on the market yet."

"It's FDA-approved. Besides, I've read the topline test results. Trust me, Genelife is completely safe."

"No side effects?"

"Nothing to speak of." Idly Kate recalled her somewhat diminished appetite, but pushed the thought aside. It could be just coincidence, and besides, she'd never looked better.

"Genelife is absolutely safe," she repeated. "And if you can't trust a doctor, who can you trust?"

Chapter 10

"I'm worried about Marianne," Avram repeated. "She's ... confused. I think she blames herself."

"Blames herself?" Steve looked at his uncle in surprise. "Why would she do that?"

"She'd been planning to leave him. Didn't you know?"

"No." Steve stirred sugar into his cappuccino. "She didn't tell me that."

"It's true. So then, when Tucker disappeared, she felt guilty, I think. Another cruller?"

"Why guilty?"

"Because she was relieved." Avram sighed, and leaned back in the plush red velvet chair. He was a large, heavy man with a shock of hair that despite his seventy-odd years was still a suspiciously uniform dark brown. "I suggested she come and live with me for a while, but ..." He shrugged and smiled. "Unlike you, this was never home to her." Avram helped himself to a cruller from the tray of pastries on the low table between them, then cut it neatly in quarters with the silver knife, engraved with a delicate "K," that lay beside his gold-rimmed plate. "Did she tell you she'd gone back to school? Columbia University."

"Yes, for a master's degree, she said. She's hoping to teach full-time, on the high school level. Actually, I was surprised at how well she sounded. Positive, determined ..."

"Well, when you see her today, remember that she's not as strong as she likes to pretend." He sighed again, deeply. "She can't be earning much with that substitute teaching. Let me know if she needs any money. I offered to pay her tuition, but you know Marianne."

Steve nodded. He wasn't surprised at his sister's attitude. He'd always felt closer to Avram than she had. Two years older than Steve, Marianne was already living at college when Steve had moved in with Avram to finish high school in New York. Ever since their parents had been killed, Marianne had been aggressive in her insistence that she could take care of herself. She'd always found it hard to accept help from anyone, family included.

He sipped his coffee and studied his uncle. Avram had aged, yet here in the rather floridly decorated town house where Steve had come to live all those years ago, his uncle seemed ageless. His Armenian accent was still soft and charming, his dark eyes still bright and kind and knowing.

"Thanks, Avram," Steve said, and meant it. He reached for a cherry turnover. Avram believed in good living. It was suddenly hard to believe that less than a week ago, he'd been deep in the African jungle.

"Three months . . ." Avram mused. "You'd have thought someone would have heard from him by now." He leaned toward Steve and lowered his voice. "Do you think perhaps it was . . . foul play?" he asked dramatically.

"You mean, did Marianne stab Tucker with a steak knife and throw his body in a landfill?" Steve grinned; Avram viewed all of life as theater.

"No, no, not Marianne, of course. But . . . he could have been mugged coming home one night."

"They'd have found his body, Avram."

Avram pursed his lower lip in a gesture that meant "maybe, maybe not." "I asked Marianne whether he had any enemies. You know what she said?"

"What?"

" 'Only everyone who knew him!' Is that true?"

"I'd lost touch with him over the years," Steve said. "I can understand some people not liking him much. Tucker was a spiky kind of guy sometimes, and it was getting worse. But kill him . . . ? Seems unlikely."

"People can make worse enemies than they know," Avram said. "I've seen it happen in the theater. For a good part, I'm certain some people would think nothing of killing. What about that place he worked? Maybe someone was jealous of him. Maybe someone lured him to a lonely spot and . . . and . . ." Avram broke off, searching for a plausible way one scientist would murder another.

"Come on, Avram, this isn't one of your plays."

"But it *is* New York." Avram turned and stared suspi-

ciously at the high windows behind him as though expecting
armed thugs to suddenly step from behind the thick bro-
cade drapes. The idea made Steve smile, despite the seri-
ousness of the conversation. He'd always felt so protected,
inside this house. "I hope Marianne is not in danger,"
Avram said darkly, turning to fix Steve with a stern look.

"I'm sure she isn't. And the police are working on the
case."

Avram raised a cynical eyebrow. "Indeed. Another
coffee?"

Steve nodded, and his uncle went to the intricately
carved breakfront with its antique marble slab, and began
tinkering with the small espresso machine. Steve leaned
back into his deeply upholstered wing chair, luxuriating in
the comfort and beauty of his surroundings.

The town house, purchased at a time when people
couldn't give such buildings away, was large and rambling,
yet somehow cozy. Over the years, Avram had invested it
with a personal, comfortable luxury. This morning, as always, it was filled with fresh flowers. Not for the first time,
Steve reflected how well his uncle matched this room, with
his impeccably cut clothes, a European manner that was
almost courtly, and a connoisseur's appreciation of beautiful things. That he was able to indulge his passion for
beauty was in large measure due to his correspondingly
selective taste in theatrical productions.

"So you think Tucker simply decided to wander away,"
Avram said.

"He's done it before."

"Ah yes, the Amazon, all those years ago. But he turned
up again, eventually."

"Right. So maybe the same thing will happen again.
Tucker never did things without a reason."

"I still think we shouldn't rule out foul play," Avram
said, handing Steve a cup of hot frothy cappuccino. "And
don't look at me like that. You'd be surprised how often
life imitates theater."

Steve sighed. His uncle had a penchant for the dramatic,
no matter how unlikely. "Speaking of plays, I loved *The
Cool West Wind,*" Steve told him, hoping to shift the direction of the conversation. "Thanks again for the pass."

"Was it a good house?"

"Packed. You need a larger theater."

"I know, I know. We're considering moving it uptown ... the Helen Hayes will be free soon, I think."

"That's good news."

"For me, yes! But for that piece of shit at the Helen Hayes, not so good!" He chuckled with pleasure. "So. You went to the show alone?"

Steve nodded. "I don't know many people in New York these days. And Marianne had a class."

"So bring your girl from Boston for the weekend. Give her a treat, yes?"

"I'm not seeing anyone right now."

"You're never 'seeing anyone.' Sleeping with someone, yes. But 'seeing someone'? Oh, no! That would be too serious."

"Stop trying to marry me off, Avram," Steve said with a smile.

"I gave that up long ago," Avram said regretfully. "How I had hoped to dangle grandnephews and grandnieces on my knee. I thought surely that Marianne, at least, would—"

"Dandle, Avram, dandle." He gazed around at the delicately embroidered throw pillows, the tasseled lamp shades, the antique Chinese carpet, and smiled. A small child could do serious damage in here. "Anyhow, my life is not conducive to long-term relationships."

"Whose life *is*?"

"The situation is not unknown, even among your friends," Steve teased. "Anyhow, I don't bug you about your personal life. How *is* your personal life?"

"Sad," Avram said, suddenly serious. "Too sad. So many friends, gone ..." Then seeing the sudden concern in his nephew's eyes, he shook his head. "No, no, don't worry about me. I'm fine. I never was promiscuous, thank the Good Lord. And now I'm an old man ..."

"Not *that* old," Steve said.

Avram guffawed. "No, not that old! Still, I'm careful. I'm discreet."

Avram was indeed discreet, Steve reflected. He'd lived under Avram's roof for nearly two years before he'd realized his uncle was gay.

As a theatrical producer, Avram had entertained often, and many of his friends had been actors and dancers and painters, artists of all kinds, a certain percentage of whom were openly homosexual. Initially uncomfortable, Steve had come to admire and enjoy the company of many of Avram's friends. Although he'd never thought of it in such terms, his innate capacity for nonjudgmental acceptance of human differences had ultimately made him a better anthropologist, and a better person.

"So. No babies to inherit my money," Avram said. "I will just have to spend it all on high living. Now tell me about darkest Africa, while I make myself another cappuccino."

Marianne carefully dished the endive salad onto two plates, then added several small pieces of goat cheese.

"Looks good enough to eat!" Steve teased. "What can I do to help?"

"You can bring the wine," she told him. "Bottle's in the fridge, glasses are in the cupboard above the sink. I'll just bring these inside, and come help you." She disappeared through the swing door into the starkly modern living-cum-dining room, carrying the salad plates.

Steve looked after her with concern. Her long dark hair had been recently styled, and she wore an attractive summer dress. But her manner was overly bright, almost jumpy. Well, the poor kid's been through a lot, he thought.

He followed after her with the wine and glasses. Marianne was retrieving a corkscrew from a drawer in the sideboard. Sunlight streamed through the large window onto a side wall, making the rest of the room seem darker by contrast.

They seated themselves at the white Parsons table, and Steve filled their glasses. "Here's lookin' at you, kid," Steve said, and she smiled.

"You're very tan," she said. "You look good."

"So do you," he replied. "I like the dress." He paused. "I'm sorry I couldn't get here any sooner—"

"You're here now," Marianne said. "That's what counts. Anyway, there was nothing you could do . . . nothing anybody could do."

"It's so weird, though . . . To disappear without a trace. The police haven't come up with anything?"

"Oh, yes. The police have come up with something just dandy."

'Steve lowered his fork. "Really? What is it?"

"They figure Tucker left me for another woman. They've dropped the investigation."

"They've—but that's absurd!"

"Which part?"

Steve sighed. "I just mean that they have no right to suggest such a thing. And they've just dropped the whole matter, you say?"

"Well, it's been over three months. There are no leads. And he didn't even take any money out of our bank account. If he had, the police could have traced him that way."

"He disappeared with no money?"

Marianne shrugged. "He could have had some put away somewhere." She took a long pull at her wine. "Maybe the police are right. Maybe he did run out on me. God knows I often thought about running out on *him*."

"Were things that bad?"

"What did Avram tell you?"

"He said you were planning to leave Tucker. That you felt relieved when he disappeared and now you feel guilty."

Marianne nodded. "You weren't in town very often, Steve. And when you were here, Tucker was on his best behavior. Such as it was. He can charm the birds out of the trees, that one."

Outside, a police siren wailed its way up West End Avenue. Perhaps it was the contrast with Avram's place, but the apartment felt sterile and forlorn.

"He was . . . driven. He stayed at the lab until all hours," Marianne said. "And even when he was home, he was thinking about that project of his, you know, the 'discovery of a lifetime'?"

"And did it turn out to be as important as he thought it was?"

"Oh, I don't know!" Marianne sighed with frustration. "Sometimes he'd talk of nothing else, not that I could understand him. He'd talk in formulas, or start to describe some esoteric theory, and then suddenly he'd clam up, as though he'd said too much. At one point he got all excited, said they were getting ready to test it. He was over the moon. But who knew how stable he was by then?"

Marianne fell silent, remembering. Steve was quiet, too, knowing she needed to talk it out, glad she was able to do so at last.

"He'd disappeared before, Steve. I never told anyone that."

Steve stared at her. "Not even the police?"

"I ... I couldn't. They wouldn't have taken it seriously now. And this time it's different. I know it."

"How can you be sure? Maybe he'll just turn up again."

"After three months? Come on, Steve!"

"But you said he—"

"A few weeks here and there," Marianne said. "And each time, I found he'd taken a suitcase, some money. I knew he was coming back. This time he took nothing."

"But where did he go? Didn't you question him? Weren't you worried?"

"Of course I was worried. Angry, too. He said it was business, and refused to discuss it."

"I can't believe you stayed with him."

"Neither can I."

"It's hard to believe he was able to function effectively in his work," Steve said. "He must have driven everyone nuts."

"Probably. The last few years, he got really paranoid, started saying someone at the lab was out to get him."

"Who?"

"He wouldn't say. And his mood swings ... Sometimes it was like I wasn't even here. God, I felt so trapped. We never saw anybody—well, you know that, we never even saw *you*—we never went anywhere ..."

"But you stayed with him .. "

"You have to understand there were actually some good times, too. Times when his mood seemed to lift for some reason, and all of a sudden he'd be the old Tucker: charming and sexy and funny ... He hadn't looked at me for months, but suddenly he was carrying me off to the bedroom ..." She broke off, blushing, and reached for her wineglass. "And it didn't happen all at once. It was gradual ... it just kept getting worse and worse. He'd always been moody, you know that ..."

"Yes, I remember when we were in college, and afterward ... he was always erratic."

"Erratic is putting it mildly. The night before he disappeared, he was ... I think he was truly deranged."

"What happened?"

"I'll never forget it. He'd gone off without a word to me

about three weeks earlier. As I told you, it wasn't the first time he'd done that, but he'd never stayed away this long before ... I was getting frantic. Of course, by then I didn't know if I was more scared that he wouldn't come back, or more scared that he would."

She drank some wine and sighed deeply. "God, it was awful! He came through that door like a madman, ranting and raving and cursing. I couldn't understand what he was saying. I don't know where he'd been, but he was physically ill, shivering and sweating. I'm not even sure he realized where he was, or that I was there, too. He finally collapsed on the sofa and sort of passed out, so I just covered him with a blanket and left him alone. By eleven or so, he was still sleeping and I was exhausted, so I went to bed. When I woke up in the morning, he was gone."

Steve's face was creased with concern. "I can't believe you've been living that way. Why didn't you tell me all this before?"

"Tucker's moods were my problem." Marianne looked at him defiantly, and again he was reminded of just how much she feared her own vulnerability. She nibbled the rim of her glass. "At first I thought it was just temporary," she said. "You know, the pressure of the research grant. Then I figured I could handle it. Eventually, I knew what I had to do ... I just kept putting it off."

"Leave him, you mean?"

Marianne nodded. "It's funny. For years, I kept hoping I would get pregnant. I even went to a doctor to see if there was something wrong with me, but there wasn't. Now I guess maybe it was just as well we never had a child." A tear tracked slowly down her cheek, but she brushed it away and stood up. "Eat up, baby brother. I'll get the fish."

Steve followed her into the small efficient kitchen. "It's okay to cry," he told her softly. "You need to let it out."

"No, I damn well don't!" she rounded on him. Then she put a hand on his shoulder. "I'm sorry."

She opened the oven and, using two bright red oven mitts, took out a covered baking dish. It smelled wonderful. She set it on top of the stove and tossed the mitts onto the countertop. "It's not emotional release that I need," she told Steve, calmer now. "It's ... closure. I need to know what happened, so I can get on with my life. Until then, I feel like I'm in limbo or something. Here, go put this on the table. I'll get the bread. Use the oven mitts."

Steve carried the dish out to the dining table, feeling helpless. What if the police never found Tucker? Soon Marianne joined him and, uncovering the dish, began spooning out the luscious-looking baked fish.

"I'm really okay," she told him, handing him a heaped plate. "It's just the not knowing that gets to me, sometimes. And also . . . sometimes I think that if I'd called the police sooner, it might have made a difference. It's just that I kept thinking he'd come back the way he'd always done before."

"You mustn't blame yourself," Steve told her firmly. "Whatever's happened, it's not your fault."

"I know. You're right. Let's talk about something else. How was Africa?"

Between forkfuls, Steve told her about the trials and tribulations of his recent trek, and by the time they were ready for dessert, Marianne was laughing.

Over coffee, Steve broached the subject of money and Avram's offer, but Marianne shook her head.

"Avram's sweet, but there's enough in our joint account to last me a while, tuition included. I do some substitute teaching. And the rent here is cheap."

"How does it feel to be back in school?"

"A little strange, but it's good therapy. It's challenging, and it gives me a purpose, something to look forward to." She lowered her coffee cup and looked thoughtful. "Steve, do you think Avram could be right? Was Tucker murdered?"

"He said that to you?" Steve said, surprised that Avram would have been so tactless.

"No, not to me. To the police. They told me."

"They questioned Avram?"

"No, he called them to suggest Tucker might have been a victim of foul play, as he put it."

Steve shook his head. "He suggested the same thing to me this morning. But who would want to murder Tucker? I mean, there've been many times when I've wanted to give him a swift kick in the ass, but . . ." He paused and studied his sister's face. "Can *you* think why anyone would kill him?"

"No, of course not," she said slowly. "Only . . ."

"What?"

"Well, it's probably nothing. But about a week after Tucker disappeared, someone tried to jimmy the lock to the apartment. I'd replaced the old lock with a Medeco a couple of days before, and they didn't get in, but it shook me a little."

"Did you tell the police about it?"

"Of course. But they seemed to think it was just another burglary attempt. We only have a part-time doorman, and there've been several break-in attempts in the building."

"I think you ought to leave here for a while. Come live with me. Or Avram."

But Marianne shook her head. "It only happened the one time. I don't think it was related to Tucker's ... to Tucker. Really, I'd rather stay here." She poured them both more coffee, and added cream to hers. "Remember when we were all at school back in Boston? They were such happy days ... Who would have thought things would turn out like this?" She sighed and stood up, stretching. "Looking back, I'd do a lot of things differently," she told him. "But when they were good, they were very, very good."

Steve poured himself more coffee. "They were," he agreed.

"Hey, that reminds me. I left these out to show you." She went to a low cabinet across the room and retrieved a shoe box, its lid secured by a thick rubber band. "I was going through a bunch of papers and stuff, doing a little reorganizing. Look what I found."

She put the shoe box on the table. It was scuffed and torn, and the rubber band snapped apart as she pulled it off. "Shit!" She threw the cardboard cover aside and began taking out small bulky white envelopes. "Check these out," she told him, opening one of the packets. "They were taken at the bon voyage party you guys threw just before you went to the Amazon." And she tossed a pile of photos across the table to him.

Steve began sifting through the photos and was suddenly overwhelmed by a flood of memories.

"These were taken at our wedding," she said, tossing him another packet. "And—hey, how'd this get in here?" Steve looked up; she was staring at a photo he couldn't see.

"What is it?"

"Nothing. Just a shot I took of Tucker."

Steve came around behind her chair and stood peering over her shoulder. "God!" he said softly. "Were we really ever that young?"

Marianne gave him a curious look. "I think some of us never grew up."

Steve took the photo of Tucker from her and studied it for a moment. "Tucker Boone, in all his glory. This old picture really takes me back."

"Old? I took it about six months before he disappeared. That's why I was surprised to find it mixed in with these others."

"But he looks so young."

Marianne nodded. "Tucker was one of those people who never seemed to age." She dropped the photos back on the table and leaned her chin in her hands. "I wish we could go back to the beginning, when it was all so good," she said. "I wish Tucker had never gotten that damn grant from the Randall Foundation."

Chapter 11

Kate lay back in the tub, luxuriating in the heat of the water and the scent of the bath oil. It had been a very busy few months. And with only five weeks until Genelife's official launch date, the following weeks promised to be more frantic still. Nolan hadn't been wrong when he'd assured her, back in September, that the pace would soon quicken. But despite the pressure of short deadlines and long hours, she felt exhilarated, excited. Genelife was going to be a real winner.

She glanced over at her watch that lay on a low stool at the side of the bathtub: nearly seven o'clock. She'd spent over half an hour in the tub, but felt too lethargic to get out. Just ten more minutes, she promised herself.

The tension in her shoulders was easing. When Nolan had explained that part of her job would be to "liaison with the press," Kate hadn't realized he'd meant she herself would have to appear on camera. Yet from a marketing standpoint, she had to admit that it made good sense. Yesterday had marked her first performance, and although it had been somewhat stressful, it had also been exciting and surprisingly enjoyable.

The MacAllister Agency had written three short promotional scripts about Genelife. Called video press releases, these three- and four-minute miniprograms would be beamed via satellite to television stations around the country, many of whom would use them as part of their "soft news" programming the day Genelife was officially launched.

Never having seen herself on camera before, Kate had been reluctant to look at the playback. But Mac had insisted. And she'd been relieved to find that she looked and sounded very good. Her delivery had been professional yet outgoing, friendly without being cute. Her hair, now cut fashionably short, had been styled to frame her face in soft tendrils, giving her a more sophisticated look. And Genelife had certainly done its part, she reflected.

The past five months at Randall Webber had imbued her with a new confidence and independence that had nothing to do with the effects of Genelife on her laugh lines. She was feeling good, professionally and personally, and that had come across on the videotape.

The water was growing cool. Time to make the big move, she thought, and forced herself up out of the tub. Standing on the thick white bathmat, she admired yet again the small bathroom's new blue and white wallpaper and soft cobalt towels, paid for by her Randall Webber salary. The new vertical blinds across the windowed wall of her living room were a big improvement, too.

She toweled off and went down the short hallway to her bedroom. She'd been renting the apartment since her divorce seven years before, but until now she hadn't had the money to do very much with it. The colorful new bedspread and matching curtains were a big improvement, she reflected.

As Kate stepped into the hallway, Cheerio raised a pale hairy ear, and her face registered the canine equivalent of "Oops!" Rising with alacrity from the middle of Kate's new bedspread, the large shaggy animal resettled herself on the carpet beneath the window and closed her eyes.

"You don't fool me, you hairy beast," Kate chided her, eyeing the dog-shaped depression in the bed.

Cheerio raised her head and looked at Kate with an expression of injured innocence.

"Must have been some other dog, right?" Kate said. She opened a dresser drawer and pulled out some underwear. Cheerio rolled over onto her back, and Kate tickled the dog's tummy as she went to the closet.

She pulled on a soft wool tunic top and fastened a snakeskin belt around her waist, then checked herself out in the mirror. She was a lot slimmer; the belt buckled two notches down from the well-worn hole that marked where her waist used to be. Well, someone once said that you can never be too thin, she thought. And those little wrinkles at the sides of her eyes certainly seemed fainter.

Her apartment was on East Seventy-sixth Street, some

distance from Victoria's West Twenty-third Street brown-stone. As her taxi splashed its way downtown through the freezing rain, early Christmas lights made colored streaks on the wet windshield. Huddled in a down coat on the sprung seat, Kate found herself in a reflective mood. What a good day today had been. Mac and Dave had driven up to Connecticut for a creative meeting and had surprised everyone by presenting the edited video press releases to Nolan. The videotapes hadn't been scheduled to be completed for several days, but Dave had worked all night to rush them through. Michael had been very pleased and had immediately screened them for the marketing and sales staffs, all of whom had echoed his enthusiasm. And the creative meeting that followed the screening had gone very well, too, aside from Jerry Lim's bizarre interruption. Afterward, Nolan had explained that Jerry had been working too hard. Well, that was certainly possible; everyone at Randall Webber was overworked at the moment.

The cab drew up in front of an attractive brownstone; a haze of warm light leaked through its curtained front windows. She pushed the doorbell and spoke her name into the small speaker at the side, and the door lock immediately clicked open.

"Come on up!" a tinny voice said through the intercom. "I'm in the studio."

Kate went into the entrance foyer, pulling the street door shut behind her. The first thing Victoria had done when she'd bought the house had been to knock down the wall separating the hallway staircase from the front room. Now, as Kate mounted the stairs that led up through the house, she glanced over at the appealing clutter of pillows, books, carpets, and artwork that filled the enlarged living room. She'd visited Victoria a number of times over the past few months, and never failed to marvel at how effectively Victoria managed to combine treasures and junk. Her unique sense of style was completely unself-conscious.

"Toss your coat on a chair and pour yourself some wine," Victoria called as Kate climbed the last flight of stairs, breathing hard. The studio made up the entire top floor of the house. The original roof had been replaced with glass paneling, and the rooms had been knocked together into one large workspace. Although it was quite dark outside, bright flat light flooded down from two giant arc lamps mounted just below the ceiling panels. Canvases in various states of completion were stacked around the paint-smeared walls.

"I got myself involved in something here and I can't stop just yet," Victoria apologized. "Still raining out, huh?"

"A real stinker," Kate said. "But even that can't bring me down tonight. I've had such a great week!" She dumped her coat and got herself some wine.

"So I've heard," Victoria said. She applied a deep magenta pigment in two thick broad swatches, and then stepped back and eyed the effect critically. "Even your receptionist sounded crazed when I called today."

"You're right about that. The excitement's getting to everybody, even the Great Stone Face."

"Who?"

"Michael Nolan, my boss."

"Oh, yes of course. Mac's mentioned him."

"And our creative meeting was a hoot. Dave was really flying!"

"Agency people are all crazy," she said. "But before a launch, they're certifiable." She filled the brush with paint and approached the canvas again.

"That could describe many of us up in Connecticut too, at the moment." Kate grinned.

Victoria stared intently at the canvas before her, brushing a wisp of hair from her forehead. "Yes, well, unlike client insanity that comes and goes, agency insanity is just a matter of degree." She added more magenta. "That's why I love them all."

"Well, they're entitled to be a little hyper at the moment," Kate said. "The advertising's looking great, the advance sell-in's phenomenal. But there's still so much to be done in the next four weeks . . ."

"Tell me about it," Victoria said. "I haven't seen Mac for days, and he's working all this weekend, too. He's over the moon, of course; he thrives on stress."

"Everybody at MacAllister does, it seems. Now, at the hospital, long hours always showed. We residents wore our tiredness like a badge. But agency people! I've never seen people work so hard and look so good."

Victoria turned and stared and Kate. "Surely you know why," she said.

"No. Why?"

"They're all taking Genelife. Not Mac, of course. He won't take an aspirin. But lots of others. Dave's been a big fan of it from the beginning."

"But ... it's not on the market yet."

"Nolan sent over a boxful, didn't you know? He said it was for photos and stuff, but he had to realize it would be used."

"He never told me ..."

"Is there a problem?" Victoria asked, suddenly concerned.

"No, not really. It's just ... Genelife's a prescription drug. It's illegal for Nolan to simply hand it out."

"If they catch him, he'll probably say Dr. Martin prescribed it. Hey, just kidding."

"Dispensing prescription medication without a medical license is no joke, Victoria. It could get the company in big trouble."

"Maybe I shouldn't have mentioned it," Victoria said. "Only I was sure you knew."

I should have recognized the signs, Kate thought. Over the past few months she'd spent a lot of time at the Mac-Allister Agency as they prepared the advertising materials needed for the launch in January. Now that she thought about it, Dave had lost some weight, and he looked fresher, somehow. And Mac's secretary had gotten a lot slimmer, not that she hadn't needed to. Well, what was done was done. She only hoped Nolan hadn't given Genelife to anyone else.

Victoria turned back to the large canvas propped against the wall. She painted a smaller swatch of magenta to one side of the others, then studied the effect. She felt silly she hadn't realized that Nolan's sending over the patches was very different from a client sending, say, a case of peanut butter. Still, Kate used it herself, so it must be safe enough, even dispensed without a prescription.

"So. How does craziness manifest itself in the world of slide rules and marketing plans? Does Nolan do the fandango on the boardroom table? Does the sales staff run amok in their underwear?"

"Hardly," Kate said, laughing. "We favor a more dignified, restrained hysteria at Randall Webber: both donuts *and* cookies in the coffee room!" Then her face became

serious as she remembered Jerry's performance that afternoon. "But a strange thing did happen today ..."

Her tone caused Victoria to turn her attention from the
painting. "Really?"

Kate paused. She knew she could trust Victoria, yet telling her felt slightly unethical. Then she reminded herself
that Mac had been there, too. He would probably tell Victoria anyway.

"Our Genelife research honcho went rogue," she said.
"It was a little unnerving, but Michael calmed him down."

"What happened?"

"Well, we'd all moved into Nolan's private conference
room after the video screening—Michael and Mac and
Dave and me. Dave was taking us through some copy
changes when it happened. I was sitting near the door that
connects the conference room with Michael's office, and I
heard Jenny, that's Nolan's secretary, arguing with someone. She was telling him he couldn't go in there, and he
was saying he had to talk to Nolan and she couldn't stop
him, and then suddenly Jerry bursts in, yelling and waving
his arms around and saying he's worried, and maybe we
should postpone everything, and Nolan's shouting at him
and Jenny's saying 'I tried to stop him, Mr. Nolan!' He
smelled like he'd been drinking."

"Who, Nolan?"

"Of course not! Jerry."

"And Jerry is ... the research boffin?"

"Right, Jerry Lim. Well, Nolan grabbed him and sort of
walked him out of the room, with Jerry still muttering
about postponing the launch ..."

Victoria stared at her. "Why would he want to do that?"

"I asked Nolan that very question. I mean, our research
results have been excellent, and of course we have FDA
approval. The whole thing was completely illogical."

"Uh-huh."

"Nolan said Jerry's been having a lot of trouble dealing
with the pressure. The size of the project scares him. And
he's afraid of success. He used to be a soldier, and now
he's a general. He simply can't handle it."

"Why doesn't Nolan replace him?"

"I asked him that, too. Apparently, Jerry's brilliant. He's
also the only scientific continuity we have with Genelife.

Jerry's boss, the guy who originally developed it, left the company under a cloud."

Both women fell silent. Victoria turned back to the small paint-daubed table that held her colors, and reloaded her brush.

"Look, I've seen the topline research results myself," Kate said. "And besides, Nolan wouldn't launch if there were any doubts about the product. It just wouldn't make sense."

"You're right," Victoria agreed. "It wouldn't."

Kate went and refilled Victoria's wineglass and then her own. Launching a questionable product would be very bad business, and Nolan was known for his business acumen. The opinion she'd formed of Jerry during the brief contacts she'd had with him over the past few months—the occasional lunch or research debriefing, always with Nolan present—was of an immature, rather nervous young man, who fit Nolan's psychological analysis quite well. Jerry was obviously one of those people who needed a strong leader, and who didn't work well under stress.

"On a brighter note," she said, pushing Jerry and his problems aside, "Nolan loved the video press releases."

"That's terrific!" Victoria turned and gave her a magenta-colored thumbs-up. "And how did you like being on camera?"

"I was *very, very* nervous at first," Kate answered. "After the first hour or so, I was only *very* nervous."

"Apparently it didn't show," Victoria said

"That's lucky. Nolan's planning to book me on talk shows to promote Genelife."

"Mac says you're a natural."

"Did he really? That was nice of him."

"No, it wasn't. I mean, Mac isn't nice that way. He's brutally honest. If he said it, he meant it." Victoria switched to a thin yellow glaze and began layering it carefully over areas of magenta. "And I understand you look wonderful on camera." She turned and gave Kate the same critical stare she used on her paintings. "You certainly look younger than thirty-four."

"Thanks." Under her tunic top, the place where the Genelife patch had been itched slightly. She should have removed it two days ago, but in the excitement of shooting the press release, she'd forgotten. When she'd peeled it off this morning, it had left a pale red ring. The adhesive, she thought. Her own damn fault. She'd try to remember to put some cortisone cream on it when she got home.

"You're awfully young to have a job like this, aren't you?" Victoria was saying. "Don't they usually drag out the graybeards for the media, to add authority?"

"I think they chose me because of the kind of drug Genelife is," Kate said. "I sort of represent both the medical establishment and the target audience."

" 'Target audience.' You're learning, kid!" Victoria flashed her a smile.

"And it's kind of nice being young for a job for a change. Back at the hospital, I always felt older than everyone else. Well, I *was* older."

"I'm older than everyone else," Victoria said. "I'm forty-two, older than Mac. And I don't give a shit."

"You're an artist."

"Doesn't matter. Artist, doctor, Indian chief. Your age only matters if you let it matter."

"My mother said that, too. But it makes more sense coming from you."

Victoria laughed. "Well, it's true, whoever says it. That's why I won't use Genelife. Oh, I'm sure it's perfectly wonderful. But I'm sick of the media constantly telling me I have to look young, young, young. I'm okay with the way I look."

"Who wouldn't be?"

"I could say the same of you. *Before* you started using those patches."

"Really?"

"Look, Kate. I don't know what your marriage and all those residents did to your ego. Sure, you may have looked a couple of years older than some of them. But I'll bet you also looked a helluva lot better." Victoria stepped back again and studied the canvas, then added more yellow. "I don't think it had to do with your looks, anyway," she continued. "You felt self-conscious because you were older than everyone else at your level, and that colored how you saw yourself. But you've changed. I've watched you. You're happier, you're a lot more confident."

"I was thinking the same thing, earlier," Kate said. "I really do feel a lot better about my life these days."

"You could throw those damn patches away and you'd never miss them."

But Kate only shrugged.

"I think that's enough for tonight," Victoria said. She went to the stone sink at the side of the room and began cleaning her brushes. "How about some food? I'm starved."

"Sure," said Kate. She wasn't very hungry, but she knew she should eat. Breakfast had consisted of half an English muffin, and she'd had no solid food since then.

"Don't you ever barge into a meeting the way you did today! Do you understand me?" Nolan's face was red with anger, and his eyes blazed. He'd waited all day to have this out with Jerry. Now everyone else had gone home, and he gave free rein to his fury. "I've had it with you, you little bastard!"

Jerry Lim went pale. He blinked rapidly and backed away toward his desk, but Nolan grabbed his shoulders hard. "The product is fine, understand? There's nothing wrong with Genelife. Tucker fixed it, remember?"

"I know. You told me that," Jerry agreed in a small, frightened voice. "I just wish . . . I wish Tucker were here."

Nolan shoved Jerry away from him in disgust. "You're a weakling! You make me sick!" He strode to Jerry's office door, which stood open to the empty corridor, and banged it hard with his fist. He turned and paced back toward the grubby sofa where Jerry sat cowering. He clenched his fists in frustration. "You have a great career ahead of you . . . money, recognition . . ." he told the frightened scientist. "But all you can do is whine about Tucker Boone."

"Tucker would know what to do."

"Do about *what,* goddammit?"

"About the Genelife launch."

Nolan kicked at a stack of reports on the floor, scattering paper across the room. It was late, he was tired, and he didn't need yet another crazy stirring up trouble. "What about the Genelife launch? What the hell about it?" he demanded roughly.

Jerry shifted uncomfortably on the sofa and scratched his ear. "I heard that Tucker . . . well, he didn't exactly . . . I mean, I heard a rumor that Tucker didn't want to go to market with Genelife. That he told you he was having second thoughts."

Nolan stared at him suspiciously. "That's ridiculous."

"Well, that's what I heard," Jerry protested weakly.

Nolan shook his head in disgust. "Think about it, Jerry! Is it likely Tucker would come to me with a problem about Genelife and I would ignore him?"

Jerry shook his head. "I guess not. Only—"

"Only what?" Nolan shook his head impatiently. "Look, you show me something wrong with Genelife, and we'll pull it off the market. You see anything in the research that bothers you?"

"No, no, the research is fine . . ."

"Then what in the hell is your problem?" Outside, a wet snow was falling. The drive back to Greenwich would be slow. Nolan paced back toward the door. Beyond, the corridor was dark and silent. Jerry was getting to be a real pain in the butt. But firing him wasn't the answer; it was safer to have him where he could keep an eye on him. He turned back to Jerry, who was scrunched into the sofa cushions, looking scared. Forcing himself to be calm, Nolan went to the desk, pushed some junk aside, and perched on the top. He smiled down at Jerry. "I'm sorry I yelled at you, kid," he said. "We're all under a lot of pressure right now."

"That's okay," Jerry said. He looked relieved.

"As I said, if you see any problems with Genelife, you come and tell me immediately. Otherwise, you have to trust me. Do you trust me, Jerry?"

"Sure, Mr. Nolan."

"Call me Michael."

"Uh, Michael."

"Good. Now, this nonsense has got to stop. First, you're upsetting my staff. And second, people are saying you're unstable. Are you unstable?"

"No sir, Mr. Nolan, Uh, Michael. It's just that . . ."

Nolan held up his hand. "No! No more! It stops right here, right now. Do you understand me?"

Jerry nodded.

"And after all, you don't want to force me to fire you just when we're all—you included—about to reap the benefits of our first real breakthrough. Do you?"

Jerry gulped and shook his head.

"Then I have your word? No more rumor-mongering, no more loose talk?"

"Yes sir."

"Okay. Now go home. It's late."

Slowly Jerry rose from the sofa and began gathering his things: a scruffy anorak, a briefcase, a woolen ski hat. Nolan waited until Jerry was ready to leave. Then he shrugged on his own dark blue cashmere overcoat and followed him into the corridor. Jerry carefully locked the door to his office, and the two men walked together to the outer door of the building.

The snow was heavier; everything was shrouded in a moist whiteness.

"Good night," Nolan said. "Get home safely." He watched Jerry cross the shoveled parking lot toward his old blue Dodge. Just before he slid behind the wheel, Jerry turned and looked back toward the entrance of the R&D building. Nolan waved.

He stood in the chilly doorway until Jerry drove off. Then he went back into the deserted building, moving quickly along the darkened corridors to Jerry's office. Using his master key, he unlocked the door and disappeared inside.

Chapter 12

January 15

"Have you seen it?" Marianne asked excitedly. "Commercials on TV, ads in magazines ..."

Cradling the phone between his ear and his shoulder, Steve stood and reached over to push his office door shut. Then he sat down again and swung his loafers up onto the scarred wooden desk. Outside, the snow-covered quadrangle was alive with students returning after winter break. "Slow down," he said. "Have I seen what, exactly?"

"Genelife. Tucker's drug!"

"Tucker's? Are you sure?"

"Well, it sure sounds like it. And it's from the same company: Randall Webber. They fund the Randall Foundation. They gave Tucker his grant."

Steve swung his feet off the desk and reached for a pencil. "Hang on a second," he said. "Start from the beginning."

Marianne took a deep breath. "I was watching *Good Morning, America,* and they were talking about this new cosmetic breakthrough called Genelife. They said it had originally been developed by the Randall Foundation, which is funded by Randall Webber."

"Are you sure it's Tucker's? Companies work on new stuff all the time."

"No, I remember the name. It's Tucker's project. What do you think it means?"

"Means?" Steve had a departmental meeting scheduled in twenty minutes; he loved his sister but he wished she would get to the point.

"Look, Tucker's working on Genelife. Suddenly he disappears. Six months later, Genelife is on the market."

"I'm sorry, Marianne, but I don't see the connection."

"Let me run something by you, okay? When Tucker first

went to the Randall Foundation, they told him he'd get a royalty on anything he developed that was eventually marketed by Randall Webber. I remember how excited we were about it. Do you think someone wanted Tucker out of the way so they wouldn't have to pay him?"

"That wouldn't make sense," Steve said slowly. "We're talking about a corporation of some size, here. Besides, just because Tucker ran off—uh, disappeared—doesn't mean the company's off the hook. They're still obligated to pay out whatever royalty his contract called for." He chewed thoughtfully on his pencil. "I wonder, though ... could Tucker have *thought* someone wanted him out of the way, and so he just took off? Exactly how paranoid was he?"

"Some days not, some days very. Anyway, if that was it, why wouldn't he have told me?"

"Who knows?" Steve glanced at his watch and began to gather up his papers. "Look, have you spoken to anyone at Randall Webber?"

"Not since Tucker disappeared. They were very nice, but no one knew anything that would help."

"Well maybe you should talk to them again, now that Tucker's drug is actually being sold. It sounds like they owe you some money. Hey, can I call you back in about—"

"Actually, I did try to call Randall Webber this morning, and I got the runaround. It was kind of strange. First they said they'd never heard of Tucker, then they said I needed to talk to Michael Nolan. He's the chairman of the company. I remember Tucker mentioning his name; he didn't like him."

"And what did this Michael Nolan tell you?"

"They said he was in conference. I didn't want to leave my name so I just said I'd call back. Steve ..." Marianne hesitated; asking for help was hard. "Could ... would *you* talk to Randall Webber for me? I have the phone number right here ..." Steve heard the rustle of turning pages. "I don't mean to be a bore about this, but I just think you'll get more information than I will. You have some perspective on this thing; I'm still too emotionally involved. Would you mind? Do you have a pencil?"

"You know I will." He knew how difficult it had been for her to make the request, and he was glad she was finally letting him do something for her. He copied down the number carefully on a Post-it and stuck it on the phone, just below the push-buttons. "I'll call today, I promise."

There was a short embarrassed silence; then Marianne said, "Thanks, little brother."

"You're welcome, big sister." From out in the quadrangle beyond his window, the old tower clock began chiming the hour. Shit, Steve thought. I'm late. "Hey, I really have to run, but I promise I'll call you later. After I talk to Nolan."

Steve hung up, an idea forming. He'd been pretty good about calling Marianne from time to time, but he'd only been back to see her once since September; he and Marianne had spent a sort of family Christmas at Avram's, and he'd returned to Boston the next day. Glancing at his appointment book, he decided that aside from a nine o'clock seminar, there was nothing scheduled for tomorrow that he couldn't change. Maybe he'd hop a shuttle and talk to this Nolan guy in person. Yes, and check in with the police, too. He and Marianne could grab an early dinner before the last shuttle back.

He'd work on it after the meeting. He picked up the stack of papers he'd assembled, grabbed his tweed jacket from its wooden peg behind the door, and headed down the hall to the divisional conference room.

It was eight in the morning, and the dining room of the Regency Hotel was crowded with movers and shakers. Bettina was already seated, sipping a tall glass of fresh orange juice. Although Nolan was five minutes early, he felt guilty for making her wait. He straightened the knot in his already-straight maroon and gray tie.

She greeted him with her usual coolness, but her eyes danced. "I must compliment you on your orchestration of the Genelife launch," she told him. "Very effective."

"Thank you."

A waiter in impeccable livery presented menus, but Bettina waved hers away and ordered fresh raspberries and a croissant. Nolan followed suit, although he'd have preferred eggs Benedict.

They made small talk as the waiter hurried back and forth with coffee and tea. Nolan complimented her on her outfit, a beautifully cut cocoa-brown pants suit with a pale lemon blouse, set off by a Liberty of London scarf.

"I've had it for years," she told him. "It's very comfortable on long flights."

"How long will you be gone?" Nolan asked her.

"Less than a week," she said. "I'm on a Swissair flight out of JFK at two today, and I'll be back in Chicago on Wednesday. My assistant will be in the office over the weekend. He knows how to reach me."

Nolan nodded. He was quite certain that even on the slopes of Gstaad, business would come first for Bettina.

Two bowls of perfect raspberries appeared on the starched pink damask tablecloth, followed by warm, buttery croissants. Bettina waited until the waiter had moved away to serve another group. Then she leaned toward Nolan confidentially.

"They've approved my plan," she said quietly. "I heard late yesterday afternoon. We're going ahead with the spin-off."

Nolan drew a sharp breath. It was what he had hoped for, but he'd never expected it would happen so fast.

"When?" he asked. His hands were shaking with excitement.

"Soon. As long as the Genelife revenues hold up, we plan to spin off Randall Webber in a public offering within eighteen months."

"That's . . . that's fantastic!" Coffee slopped over the rim of his cup.

"Your stock options will make you an exceedingly rich man, Michael." She glanced at the spilled coffee with disapproval. She'd never cared much for Nolan, but he had certainly delivered the goods. "You're looking at a payoff in the millions. As long as Genelife stays strong."

"It will," he assured her. "We've already exceeded the first month's projections. We can't lose!" He set down his cup and wiped his wet hand on the large pink napkin.

"Let's hope not. You have the flash report for me?"

Nolan reached for his briefcase, his heart singing. A public offering! The years of toadying up to Clark Randall, the secret dealings with Omni, and all the rest of it were finally going to pay off.

Bettina reached for the papers but didn't look at them. Instead she locked eyes with Nolan and held him as a snake holds a bird. "This is the big one, Michael," she said quietly. "Don't fuck up."

January 16

The precinct was housed in a low, pale brick building on a side street between West End Avenue and Broadway. Police cars, some with spectacular damage to their body-work, were parked along both curbs as well as across the sidewalk on either side of the entrance.

Steve pushed through the door and stopped at the metal reception desk where a large, bored-looking police officer was drinking a can of soda and reading the *Daily News*.

"I have an appointment with Detective Malley," he said.

The man nodded and reached for the phone. He spoke briefly and hung up. "Be right witcha," he told Steve. "Somebody steal ya car?"

"No."

"Break inna ya car?"

"No."

"Break inna ya apartment?"

"No."

The officer studied him for a beat. "You from outta town, huh?"

Steve nodded.

"Figures." The officer gulped the last of his soda, slam-dunked the can in a giant trash basket with a hand-lettered sign reading "Recycle Only," and went back to his paper.

A short, stocky man of about Steve's age, dressed in plainclothes, appeared in the doorway leading into the precinct offices.

"Steve Kavett?"

"That's me."

The detective held out a hand. "I'm Bob Malley. Come on in."

Steve followed the man through a maze of desks, officers, and high-decibel confusion.

"Quiet here today," Malley told him, and led him into a tiny windowless cubicle containing a rickety desk, several filing cabinets, and two unmatched chairs. "Have a seat. Want some coffee?"

"No thanks."

Malley lowered himself into the metal chair behind the desk and reached for a manila folder. "Tucker Boone," he said. "I pulled the report when you called yesterday. His wife—your sister, right?—reported him missing on June second. So what can I do for you?"

"I was out of the country when it happened. It's been over six months now, and we haven't heard anything. My sister's very worried."

The detective opened the folder. "I wish I could help," he said. "But frankly, we've run out of leads on this one. Fact is, there weren't a whole lot of leads in the first place. You want me to take you through it?"

"I'd appreciate that."

"Okay. Mrs. Boone calls, says her husband hasn't come home. Most situations like that, the husband turns up sometime in the next day or so. He got drunk, went home with some bimb—uh, a buddy. In this case, the guy didn't turn up. So . . ." Malley leafed through the sparse contents of the file. "We checked the hospitals and the morgue. Then we talked with anyone who might have seen him the day before. We started with his place of business."

"Randall Webber."

"That's right."

"And they were cooperative?"

"Oh, yeah. They were upset to lose him." Malley consulted a roughly typed page of notes. "Our boys talked to people in the lab where he worked . . . also a guy named Michael Nolan."

"He's the chairman of the company."

"Uh-huh. Says here he offered our guys a reward if they could find him. Said Mr. Boone was working on something important and he needed him back."

"So no one had any idea where Tucker could have gone?"

"No. He was a moody cuss, apparently. Well, you knew him, of course." Malley checked his notes again. "People said he was reclusive, kept to himself, didn't say much. Had a powerful temper, too. People tried to stay out of his way. Seems he even had an argument with the chairman, this Nolan guy, just before he disappeared."

"What did they argue about?"

"Hang on . . ." Malley leafed through the papers. "One of our guys talked to Nolan just after . . . Ah, here it is . . . Nolan said they argued about corporate politics. Said they'd had the same argument several times before."

"Politics? Doesn't sound like Tucker."

"No? Well, that's what Mr. Nolan said. Apparently the

company had recently been taken over by a conglomerate and Tucker didn't like it." Malley shrugged his shoulders. "Office politics. Happens everywhere."

"And Nolan offered a reward for Tucker, even though they'd been arguing?"

"Nolan said the argument wasn't important. Tucker's work *was*."

"Yes, it was. He was working on Genelife. You know, the new cosmetic drug that just came on the market?"

"No kidding! My wife's just started using it! No wonder Nolan wanted Tucker back!"

"My sister wondered whether there could be a connection between Tucker's disappearance and the marketing of the drug."

"What kind of connection?"

"I don't know, exactly. He was supposed to be paid royalties. I have an appointment to talk to Nolan about it this afternoon." Steve took a deep breath. "There's something else," he said tentatively. "I know this may sound kind of silly, but my uncle Avram seems to think there could have been . . . foul play."

Bob Malley smiled. "Oh, I don't think so. I mean, where's the motive? I remember talking to your uncle on the phone . . . an excitable man. No, I just don't see it. Unless you have some new information?" He looked at Steve hopefully. But Steve shook his head.

"No threats on his life that his wife forgot to tell us about? No recent blackmail attempts, or large withdrawals from his bank account?"

"No, nothing like that."

"Frankly," Malley said, "I think it's pretty simple, what happened. Mr. Boone ran out on his wife. Hey, I'm sorry, I know it's your sister we're talking about. But it does happen. I understand their marriage wasn't too happy."

"No, it wasn't. Still, I can't see Tucker just going off and not telling anyone . . ."

"He's never done anything like that before?"

"Well . . . actually he has. But it was a long time ago. And a completely different situation."

Malley studied him. "Want to tell me about it?"

But Steve shook his head. "It was completely different," he repeated.

The detective shrugged. "If you say so," he said neutrally.

"So what happens now?" Steve asked.

"Happens?"

"What do you do next?"

Malley shook his head. "Nothing," he said. "We've gone as far as we can."

"That's unacceptable!" Steve stood up angrily. "You can't just stop looking!"

"Please, Mr. Kavett. Sit down. Try to understand our position. We've talked to his wife, his business associates, the bars and stores and restaurants near his home and his office, even the guy who laundered his shirts. We've put out an APB on his driving license. We've alerted his bank, his credit card company, the United States Passport Service. If he'd cashed a check or rented a car or charged a meal or tried to leave the country, we'd have been able to track him down. But he hasn't done any of those things. He's left no traces for us to follow." Malley stacked the papers neatly together and put them back into the folder.

"Well, doesn't that seem suspicious? Jesus, it seems strange as hell to me!"

"Not really. If a guy really wants to disappear, it's not as hard as you might think. New ID, bank account under a false name ..."

"Okay, okay. But not using his money or his driver's license ... couldn't that also point to something ... worse?"

"Like maybe somebody chopped him up and dumped him in the Hudson River?" Then seeing Steve's face, he put a hand on his arm. "Sure it's possible, but it's not very probable. Look, I'm not saying we don't want to do anything further. It's just that we've run out of things to do."

Steve nodded and stood up. "I understand. Thanks for your time."

Malley stood, too, and came around the side of his desk to shake Steve's hand. "I'm really sorry, Mr. Kavett," he said. "If you come up with anything new, anything at all, believe me, we'll follow it up. But right now, the trail is not only cold, it's nonexistent."

The day was bright but frigid. As Steve came out of the precinct house and headed uptown, a biting wind made his eyes water. He'd left his gloves in the car he'd rented at La Guardia, and he walked the two blocks to the parking garage with his hands shoved deep into the pockets of his sheepskin coat. It was just after two o'clock, and his appointment with Michael Nolan in Connecticut was for three. He stopped at a street stand and bought an apple and a banana to eat on the drive north.

He ransomed his car and headed across town, picking up the FDR Drive at Ninety-sixth Street and skimming across the Triborough Bridge. A tractor-trailer accident had slowed the southbound traffic on I-95 to a crawl, but the northbound lanes were moving well. As he crunched his apple, he thought about what the detective had told him. His earlier anger at the NYPD's lack of success in finding Tucker had dissipated; he had to admit there really wasn't much to go on.

As he neared the Randall Webber exit, he wondered whether he was on a wild goose chase; it seemed unlikely that Michael Nolan could add anything to what he'd already told the police back in June. Well, at least Steve could do something about those royalties. Sooner or later, Marianne would need them.

He followed the winding road through the trees and meadows of the corporate headquarters and pulled into the parking lot for the executive building.

A neat gray-haired receptionist took his coat and directed him to a comfortable chair in the atrium lobby. He'd barely begun to rummage through the magazines on the glass coffee table when he heard his name. Looking up, he saw an attractive middle-aged woman in a business suit and sensible shoes.

"I'm Jenny," she said. "Mr. Nolan's secretary. Would you come with me please?"

Steve rose and followed Jenny along a short side corridor and into a work area bustling with activity. As they passed a row of offices, a pretty red-haired woman emerged from one of them. She was carrying a pile of reports. "Jenny!" she called. "Has he got a minute for me around four?"

Jenny turned and so did Steve. "I'm not sure," Jenny told the woman. "He's leaving early today. I'll see what I can do."

"Thanks." Kate started down the corridor in the direction from which Steve and Jenny had just come. She flashed Steve a smile as she passed him—who's the tall dark stranger? she wondered idly—and disappeared around a corner. He stood looking admiringly after her.

"Mr. Kavett?" Jenny had continued through the work area and now turned back, waiting for him. "This way, please."

"Sorry," he said, catching up with her. "Er, who was that?"

"Dr. Martin," she said. "Do you know her?"

"She, er, looks familiar."

"You've probably seen her on television."

"Actually, I don't watch much television. Maybe I ought to start."

Jenny gave his remark the weak smile it deserved, and ushered him into Nolan's conference room.

Nolan was in excellent spirits. Everything was falling into place. Soon he too would be making trips to Switzerland. He would visit his money.

He greeted Steve with a smile and a firm handshake. So this was the man who'd been in the rain forest with Tucker Boone. Nolan wondered how much he knew. Tucker had said he'd told no one, but Tucker was off the wall. He studied the tall, deeply tanned man in front of him. Take him out of the tweed jacket and give him a hat rimmed with corks on strings, and he could pass for a dark-haired Crocodile Dundee, he thought. The image amused him.

Steve studied Nolan in turn. Expensive three-piece suit. Silk tie. Smile like a shark. Tucker had probably been right to dislike Michael Nolan, he decided.

Nolan ushered him to a chair and offered coffee. They spoke in generalities at first, attempting to get each other's measure: the drive up from New York, the cold snap, Randall Webber's picturesque setting.

"Milk?" Nolan offered as he filled their china cups.

"No, thanks."

"So Mrs. Boone is your sister?" Nolan said at last. "I feel deeply for her; such a tragedy. How is she?"

"She's okay," Steve said. "Of course she'd be better if we could find Tucker."

"Wouldn't we all?" Nolan replied. "Of course, the man was extremely erratic. I suppose his disappearance can be seen as a symptom of his disintegrating personality."

"Had he really gotten that bad? I mean, I know he wasn't the easiest person to get along with, but I can't believe he went over the edge . . ." Steve trailed off. He hadn't actually seen much of Tucker over the past ten years. And Marianne had described a Tucker far worse than the moody young man who had walked out of the rain forest years ago. How could Steve know what Tucker had become?

Nolan sipped his coffee. "When Tucker disappeared, the police talked to me, and to the people who worked with him

in the lab. They all spoke of his tantrums, his emotional inac-
cessibility. He was unreliable. He'd forget that certain research had already been completed and order it done again.
He'd yell at people one day, compliment them the next . . .
Surely your sister witnessed similar personality shifts."

Steve nodded reluctantly.

"None of us were immune," Nolan told him sympathetically. "Not even me."

"Yes, I understand you and Tucker had quite an argument just before he disappeared," Steve said. Nolan looked
surprised. "The police file," he explained. "I was over at
the precinct today."

"I see." Nolan refilled his coffee cup. "Then you also
know what we fought about."

"Office politics."

Nolan smiled wryly. "You could call it that. Sorry, would
you like more coffee?" Steve shook his head. "It all goes
back to the time when Randall Webber hired Tucker out of
the Randall Foundation to develop Genelife commercially.
Clark Randall was chairman then; I was his executive officer. Clark took a liking to Tucker, despite, or maybe because of, his eccentricities. And Tucker seemed to find a
father figure in Clark. Now, Clark was a very nice man, but
not exactly a forward thinker. It was a family-owned company then, and the family pressured Clark into taking it
public so they could cash in. So now the family was happy;
they'd made their pile and didn't really care what Clark
did with the company after that. But the new stockholders
wanted to see some action: they wanted Randall Webber
to market some new, modern products and make a big
profit. Clark was too timid. He let the company languish,
and soon it was ripe for a takeover. Ever hear of Omni?"

Steve shook his head.

"Omni's a huge Japanese conglomerate. Omni took over
the company, gave Clark Randall a golden handshake, and
promoted me to chairman."

"And Tucker didn't like that."

"Not one bit. He blamed me for Clark's being fired, not
that I could have done anything about it. Actually, I was
happy to see Clark go; he *was* too timid, and he held the
company back. But I really had nothing to do with it. The
decision was Omni's."

"And that's what you argued about?"

"Constantly. Tucker didn't like Omni. He didn't like losing Clark. And he didn't like me."

"Did you like him?"

Nolan thought a moment. "No," he said. "I didn't. But that didn't affect my being able to work with him. I didn't have all that much contact with him, day to day."

"You had enough contact with him to fight with him."

Nolan smiled bleakly. "I didn't fight with him. He fought with me."

Steve took a sip of coffee. It had gone cold and he put the cup down again. "If Tucker was so unhappy, why didn't he leave the company?"

"Genelife was his product," Nolan said. "He'd been working on it for years. He'd never abandon it."

"But he did abandon it, didn't he?"

"You're right," Nolan agreed. "He did. Of course it was fully developed by then. Still, it's a pity he left when he did. He missed the launch . . . the rewards of his years of effort."

"Actually, that's one of the things I wanted to discuss with you. I understand Tucker's contract with the Randall Foundation included royalties. I'd like to arrange for you to pay them to his wife in his, er, absence. I've spoken to an attorney, and there doesn't seem to be any legal problem—"

Nolan's face took on a look of deep commiseration. "Actually, there is," he said. "You see, the contract Mr. Boone signed with the Randall Foundation did indeed entitle him to royalties. But only if he was still working for either the Foundation or Randall Webber when his product was first marketed." He reached behind him to the phone that sat on a small side table and punched the intercom button. "Jenny! Bring me a copy of the Tucker Boone contract, please. It's in a blue folder on my desk. Mr. Boone, uh, Tucker, left the company at the end of May," he continued, turning back to Steve, "and the product was launched in January. No royalties are, in fact, due."

"But he didn't leave the company," Steve protested. "I mean, he didn't resign. He just disappeared."

"If we'd had this discussion back in September, I would have agreed with you. That is, I would have said we should wait and see if Tucker returned. But it's been nearly eight months, Mr. Kavett. He's gone."

"But that's . . . that's not fair!"

"It's perfectly fair. I've reviewed the situation with our

corporate attorneys. What they've advised is that we deposit Tucker's royalties in an escrow account for a year. At the end of that time—that's four months from now, if you're counting—if he doesn't show up with an explanation of his absence that could cause us to reinstate him in the company retrospectively, we'll petition the court to release the money to us. It's all perfectly legal, I assure you."

"It may be legal, but it's not right! Marianne should have that money. She needs it."

A discreet knock on the conference-room door interrupted him. Jenny entered and handed Nolan a blue folder. "Here's the original and a copy," she told him in a low voice. "And your three-thirty appointment has arrived."

"Thanks, Jenny. We're nearly through here." He waited for her to leave before continuing. "Mr. Kavett, uh, Steve, I don't mean to sound unsympathetic. But I am chairman of this corporation, and as such, I must act in a fiscally and legally responsible manner. As far as Mrs. Boone's financial situation is concerned, my attorneys have advised me not to continue to pay Tucker's salary; surely you can understand their reasoning. However, I do empathize with Mrs. Boone's situation. And I would be quite willing to make her some kind of lump sum payment, right now, in exchange for her relinquishing any claim against the escrowed royalties. Not that I think she'd win such a claim. But I'd prefer to avoid the legal costs, and frankly, the embarrassment such a case could cause."

"I suppose I could ask her," Steve said slowly.

"I assure you, I really do want to help." Nolan got up, signaling that the meeting was over. Steve rose too, and followed Nolan to the door of the conference room.

"Jenny will show you back to the lobby," Nolan said. "Nice to meet you. Let me know what Mrs. Boone wants to do. Jenny? Mr. Kavett is leaving." He turned back to Steve and extended his hand.

But Steve, studying Nolan's face, ignored it.

"You're certain he's not coming back, aren't you?" he said to Nolan. "What do you know that I don't?"

For a moment Nolan didn't answer. Then he sighed and shook his head. "I know no more than you," he replied softly. "But I would be very surprised to see Tucker again."

Chapter 13

He was small and frail, with a freckled, balding pate. Many months of depression and disappointment had bowed and diminished him, and he looked older than his seventy-two years.

He sat before the television set in the small gray morning room of his big empty house, and picked at the food on the tray in front of him. Food had never interested him much.

He'd always thought of the company as his personal property, despite the public offering and the takeover. His sudden ouster had been a shock he'd never recovered from. Never would.

At first he'd tried to put a good face on things. He'd talked about golf, about fishing. He'd toyed with the idea of moving south to Florida, west to Arizona. Someone suggested he write his memoirs, and he'd actually spent several days in front of his keyboard before giving up in frustration. He knew he was no writer. He wasn't even much of a golfer. He'd been the chairman of a well-known corporation, and now he was nothing.

He pushed the peas around on the plate. Peas. He hated peas. Maria knew he hated peas. Why did she keep serving him peas?

He stared at the television, but didn't see it. Maria always turned on the television for him when he ate. To keep him company, she said. Some company. He preferred his thoughts.

He leaned back, a shriveled figure in an overstuffed chair. He didn't feel well. He hadn't felt well for a long time. Not sick. Just . . . weary. No energy. No life. No wonder; Randall Webber had been his life.

His wife had kept making suggestions: let's go to Europe, she'd said. Let's visit the kids in Chicago. But he hadn't had the heart for it. Eventually she'd stopped asking and just went herself. Not that he blamed her. She was in Chicago now. Or somewhere.

Suddenly something brought him upright, his heart pounding. He was sure he'd heard it, but who had said it? He looked around suspiciously, then realized it must have been the television. Why would they say it on television?

He leaned forward across the tray to raise the volume. Peas and mashed potatoes cascaded onto the floor, but he barely noticed. Someone had just said it again. Genelife.

A pretty woman was talking. Something about a cosmetic effect. There were words along the bottom part of the screen: "Dr. Kate Martin. Medical Consultant, Randall Webber."

Fools! he thought. They'd actually done it. "Fools!" he shouted at the screen.

The pretty woman smiled and talked. "I use it myself," she said.

"No! No!" He banged his fists on the arms of the chair. Nolan had promised him! And Boone—how could Boone have allowed this? "God damn you, Nolan!" A searing pain engulfed his chest, and he gasped and clutched at his shirt.

The woman had stopped talking. There was music now, and on the screen was a picture of a package. Introducing, a voice said. *Amazing breakthrough.*

The pressure in his chest was intense; he could barely breathe. Then a blinding pain exploded in his chest and his leg shot out, kicking over the tray table with a crash.

Through dimming eyes he saw Maria's face, dark with concern. "What happened?" she said. "Are you all right, Mr. Randall?"

He pointed toward the television. "Genelife!" he shouted, but it came out in a whisper.

"I know," she said. "Isn't it wonderful? Makes you young. Like the fountain of youth." He had slipped down onto the floor now, and she tried to prop him upright against the chair.

Fountain of horrors, he tried to tell her, but no words came out. The pain was unbearable. He felt himself slipping away . . . from the pain, from the room . . .

Maria gasped and hurried to the phone. She dialed 911. On the television, people were talking about Genelife.

"Quick, send an ambulance," she begged. "A man is dying."

He was quite still now, his head lolling backward against the seat of the chair. Maria had only worked here for two months. Now she would have to find another job. She shook her head, and tears welled up. Poor Mr. Randall. Genelife had come too late for him.

PART THREE

Chapter 14

"The age spots on my hands are much paler!" exclaimed the woman in the acid-green blouse. "And I've lost eight pounds!"

"The wrinkles around my eyes are almost gone. It's made a real difference in how I feel about myself," another woman stated.

"This poignant moment," Dave announced, "was brought to you courtesy of Randall Webber, maker of—"

" 'Once I was fat and old and ugly, just like you,' " Louise interrupted. " 'Then I tried Genelife. Now my life is rich and beautiful!' "

"Come on, guys! You're supposed to be taking this seriously," begged Amy Treeson. Amy was the MacAllister Agency's head of research, and she was finding Dave Randazzo and his art director Louise Kramer extremely trying. She glanced over at Kate, who was grinning at their antics. It was lucky the client had a sense of humor.

"I don't know why we just can't look at the tapes in the office," Louise said for the millionth time. "I hate sitting in these cramped little rooms, spying on people."

"What's the matter? Don't you like traveling?" Dave asked her. " 'Join the MacAllister Agency. See the world.' "

"Some world. Two days each in St. Louis and Dallas . . ."

"And San Francisco," Dave reminded her. "Aren't you enjoying San Francisco?"

"We're not in San Francisco, Dave. We're in a small, overheated room in a shopping center, looking through a one-way mirror as a bunch of our less articulate peers attempt to describe the ecstasies of using Genelife."

"Don't mind Louise," Dave told Kate. "She's bitter be-

yond redemption. It all started when she learned the Jolly
Green Giant was gay."

"Very funny," Louise said. She reached for a can of soda
from the stack on the side table, and popped the top loudly.
"I still don't know why we all had to come and experience
this firsthand. The tapes would have been enough. More
than enough."

"You're here in case you want to ask the focus group
participants any questions," Amy Treeson told her sternly.
"You know, anything the moderator doesn't ask. Or something you want to follow up on." Despite Louise's negativ-
ity, Amy was enjoying being back on the road. As the
department head, she nearly always sent a member of the
staff on such excursions. It was good to be back in the field
again. "Is there anything any of you would like the moderator to ask the women?"

"Yeah, I have a question," Louise said. "Where does the
one with the 1950s beehive get her hair done, the twilight
zone?"

"The Twilight . . . Is that a salon? Because I don't think
you'll have time for—"

"God, Amy, forget it!"

Amy looked at Louise suspiciously. "You're not taking
this seriously, are you?"

"No shit, Sherlock."

Kate smiled. Much of Louise's bitching and moaning was
strictly for effect; she and Dave had already found some
interesting material in these sessions that they could build
into the body copy of their new ads. And having now sat
through eight of these sessions, she realized that the banter
kept everybody from killing each other out of sheer unre-
lieved boredom.

"—not sure it's safe."

Kate swiveled around. What had the woman in the pink
sweater just said? The others had stopped their clowning
and had also turned toward the one-way mirror.

"Why is that?" Pat, the moderator, was asking.

"I have a friend who had to go to the hospital because
of Genelife," Pink Sweater replied. "She couldn't eat, she
got weak, she fainted a couple of times . . ."

"Excuse me," the moderator broke in. "I thought everyone here was a Genelife user."

"I am," Pink Sweater said. "I mean, I was when you

asked me to be in this group. But then my friend had to go to the hospital a couple of days ago, so I stopped."

Pat cast a surreptitious look toward the one-way mirror. Okay, guys, how do you want me to handle this one? it said.

Amy began scribbling furiously on a scrap of paper.

"Are you sure it was because of Genelife?" One of the other women asked.

"Absolutely," said Pink Sweater. "Her doctor took her right off it." She turned toward the woman in the acid-green blouse who had talked earlier about losing weight. "See, you lost eight pounds, right? Well, that's because this Genelife stuff kills your appetite. But if you don't eat, you get weak. You don't have any energy. That's what happened to my friend. That and some other stuff."

"Other stuff? What other stuff?" The women were becoming alarmed.

"Now, I'm sure there were other factors—" Pat attempted to break in, but the women were all talking at once.

"She got very nervous," Pink Sweater explained. "You know, jumpy. And—"

"I get jumpy, sometimes, too. I never did, before—"

"A friend of mine had a miscarriage when she was taking Genelife—"

"You're not supposed to take it when you're pregnant!"

"Well, she did, and—"

Kate looked at Dave in alarm. "What the hell's going on?" she said. They'd heard some mildly negative comments in several of the other focus group sessions, but nothing like this.

"Don't worry," Dave said. "There's always one woman in every group that sets the tone, you know, leads the reactions of the others. This woman happens to be very negative and very strong. So you'll hear more negative stuff with her in the room."

"Yes, but if her friend really was hospitalized because of Genelife . . ."

"Hey, don't sweat it. Your research says the drug is fine. You don't know what was wrong with the woman before she started taking Genelife."

"—never sick a day in her life," Pink Sweater was saying.

"Oh, swell," Louise said. "Blame it on the product that pays my salary!"

"Shhh! Quiet!" Kate ordered. "I want to hear what else she has to say."

But Pat, having received Amy's scribbled note, now brought the group under control again, explaining that there was a certain percentage of the population that experienced side effects with any drug. Certainly, if any of them were concerned, they should see their doctors. Then she went around the table, asking each person to summarize the benefits they felt they'd gotten from using Genelife. Pink Sweater scowled.

"Why is Pat doing that?" Kate complained. "I want to know who else is having trouble with the drug."

Dave glanced at Amy who shrugged and scribbled another note, then left the room and appeared on the other side of the one-way mirror as she went into the research room and handed Pat the folded paper.

Pat glanced at the note: did they really want her to pursue the side effects issue? "Now let's go around the table and summarize any, er, little problems you may have had with the product," she said reluctantly. Pink Sweater opened her mouth, but Pat immediately pointed at a woman well down the table from her. "Let's start with you, Cathy."

"Well ... I don't know. I guess I don't eat as much as I used to, and sometimes I get these headaches ... but I really feel okay ..."

"I'm a little more nervous, I think ... My kids say I yell more. But they also say I look prettier ..."

"I've been trying to get pregnant for six months now, and nothing's happened. I think that might be because of Genelife."

"I'm sure it is. Didn't your doctor tell you not to use Genelife if you're trying to get pregnant?" Pat asked.

"Yes he did, but—"

"I don't think you can blame Genelife if you use it wrong," said the woman in the acid-green blouse.

Pat looked at her watch. "Well, ladies," she said, "I think we're about through. Thank you all for participating in this very helpful discussion."

Behind the one-way mirror, the women began to file out. There would be a twenty-minute break before the last focus group session of the day, an assortment of men aged forty-four to fifty-five, with a male moderator.

The four people in the cramped observation room stood and stretched. Amy went out to make sure the new moderator had arrived. Louise announced she needed a bathroom break. "I still say we could have watched the damn tapes back in New York," she repeated as she left the room. "Hey, dibs on that 7-Up."

"Want a soda?" Dave asked Kate.

"Ginger ale, please."

Dave tossed it over. "So, have these discussion groups been useful?"

"Actually, they have. It's good to hear about people's experiences with Genelife, firsthand."

"When Mac suggested you might want to come along, I didn't think you'd be able to spare the time for a week-long research trip. I mean, to tell the truth, *I* didn't have the time. Of course, once Mac knew you were coming, he figured he'd better send the big guns along with you."

Kate laughed. "I see. So I'm to blame for you and Amy having to endure all this."

"Oh, Amy loves being out of the office. And I guess it's good for me to go to these things once in a while. The atmosphere gets a little rarefied as you move up the corporate ladder. This puts me back in touch again."

"Very diplomatically put. The truth is, I was kind of surprised that Randall Webber could spare me. Michael Nolan used the same words you just did when he urged me to go. It would put me in touch with real people, he said. Only he didn't say 'real people.' He called them 'the great unwashed.'"

Dave laughed appreciatively.

The sound of a chair being knocked over made them turn back to the one-way glass; men were filing into the room and seating themselves around the white laminate table.

Just then, Mac burst into the observation room, bringing on his trench coat a welcome gust of fresh air and a spattering of rain.

"How'd the pitch go?" Dave asked.

Mac gave him a thumbs-up and a wide grin. "We are now agency of record for Crystal Coolers!"

"No shit?"

"No shit."

"All right!" Dave hopped off his stool and punched the air a few times. "Two years we've been after that account! When do we start?"

"Right away." Mac patted his attaché case. "I've got a briefing document here, and they're FedExing a whole bunch of stuff for tomorrow."

"Congratulations," Kate told him.

"Thanks. So, how have the groups been?"

"Interesting," Kate said. "Nothing really unexpected, except for the last group. They talked a lot about side effects. One woman said a friend was hospitalized."

Mac's grin faded. "Jesus. Do we have a problem here?"

"I don't think so . . ." Kate said slowly. "We shouldn't have. The research is fine, and there's always a certain percentage of people who'll have an adverse reaction to something." She saw the concern on Mac's face. "I can't believe it's really significant," she said. "Let's see what these guys have to say."

The men's group went well. They all mentioned that wrinkles and lines were smoothing out, and skin was becoming younger and fresher-looking. Several men said it was good for business; one had actually beaten out an older-looking man for a promotion. Although there were several mentions of weight loss, no one complained of headaches or faintness.

"Maybe there are fewer side effects among men," Kate said thoughtfully, trying to remember whether the research she'd seen had indicated any such phenomenon. She didn't think it had.

"Or maybe men are just reluctant to talk about their ailments," Mac said. "You know, stoic."

"Macho," said Louise.

"Well, let's ask them," Kate said. "Amy, can we ask the men specifically about the side effects? 'Have you been having headaches?' 'Do you ever feel faint?' That sort of thing."

Amy gave her a horrified look. "You really want to put ideas like that in their heads?" she asked.

"I want to know what's really going on," Kate told her firmly.

But even when asked, the men maintained that any side effects were minor; nothing that they couldn't handle.

It was only when they were specifically asked about changes in their love lives that one man admitted he had a lot less sexual drive. But if the others had had the same experience, none of them were saying so. Embarrassed, the man said very little for the rest of the session.

Afterward, Kate and the agency people all piled into the waiting taxis and sped off to the airport to catch the last direct flight back to New York. Seated next to Mac in first class, a celebratory glass of champagne in her hand courtesy of MacAllister's new wine cooler account, Kate found herself thinking again about Genelife's side effects.

". . . puts the end of his tie in his mouth and starts chewing. Well, I'm trying not to stare, but soon about half his tie is bunched up in his mouth, and meanwhile this other guy is sitting there casually rooting in his ear with a paper clip, and all I can think is, these two guys actually control seventy-two million dollars in billings—am I boring you?" Mac asked suddenly.

"What? Oh, I'm so sorry! I was just—"

"Preoccupied. What gives?"

"Just thinking about the focus groups."

Mac's face became serious. "You're not really worried about what those women said, are you?"

"Of course not," Kate said quickly. "I mean, we knew, going in, that there were certain side effects associated with Genelife. Headaches, diminished appetite, a drop in sexual drive."

"I remember that from your briefing," Mac agreed.

"What I don't understand is, the long-term research doesn't show anything nearly as strong as what some of the people in the women's focus group told us."

"Shit."

"Oh, I don't think it's so bad," Kate said, trying to reassure them both. "I mean, we've seen—what?—a hundred and sixty people? It's not statistically significant. And Dave says people tend to follow the leaders in these sessions. We had one really strong woman today who had a problem with Genelife, and the rest just followed along."

"Yes, that happens a lot."

They both fell silent. Mac refilled both their glasses, but left his untouched. Getting the wine cooler assignment was great, but it was only a small part of the large Bello Wine account, and it didn't bill much. If the MacAllister Agency was successful with this small assignment, Mac could push for a bigger slice of the Bello business. But meanwhile, bills needed to be paid, and Genelife was paying them. Mac prayed fervently that this side effects thing would turn out to be nothing. Don't let this one blow up on me, he prayed. I need this account.

Kate, too, was hoping the side effects were not representative. Based on the research studies, they shouldn't be. Although she hadn't developed Genelife, she felt ethically and morally responsible for its safety. She'd helped publicize it, she'd written articles on it for several medical journals, she'd spoken to doctors' groups about it. She'd actually stood up on television and recommended it. Hell, she used it herself. She felt a sudden jolt of fear—what if there really was a problem? Those headaches she'd been having recently ...

But no, she was suffering from overwork, that was all. These small focus groups weren't statistically significant. She glanced over at Mac, who was scowling into his glass.

"I really don't think we need to start panicking just yet," she told him lightly. "Not on the basis of a few isolated reactions."

"You're right, of course," Mac agreed, brightening. "Let's not blow a couple of comments out of proportion."

Chapter 15

The automatic revolving doors were new, two huge circles quartered by glass dividers. From outside, they appeared to be a major improvement over the narrow double doors they'd replaced. Inside there was still the same old bottleneck as doctors, nurses, and aides attempted to separate themselves from the "Visitors" line that was led via stanchions and chains past the security desk. Automatically, Kate headed for the "Staff" sign and the open stairs beyond.

"Excuse me, miss, you can't go that way!"

Kate stopped and turned toward the guard who stood off to one side, scanning the crowd.

"Hello, Carlos," she said.

"Hey, Dr. Martin? That you?"

"It's me," Kate assured him with a smile.

"Sorry, I didn't recognize you at first."

"Well, it's been a while. I see you've got new uniforms. Looking good!"

"Back at you. Hey, I saw you on TV! I said to the Missus, I know that lady! So, you working here again?"

"No, just visiting."

"Well, have a good one!" He waved her through the staff line.

Kate climbed the short flight of marble stairs and walked across the atrium that connected New York General's three main hospital buildings. As she went through the glass doors into Bennett, the distinctive hospital smell filled her with a sudden nostalgia that surprised her.

At Seven West, two very young men in white coats, with stethoscopes slung casually around their necks, bustled onto the elevator. "He presented around two A.M. in the ER,"

one was saying to the other importantly. "Your typical
LOM, with SOB and CP."

"An MI?"

"Bet your ass. Carlin sent him to the CCU."

"Respect Patients' Privacy," warned a prominent sign on
the elevator wall. "This Is Not the Place for Discussion."
But the young men ignored it; only another medical professional would understand from their conversation that a little old man with shortness of breath and chest pain had
been admitted to the emergency room with a heart attack.
Carlin was one of the senior cardiology residents; he'd
transferred the patient to the cardiac care unit.

"Status?" the second young man asked.

His friend shrugged. "Basically, he's CTD."

Kate turned and scowled at them. CTD meant "circling
the drain."

Harold Gould's office was on Nine, around the corner
from the ambulatory surgery corridor. Several patients in
striped hospital gowns and fabric slippers were padding
along the hall between the admitting office and the pre-
surgery waiting room. Beyond, the doors to the operating
theater opened and a young woman in green surgical scrubs
hurried out.

For a moment Kate felt a pang of—regret? No, of course
not, she told herself. She hurried around the corner to Harold's office.

As department chief, Harold Gould rated a window office with a view of the park. He emerged when he heard
her voice in the anteroom, and ushered her inside, complimenting her on her clothes, her haircut. "And I've seen
you on television," he said.

"I'm afraid you'll be seeing rather more of me in a couple of weeks," Kate told him. "We're doing a big press
event, and they've got me booked on all the local talk
shows."

"Well, you come across very well."

"Thanks. I know it's not really medicine, but—"

"It's a legitimate job. Stop apologizing." Gould patted
her hand in a fatherly way. Then waving her to a chair
across from his desk, he settled back in a creaky brown
leather swivel chair and folded his arms behind his head.
"I don't mean to rush you, but as I told you when you

called, I've got a consult at eleven-thirty. So why don't you jump right in and tell me what's bothering you."

Kate sighed; where to start? "I'm probably just blowing smoke," she said. "I mean, all the research on Genelife says it's fine. And most of the users we've spoken to love it. It's just that a couple of people . . ." Kate broke off, aware she was rambling. Pretend you're a medical student again, she told herself. Stick to the facts. She began again. "Briefly, Genelife's a transdermal drug that produces a cosmetic effect. You've seen me on TV, so you know that. It produces this effect by way of the enzyme superoxide dismutase, which is—"

"I know what SOD is," Gould interrupted.

"Yes, of course. Well, we knew there would be some side effects. The research I saw mentioned headaches, diminished appetite, lowered libido. In most males, the sperm count dropped. Some people exhibited a certain nervousness. But aside from the sperm count, the effects were within acceptable levels of strength and frequency."

Gould nodded. The effects would have had to be at a level the FDA found acceptable, otherwise the drug would not have been allowed to be marketed.

"I've just sat through a week of what they call focus group research," Kate explained. "We listened to about a hundred and sixty people talk about their experiences with Genelife."

"Not exactly statistically significant," Gould offered.

"I know. And actually, a lot of people were just fine with the drug. Sure, they sometimes had headaches, and didn't eat as much as they used to. But they all praised the cosmetic effects. One woman brought a photo of herself taken before she started on Genelife. The difference was incredible!"

"After only—what?—barely three months?"

"I know. It seemed to work a lot faster in her case."

"That can happen with a drug sometimes. It's unusual, but not unheard of. Were her side effects stronger, too?"

"Yes, they were."

Gould nodded. "For some reason her body chemistry is more receptive to the drug's effects, both good and bad. But she'll be the exception, not the rule."

"That's true. Most of the people in the groups didn't have any real side effect problems."

"So what's bothering you?"

"Well, in the groups with people that did have problems, it seemed to me the problems were stronger than I would have expected from the research. One woman said a friend had actually been hospitalized."

"Of course you don't know her medical history prior to starting Genelife."

"Yes, but the point is, once this woman sort of broke the ice, the others admitted they'd had problems with it, too. Not hospitalization," she said hurriedly, seeing Gould's expression. "But statistically, more people in that room exhibited side effects than they should have."

"I thought you said these sessions weren't statistically significant."

"They're not, that's the problem. I'm not sure how much of what I'm seeing is aberrant."

Gould studied her. "You're still using Genelife yourself, aren't you?" he said gently. "Are you sure that's wise?"

"Look, Harold, this is only a vague feeling of disquiet, not a major panic," she told him. "I don't really think anyone's at risk from the drug. I'm just trying to figure out why I could be seeing what I'm seeing, if I'm actually seeing it."

Gould thought for a moment. "What form of SOD is being used?" he asked. "What's its sourcing?"

"It's a synthetization," Kate explained. "Developed within Randall Webber and manufactured for them in bulk by a Swiss company called Chemstra."

"Chemstra . . . I don't know them."

"The company's about five years old and fairly small, but well respected."

Gould pursed his lips. "Not everything can be successfully synthesized," he said. "And not every synthetization remains stable over time. Perhaps what you're seeing is your synthetic SOD starting to behave erratically."

"Wouldn't that have shown up in the long-term usage test results that went to the FDA? And wouldn't they have required correction of that before they approved Genelife?"

"Yes, if the research turned it up. Did Chemstra synthesize the original batches of SOD, the SOD used in the early research? If they've only been around for five years . . ."

"The top-line report says they did."

"Hmm ... And the original clinical trial data, does that agree with the topline results?"

Kate blushed. "I never saw the original clinical material," she admitted. "Genelife was practically on the market, the FDA had approved it ..."

"Of course," Gould said. "And I'm sure it says the same thing the topline does. It would have to, wouldn't it? Still, have a look at it, just for your own peace of mind. And you might want to check out Chemstra, too. Something may have changed in the manufacturing process."

"If it had, shouldn't it have been reported?"

"Not necessarily. Not if your people were certain it wouldn't impact the action of the drug in any way. Talk to your friends in R&D."

"Actually, I don't have a lot of friends in R&D," Kate admitted. "Nolan keeps me pretty busy with a lot of other stuff, and I spend a lot of time at the advertising agency. As Michael says, the work on Genelife is completed ..." She trailed off; it was almost as though Nolan was subtly discouraging her from spending much time there.

"How about the people who developed it for Randall Webber? Have you spoken to them?"

Kate shook her head. "The guy who came up with it is gone. He left the company back in May."

"Well, find out where he went. Call him up. Go see him."

"Not so easy. He sort of disappeared."

Harold's left eyebrow arched up, giving his face a look of cynical surprise. She remembered the expression well, from her training. "Getting the eyebrow" meant that Dr. Gould was not at all satisfied with the response a student or resident had given to one of his always-tough medical questions. A certain amount of humiliation invariably followed.

"He had some kind of emotional problem," Kate explained. "He left the company suddenly. Nolan implied that he had a drug problem, too. He entered some kind of rehab program, apparently. No one seems to know where."

"Surely there must be other people who worked with him."

"Jerry Lim was his assistant. Talk about Tucker Boone seems to upset him, at least Nolan says so. They were very close." Kate paused. She'd called Jerry on her return from San Francisco, and he'd assured her there was nothing to worry about. "He says he wasn't involved much in the original development of Genelife, but that the research says the drug is fine, so there's no need to be concerned." Jerry had ended their short conversation abruptly, she recalled.

The phone on Harold's cluttered desk buzzed. He leaned forward and depressed the intercom button. "Yes?"

"Dr. Gould? Dr. Burton is here," a female voice said.

"Thanks, Ann," Harold said. He glanced at his watch. "He's a tad early, but not that early." He stood up, and Kate rose too. "Check out Chemstra," he told her. "And the clinical trial data."

"I will. Thanks."

Harold gave her a smile as he ushered her out. A tall, bearded man with a briefcase stood waiting in the anteroom. "Dr. Burton? Please come in. Good to see you, Kate." Dr. Gould disappeared back inside his office, and Kate slowly retraced her steps to the elevator. It was nearly eleven-thirty. She had over two hours before the research meeting, time enough for a few phone calls, at any rate.

Outside, she retrieved her car from the expensive hospital parking lot, and headed toward the FDR Drive.

"Overall, the consumer response is excellent," Amy Treeson began.

Nolan smiled. He'd expected nothing less.

Mac smiled too, and gave Nolan a thumbs-up. He'd reviewed Amy's report at the agency the day before, and had been pleased and relieved to see that despite the negative comments Kate had mentioned to him, the dominant mood of the recipients had been most positive.

Amy was halfway through her review of the topline focus group research when Kate slipped into the room. Nolan frowned at her, and she shrugged her shoulders apologetically. It had taken her several tries to get someone on the line at Chemstra who spoke English.

Kate listened carefully to Amy as she riffled through the blue folder that contained the written version of her report. Reading the verbatims (as the quotes from the various focus group participants were called) was reassuring. The positive responses far outweighed the negative.

Amy finished with a flourish of praise for Genelife, and Nolan reached across the wide table to shake her hand and then Mac's, congratulating them for a job well done. "Not exactly a surprise, of course," he beamed. "We all knew Genelife was a winner."

"Actually, there were a few surprises," Kate broke in. "Several women talked about experiencing some fairly serious side effects."

Nolan scowled at her. "Not according to this report," he said.

"Actually, it *is* in the report," Amy told him. "But those women were very much in the minority. We don't feel they're statistically significant."

"Kate?" Nolan turned to her almost challengingly.

"Well, that's true, of course," Kate agreed. "But I don't think we should just write them off. I mean, I found them a little worrying."

"Well, you can stop worrying," Nolan told her firmly. "That's what I get paid to do." He gave a small chuckle. "You have a lot more important things to concentrate on just now."

More important? Kate thought. What could be more important than a possible problem with Genelife?

Catching her thought, Nolan gave her a high-wattage smile. "I'll put Jerry on this immediately," he assured her. "He can check it out. Meanwhile, the upcoming press event is of vital importance to this company. And we're counting on you to make it sing. Right, Mac?"

Mac nodded; he needed a lot of Kate's time during the next ten days.

"How about some lunch?" Nolan asked expansively. "You folks must have been on the road since noon." He rose and began gathering the folders into a neat pile, Kate's included. She reached out to take it back, but Nolan quickly picked up the stack. Holding them close to his chest, he started for the door to the corridor.

"How soon can we put Jerry on it?" Kate heard herself say.

Nolan stopped and turned back to her. He didn't look pleased. "Why don't we stop at R&D right now?" he said pleasantly, but his face was tight with controlled anger. "I'll give him a copy of the report and get him started on it right away." He turned toward the agency people. "You don't mind a little detour, do you?"

"No, of course not," Mac said. "And lunch would be nice. Thanks." Strange vibes, he thought. Probably just some jurisdictional conflict between Kate and Jerry. Doesn't concern us.

Nolan dropped all but one of the folders on his secretary's desk and led them down the hallway. Mac looked questioningly at Kate as they followed Nolan out to the lobby to pick up their coats, but she seemed lost in thought. She too had picked up unsettling feelings in the air.

As their carts deposited them at the front entrance to the research and development building, Kate realized with a shock that it had been nearly two months since she'd been inside. Nolan had given her a computerized passcard, but thanks to the guards who had suddenly taken root at both front and rear entrances back in September, she hadn't had to use it. One look at her employee badge and the guard had admitted her.

Now Nolan waved the beefy uniformed man away and fitted his own passcard into the lock set flush in the steel door. Kate smiled a greeting at the guard as she followed the others inside, but he looked blankly at her. Again, it gave her an odd feeling to realize that she hadn't been here often enough for him to remember her.

They came upon Jerry in the corridor outside his office. He looked even more disheveled than usual, and seemed reluctant to invite them inside. When a scowling Nolan pushed past Jerry and swung the door open, Kate realized why. The unmistakable scent of stale alcohol welled out into the corridor. She didn't remember Jerry's office smelling that way before.

"God, Jerry, air the place out!" Nolan said testily. Mac and Amy exchanged embarrassed glances. "We just came by to bring you up to date on the agency's focus group report," Nolan continued briskly, clamping a hand on Jerry's shoulder and propelling him through the door. "I seem to have left the folder in the cart, but the results are excellent. Remind me to send it to you." He turned back toward the corridor. "Okay, everyone, let's go get some food."

Kate looked at him aghast. This was Nolan's idea of "getting Jerry started on it right away"? "Actually, I'd hoped to get some follow-up on the negative comments," she told Jerry as she stepped into the room, blocking Nolan's exit.

"Negative?" Jerry squeaked, looking at Nolan.

"Nothing major," Nolan assured him. "Well within acceptable limits, but of course we should check them out.

I'll call you later. Come on, Kate, our friends are waiting." He circled around her toward the open door.

But Kate didn't budge. "Jerry, could you get me a copy of the original clinical trials?" She asked. "Maybe I could just borrow your set. I won't need them long."

Nolan stopped, then turned to stare at Kate.

"Uh, I don't have the original clinicals," Jerry said. "I never had them. Uh, Mr. Nolan?"

"I'll get them for you," Nolan told Kate impatiently. "Not that you need them. And if there's anything else you want, I wish you'd go through me and not bother Jerry here."

"Sure," Kate said, trying to remain calm. How dare Nolan treat her with such condescension? And what was the big deal about asking Jerry for the clinical trials data, anyway? "From now on, I will." Her face was stony.

"Good, good." Nolan turned to Mac, who was hovering just outside the office door. "This is all routine stuff, you understand."

"Absolutely routine," Kate agreed. "I should have asked to see the clinical trials before."

"I can't think why," Nolan growled. Amy glanced toward Mac, embarrassed. Mac shook his head warningly and retreated a few steps down the corridor, out of the line of fire. Not our fight, his look said.

"Because it's part of my job," Kate said firmly. "By the way, I talked to Chemstra this morning."

Nolan froze for a beat, then went to the door and looked down the corridor toward the agency people. "Would you excuse us for just a moment?" he asked, swinging the door shut with a bang. Then he turned and fixed Kate with an icy stare. "You called Chemstra. Go on."

Kate felt suddenly nervous. She'd obviously stepped out of bounds with this one. Yet why shouldn't she talk to the company that produced Genelife? "I asked for a quality control analysis of the manufacturing process," she said. "Perhaps there's been a change in the way SOD is being synthesized. That might account for—"

"How dare you take such a request upon yourself, without my authorization!" Nolan's face was red with fury. "Do you have any idea of the cost of such an analysis? Do you? Not to mention the message it sends to Chemstra! Now I'll have to call them, calm them down . . ."

"Calm them down? Why?"

"You're implying there's a problem with their procedures!"

"That doesn't necessarily follow, Michael. But if there *is* a problem, shouldn't we—"

"There is no problem with Chemstra. Nothing has changed since they did the original testing."

"Chemstra did the original testing? I thought they were the manufacturing laboratory."

"They are. They're also a testing lab."

"You mean the testing was done by the same people as the manufacturing?"

"Yes. Uh, no, not exactly. The testing was done by their subsidiary."

"I had no idea you weren't doing the testing yourselves."

"Of course we're not. It would be far too expensive for us to staff up for one-time projects like Genelife. We'd be crazy to spend money on field research when we can use the same money to fund basic research. The kind of research that developed Genelife in the first place."

Jerry nodded. "He's right. Merck, Ciba, Miles ... It's done all the time."

"You're new to all this, Kate," Nolan told her, "but I assure you, sending out clinical research to contract labs is very common."

"Okay," Kate conceded. "But why would you have a problem with my calling Chemstra?"

"Because talking to Chemstra is not part of your job! It's part of *my* job. Now come and help me entertain the agency."

Entertaining the agency is part of my job, Kate thought angrily, but talking to the contract lab isn't. She thought of the scrub-suited woman coming out of the OR near Dr. Gould's office, and the familiar smell of hospital disinfectant. What the hell am I doing here? she wondered, as she followed Nolan out into the hallway.

Chapter 16

"I'm not sure I should go through with it," Kate repeated.

Richard Day looked at her kindly. "So you said. But isn't it a little late for that?"

Kate nodded. The press party was only hours away, and reporters and crews from the major news programs would be there to tape an interview with her.

Nearly two busy weeks had passed since her run-in with Nolan in Jerry's office, but the troubling uncertainty she'd felt still lingered. Nolan had grudgingly approved the analysis she'd requested from Chemstra but told her to be patient; Chemstra had far more important things to do. And although Nolan said the clinical trials data were on their way, the report still hadn't surfaced.

And yet, as she'd studied the focus report Amy Treeson had prepared, she'd been reassured by the small number of people who'd actually reported the more serious side effects. In fact, based on the final focus group research tabulations, Nolan was right about the side effects being nearly within acceptable limits.

What had been troubling her for the past week, what continued to rankle, was Nolan's seeming lack of respect for her as a professional. How could he countermand her orders for data? The more she fumed over his treatment of her, the more she began to question his business ethics.

This evening she would stand before the assembled press and sing the praises of Genelife. She'd been briefed, both by a tight-lipped Nolan and an encouraging Mac, and in the course of those briefings had learned little that was new, aside from the fact that Tucker Boone had brought the original idea for Genelife out of the rain forest years ago. This was interesting but not significant; over a quarter of modern prescriptive medicines had been developed from rain forest plants. Still, it was the kind of thing the press could play with.

"A penny for them," Richard's voice brought her out of her reverie, and she smiled an apology.

"Sorry. It's just ... I'm beginning to wonder whether I made a big mistake in taking this job."

"You can always quit," Richard said reasonably.

"You mean, after the press event?"

"Surely not before it." He smiled encouragingly. "I thought you loved the job. What's changed your mind?"

"I haven't exactly changed my mind ..." She ate a forkful of lettuce. How did she really feel about her job at Randall Webber? About Genelife? She could still say in truth that she used the drug herself. She believed in its efficacy, and had been reassured about its safety. She was still comfortable recommending it. But the job at Randall Webber was something else. I'm supposed to be a doctor, not a shill, she thought. When did I become a spokesperson instead of a scientist? And then there was that business with Chemstra ...

"Richard, you know the drug business, right? You've worked with other clients like Randall Webber?"

"Yes. In fact, I started out on the client side with Miles Laboratories."

"Then tell me, is it true that drug companies routinely use contract labs to do their clinical research?"

Richard's eyes narrowed slightly. "Yes, it's true. All the majors do it. Why?"

"Randall Webber uses a company called Chemstra, in Switzerland."

"Chemstra ... I don't know them."

"They're only five years old. They also manufacture Genelife. Is it kosher to use the same lab that does your testing to do your manufacturing, too?"

"If they're up to it, sure. Although I'd think it would be economically unfeasible to manufacture abroad and then import—" He broke off abruptly. "Chemstra does both?"

"Through a subsidiary, yes."

Richard nodded. "I see." He didn't see at all, but he was curious to hear more. "If that's all that's bothering you, you can go do your press interviews with a clear conscience." He looked at her questioningly.

"No, that's not all. But I can't really talk about it."

Richard nodded. "I understand," he said. "You're in a delicate position. Something's obviously troubling you, but you don't want to talk about anything that should be kept confidential. I admire that. But I'm out of the loop on this thing. I have been, ever since the business went to Mac-Allister. So, if you want to unload on me, I hope you know that I would never betray your confidence."

"I appreciate that."

Richard poured them both more wine, while Kate picked at her chicken. It was nice of Richard to plan this celebratory lunch. She hadn't seen much of him over the past few months, although they'd spoken on the phone now and then. When he'd suggested they celebrate her appearance at the press event, she'd been flattered. No one at Mac-Allister had suggested such a celebration. Well, they'd been awfully busy lately.

"Genelife is a helluva product," Richard said, watching her carefully. "Lots of people at our agency are using it. Only—"

Kate looked up. "Only what?" she asked quickly.

"Nothing," Richard said.

"No, you were going to say something. What was it?"

"I was going to say that I'm glad our agency didn't get the account."

Kate stared at him. "Why?"

"You know why."

"I don't!"

"I think you do," he said. And waited.

"The side effects," she breathed. "You heard about the side effects."

Richard tried to hide his surprise. "Exactly," he said. "Some of our people have experienced ... uh, all sorts of things. Why, one of the secretaries actually had a miscarriage."

"I can't believe a doctor would prescribe Genelife for a pregnant woman! That's ... criminal!"

"Her doctor didn't prescribe it. She got the patches from someone else. This is a dangerous drug you're dealing with."

"Any drug can be dangerous if it's misused," Kate told him. "That miscarriage was not Genelife's fault."

"Of course it wasn't," Richard said soothingly. "So

you're thinking of jumping ship because the side effects are going haywire?"

"They're not going haywire, Richard! It was only a few people in the focus groups. Don't put words in my mouth."

"Sorry. You were the one who said—never mind. Look, maybe you should talk to Nolan about it."

"I tried," Kate said angrily, her hackles rising as she once again recalled the way Nolan had spoken to her in Jerry's office. "He doesn't want to hear about problems, only about profits."

"Yes, Nolan's fixated on money, I hear. So's Mac. They're well matched, aren't they? Anything for a buck."

"Nolan, maybe. But surely not Mac. No, he's—" Suddenly Kate flushed. How could she discuss Mac and Nolan with Richard? She tried to remember exactly what she'd said. Had she been terribly indiscreet? "Look, Richard, I think we should just change the subject, okay?"

"Sure," Richard said easily. "Have you seen the Met's new production of *Don Giovanni*? A little too modern for me, but worth seeing . . ."

The conversation lightened, and with it, Kate's mood. Surely Richard had been the one to bring up the side effects issue, hadn't he? And she'd assured him everything was fine. She may have said a few things about Nolan she probably shouldn't have, but she was certain Richard wouldn't repeat them. Who could he repeat them to? Certainly not to Michael himself; Richard had no contact with Michael Nolan. And repeating her remarks to anyone else wouldn't really matter.

As far as her own relationship with Nolan was concerned, she'd just have to become more assertive. Yes, that was it. Try to do less selling once tonight's press conference was behind her, and more science. Perhaps Randall Webber had another drug in the pipeline, something less fully developed than Genelife, that she could get involved with.

But what if he refused to give her another project?

She sipped her wine absently. Despite Amy's reassuring report, what had felt so right back in July was starting to feel very wrong.

Damn! She set her wineglass back onto the table with a bang that startled them both. How many times do I need to change my life, she wondered fiercely, before I get it right?

* * *

"... use it yourself?"

"That's right," said the pretty red-haired woman. "I've been using Genelife for nearly a year."

"But it's only been on the market since January," observed the male reporter.

"True. But we've had FDA approval for over a year. I self-prescribed it as soon as I joined Randall Webber."

"And it obviously works," the female member of the news team said. She herself had been using Genelife for several months, though she steadfastly denied it. Better for her image. "Dr. Martin, I understand Genelife was originally discovered in the rain forest of Brazil. Could you tell us a little about ..."

Steve lowered the senior thesis he was grading, and turned toward the television set that sat on the built-in bookshelves along one wall of his apartment. It was his habit to catch the eleven o'clock news each night. He'd set the sound low, as he plowed through the paperwork that was his least favorite part of teaching. Now he got up and went to the TV. I know that woman, he thought. He raised the volume.

"... a brilliant young scientist named Tucker Boone. He drew his inspiration from a trip he made to the Brazilian interior ..."

Tucker? How did this woman know Tucker?

"And isn't it true, Dr. Martin, that Genelife is actually made from a rain forest plant?" the male reporter asked.

Dr. Martin, of course! Steve thought. The pretty woman at Randall Webber. The woman that Nolan's secretary thought I'd seen on television. So she knew Tucker!

"Not exactly," Dr. Martin was saying. "Genelife uses a synthetic version of a chemical compound that occurs in a rare rain forest plant. Actually, over twenty-five percent of today's prescriptive drugs ..."

Steve rushed back to his desk for pencil and paper, banging his shin on the low glass coffee table. Shit! Hobbling back to the TV, he scribbled "Dr. Martin" with one hand while rubbing his throbbing leg with the other. Now her name was superimposed on the screen, and he added "Kate."

The interview concluded soon afterward, and Steve switched off the TV. He glanced at the large old English wall clock ticking softly beside the bookshelves, and decided it was still early enough to call Marianne. She'd been so despondent lately, living in a limbo of uncertainty and guilt. He was sure it would perk her up to hear that he'd found someone new, someone not interviewed by the police or mentioned by Nolan, who apparently had known Tucker. Ever since his meeting with Michael Nolan, Steve had been keenly aware that in addition to his sister's peace of mind, there was quite a lot of money at stake.

He'd contact Dr. Martin first thing in the morning. The search for Tucker was on again.

An uncertain moonlight spilled through the windows, casting strange shadows. Dark shapes lurked in corners, and the staircase took a jagged bite from the dark pool of carpeting. The elevator door opened with a sudden whoosh that echoed in the deep silence, and disgorged two figures.

They stood for a moment, silhouetted against the bright interior of the elevator, then began making their cautious way along the dimly lit hallway. Office doors stood open and vulnerable; chairs and desks were empty, abandoned.

"Stay close and don't trip over anything," Mac told her. "Where's the damn light switch?"

"It's spooky," Kate said.

"It's cost-effective," he explained. "The cleaners are instructed to turn out all the lights as they finish with each section of the building. Don't come any farther. You'll break something." Mac stepped out into the large unlit work area that housed the market research department, and began working his way over to the far wall. There was a loud crash, followed by the tinkle of broken glass. "Goddammit!"

"You all right?"

Mac's fingers scrabbled along the wall and found the light switch; a cool fluorescence lit up the work area. "Shit!" he exclaimed with real feeling. A small PC monitor lay smashed in the middle of the carpet. "Well, come on!" he said impatiently. "Walk around it and let's get started."

"I still don't understand why you didn't tell me sooner," Kate said, anger coloring her voice.

"If I had," he said tiredly as he booted up the computer system, "you'd never have gotten through the press interviews."

"Damn right!"

"Calm down. It's a little unsettling but it's not definitive."

"And that's why you're sneaking into your own office at ten-thirty at night."

"I just don't want to start a panic. It could be nothing."

"Then why are we here?"

"To cover my ass in case it *is* something," Mac said. "You did great with the press people, by the way."

"Thanks. The AMA can cite the tapes when they revoke my license to practice medicine."

Kate massaged the back of her neck. She was tired. Performing for the press had been exhausting, and afterward Nolan had hosted a dinner at Bouley for key company and agency personnel. When the party broke up around ten, Mac had suggested he and Kate share a cab uptown. It was then he'd suggested they stop at the agency so he could show her some new data he'd turned up.

The system was up and running now. Mac hit a series of keys and scrolled through the information that appeared on the screen.

"As I told you, I saw most of the original stuff for the first time this morning," he explained. "Our public relations people have been putting together information packets for tonight. They requested things like user profiles from the market research department, promotional video clips from the creative department. Everything was pulled piecemeal by a bunch of different departments. I wanted to make a few last-minute revisions to some of the pieces, and asked to see the various source materials. That's when I began to worry a little."

"Dave didn't worry about it? Or Amy?"

"To Amy, the numbers didn't look so bad. And in fact, they don't. Dave's in denial on this thing. He won't hear a word against Genelife."

"I missed him at the press party."

"He hasn't been well. He went home early." Mac looked as though he were going to say something, then stopped himself.

"Is he okay?"

"I hope so. Here, look at this." Kate bent closer to the screen as Mac scrolled through the data that a less formal but wider-reaching research poll had collected.

The reported incidences of headaches, appetite loss, and debilitating weakness seemed definitely higher than expected, though not a lot higher. More chilling, there were three reported deaths. "Jesus," Kate breathed. "I don't like this at all. Can I get a printout?"

Mac hit some keys, and the printer began chattering. "It'll take a little time," he said. "Meanwhile, there's something else I want to show you."

He led her out of the research area and down the darkened stairs to the creative floor. This time he found the light switch on the first try.

"You know those on-camera testimonials we use in the new campaign?"

Kate nodded. "You included a video of some of them in the press kit, too."

"Right. Well, before Dave took off, I had him show me the original uncut screening tapes. I think you should see them, too. It'll make me feel less guilty. Not that we don't cut testimonials this way all the time."

Mac opened the door to a small screening room. Inside were several chairs, a TV monitor, and a VCR. At least two dozen videocassettes were stacked on a small side table. On top of the cassettes was a clipboard with a thick sheaf of paper. "The shot log," he explained. He checked the list, then switched on the machines and inserted one of the cassettes.

"This is Kathy Howe, the woman in the blue dress," said Mac, pressing PLAY.

Kate nodded. "I remember her. She said some great things."

"Yeah," Mac said. "And some not so great things, too. The creative group cut them out."

A small rectangular cutout containing constantly changing time-code numbers was superimposed over the image on the screen. "Those numbers let us locate different parts of the tape fast," Mac explained as he forwarded through the material. "We also use them in post production, when we cut different takes together." Kate glanced at the log sheet in Mac's hand. Time-code numbers ran down the left-hand side of the page; on the right were descriptions of the action or words that occurred at that point on the tape.

". . . not really that bad." Kathy Howe's voice suddenly boomed out of the small speaker as Mac released the forward scan button. He quickly lowered the sound. "But the headaches are awful, sometimes. It just pounds and pounds ... but it's worth it ..."

"Here's the clip we used," Mac told Kate as the woman in blue began speaking again. "I look ten years younger, without surgery! It's just incredible! I just wish I didn't have these headaches all the time, though. Sometimes I ..."

"I don't remember the part about the headaches," Kate said.

"Of course not. They cut the video right after she said 'It's just incredible!' As I said, we do it all the time, with testimonials." He popped out the cassette and inserted another. "This is Stacy Lewis."

"Who?"

"You'll recognize her."

Again he scanned through the video, referring to the log for the time-code number. "Thirteen twenty-two ... thirty ... here we go."

"Yes, I did," Stacy Lewis told the camera. "I sort of stopped eating and I lost a lot of weight. My doctor says I've lost too much weight, but I don't care! I wouldn't stop taking Genelife for anything! It's a little miracle!"

" 'A little miracle,' " Kate repeated. "I thought that was such a great line. I never would have guessed she had problems with Genelife."

"She doesn't think she does."

"Are they all like this?"

"A few," Mac admitted. "But most people gave us good, solid testimonials. Most of them didn't have side effects."

"Like me," Kate said. "Let's go get the computer printout. Can you run me a statistical tabulation on the market research in the morning? I'm going to need some hard numbers to take to Nolan."

"You're going to Nolan?" Mac asked.

"I'll have to. We need to check this out. Don't panic," she added, seeing his face. "We're not pulling Genelife off the market yet."

"We'll get you anything you need," he assured her. "But please, let's keep it quiet, okay?" He shoved his hands in his pockets and paced the length of the small room. "The side effects tabulations may be a little higher, but I don't think they're that much higher." He paused, searching for words. "Ordinarily, I wouldn't have mentioned it, much less brought you up here in the dead of night to show it to you. It's just that this, coming on top of that focus group ..."

"I'm glad you told me."

"Frankly, you're more than a client. You've become a friend. If we really do have a problem here, I want us to be able to help each other."

"I appreciate that. I'll keep you posted. Nolan's out of town tomorrow, but I'll get to him first thing Wednesday."

Mac turned off the video machines.

"How bad do you think it is?" he asked.

Kate shrugged. "Maybe not very bad at all," she said. "A colleague of mine suggested we may be seeing the results of an unstable synthetization. If so, the situation is messy but correctable, at least from the medical perspective."

"But it'll mean pulling Genelife off the market, won't it?"

"Pulling the old stock, yes, but not necessarily the drug itself. But that may not be necessary. Don't forget that we have FDA approval, based on clinical trials with this same formulation." Kate shook her head in frustration and puzzlement. "It just doesn't make sense. Chemstra ..." She broke off.

Mac was replacing the cassettes in their plastic boxes. "Who's Chemstra?" he asked. "What's their involvement in all this?"

Kate was silent for a moment. When she spoke it was more to herself than to him. "That," she said softly, "is what I need to find out."

Chapter 17

April 9

The alarm clock rang at six-thirty as usual, dragging Kate from a deep, dreamless sleep. Blinking in the morning light, she reached out to the bedside table, fingers scrabbling for the round object. Grasping it firmly, she hurled it at the far wall; with a yelp of joy, Cheerio bounded after it. The loud raspy clanging ceased upon impact as it was designed to do, and the dog caught it on the rebound. Carrying it carefully in her mouth, Cheerio returned the tennis-ball-shaped clock to Kate, then bounced around hoping for a replay.

"Only one to a customer," Kate told the dog, wiping the clock with a tissue and replacing it on the bedside table. Cheerio nudged it with her nose and wagged her tail.

Kate's father had given her the clock as a sort of joke gift, when she'd been accepted into medical school. "There'll be many a morning you'll be so exhausted, you'll want to throw the damn thing at the wall," he'd said. "Now you can." Kate had always found it a very satisfying way to wake up.

"Breakfast, girl!" she announced, and padded into the kitchen to spoon out Cheerio's food—the Chow-Down Dave had sent had been a big success—and to put on the coffee.

As she measured the water and ground the beans, she reviewed the plan she'd formulated last night. It seemed simple enough. She glanced at the oven clock: nearly seven. It would be one o'clock in Switzerland. She decided she had time for a shower to clear her head.

The first thing she did when she'd toweled off and dressed was to call the office and leave a phone-mail message saying she had a morning meeting in New York, and would arrive at Randall Webber around noon. Then she went back to the kitchen, poured a mug of coffee, and went back into the living room. Taking a large yellow pad and a pencil from her briefcase, she set them on the small square dining table alongside the coffee mug.

Kate's telephone was a reasonably sophisticated instrument with a built-in answering machine and various convenience functions. It sat on a low Lucite table beside the green chintz sofa across the room. Uncoiling its extra long extension cord, Kate carried the phone to the table, then pulled out one of the rush-seated dining chairs and sat down.

She hesitated for a moment, sipping the hot, fragrant brew and wondering if she could pull it off. Then she figured what the hell, and began to dial.

Once again, it took some time for the Chemstra receptionist to locate an English-speaking operator, but Kate held on gamely.

"*Bonjour,* hello!" said a perky female voice at last. "I am Madame Berthold. May I help you?"

"I hope so," Kate replied. "My name is, uh, Joanne Kennedy. I'm a reporter with the *Wall Street Journal,* here in New York. I specialize in science and medicine. I'm preparing a story about Genelife, and I'd like to ask a few questions, if I may."

There was a long pause. "I'm sorry, madame," the woman said. "You must speak with Randall Webber."

"I've already spoken with them," Kate replied, managing to sound both perplexed and annoyed. "A Mr. Michael Nolan. He was most cooperative. In fact, he was the one who suggested I call Chemstra."

"I see. One moment, please. I must ask you to wait." Kate heard a click as the woman put her on hold.

She's calling Nolan, Kate thought. But of course he won't be in. She sipped her coffee and waited.

After nearly five minutes, the woman was back on the line. "I am so sorry," she told Kate. "I understand there was a press conference yesterday, no? And that is why you are calling?"

"That's where I spoke to Mr. Nolan, yes. But I'm on a very tight timetable, Madame Berthold. I must file my story today or ... or the paper will run another story instead. Mr. Nolan is quite anxious for this article to appear. It's a very positive picture of the whole, um, operation."

"Unfortunately Mr. Nolan is not in his office, so he cannot confirm your statement. Perhaps when he returns tomorrow—"

"Pardon me, madame," Kate broke in angrily. "But when he returns tomorrow, he will be most unhappy to learn that an extremely positive and important news story about his company failed to run in the world's most influential financial publication because your company will not answer a few simple questions."

This time the pause was shorter. "I think you must talk with Monsieur Fanning," the woman said. "He is the one who can answer your questions. Unfortunately, he is not here at the moment."

"When will he return?"

"A little after four, I believe."

Kate calculated quickly; that would be ten o'clock New York time. "If you would be kind enough to give him my name, I will call him back."

"I think he would prefer to call you at the *Wall Street Journal*," the woman told her.

"Of course," Kate said. "I'll give you the direct line for the science department. Do you have a pencil?" She recited her home number, then thanked Madame Berthold and hung up quickly. If Monsieur Fanning—not a Swiss name, surely?—didn't call her by ten-thirty, she'd call him.

Meanwhile, she had two and a half hours to kill. She didn't dare leave the apartment, in case Fanning got back earlier than expected. She did a halfhearted cleanup, fluffing the quilt on her double bed, changing Cheerio's water, sweeping the spotless kitchen floor. The morning paper was sitting on the mat outside her front door. She brought it in and tried to read, but found she was too tense to concentrate. Was there some office work she could do? Or perhaps she should call Mac and remind him about the tabulations. No, it was too early, and besides, he wouldn't forget. She played catch with an ecstatic Cheerio in the hallway between living room and bedroom, then brushed the dog's long pale hair. She picked at an English muffin. She drank more coffee. She had another go at the paper. Finally, just after ten, the telephone rang. She took a deep breath and picked up the receiver.

"*Wall Street Journal*, Science and Medicine," Kate announced with a nasal New York drawl, hoping it wasn't her mother on the other end of the phone. "Can I help you?"

"Joanne Kennedy, please," said a male voice with a British accent. "Barry Fannon from Chemstra returning her call."

"One moment, please," Kate said, and pushed the hold button. She'd noted down her questions on a yellow pad; now she ran her eye over the list nervously before hitting the hold button a second time to release the call.

"Hello, Mr. Fannon," she said in her normal voice. "This is Joanne Kennedy. I'm writing an article about Genelife, and—"

"Yes, Madame Berthold explained. How can I help?"

Kate thought for a moment. Reporters always needed to identify their sources, didn't they? "May I have your exact title, please?" she asked. "For my records."

"Of course. I'm Director of Client Services."

"I see. And how long has Chemstra been involved with Genelife?"

"Since we began. Genelife was our first account."

"A rather large assignment to give a start-up company, wasn't it?"

"Mr. Nolan was familiar with the work of several of the scientists we agreed to recruit for the project. And of course he had worked with Henri Koch years ago in the United States."

"And Henri Koch is . . . ?"

"Our managing director. He founded Chemstra."

Kate was scribbling notes. "And you produce the synthetic SOD-2000 that's used in Genelife?"

"Correct."

"And you run the testing program?"

"Yes."

"Have you changed the formulation of the synthetic enzyme over time, based on clinical findings?"

"Not that I'm aware of."

"And have your long-term tests revealed any unusually strong or recurring side effects?"

"I don't quite understand your line of questioning, Miss Kennedy. I thought this was to be a positive article."

"Oh, it is, it is!" Kate gushed. "I use Genelife myself. It's just that I've, we've been hearing some reports of recurring headaches, physical degeneration due to food aversion . . . several people have died."

A short pause. Then, "No drug is without some side effects, Miss Kennedy. But ever since we switched to the synthetic, those side effects have been well within—"

"Excuse me. Since you *switched* to the synthetic? What were you using before?"

"Why, the plant derivative, of course. And yes, we ran into some problems there. But substituting the synthetic brought the side effects well in line with FDA requirements."

Kate's head was swimming. She'd assumed the synthetization's instability had been causing the problems she and Mac had been seeing, but now Fannon was telling her the plant derivative had been worse. "Listen, I'm sorry if I seem dense, but which form of Genelife did the FDA approve?" she asked.

"Which form?"

"The plant derivative or the synthesized enzyme?"

"Why, the synthesized version, of course. That's what's on the market."

"And you supply synthetic SOD-2000 to Randall Webber."

"Precisely."

"The same synthetic SOD-2000 the FDA approved."

There was a brief icy pause. "What are you implying, Miss Kennedy?" he asked tightly.

"Oh, nothing at all," she said hurriedly. "Just getting my facts straight. Uh, for the record."

"Well, for the record," Fannon said stiffly, "yes, we do supply the same synthetic SOD-2000 the FDA approved. Now, I really think—"

"Just one more question. How many clients does Chemstra have?"

"I fail to see . . ."

"It's just background."

"Well, we handle projects for a number of other pharmaceutical companies. But Randall Webber is naturally our most important client."

"You mean, because of the size of the Genelife assignment?"

"That, and because of the relationship between our two companies, of course."

"Of course. And that relationship is . . . ?"

There was a moment of silence. "As I told you, Genelife was our first account. Now, was there anything else you wished to know?"

An idea entered Kate's head stage left and began leaping around.

"Who owns Chemstra, Mr. Fannon?"

"That is privileged information, Miss Kennedy, and not relevant to our discussion."

"Our research department can find out easily enough," Kate told him.

"Then by all means ask them to do so. But I should warn you that in Switzerland private companies are not required to register the names of their directors or investors. I find your question most intrusive."

"Chemstra is a private company?"

"I'm afraid I must take another phone call. Please send us a copy of your article. Good-bye." *Click.*

Kate sat for a while, staring at the page of notes. Then she took a fresh sheet of paper and began to list what she had learned.

Fact: Chemstra is a private company, probably financed by Randall Webber.

Fact: Chemstra's research results showed a reduction of side effects when synthetic SOD was substituted for a plant-derived enzyme.

Fact: The FDA had approved the use of the synthetic, which Chemstra was now supplying to Randall Webber.

Now the side effects were on the rise. Why?

Kate arrived at the office around noon to find her desk covered with a pink snow of message slips. She'd gathered them into a neat pile and was just starting to sort through them when her phone rang.

"Jesus, Kate, I've been calling you since ten-thirty!" Mac's voice exclaimed.

"I, er, had an appointment outside the office," she told him. "What's up?"

"Dave's in the hospital. He collapsed during a meeting this morning. I thought you'd want to know."

"My God! Is he all right? What happened?"

"No one's quite sure. But . . . could it be Genelife?"

"Shit! What does his doctor say?"

"I don't know. Will you go and see him?"

"Of course." Kate flipped over one of the pink slips and scribbled the information Mac gave her on the back. "I'll leave right away," she said. "Be there as soon as I can."

"I'll meet you there," Mac told her, and disconnected.

Kate's intercom was buzzing. She stabbed at the button with a shaky finger. "Yes?" she asked impatiently.

"There's a Steve Kavett on three," said the secretary Kate shared with the sales staff.

"Who? Never mind. Tell him to leave a number and I'll get back—"

"He's already called twice," the secretary told her. "He says it's important. Something about Tucker Boone."

"I'll take it." Cradling the receiver under her chin, Kate shoved the paper with the hospital information into her jacket pocket with one hand while hitting the flashing phone button with the other. "Kate Martin here."

"Dr. Martin? My name is Steve Kavett. I saw you on television the other night. On the news."

"Yes?"

"You talked about Tucker. I need to find him. I was hoping you could help."

"I'm sorry, but I really don't think—"

"Let me explain. I'm the guy he went to the Amazon with, back in '82. He married my sister."

Slowly Kate lowered herself into the big desk chair. "Tucker found Genelife in the rain forest," she said softly. "You were there?"

"No. Yes. I mean, I was there, but I never knew what he'd found. He stayed on for months after I left. It's a long story. The thing is, my sister's very anxious to find him."

"Find him ... ? I'm a little confused here. I thought he ... and why should you think I could help?"

"You knew him, you worked with him. You might have some idea of where—"

"Oh, I see. You thought ... Sorry to disappoint you, Mr. Kavett—"

"Steve."

"Steve—but I joined the company a good month after Tucker left. I'm afraid I never met him."

"Shit!"

"You'll have to excuse me," Kate said, "but we have kind of a crisis here. A friend of mine's just been hospitalized. Perhaps I could call you back when things aren't so crazy."

"Sure, of course." Steve gave her both home and office numbers, feeling extremely depressed. He'd been so sure he'd uncovered another lead.

"I'm sorry I couldn't help," Kate said, hearing the disappointment in his voice. "I have no idea what happened to him after he left the company, but I'll keep my ears open."

"But he didn't le—"

"I really have to run, uh, Steve. I'll call you back soon, I promise. G'bye."

Kate slammed down the phone and headed for the door. The secretary looked up in surprise. "Going out again?" she asked.

"Yes," Kate said shortly. "And I probably won't be back today."

Too bad Steve Whatshisname doesn't actually know what Boone found in the rain forest, she thought as she hurried down the corridor. Still, she'd shoved the message slip with his phone numbers into her handbag. There might be some way they could help each other on this thing. She rushed through the atrium lobby and into the parking lot, dredging her car keys from the depths of her purse as she ran.

They'd taken Dave to the emergency room at Beacon Hospital, the medical facility closest to the MacAllister offices. The waiting area outside the ER was crowded, as it was in every hospital Kate had ever been in. She looked for Mac but instead found Victoria, huddled in a chair near a narrow window, looking miserable.

"How is he?" Kate asked anxiously.

Victoria looked up at Kate with relief. "I'm so glad you're here," she said. "They won't tell me a thing. Just that he's stable, which is a strange description of Dave when you think about it." She smiled weakly.

"What happened?"

"He was giving a new business presentation. Apparently he'd been up all night reviewing the material at home, making some changes . . . He got his secretary in early and they revised the storyboards and the print ads together. Then the client called and delayed the meeting an hour. Mac said Dave looked exhausted when they finally got started."

Several white-coated figures approached them, and Victoria looked up hopefully.

"Mrs. Rivera?" one said tentatively.

Victoria shook her head.

"Sorry." The doctors disappeared down the hall.

"Where was I?" Victoria asked.

"Client was late, Dave was exhausted."

"Right. Well, Mac said that Dave was in the middle of the creative presentation. He was going great guns when suddenly he winced and grabbed his forehead. Then he sort of slid slowly down onto the floor. The client thought it was some kind of tasteless agency joke."

"Was he conscious?"

"Oh, yes. Mac said he was still pitching the print ads as the EMS team carried him onto the elevator."

Kate smiled. "Sounds like Dave."

"Yeah." Victoria stood up and went to the narrow window. Below, people were carrying groceries, hailing cabs, walking dogs. "Kate, was it Genelife?"

Kate sighed. "Maybe. Maybe not. I'd need to see his chart, talk to his doctor, look at the various test results . . ."

"Mac thinks Dave's trying to live up to the way he looks these days, pretending he's twenty-five again."

"Is that so bad?"

"Honey, the man is fifty-two and he's running on empty. He's getting maybe three hours of sleep a night, he's living on coffee as though it were a three-course meal, and he's working nonstop. He's killing himself."

"That sounds more like a psychological symptom of using Genelife than a medical one."

Victoria fixed her with a steely eye. "That may be," she said, "but the result is, he's in hospital."

Kate nodded; her head had started to throb painfully. "Look, I'm going to see what I can find out. You know, doctor to doctor. Do you have any aspirin?"

Victoria eyed her with concern. "Not you, too!"

"No, of course not! I'm just a little stressed out at the moment."

Victoria appeared unconvinced, but she rummaged in her purse and came up with a small tin. "Help yourself. Oh, and Mac said to tell you he'll be here as soon as he can. He wants to talk to you."

"Thanks." Kate dumped two of the pills into her palm. "I'll be back with an update."

Once Kate had left the room, Victoria sat down again on the hard gray chair and replaced the tin of aspirin in her purse. Then she took out a tissue and dabbed at her moistening eyes.

Kate swallowed her aspirin with water from a drinking fountain in the hallway. Then she approached the information desk, introduced herself, and asked to speak with the senior resident in charge of the ER room. A few minutes of phone conversation and the resident, whose name was Alan, buzzed her in through the one-way ER doors.

Alan had a buddy doing a residency at New York General and Kate recognized the name. This formed a bond, and Alan became more forthcoming. Mr. Randazzo's pressure had been way down when the EMS team had brought him in, Alan explained, and his cbc had revealed a dangerously low hemoglobin. They were transfusing him now. Other test results hadn't come back from the lab yet, but the physical exam hadn't turned up anything. "Nothing significant in the medical history. He's not on any medication," he said, consulting Dave's chart. "Malnutrition and stress, that's my guess."

"But he *is* on medication," Kate said. "He's on Genelife."

"Really? He didn't say so." Alan scribbled a note on the chart.

Dave's in denial, Mac had told her last night. "Okay with you if I go in for a minute?" she asked.

"Sure, go ahead. Room D."

Dave managed a weak grin when he saw her, but Kate didn't smile back. The red IV tubing that snaked down from the blood bag hung on the metal stand beside the bed was the only bit of color in the room. Dave, the blanket that covered him, and the walls around him were all a uniform off-white.

"Why didn't you tell the resident who took your medical history that you were on Genelife?" Kate demanded.

"Nice to see you, too," Dave said. "I feel much better, thank you."

"This is serious, Dave. You could have died."

"Yeah, right. You doctors panic so."

"Dave, I want you to promise me something. Stop using Genelife."

"What for? You think Genelife put me here? Get real, Kate! I've been working too hard, I forget to eat ..."

"Mac showed me some research data at the agency last night. It seems to indicate that side effects could be higher than we expected. Not astronomically higher, but the trend is there. And you have the classic symptoms: headaches, lack of appetite—"

"I didn't see *you* putting away the mashed potatoes and gravy during the focus group trip," Dave interrupted.

"That's right, you didn't. Genelife kills the appetite. But I force myself to eat a little, even when I don't want to. Sure, I've lost weight. But I bet my hemoglobin's at least four points higher than yours. Some people are more sensitive to certain drugs. You happen to be sensitive to Genelife."

"I'm sorry, Kate, but I don't believe it. Aside from what you call the classic symptoms, I feel terrific. My muscle tone's improved. Even my eyesight's better. Genelife is the best thing that ever happened to me."

"How can you say that?"

"Look at me, Kate. How old do I look to you?"

"This is silly ..."

"Humor me."

Kate studied the face on the pillow. A faint blush of pink was visible now as the transfused blood began to suffuse the tissues. Dave certainly didn't look fifty-two. She tried to forget his real age, to look at him as she would a stranger. "Thirty," she said at last. "Thirty-five, tops."

Dave beamed at her. "Exactly," he said.

"But why should it matter? You looked fine before." Her words sounded familiar somehow. Hadn't Victoria said something similar to her? I'm a great one to talk, she thought ruefully.

"It's not vanity that keeps me using Genelife," Dave said. "It's business." He shifted slightly on the bed. "Would you mind taking this blanket thing off?" he asked. "It's getting warm in here."

"That's the blood working." Kate stripped off the thin cotton blanket and folded it across the foot of the bed. The outline of Dave's body beneath the sheet looked awfully thin.

"See, advertising's a very young business," he continued. "Especially on the creative side. I would guess maybe eighty percent of the creative department at MacAllister is under thirty-five. And of those, probably half are in their twenties. Even Mac is under forty. It's that kind of business."

"But you're the creative director. You're in charge. It's not the same for you, is it?"

"Sure it is. Youth respects youth. A few more years, a few more lines, and unless you're some kind of legend—which I'm not, believe me—you're an oldster. You're unhip. Agencies are looking for the young turks out there, the young crazies, not the old guys."

"Mac doesn't feel that way. He thinks you're wonderful."

Dave smiled. "I love that guy. Yeah, Mac's different. He has this fierce sense of personal loyalty. Once he makes a personal commitment to you—as a friend, a lover, an employer, whatever—he'll defend you to the death. And he expects the same commitment, the same unswerving loyalty, from you. No, I'm okay with Mac. But let's say his little shop goes bust and I have to find an honest job. No one's gonna hire me at fifty-two, babe. But at thirty-three, the world's my fucking oyster."

"You may look thirty-three. You're still fifty-two."

"Ah, but that would be my little secret."

A knock at the door; Alan stuck his head inside. "We're going to transfer you upstairs, now," he told Dave. "We'd like him to be our guest for a day or so," he said to Kate. "Just to be safe." Kate nodded.

The rattle of a gurney announced the arrival of Dave's transport. "Victoria's outside," Kate told Dave. "And Mac'll be here any minute. We'll come see you when you get settled."

Dave smiled. "Good old Vic," he said.

Kate leaned over and kissed his now-rosy cheek. Transfusions worked their magic amazingly fast.

Back in the waiting area, Mac had joined Victoria, and people were eyeing them curiously; haven't we seen them on television?

"He's fine," Kate announced. "They're keeping him overnight so they can keep an eye on him. He'll probably go home tomorrow."

Now the stares were transferred to Kate; was she Somebody?

Victoria looked relieved, but Mac scowled. "What the hell *is* this drug of yours, Kate?" he said angrily. "What the hell are you selling?"

"Hey, I didn't invent it," Kate retorted. "I didn't develop it, I didn't test it. And you can't expect me to know more about it than the FDA!"

"Guys, guys!" Victoria broke in. "We're all upset. Let's not take it out on each other, okay?"

"Sorry," Mac said. "It's just . . . I'm worried."

"I know," Kate said. "Me, too."

"How about some coffee?"

"Good idea."

Across the street from the hospital was a large coffee shop, nearly empty now that the lunch crowd had gone. They settled into a booth and ordered, and Kate told them what Dave had said about the advertising business.

"He's right," Mac said sourly. "It sucks, but it's true."

A waitress brought coffee and they sipped in silence for a while. Finally Mac spoke. "This thing is starting to scare me," he said. "I'm between a rock and a hard place. I can't afford for the agency to be caught in a scandal. And I can't afford to give up the Genelife business, not if there's a chance it'll turn out okay. So tell me: Do we have a great drug with some aberrant research? Or do we have a breast implant situation? Help me here."

"I wish I could. I just don't know. Chemstra says they haven't changed the formulation of the enzyme since the FDA approved it. And the FDA *did* approve it. Something's wrong, but I can't figure out what."

"Should we resign the account?"

"God, no!" Kate exclaimed. "The problem could turn out to be something simple, something correctable."

"What if it isn't?" Victoria asked. "Will you tell him if things start to get too hot? Can you help him get out in time?"

Kate smiled. "What's that old joke about a guy on a bus asking another guy where Maple Street is? The second guy says, 'Watch me and get off two stops before I do.' Yes, I'll warn you if it starts to look bad."

"Thanks."

"Dave should be settled in his room by now," Kate said. "You want to go and see him?"

"Of course." Mac reached for the bill and slapped a dollar on the table. Then he slid out of the booth and headed for the cashier near the front door. Victoria followed. But Kate remained where she was, facing the swinging doors to the kitchen at the rear of the room.

She knew what she had to do, what she'd advise any patient of hers to do in the circumstances. She reached her hand under the neck of her pink striped summer sweater until she felt the smooth circle below her collarbone. Regretfully she began to lift the patch. Then she hesitated; was this absolutely necessary? Was she just panicking because of Dave? After all, she hadn't experienced any really strong side effects.

"Coming, Kate?" Mac called from the doorway.

The research might be aberrant, she told herself. The headaches I've been getting might just as likely be caused by worry and stress. She looked down at her plate with its lightly nibbled muffin. I like being so slim, she thought.

She began to withdraw her hand, then stopped. Who was she kidding? Lifting the adhesive with her nail, she ripped the patch from her skin. Then she folded it in half and dropped it into the ashtray.

Chapter 18

"Impossible!" Nolan scowled at Kate and slashed the air with his arm. "He must have been on something."

"He was!" Kate retorted. "Genelife."

Kate had been trying to talk to Nolan since his arrival in the office first thing that morning, but it was nearly twelve-thirty before Jenny could fit her into his schedule. He'd been sweetness and light when she'd first stepped onto the oriental carpet that was the focus of his large, airy office. He'd held his hands out to her, kissed her lightly on the cheek, and showered her with praise for her part in the press party and subsequent news coverage. But when Kate had waved away the compliments and broken the news of Dave's hospitalization, his eyes had narrowed suspiciously. And to her suggestion that Genelife might have had something to do with the situation, Nolan pulled back as though she'd struck him, and professed not concern but disbelief and anger.

"He was on Genelife, Michael!" Kate repeated.

"I meant something illegal," Nolan told her. "Like cocaine. Sure, he's probably a coke head. All those creative types are. Helps them concentrate."

"Not Dave."

"And what makes *you* so smart?" Nolan sneered.

"I'm your medical consultant, remember?" she said angrily. "By the way, I never got those clinical trial results you promised me."

"I told Jerry to find them for you. I'll tell him again." Nolan glanced at his watch. "I really don't have time for this nonsense, Kate."

"It's not nonsense. It could be the start of some real problems, Michael. I can't understand how you can be so . . . resistant."

Nolan stood and walked around his desk to her, his attitude now one of infinite patience. "Kate, my dear, overwrought, overworked Kate ... I've seen all the research, and believe me, we have no major problems with Genelife." He gave her a patronizing little pat on the shoulder. "And the last thing we need is for you to start spreading rumors about Randazzo."

"Rumors?" Kate replied hotly, stung by his tone. She stood up and began to pace. "Is it a rumor that he used our product? Is it a rumor that he's in the hospital?"

"Enough!" Nolan held up a hand. "I already have Jerry checking out those focus group side effects you were so worried about. I'll tell him to add Dave to the list, okay? If we have problems, nobody will be more eager to identify them and solve them than I will. But you really don't help things by going off half-cocked, encouraging fears ..."

Nolan's intercom buzzed. "Yes?"

"Henri Koch is holding for you on two, Mr. Nolan."

Asking about Joanne Kennedy? Kate wondered.

"Tell him I'll be right with him." He took Kate firmly by the elbow and walked her to the door of his office. "Now, Kate, I want you to keep quiet about this thing. We'll get it straightened out, whatever it is. But no loose lips. You work for us, not MacAllister, remember?"

"There's something else. Mac and I were going over some—"

"Later. Jenny? Send a basket of fruit to Dave Randazzo at Beacon Hospital. Kate'll give you the address." He propelled Kate firmly into the corridor and shut the door behind her.

Furious, Kate gave Jenny the hospital address and stalked off down the hallway. That bastard! She stormed into her office and swung the door shut with a satisfying bang. She flung herself into her desk chair but couldn't sit still, and got up again almost immediately and went to the window. It was one of those rare and perfect early spring day, trees covered with a green gauze of new buds, the sky a cloudless blue. I've got to get out of here, she thought.

She followed the asphalt path around the executive building, kicking viciously at stray twigs and leaves. Crocuses— yellow, blue, and purple—beckoned gaily, and she kept telling herself that nothing would be gained by grinding them into the dirt.

The path divided and absently she chose the right fork. Some distance on was a small crossroads, and this time she turned left. For nearly half an hour she wandered unaware of her surroundings, deep in thought, along roads that meandered through woods and meadows, crossing and recrossing. Then a change in the feel of the road under her feet shifted her attention from within to without; where was she? She looked around. The asphalt paving had become rutted dirt some fifty yards behind her. Off to the left she could see the redwood facade of the gymnasium building through the budding trees. It seemed surprisingly far away.

Ahead of her, the dirt road twisted to the right and disappeared into a copse of giant evergreens. Curious, Kate followed it around the bend into the shadows of the tall firs, shivering in the sudden coolness. Though rough and stony, the road was wide and bore the imprints of large deeply treaded tires in its dried mud surface.

She was calmer now, and felt a little silly having walked quite so far. It would be a long trek back. She had decided to abandon her halfhearted exploration of what was obviously some sort of maintenance road, and had turned back the way she'd come, when the roar of a diesel close behind her made her jump. She scrambled onto the shoulder as a mud-spattered truck careened past. Kate looked for the Randall Webber logo on the side as it sped by, but the truck was unmarked. Suddenly it screeched to a stop. The door opened, and a man got out.

He was tall and beefy in his jeans and denim jacket; as he approached, Kate noticed he was wearing a Randall Webber security badge pinned to his lapel. "Hey! You!" he barked. His sunglasses were opaque mirrors as he strode back toward Kate. She'd never seen any of the guards wearing glasses like these. Was that why she didn't recognize him? "Who the hell are you?" he demanded. He'd been eating a candy bar; now he tossed the bright red wrapper into the ditch.

"I'm Dr. Martin," Kate told him firmly. "I work here." She dug her ID badge out of her pocket and handed it to him. He examined it carefully, his eyes invisible, before handing it back to her. His hands were strong and rough-looking. There was dirt under the nails.

"You're a long way from home, Dr. Martin," he said suspiciously.

"I went for a walk," she said.

The man stared at her through his silvered lenses. "Get in," he said at last. "I'll drive you back."

"I don't want to be driven back," Kate told him.

"It's too far to walk."

"Not for me."

He grabbed her arm. "Come on," he said. He began pulling her toward the idling truck. "Let's go."

She stared at him in amazement and fear as he dragged her along. Was this really happening? "Okay, okay," she said, softening her voice. "You can let go of me. I'll come quietly." She gave him a meltingly sweet smile, but he ignored her, continuing to haul her along. "My arm!" she cried. He seemed to hesitate. "I'll come with you. But please, stop hurting me!"

She felt his grip loosen slightly, and she spun free and ran for the woods, pushing her way through the sharp needles. Was he behind her? She didn't dare take time to look, but kept going, gasping with fear, her heart pounding. Soon she could see daylight through the trees ahead. She stopped just inside the line of trees and looked behind her; no one. Her knees felt weak with relief. She turned back; just beyond the trees, a low cement-block building with several high, small windows squatted in the middle of a scrubby clearing. The area seemed deserted.

The man in the sunglasses ventured several steps into the evergreen woods, then hesitated. The woman was probably back on the main road by now. Besides, he knew her name. Better to simply report the incident and let them take care of her. He kicked at the dirt in frustration. He'd been stupid to have offered to drive her back. They'd warned him to stay off the company roads; he'd have lost his job if they'd caught him around the office buildings. But he'd panicked when he'd seen her, and his only thought had been to get her out of there. Well, fuck it. He climbed back into the cab of his truck, engaged the clutch, and continued down the dirt road.

Kate's hands were bleeding, her arm was bruised from the man's grip, and she could feel a long scratch along one cheek. Staying inside the tree line for cover, she worked her way around the perimeter of the clearing until she came to where the dirt road entered the clearing. Then keeping the woods between herself and the road so as not to be seen by anyone who might be in the depot building, she backtracked toward the junction with the asphalt section of road, listening for the sound of the truck. To her relief, she soon heard it accelerate and then fade. Up ahead, the road curved out of sight; when she was sure she would not be visible from the clearing, she stepped out of the trees and increased her pace toward the main road.

Turning sharply onto a narrow track cut into the woods, the driver maneuvered the heavy truck up a small rise. Hell, the woman wasn't his problem. He slowed as he approached the hidden gate, inserting a plastic card to raise the steel barrier, and drove through; the barrier clanged shut behind him. Half a mile along, he swerved onto a municipal feeder road, exiting the Randall Webber complex three miles past the company's main entrance. He unclipped the security badge and shoved it under his seat, then switched on the radio and turned up the volume. The cab reverberated with the hard, driving music, and he beat out the rhythm on the steering wheel. Some twenty minutes later, he swung onto I-95, heading south. A large flask of strong coffee nestled beneath the passenger seat, and the glove compartment was filled with his favorite chocolate bars. Thirteen hundred miles nonstop took a lot of caffeine.

Fear turned to fury as Kate marched back toward the executive office building. I'll have his job, she vowed. I'll have his hide! Ignoring the receptionist's startled glance, she headed for the ladies' room to catch her breath and remove the worst of the blood.

"Kate!" Freda Pershing, freshening her makeup at one of the washbasins, greeted her arrival with enthusiasm. "I saw you on TV the other night, very—" She stopped dead as she noticed Kate's torn lapel and scratched face. "What in hell happened to you?"

"I went for a walk," Kate told her. "Up that dirt road near the truck depot."

"The what?"

"You know, that building where they keep ..." Kate paused. It was obvious that Freda had no knowledge of the place. "Anyhow, a guard threatened me and I ran into the woods."

Freda stared at her. "You were attacked by one of our

own security guards?" she asked in horror. "My God, you're bleeding!" She took a wrinkled tissue from her handbag and dabbed at Kate's cheek. "Have you reported this?"

"No, but you bet your ass I'm going to!"

"Oh, you *have* to! Where exactly were you when it happened?"

"On the dirt road over by the truck depot. This guard was driving past me and he stopped and tried to make me get in ..." Kate stopped; Freda was staring at her, an expression of deep puzzlement on her face.

"We haven't got a truck depot," Freda said.

"Well, shipping and receiving, then. It doesn't matter—"

"Well, it does, actually," Freda told her. "Shipping and receiving is over behind the cafeteria, not on some dirt road. Surely you've passed it?"

Kate shook her head. "No, I never—"

"George Gallagher's been on duty there for as long as I can remember," Freda continued. "He's a testy old bastard, but I can't believe he'd actually—"

"No, this guy was young, about thirty. And strong." Kate's bruised arm still throbbed.

"And he was driving one of our trucks, you say? I never saw a Randall Webber truck around here. Just suppliers' trucks making deliveries. I mean, the only thing we produce around here is paper, and while I'm sure it would fill a whole *fleet* of trucks—"

"Actually, the truck didn't have any markings on it at all."

Freda leaned against the sink. "I can't understand it," she said. Then her face brightened. "I know! You must have wandered over the property line, kid. We're in the boonies out here, at least as compared to the Upper East Side. You probably surprised one of our rustic neighbors."

"Yes, but Freda, he had a Randall Webber security badge."

"Well, that *is* strange," Freda agreed. "Of course he might have stolen it ... Look, I'm not trying to diminish what happened to you. It's just that it doesn't sound like any part of Randall Webber I ever saw, and I've been here fifteen years." She shrugged her shoulders. "Of course you have to report it."

"I will."

"Talk to Marge Hanson in Personnel. And stay out of the woods for God's sake! If you're short of work, come and see me. I've got more than I can handle!" Freda put an arm around Kate's shoulder and gave her a little hug. "At least you weren't badly hurt. And don't forget to call Marge," she added as she headed for the door.

"Yes, mother," Kate told her with a smile, brushing the last of the pine needles off her skirt. Alone in the bathroom, she stared at herself in the mirror. Aside from the scratched cheek and the slightly wild hair, she didn't look too bad. Now, who was it Freda had told her to see? Marge somebody . . .

And yet . . . was it really such a hot idea to report the incident? Might it actually be dangerous to admit having been anywhere near the depot? Despite what Freda had said, it was quite obvious to Kate that she hadn't crossed any property lines. The truck, the road, the guard, the building; all were part of Randall Webber, a part nobody else seemed to know about. And the reaction of the guard to her presence on the dirt road seemed to indicate that it would be in her best interest to pretend she didn't know about it, either.

Or am I just being paranoid? she wondered. She'd been through an awful lot in the last forty-eight hours: the huge press party, Mac's scary new research tabulations, Dave's sudden illness, and her set-to with Nolan this morning. Quite possibly she was overreacting. Surely the cinder-block building was simply part of the maintenance operation. The guard ought to be fired. She'd call this Marge woman immediately.

And yet . . .

She pushed open the door of the bathroom and stepped into the hallway. To the right was the corridor to her office; to the left, the atrium lobby and rear exit that led to the golf cart parking bay. Pausing for only a moment, she turned decisively left and made her way out of the building through the back door.

She climbed into a waiting cart and pressed the accelerator. The cart rolled slowly out of the parking bay and onto the smooth asphalt path.

Nolan had warned her against loose lips. Well, she'd take his advice and leave the attack unreported, at least for now. She wanted to know a lot more about what was going on at Randall Webber before she showed her own hand. And she knew just where to start digging.

It was called The Three Pheasants. Its hundred-year-old clapboard siding was stained a colonial blue-gray; wood-smoke curled from its chimney despite the warmth of the afternoon. An old sleigh filled with boxed flowers was set out on the front lawn. Around the back, three cars sat in the white-graveled parking lot. Two of them belonged to the staff. As it was nearly three in the afternoon, this was not surprising. The middle-level executives who brought business associates or friends here for a taste of atmosphere were long gone. Two-hour lunches didn't go over well with the boss in these days of economic recession, not even when there was a client involved.

Jerry Lim sat crouched over the polished cherrywood bar, his head in one hand and what was left of his fourth drink in the other. Down at the far end of the room, the barman was polishing glassware and attempting to avoid being drawn into conversation. This was not the first afternoon Jerry had spent at The Three Pheasants.

Jerry drained his glass and set it down with a bang. "Hey, Brad! Fill 'er up!" He favored Brad with what he thought was an engaging smile.

Brad shook his head. "Sorry, Mr. Lim," he said. "Afraid I can't."

"Why in hell not?"

Brad put down the dishcloth and walked slowly up the bar toward Jerry's slumped figure. "Please, Mr. Lim. You've had enough. I could lose my license."

Jerry nodded. "Sure, I unnerstand. Wouldn't want you to lose. License. Course not. Okay."

Brad nodded and started back down the bar.

"Hey!" Jerry reached for his empty glass and waved it toward the barman. "How about just one last teeny-tiny refill? It'll be our little shee . . . secret." He tossed the glass in Brad's direction but miscalculated the angle. The glass crashed to the wooden floor.

"Shit," said Brad, and went for the hand broom.

"You gotta learn to catch better than that, you wanna play in the majors, buddy," Jerry told him with a giggle. Go to hell, Brad said with his eyes, but his mouth said "Right you are, Mr. Lim," and smiled. Lim was a lush but he was one hell of a tipper. Brad bent down and swept the shards into a metal dustpan.

Behind Jerry, the door opened and footsteps approached the bar.

"They told me I'd find you here," said a voice.

Jerry turned. "Hey, it's Kate! Hiya, Kate! Have a drink, Kate! How'd you know I was here, Kate?" He turned to Brad who had risen from the floor with a dustpan full of glass. "Brad, this is my friend Kate."

"Nice to meet you," Brad said. "You come to take him home or what?"

"What," Kate told him.

"Huh?"

"Never mind. Could I have a club soda or something? Are you still open?"

"For you, sure."

"He could lose his lishence," Jerry explained carefully.

"And I hate to bother you, but do you think you could get him some coffee?" Kate added.

"Now that'll be a pleasure," Brad said. "Be right back."

"Nice of you to drop by," Jerry told her. "You come here often?"

"No, but your friends at R&D said that you do."

"Home away from home."

Brad arrived with a steaming mug, a milk jug, and packets of sugar on a tray, then poured a club soda for Kate, who picked out one of the ice cubes and added it to Jerry's coffee. "Drink," Kate told him, then turned to Brad. "You have any more of this somewhere?" Brad nodded and went to fetch the pot.

Jerry put down the half-empty mug. "I feel mush better," he said.

"Keep going," Kate ordered, drumming her fingers on the bar impatiently. She waited until he'd drained the mug, then handed it to Brad, who refilled it and moved down the bar to his dish towels and glassware.

"How do you feel?"

"Okay, I guess," Jerry said, still somewhat glassy-eyed.

"Good. Now I'm going to ask you some questions, and I want you to answer them, okay?" Jerry nodded. "What is it about Genelife that makes you so nervous, you have to drink your lunch every day?"

Jerry looked shocked. "You think I do this every day? That's absolutely—"

"Come on, Jer. I had a long talk with the boys and girls in R&D. Nobody ever sees you after eleven-thirty in the morning, these days."

"I'm under a lot of pressure."

"What kind of pressure, Jerry? You're worried about Genelife, aren't you?"

Jerry shrugged. "Not me. I think it's just great."

"No, you don't. You told Nolan you didn't think he should launch Genelife, back in December. I was there, remember?"

But Jerry was silent.

"Look, if you're afraid someone will find out, I promise I'll never tell anyone about this conversation. I swear it." She took a sip of club soda and decided to try another approach. "Just between us," she said, lowering her voice, "we may have some problems with Genelife. I don't mean the focus group research Nolan asked you to check out. This is different research."

"Focus group research? Nolan never told me to check out the focus group research."

"You sure?"

"I may be a little drunk, but I'd remember if Nolan told me to check out a problem with Genelife. Hell, why do you think I drink every day?"

"I don't know. Why *do* you?"

"Because I'm scared of Genelife, and I'm scared of losing my job, and I don't know who to believe anymore." He took a large swallow of hot coffee. "Maybe Tucker was right, after all."

"Right about what?" Kate asked, but he didn't reply. "Come on, Jerry! Maybe Tucker was right about what?"

"He said we should delay the launch," Jerry said at last.

"Why?"

"That's what I can't be sure of.

"A problem with Genelife, surely."

Jerry shook his head. "It's not that simple," he said. "Tucker was a complicated guy, with a lot of anger. There were other reasons he could have been pushing for a delay."

"Like what?"

"Like Nolan. See, he and Nolan hated each other.

Tucker could simply have been trying to fuck Nolan for fucking Clark Randall. He was perfectly capable of doing something like that."

"Hold on! Explain the part about Nolan and ... who's Clark Randall?"

"Clark Randall is—was, he died back in January—chairman of Randall Webber for years. Nolan was his second-in command. Then Omni bought Randall Webber and fired Clark and moved Nolan up."

"Why should Tucker care?"

"You don't understand. Clark was on the board of the Randall Foundation, back when they gave Tucker the grant to develop Genelife years ago. Clark thought Tucker was some kind of warped genius, and he became Tucker's champion. It didn't matter what Tucker did—and he could be a real bastard sometimes—Clark defended him. And Tucker developed a kind of father thing about Clark; he worshiped the guy. He was furious when Clark was canned. He accused Nolan of engineering the Omni takeover and getting rid of Clark. He used to tell people about how wonderful Clark was, and how Nolan had fucked him by giving the company away to Omni to assure his own future."

"That must have made him popular with Nolan."

"Oh, yeah. Nolan loved it." Jerry smiled wryly.

"So you think maybe there really wasn't anything wrong with Genelife? That Tucker's trying to delay the launch was just his way of getting back at Nolan, of trying to prevent him from having a big success? But surely he'd have to have some evidence of a problem in order to make a case for a delay?"

"At first he had. The clinical trials turned up side effects in excess of what was acceptable to the FDA. But those problems had been solved by Chemstra before Tucker left the company."

"What was Tucker's reaction to that?"

Jerry thought for a moment. "You know, I'm not really sure. I don't remember ever discussing it with him. He wasn't around much last year, you see. Traveling a lot. I don't know when they told him. But I bet he didn't like it when he found out."

"Why not?"

"Well, it turned out that Nolan got Chemstra involved in the project secretly, over five years before. Tucker'd been having trouble with the synthetization, and Nolan wanted a backup. None of us at Randall Webber knew anything about Chemstra's involvement until after the FDA approval came through. The idea of Nolan quietly going behind his back to Chemstra must have made Tucker sore as hell."

"But wouldn't he have been glad the problems had been solved?"

"You didn't know Tucker. He'd see it as someone else tampering with his invention. And getting the glory, too. He'd want to be the one to fix the side effects, and now someone else would have done it first."

"Could that have been enough to put him over the edge last May?" Kate mused.

"Who knows? Tucker was really unstable. I mean, I worked for him for three years, and the man was brilliant, but . . ." Jerry gave a thumbs-down. "And when he came back from the Amazon at the end of May, he was a madman!"

"Last *May*? I thought he discovered the drug in the rain forest ten years ago. Isn't that when he brought back the plant material he used in the original development of Genelife?"

"That's right. But he went back again last spring."

"Why?"

"Who knows? Tucker was a secretive guy, even with me, and I worked for him. I mean, he never told anybody in the department about his trips. He'd be here, he'd be gone, he'd be back . . . If you questioned him, he'd growl at you. And he only gave you pieces of things to work on, never enough to really understand the whole—"

"Then how did *you* know about the trip in May?" Kate interrupted. "Why did he tell you?"

"He didn't mean to," Jerry admitted. "See, I was in his office one day—we were working on something, who remembers what?—and all of a sudden he looks at his watch and pulls out this little bottle and starts popping pills. I asked if they were for his ulcer—you know, teasing him a little—and he said no, they were malaria pills. 'Going back to the jungle?' I asked him, just kidding around. I could do that with him, sometimes. But Tucker being Tucker, he got pissed off and said actually he *was* going back, but if I told anybody, he'd have my job. I guess I looked surprised, because he started muttering about industrial espionage. A week later, he was gone."

"Did Nolan know?"

"Oh, absolutely. In fact, the afternoon Tucker got back, he and Nolan had a huge fight."

"Really? How do you know about it? What happened?"

"Well, it was Friday afternoon before the Memorial Day weekend. I remember that because the place was practically deserted; everyone had left early. I was finishing up some work in my office—not the office I have now, of course—and I heard shouting. So I went to see what was going on. I saw Nolan and Tucker standing in the hall just outside my—uh—Tucker's office. Tucker's old battered suitcase was sitting there on the floor—he must have come straight from the airport—and they were really going at it."

"What were they saying?"

"Tucker was yelling that Nolan had no choice but to stop the launch, and Nolan was yelling that Tucker was trying to destroy him and Randall Webber. Then Nolan turned around and saw me and started shouting at me to get out of there, to go home, and Tucker was shouting that I should stay and listen, and Nolan grabbed him—Tucker was tall but very skinny and weak-looking—and pushed him into the office and banged the door behind them. I took off fast, I can tell you. I didn't want any trouble with Nolan."

"So Nolan fired Tucker and promoted you."

"He didn't have to fire him. Tucker broke into the lab over the weekend when it was empty. Apparently he tried to destroy a whole bunch of material, even his own original data that went back years. The story is, he was raving like a lunatic, throwing things out of the window ... The security guards tried to calm him down, but he broke away and ran ..."

"And then ... ?"

"Nothing. That was the last anyone saw of him."

"But I thought he had a drug problem, that he left the company and went into some sort of recovery program. At least, that's what Nolan told me ..."

"He mentioned something about a drug recovery program to me, too. It seemed pretty straightforward at the time ..."

"So what are we going to do?"

Jerry looked surprised. "Do? Do about what?"

"About the Genelife side effects, Jerry! We have to figure out what's gone wrong."

Jerry sighed and pushed the half-empty mug away from him. "I need a drink," he told her. "Brad?"

"Come on, Jerry! You're a scientist for Christ's sake. You're supposed to be in charge of this thing. Will you help me?"

"Will he help you with what?" asked Nolan.

Chapter 19

Kate spun around in stunned surprise. Nolan smiled grimly at her expression, then glanced over at Jerry who cowered on his bar stool. "Help you with what, Kate?" he repeated, his eyes boring into Jerry's. Lim looked away guiltily, and Nolan turned his attention back to Kate.

How much had he heard? she wondered fearfully. Well, her best defense was probably a counterattack. "I asked Jerry to help me investigate the new side effects tabulations the MacAllister Agency turned up," she answered boldly. "I tried to tell you about them earlier today, but you wouldn't listen."

Nolan frowned. "I thought I told you to forget that nonsense."

"You also told me you'd put Jerry on to the focus group research, but he doesn't know a thing about it."

"That rummy doesn't remember what he had for break-fast." Nolan glanced at Jerry, who blushed.

"Then why do you keep him—" Kate caught herself in time; why hurt Jerry any more than he'd already hurt himself?

"We need to talk," Nolan said. "Privately." He turned to Jerry. "Isn't it about time you went home?"

Relieved to be let off so easily, Jerry scrambled from his stool. "Yes sir, Mr. Nolan," he said. "I didn't know it was so late! Lots to do back at the lab, so I'll just—Brad! My tab!"

"I'll take care of your bill," Nolan told him. "You go on home and sleep it off."

"Good idea," Jerry said. "Uh, thanks." He fumbled his jacket off the wall peg beside the bar, searching in the pockets for his car keys. Nolan watched as he finally retrieved them from his trouser pocket.

"Do you think he's okay to drive?" Kate asked Brad,

who shrugged. "Michael, do you think one of us should drive him—"

"He'll be fine," Nolan said roughly. "He rents a condo not far from here."

They watched as Jerry lifted the mock antique latch on the front door. He turned back and gave them a little wave, then stepped out into the late-afternoon sunlight, closing the door imperfectly behind him. Brad sighed and went to shut it properly.

Nolan guided Kate to a table across from the bar. "Sit down," he said. "Please. What are you drinking?"

"Club soda," Kate said. "But—"

"Two club sodas," Nolan called to Brad, who nodded and began to fill two newly polished glasses. "You're very pissed off with me at the moment, aren't you?"

"I'm not sure 'pissed off' is exactly—"

"Well, you have every right to be. And I owe you an apology." He sighed deeply. "It's been a helluva six months, and I know I haven't been as appreciative, as responsive, as I might have been. Should have been."

Brad delivered their drinks, and Kate sipped hers. Nolan looked at her for a reaction, but she gave him none.

"I haven't been completely honest with you, either," he continued at last. "I didn't ask Jerry to check out the focus group side effects. You can understand why." He waved a hand toward the bar. "It would have been a waste of time. I put Chemstra on it instead."

"Chemstra?"

"Of course. They're our clinical research arm. They're the logical group to check out any . . . abnormalities."

"Why did you tell me you asked Jerry to do it?"

Nolan shook his head. "Who the fuck knows?" he said tiredly. "Frankly, I just wanted to get you off my back. And most people at R&D resent Chemstra. My fault, really."

"Because you went to them behind Tucker's back for the synthetization?"

Nolan blinked in surprise. "How did you— Oh, Jerry told you, right?" Kate nodded. "What else did he say?"

"Nothing much. At least, nothing I could make any sense of. He'd been drinking, of course. He was practically incoherent." *You bullshit me, I bullshit you.*

"I've been under a lot of strain," Nolan continued. "It's good strain, don't get me wrong. Genelife's numbers are going through the roof, and Omni's absolutely delighted. But even good strain takes a toll. I never meant to take it out on you. Now, about the tabulations you discussed with Jerry . . ."

"I didn't get to discuss them with him," Kate said. "I mean, I couldn't, in his state. But I think you should know that they show a higher incidence of side effects than one would expect from the FDA report."

"How much higher?"

"Statistically, not very. But they could be an indicator of a very worrying trend."

Nolan patted her hand and gave her a Mr. Charming smile. "Chemstra assures me that we have nothing to worry about. Some statistical peaks and valleys are to be expected with a drug of this kind. It's the averages over time that count. And I promise you, the averages are fine."

"Don't you even want to see the new tabulations?"

"Of course, of course. But I can tell you right now, I'm not inclined to treat them very seriously. Don't look so shocked," he added. "I've lived with Genelife a lot longer than you have."

Kate studied him; dark rings rimmed his eyes, and he looked every day of his forty-five years. "You don't use Genelife yourself, do you, Michael?"

Nolan took off his glasses, rubbed his eyes, and put his glasses back on again. "No, I don't," he admitted. "Maybe I should start. Look, we got off on the wrong foot today, and I'm really sorry. You're a strong member of my team, and I need you. I promise to be more responsive to you, okay?"

Kate nodded guardedly.

"But you need to make me a promise, too. You have to trust me more. You have to stop going off half-cocked, panicking people like Jerry."

"But I—"

Nolan held up a hand. "Hear me out. The corporate world is different from anything you've experienced before. It's important to be a team player. That doesn't mean following along blindly. But it does mean trusting your . . . er, coach. Letting him call the play. You understand what I'm saying?"

"Yes, of course. I . . . I guess I never thought about it

that way before." The fertilizer certainly is getting deep in here.

Nolan gave a satisfied little nod. "And if you have any questions, any issues you want to discuss, I want you to promise to come to me, not Jerry or your pal Mac or—"

"Actually, Mac came to me with the tabulations."

"He did?" Something flickered briefly in Nolan's eyes, then disappeared. "The point is, bring your questions to me from now on."

"I will." Kate watched his face carefully. "Michael, why did Tucker Boone go back to the rain forest last spring?"

But Nolan's face showed nothing but mild surprise. "Jerry told you about that, too?"

"Yes. And if Genelife is being made synthetically, why would—"

"Of course Genelife is a synthetic!" Nolan exclaimed. "Whatever Tucker went back to the rain forest for, I assure you it had nothing to do with us. He was always a secretive bast—uh, guy. One of his less endearing personality traits. He decided to go and off he went."

"And you just let him? During a key development stage of a major new drug?"

"You bet I did. Chemstra was doing the real work, had been for some time. Believe me, it was a relief to get Tucker out of the way just then. He'd have gone rogue if—" Nolan broke off and looked toward the bar. "Brad? Can we have a check here, please?" He stood and reached for his wallet. "I hope you'll excuse me, but it's getting late, and I have an appointment."

Kate rose, too. "Of course," she said. "I should be getting back, too."

"No, stay. Finish your drink. No need to come back to the office today; it's nearly five. You might as well go straight home. I'm glad we had this little talk."

"Yes, so am I." Kate smiled at him sweetly. "I understand you so much better now."

Nolan dropped two twenties on the table. "This should cover Jerry's bar bill, poor bastard. He used to be a good man." He shoved his wallet back in his pocket and headed toward the door. "See you in the morning, Kate."

"Michael, wait." Nolan turned back with an air of controlled impatience. "Why did you come looking for me, just now? How did you know I was here?"

"I didn't start out looking for you, Kate," he said. "You were a bonus. I was actually looking for Jerry. The lab boys told me he was here, and that you'd been asking for him. So I figured it would be a good chance for me to apologize to you, and get us back on the same side." He favored her with a warm smile.

"Oh, we are," she lied, returning his smile with interest. "But ... what did you want with Jerry?"

Nolan's face took on an expression of concern and sympathy. "It's really too bad," he said regretfully. "Such a waste. The truth is, I came here to fire him. Have a good evening."

Kate watched him openmouthed as he strode out the door, pulling it closed behind him.

"Nice guy," Brad observed, scooping the money from the table. "Friend of yours?"

"Not hardly," Kate said. "You have a phone around here?"

"Straight back and to your left."

"Thanks." She pulled the wrinkled pink message slip from her purse; office or home? It was nearly five; she might still catch him at his office. If she missed him there, she'd keep trying his home number. She suddenly felt she and this Steve Kavett had a lot to talk about.

"Anthropology," announced a young female voice.

"Uh, is this the right number for Steve Kavett?" Kate asked hesitantly.

"Yes, but I think Professor Kavett's gone for the day. Hold on and I'll check. Who's calling?"

"Kate Martin. He called me this morning."

"Hang on!"

Several clicks and thirty seconds later she was back. "Caught him halfway down the stairs," she said. "Here he comes."

More clicks. Then Steve came on the line, sounding breathless. "Dr. Martin? Glad you caught me. Did you remember something about Tucker?"

"Not exactly. But I think you and I might be able to help each other. By the way, where am I calling you?"

"Boston University. I'm a professor of anthropology."

"An anthropologist ... and that's how you happened to be along on Tucker's rain forest trip?"

"Actually, it was my trip. Tucker came along with me."

"And were you with him when he went back last May?"

"Last *May*? Tucker went back last May?"

"You didn't know?"

"Hell, I haven't seen Tucker for years. He went back to the rain forest in May ... Funny, Marianne never mentioned it."

"Marianne?"

"His wife. My sister." Steve paused. "I wonder—Look, I think we should meet."

"I think so, too. Is there any chance you could come to New York?"

"Is Friday soon enough? If not, I can cancel a seminar tomorrow and—"

"Friday would be just fine."

"Good. I'll fly down in the morning. You know where the Explorers Club is?"

"Never heard of it."

Steve chuckled. "Most people haven't. Do you have a pencil?"

Kate smiled to herself as she copied down the address; he had a very nice voice.

"They don't have a dining room, but we can have a drink and then go somewhere else for lunch, okay?"

"Fine."

"I'll meet you around noon at the polar bear."

"The what?"

"You'll see! Till Friday."

"Till Friday."

She hung up, still smiling: meet him at the polar bear? Then something tickled at the back of her mind, and she pulled out her little appointment book. Sure enough, she'd arranged to have lunch with Richard on Friday. Well, she'd just have to cancel. She picked up the receiver again and dialed his number from memory.

Richard was very nice about it. Yes, he understood completely. How did next week look for her? Could they reschedule?

"That's sweet of you, Richard, but I'd rather not plan ahead at the moment. I ... don't know what the week will bring."

"I understand. Still sweating the side effects, huh?"

"Sort of ... And some other stuff."

"Have you discussed it with Nolan?"

"He keeps assuring me there are no problems."

"Yeah. Sure."

"Something isn't right, Richard, I can feel it. And yet . . . Maybe I'm being paranoid. Nolan says that Chemstra checked out the focus group material and it's okay."

"Chemstra?"

"The Swiss company that did the clinical trials. They say even the increased numbers in MacAllister's research tabulations are normal."

"So MacAllister's been doing some sleuthing, too, huh?"

"I wouldn't call it sleuthing. But you can't blame them for worrying. No one wants to get burned."

"Has Mac been bugging Nolan about the side effects?"

"Not exactly. He told me about their research and I told Nolan."

"And that's when Nolan told you everything was all right?"

"He said it's the averages that count, and on average, Genelife is safe."

"And you believe him?" When Kate didn't answer, Richard pressed harder. "Come on, Kate, this is me, your pal Richard. You and Mac have to keep at him. You've got to protect your professional reputations."

"Not to mention the millions of people who are using Genelife. You're right. Richard. I have to keep digging."

"You bet you do. And for encouragement, I'll leave you with three little words: silicone gel implants. Bye, sweetie."

God, I hope not! Kate thought. She gathered up her jacket and purse and headed back to the bar. Brad was busy with the early evening crowd, but he waved good-bye to her as she left.

As she walked to her car, she berated herself for having said so much to Richard. What in the world had gotten into her? Exhaustion and stress were no excuse; although she was certain she could trust Richard, it had been very unprofessional. She felt awfully tired. A nice hot bath, she thought. Maybe an omelette. And an early night. Definitely.

Nolan skidded to a stop in the parking lot, slammed the door of his new Lexus, and stomped in through the atrium entrance. The receptionist was just leaving, and gave him a bright smile, but he ignored her. His secretary was also gone; he riffled through her Rolodex until he found the tab to which she'd stapled Mac's card. Slamming into his office, he punched out the number for Mac's private line angrily.

"MacAllister?" Nolan roared as soon as Mac answered. "This is Michael Nolan. We have a problem."

"You mean the new tabulations. Yeah, I thought you'd be—"

"Not the tabulations. *You're* the problem."

"Excuse me?"

"What are you, some kind of troublemaker? Starting rumors, upsetting my staff—"

"Hold on a minute!" Mac said hotly. "What are you talking about?"

"Those goddamn research findings you dreamed up."

"I did not dream them up! They're absolutely legitimate, and they show that—"

"I know what they show. Or rather, what you *say* they show. I've just had a long talk with Kate Martin."

"Then you also know that she agrees with me!"

"I know no such thing. What I do know is that you've managed to frighten her rather badly. What I can't figure out is why you're trying to sabotage my business!"

Mac took a deep breath and tried to control his temper. He wasn't used to being spoken to like this, no matter how important the client. On the other hand, Nolan *was* an important client. When he spoke at last, it was in a calmer tone. "Let's start this conversation over again, shall we? I take it Kate showed you the tabulations and you don't agree with them?"

"I didn't need to see your damn tabulations. Look, we've had a top-notch company conducting long-term clinical trials for years. And based on their findings, the FDA has approved our product. You think you know more than they do?"

"I didn't say that. I just—"

"Are you with us or against us?"

"With you, of course. And part of my being with you is to send up a flare if I see a problem—"

"A problem with the marketing. A problem with the advertising, the p.r. But not the product. That's our area."

Mac gripped the edge of his desk, hard. He wanted to tell this sonofabitch to shove his product up his ass. But he couldn't afford that luxury. Genelife was a very profitable account, and those profits paid a large chunk of what it cost to keep the MacAllister Agency in business. Until another large account came in the door, he needed Nolan more than Nolan needed him.

And yet, if he and Kate were right about the implications of the research, he'd be wise to get out while he could, before any sort of scandal could dirty him by association.

On the other hand, Kate had promised to tell him in time to jump ship. And he was pitching some General Foods business next month. If he could hang on just a little longer . . .

Gritting his teeth, he tried to formulate an appropriate reply. "I'm sorry if I stepped over the line, Michael," he said at last, hating himself. "It's just that the tabulations seemed a little high, and then Dave was hospitalized—"

"I know," Nolan said, sounding somewhat mollified. "I sent him some fruit. How's he doing?"

"A lot better. They're sending him home tomorrow morning."

"Glad to hear it. He's a good man."

"Yes, he is."

Neither mentioned the fact that Dave had been using Genelife.

"Well, I'm glad you understand where you went wrong," Nolan said. "What was that bang?"

"What bang?" Mac said tightly as he smashed the heavy metal Clio Award into the telephone again, this time shattering its plastic top and exposing an interesting array of wires.

"I thought I heard a . . . never mind. Just to be completely clear about this, let me go on record as saying that we at Randall Webber are convinced there is absolutely no problem with Genelife, and we expect you to support that position. I've already spoken to Kate, and she agrees. Do I have your support?"

"Yes. Of course."

"That's settled, then. Good night."

Mac remained at his desk for several minutes after Nolan hung up, contemplating his wrecked phone and thinking of all the things he'd have liked to have said. Expletives predominated. Then he yanked open his top drawer and pulled out the original printout of the tabulations. If I'm going to suck up to this bastard, he thought, I'd better cover my ass.

Waving away his secretary's offer of help, he went down the hall and made a copy of the tabulations, then scribbled a neutral but detailed covering letter and copied that, too. He slid the original of the letter and the copy of the tabulations into a manila envelope, addressed it to Michael Nolan at Randall Webber, and shot it into Beth's out box.

"Want me to take this down to the mail room on my way out?" She shrugged into her leather jacket and took her handbag from the lower desk drawer. "The last pickup was at five."

"Nah, it can wait till tomorrow, thanks."

"Well, good night."

Mac watched her hurry down the hall toward the elevators, just one of the many nice people who depended on the MacAllister Agency for the rent money. Damn Nolan.

"Hey, Beth?" he called after her. "I think there's something wrong with my phone. See what they can do about it in the morning, will you?"

Nearly forty minutes had passed since he'd finished his conversation with Kate, yet Richard was still sitting at his desk, thinking furiously. Was this really the way to handle it? The situation definitely called for action. But he had to tread carefully.

Once again he reviewed the notes he'd made, scratching out a line here and there, adding something more.

He reached for the phone, then hesitated. When he'd dialed the number earlier, it had been busy. It was getting rather late; perhaps he should leave it until tomorrow morning? No, it was too important. He'd give it one more try.

This time when he dialed, a voice answered.

"This is Richard Day of Imagemakers," he said.

"Richard Day . . ." the voice said. "What can I do for you?"

"I'd like to set up a meeting as soon as possible. There's something I think you ought to know."

Chapter 20

The huge bear stood poised at the top of the stairs on its hind legs, claws extended, eyes glaring. Its fur, more yellow than white, glowed in the dim light.

"Hiya, Kate," it said.

"Hiya, yourself."

Steve stepped from behind the behemoth and bowed slightly. "Welcome to the Explorers Club," he said with a grin.

"Thanks. Which one of you is Steve Kavett?"

Steve gave her a little bow. "That would be me. People often confuse us; the thing to remember is that he's taller."

Kate examined the stuffed bear with amusement. "He certainly is impressive. How did he get here? Did he follow someone home?"

Steve smiled. "Actually, a prominent member shot him back in the fifties and sent him along to the club as a donation, sort of an offer they couldn't refuse. He's become quite famous."

"I'm not surprised."

"The members' lounge is back downstairs I'm afraid, but I felt you had to see this guy; he sort of sets the tone."

Kate followed him back down the stairs, feeling pleasantly surprised. The word "professor" had conjured up a stereotypically dry, balding scholar. *He's quite good-looking,* she thought. *And he has a sense of fun, which is rather a relief.*

They walked together through the open-plan ground floor and she found herself studying his face.

"You look so familiar," she told him, puzzled. "But I'm sure we haven't met."

"Actually, we did. Well, almost. I was at Randall Webber to see Michael Nolan in January, and I noticed you coming out of an office. I mean, you're kind of hard to miss." Kate smiled at the compliment. "Uh, maybe you noticed me, too," he added hesitantly.

"That's probably it," Kate agreed politely. Then suddenly she made the connection. "Wait! You were with Jenny! I *do* remember." The tall, good-looking stranger. "You turned around and stared at me."

He grinned. "And it only took three months for us to find each other!" Kate blushed slightly; he was making this sound like a date, which of course it wasn't. Although the idea did have a certain appeal ...

"Why did you go to see Nolan?" she asked, trying to ignore her attraction to him and put things back on a professional footing.

Steve gave her an amused look. "I wanted information about Tucker."

"Bet you didn't get any," Kate said.

He led her into the cozy members' lounge off the small marble lobby. Like the rest of the first two floors of the mansion building that housed the club, the walls were paneled in old, dark wood. Two tall ivory tusks rose up from either side of the fireplace, dwarfing the mantel. In front, a leather sofa and two tapestry chairs were set around a highly polished wood slab of a coffee table.

"I like this place," Kate said. "It feels homey."

Steve smiled. "It is. There's a kind of musty quality about it that I love. It's definitely a working club." He rose and went to the small self-service bar set up in one corner. "Soft drink? Wine?"

"Mineral water would be fine," Kate said. "Or club soda." While he fixed the drinks—Perrier for her, a Coke for him—she admired the mullioned windows and the worn oriental carpet. "So how come nobody knows about this place?" she asked.

"Well, aside from the monthly lectures, it's not open to the public. And it hasn't got the rarefied social cachet of, say, the New York Yacht Club. But among the fraternity of actual explorers, it's in a league of its own." He returned with the drinks and set them on the coffee table.

"I had a look at the leaflet at the front desk when I came in. Thor Heyerdahl ... Scott Carpenter ... Sir Edmund Hillary ... I'm impressed. I didn't realize you were one of such an august group."

Steve waved away the praise. "Oh, Tucker and I got lucky back in '82. We ran into a tribe that had never been contacted, and we lived with them for nine months. Actually, Tucker stayed longer."

"How come?"

"He refused to leave with the missionary team that found us. He wanted to investigate a ceremony we'd both seen, involving what I'm now practically certain was the original Genelife."

"That's fascinating!"

"Fascinating but nuts! I never thought he'd make it out alive, but by God, he did."

"Holding a test tube of Genelife and shouting 'Eureka'?"

"Holding a fistful of leaves and shouting 'Where the fuck am I?' more likely."

Kate smiled. "And then he got a grant from the Randall Foundation, developed Genelife, and went to work at Randall Webber."

"Right. And then he disappeared."

"Steve, why do you think he went back to the rain forest last May?"

"Maybe he ran out of leaves."

"Very funny."

"No, really. Maybe something happened to the root stock. Maybe he went back for more plants."

"No way. Genelife is a synthetic. But maybe ... look, what I'm going to tell you is confidential, okay?" Steve nodded. "Recently we've been seeing an increase in side effects, both the frequency and the intensity. Chemstra—they did the FDA tests—Chemstra says they saw high levels of side effects with the plant-derived enzyme, but when they switched to the synthetic, the side effects subsided. Maybe Tucker went back to try to figure out why the plant derivative was causing the side effects."

Steve thought for a while. "I suppose it's possible. But ... wouldn't he know about the synthetic?"

"I'm not so sure. Jerry Lim—he worked for Tucker—says that Nolan made sure Chemstra's development and testing of the synthetic was kept secret. He isn't sure when they told Tucker. Maybe Tucker went back before he knew about it."

"Well, why would Nolan let him? Nolan knew about the synthetic."

"Yes, but he wanted Tucker out of the way. At least, that's what he told me. He says Tucker would have gone rogue if—"

"If what?"

But Kate was replaying her conversation with Nolan. "That's exactly what he said ... 'Tucker would have gone rogue if—' "

"I don't get it."

"He stopped in midsentence, paid the bill, and ran. Don't you see? Nolan *never* told Tucker about the synthetization!"

"So Tucker could have gone off, looking for a way to fix the side effects, not knowing Nolan and—?"

"Chemstra."

"—and Chemstra had already fixed them."

"Yes. Yes, that makes sense. Except, why *wouldn't* Nolan tell Tucker?"

"Because Tucker was a crazy paranoid sonofabitch and he didn't want to tangle with him?" Steve suggested.

"Doesn't make sense. First of all, he couldn't keep him away from the lab forever. Sooner or later, Tucker would find out. Second, Nolan now had his drug and his FDA approval. Why should he give a damn what Tucker thought or said?"

"So why didn't he tell him?"

Kate shrugged. "I just don't know." She sipped her Perrier thoughtfully. "I do know that Tucker and Nolan had a huge fight when Tucker came back from the rain forest."

Steve leaned forward. "What happened?"

"I think Jerry Lim was the only one who saw it, and he didn't see much. It was the Friday before Memorial Day ..."

"Wait, that was just before he disappeared. Nolan told me about the argument, too. Tucker thought Nolan had betrayed Clark Randall, and—"

"Hold it. *That's* what Nolan said the argument was about?"

"Yeah. He told the police that, too."

"Police? Where do they come in?"

"Marianne filed a missing persons report. The police investigated, but couldn't find a trace of him. Nolan said he disappeared after their argument."

"Steve, something's really wrong here. Nolan told me

Tucker had a drug problem, that he'd gone into a rehab program."

"What? No way!"

"And Jerry Lim says he broke into the lab over the weekend, just before he disappeared. He tried to destroy his files."

"Jesus!"

"There's more. Jerry overheard part of the argument with Nolan. It wasn't about Clark Randall. It was about the Genelife launch." She recounted what Jerry had told her at The Three Pheasants.

They looked at each other in silence, their thoughts racing.

"What does it mean?" Steve asked at last.

"I'm not sure. But I have to believe the side effects we've been seeing are tied up in all this, somewhere." She thought for a moment. "I think we should join forces, Steve. You want to find Tucker and I want to find out more about the side effects. I have a strong feeling that the more we learn about one, the more we'll learn about the other."

Steve nodded slowly. "Okay," he said. "Count me in. Where do we start?"

"Marianne, for one thing. She might know more than she thinks she does. Can I meet her?"

"Sure. She's in Minneapolis right now, visiting an old school friend, but she'll be back on Monday. I'll call her tonight and set something up."

"Good. Then for now, let's start with the side effects. You said you and Tucker saw the drug in action, in the rain forest. Did you notice any side effects?"

"You don't understand," Steve told her gently. "Not everyone got to drink the stuff. Only the chief and his wife."

"Tell me about it."

"Okay. Only, if we're going to have lunch, we ought to get moving. There's a little bistro—"

"Forget lunch! Tell me about the ceremony."

Steve leaned back in his chair. God, it seemed a long time ago. He began to describe the calabash ceremony he and Tucker had witnessed together. He spoke slowly at first, but more excitedly as memories began flooding back. He described the weirdness of the place, the strange bees, the trees that Tucker was sure they hadn't seen anywhere else in their journey through the rain forest. "He grew up half wild in rural Kentucky," Steve explained. "He knew trees."

"Did you actually see them prepare the leaves?" Kate asked.

"I didn't. Tucker did, and they practically lynched him for it. He sneaked into the hut where they were preparing the mash. We saved him by pretending he was looking for food, but it was close. Later he told me that the elders had been mashing the leaves with wooden staffs, and diluting them with water from the river. He said the fumes were terribly strong."

Kate was fascinated, her eyes shining with excitement.

"Later, they passed around a calabash and we all pretended to take a sip, but only the chief and his wife really drank. I remember being very relieved when I realized I didn't have to; that stuff smelled horrible." Steve leaned forward and took a sip of his Coke, as if to wash away the memory.

"It's so incredible that you were actually there!" Kate exclaimed.

He smiled at the intensity of her expression. For a moment their eyes locked, and each felt a thrill of excitement that had nothing to do with the rain forest. Then Kate colored slightly and looked away, and Steve put down his glass and continued.

"It was some time before I realized there was more than just a ceremonial reason no one else was allowed to drink. But the more I thought about it, the more it made sense. See, chewing was the usual way the tribe processed leaves for consumption. For example, when the tribe made a sort of beer sometimes, the women chewed the leaves— different leaves, of course—and spat them into a calabash to ferment."

"Sounds disgusting."

"It was, very. But this time the elders were mashing the leaves with sticks. Chewing them was obviously a no-no. And the fumes Tucker mentioned ... I think they must have added something to the mixture to make it smell so bad. I think the point was to make it smell so terrible, no one would *want* to drink."

"Did Tucker ever tell you what he thought was in the calabash?"

"You mean, what the leaves contained?" Steve shook his

head. "He muttered something about the discovery of the century, but said it was more in his line than in mine. He talked about the need for research ... Hell, neither Marianne nor I could be sure whether he was really onto something or simply raving. He was in real bad shape."

"So only the chief and his wife drank from the calabash. What were they like?"

"Young," said Steve. "Young and vigorous. I remember being surprised the tribe had chosen such a young man to lead them."

"Genelife," Kate said softly.

Steve nodded. "I see that now. At the time, of course, I had no idea." He reached again for his Coke, then stopped, his hand halfway to the glass. "Kate, if their version of Genelife made the chief and his wife so young, why wouldn't they give it to everyone? A strong young tribe would improve everyone's chances of survival."

Kate stared at him. "Then why didn't they?"

"Maybe because making people younger wasn't the only thing Genelife did. Kate, what sort of side effects have you been seeing?"

"Loss of appetite leading to physical degeneration due to malnutrition—sorry, I'm talking like a doctor. Headaches, bad ones sometimes ... a few people reported deep depression .. a lowering of the libido, the sex drive ... the inability to conceive ..."

"That's it!" Steve interrupted excitedly. "If Genelife makes people sterile, it couldn't be given to everyone or the tribe would die out!"

But Kate shook her head. "The inability to conceive isn't permanent. It goes away when you stop taking the drug."

Steve's shoulders slumped with disappointment. "Sounded good there for a minute," he said. "Thinking back, I didn't notice the chief and his wife holding their heads in pain or not eating. Of course, the tribe subsisted on very little; their bodies were used to a low nutrient level, far lower than the rest of us. Maybe that's why they didn't react the same way."

"Maybe."

Steve stood and stretched. "Speaking of low nutrient levels, mine could use a boost. Any interest in lunch?"

"Sure," Kate said. She wasn't really interested in food, but she was very interested in this rugged, fascinating man.

He collected their empty glasses and dropped them in the bin beneath the service bar, then retrieved her trench coat and his jacket from the rack behind the reception desk.

"Do you like Russian food?" he asked as they stepped out into the breezy April sunshine.

"Russian? I'm not sure I've actually tasted any. But I'm game to try."

"Good. I know a great little place on Madison."

"I thought you were from Boston. How do you know about great little places on Madison?" she teased.

"I grew up about eight blocks south of here," he told her. "My parents died when I was young, and I lived with my uncle Avram all through high school." He glanced over at her. He liked the way her red hair curled around her face, framing her intelligent blue eyes and her wide, generous mouth. "Avram's a theatrical producer and a real character. You'd enjoy him."

"I'd like to meet him," Kate found herself saying.

"That can be arranged." Again their eyes met, and this time Kate didn't look away. "Are you free tomorrow?" Kate nodded. "Good. We'll have brunch with Avram and go to a matinee. Choose a place you like for dinner, okay?"

"Okay. What kind of food do you like?"

"I've lived on agouti and termites and french fried grasshoppers. I can eat anything."

"French fried grasshoppers sound rather good," said Kate, amused. "But . . . agouti?"

"Picture a really large hamster."

"Yechhh!" said Kate. "Double yechhh! I think perhaps French."

"An excellent choice."

They walked to Madison Avenue, then turned right and headed uptown. "Just four more blocks," Steve said apologetically.

"That's okay. I like to walk."

Kablinka was nearly full, but the young ponytailed waiter found them a little table along the wall near the window.

Kate studied the menu. "You'll have to guide me here," she told Steve with a smile. "I mean, I recognize chicken Kiev and shashlik, but the rest is a mystery."

He began to describe some of the more exotic dishes, and had gotten as far as the soups when he broke off. "I just remembered something," he said. "At that first calabash ceremony, the one Tucker and I both saw, the chief chose two teenagers, but we couldn't figure out why. They moved in with the chief and his wife. But we never saw them drink out of the calabash. After Tucker was rescued, he said he'd finally figured out what the chief wanted with the boys."

"And that was . . .?"

"At the second calabash ceremony, the one Tucker saw but I didn't, the chief chose one of them to be his . . . Tucker used the word 'successor,' but that could be wrong. Their language was like none other I'd ever studied. Even when we thought we understood what they were saying, we could never be sure we really got it."

"So the chief chose a successor. That makes sense. After all, if he and his wife were taking some form of Genelife, they couldn't conceive a child of their own."

"But you told me the effects wore off if you stopped taking the stuff," Steve said. "So why didn't they stop, have a child, and then start taking it again?"

"Maybe they couldn't risk having the chief vulnerable to aging for the period of time it would take for the drug to wear off."

"Or maybe it doesn't wear off. Maybe it's permanent."

Kate looked at him in horror.

"That's not possible!" she said. "The research says . . ."

"The research also said the side effects would be lower, right?"

"Jesus . . . !"

"And there's something else. You guys are calling this thing a cosmetic age retardant. What the hell does 'cosmetic' mean?"

"It means . . . well, that the effect is only skin-deep. You look younger, but you're not actually—"

"I wouldn't call that the discovery of the century, would you?"

"Well, no, but—"

"Tucker wouldn't, either. Believe me, Kate, he wouldn't waste time on a cosmetic."

Kate stared at him in disbelief. "You're suggesting that Genelife actually makes you stop aging? That it produced perpetual youth? My God, that would be . . . I can't believe it!"

"Tucker believed it. I'm certain he did."

"Wait a minute! Hold it! If it really does keep you young forever, why did the chief need a successor at all?"

"Shit!" Steve said forcefully. "I didn't think of that."

The waiter deposited a basket of warm dark bread on the table, and Kate took a slice. She broke off a piece and began making bread pills. "When I took the job at Randall Webber," she said, "it all seemed so ... straightforward. The company had developed a breakthrough cosmetic drug, the FDA had approved it, we were about to start selling it ... Now all of a sudden I feel there's so much we don't know. About the drug, about Tucker, about Nolan and Chemstra ..."

"But at least we *know* that we don't know," Steve said. "There are worse places to begin. And we each come at the thing from a different angle. You're the medical expert, I'm the anthropologist." He smiled at her. "I think we'll make a good team."

"I think we will."

"I have to fly back to Boston Monday evening, after we talk to Marianne. But my teaching schedule is light this semester. I can arrange to get back down here often."

"Good. It'll be wonderful to have someone to plan with, to talk with openly about all this." She paused. "I'll have to be very careful at work."

Steve looked worried. "You bet you will! You haven't mentioned your suspicions around the office, have you?"

For a guilty moment Kate thought of Richard. I can deal with him, she thought. I'll call him and tell him I was wrong, that everything's fine. "No," she said. "Not really."

"Good. Don't." He took some bread and broke it in half. "I originally got into this for Marianne's sake," he said slowly. "But now I'm in it for myself, too. And for Tucker, God help him. I want to get to the bottom of this."

"Me, too. And fast!"

"Agreed. Only ... don't do anything dangerous."

She thought of the guard with the truck. "I'll be all right," she assured him.

"I hope so. I don't want *you* to disappear, too." He said it lightly, but neither of them smiled.

The waiter approached with his pad and pencil at the ready. "Have you decided?" he said.

Steve's dark eyes were serious as he looked into Kate's. "Yes," he said. "I think we have."

*   *   *

The late-evening sunlight crept over the windowsill and striped the polished wood floor of Kate's bedroom as she emerged from the bathroom, wrapped in a towel. She padded barefoot to the kitchen where she poured a little water into a small kettle and turned on the burner. Then she padded back to the bedroom and exchanged the towel for an oversize tie-dyed shirt. Cheerio followed her progress with interest, giving several little ladylike barks to remind Kate that it was nearly doggie dinnertime.

The whistle of the kettle drew Kate back to the kitchen, where she poured the now boiling water over a raspberry teabag. Then she headed for the living room and settled herself on the green and white chintz-covered sofa.

Cheerio followed, positioning herself near the foot of the sofa and eyeing Kate soulfully.

Setting the steaming mug on a magazine, Kate reached for the novel she'd been saving for just such a quiet evening. She opened it and began to read. She'd been looking forward to the book, but somehow she couldn't get into it.

Cheerio jumped off the sofa and trotted over to the kitchen door. Then she came back and nudged Kate's arm with a cold wet nose. "I'm the hungriest dog in the free world," her eyes said.

"Oh, all right, you great hairy beast," Kate sighed, ruffling the dog's head. She closed the book and went back to the kitchen. Cheerio followed closely behind, tail wagging.

"I met the most interesting man today," she told the dog as she spooned food into a bowl. "I think you'd like him, too."

She put the food down in front of the dog, who attacked it with enthusiasm.

"In fact, you'll get to meet him tomorrow," she continued. "I wonder what I should wear . . ." Cheerio looked up and gave a little bark. "Oh, what do you know about fashion? All you ever wear is beige and brown." She gave the dog a little pat and went back to the living room.

The sun had disappeared beneath the rooftops and she switched on a table lamp. Sprawled on the sofa again, she read a few pages, then dropped the novel into her lap and stared off into space. It had been a very long time since she'd been so attracted to a man. She thought about the crinkles around his eyes, and his strong, capable-looking hands.

She forced herself back to her book again. That lowered libido effect Genelife produced was sure wearing off.

The telephone rang.

"How do you feel about barbecue?" Steve asked.

"I'm for it."

"Well, I know a great rib joint on 101st Street, but they only do takeout. And there's nothing sadder than a middle-aged bachelor, sitting alone in his sister's apartment, eating takeout in front of the television."

Kate hesitated for a good two seconds.

"Come on over," she said.

Chapter 21

Michael Nolan was feeling expansive. He lolled back in the deeply cushioned wicker settee and gazed out at the expanse of lawn rolling gently down to Long Island Sound. Off to one side of the paved area beyond the wide veranda, a line of freshly washed golf carts sparkled in the sun. The distant *pock* of a driver connecting with a ball, followed by an exclamation of chagrin, wafted to him on the breeze. From the interior of the clubhouse, a young waiter approached with a silver coffeepot and silently refilled their cups.

Both Nolan and his guest were informally dressed, though only Nolan was scheduled to play once their business was concluded. He glanced at his watch; a quarter to eleven, and he still had to call Bettina. Well, they were just about through. He set down his cup.

"I have a good feeling about this," he told his guest, who nodded in agreement. "And . . . we understand each other."

"Yes indeed."

"Then go ahead and get things started from your end, but for God's sake be discreet. We don't want any leaks."

"We certainly don't," his companion agreed. "So you definitely want me to go ahead?" He seemed surprised things were moving so fast.

"That's what I said," Nolan replied testily. "I assume you realize I can't advance you any funds at this point."

The other man frowned. "Yes, I suppose so. Um, at what point can I expect—"

"The day we announce," Nolan said. "But don't worry about the money. Just go ahead and make your financial commitments. You've got the backing of Randall Webber. And my personal guarantee."

"Good." The man rose and Nolan did the same. "How long do you think it will be?"

"Soon," Nolan assured him. "Very soon."

They shook hands. "I'm looking forward to working with you," his companion said.

"So am I," Nolan told him. "Thanks for coming out here on a Saturday. It's more discreet than a meeting at my office."

"I agree."

"Well, have a pleasant drive back." He watched as the man retreated into the clubhouse and disappeared. The smile faded from his face as he thought about how the situation had changed over the past few days.

He snapped open the briefcase that stood on the floor beside him and extracted a slim cellular telephone. With a quick look around to make sure he wouldn't be overheard, he dialed a number. "Good morning," he said to the person who answered. "You know who this is?"

"Yes."

"Good. Now, listen carefully . . ." Nolan spoke softly for a few moments. When he disconnected, he felt much better.

He beckoned to the hovering waiter, who removed the coffee service. Congratulating himself on how quickly he'd applied the appropriate damage controls, he dialed Bettina in Chicago.

"Mrs. Hollis's office," her assistant announced perkily.

So she even brings her staff in on weekends, Nolan thought admiringly. Maybe I should start doing that. "Mrs. Hollis, please. Mr. Nolan calling." He decided to pretend he was calling from his office. "Uh, from Randall Webber," he added.

"One moment please."

Bettina left him on hold for only a minute or so. "Michael!" She greeted him effusively; the numbers had been good this week. "Sorry you had to interrupt your golf game—Greenwich is so beautiful this time of year, isn't it?—but I wanted us to touch base before I fly to Tokyo tomorrow."

"Of course," he said stiffly, irritated that she'd assumed he was calling from the club and not his office, and, worse, that she'd been right. The waiter approached, but Nolan waved him away as he began reviewing the current sales figures and projections for Bettina. Her questions were incisive and rapid-fire, and he found himself almost gasping as he tried to keep up.

"So," she said, satisfied at last, "anything else Omni should know?"

Nolan paused, searching for the most innocuous phraseology. "Well, er, I'm considering changing our advertising agency."

"You mean, fire MacAllister? I thought their work was excellent. And the product is leaping off the shelves."

"Bettina, that product would leap off the shelves with *no* advertising."

"That's as may be, but the fact is, MacAllister helped get it to that point. Now, what have they done to make you so angry?"

Nolan bristled at her implication that he was acting out of pique. "They're getting too expensive," he told her.

"Really? Don't they have a contract?"

"Yes, of course, but their print and television production budgets have gotten way out of line ... and their research program, too."

"Well, rein them in."

"I've tried. They accuse me of trying to compromise the effectiveness of the marketing communications, or some such bullshit. And ..."

"And?"

"They're asking too many questions," he told her. "Questions that are none of their business. They're upsetting my staff and wasting everybody's time."

"What kind of questions, Michael?"

"Oh, stuff about the product testing procedures, the research. They've come up with some wacky research results on their own, and they're using it to upset my staff."

"You mean, they're seeing problems with the product?"

"Oh, no! Not at all. I mean, our test results are beautiful. Hell, you've seen 'em, the FDA's seen 'em. MacAllister's research department is incompetent. And Mac ... I don't know what MacAllister himself is playing at, but sometimes I get the feeling he's trying to sabotage us."

"Why would he want to do that?" she asked, suddenly concerned.

"Damned if I know. But I just don't have a good feeling about them anymore. Another thing: they're pitching a whole lot of other business these days, and I don't feel we're getting the time and attention a major product like Genelife deserves. They're charging us more and giving us less."

"I don't like the sound of that," Bettina agreed.

"I haven't made up my mind for sure," Nolan cautioned her. "I'm just kind of thinking out loud here ... I wanted to put you in the picture, in case I do decide to make a change."

"It's very important to me that the marketing effort be maintained," Bettina said firmly. "I assume you have an alternative in mind?"

"Yes, I do. An excellent alternative."

"One of the other agencies that pitched the business last year?" Bettina asked doubtfully.

"Definitely not," Nolan told her. "What I envision is a start-up operation that will actually be designed to handle our business."

"An in-house agency?"

"No, what I have in mind is an independent agency that would act like an in-house agency. We'd have top professionals working for us, and we'd pay a reduced commission."

"Sounds interesting," Bettina said, thinking of the bottom line. "As long as you're sure we'd get the same high quality marketing expertise we're getting now."

"No question about it," Nolan assured her.

"I hope not. By the way, the press event went brilliantly. You got my telegram?"

"It's framed and hanging over my desk," he told her truthfully.

"I thought that Martin woman came across very well," Bettina continued. "I must admit you were right about her."

"Yes, she has been useful," Nolan said slowly. "But I wonder if we really need her anymore, at this point."

Bettina was silent.

"I mean, she's been very effective on television, but I doubt we'll want to mount another p.r. event like this week's. And as you yourself pointed out, she is rather young ..."

"What's *she* done to make you angry, Michael?" Bettina asked, a slight smirk in her voice. The asshole probably came on to her and she turned him down, Bettina thought. Well, good for her.

Bitch! he thought. "Frankly, she's become a bit of a prima donna," he said. "All that television exposure has gone to her head. She's very difficult to work with, comes in late, goes home early, spends a lot of time over at Mac-Allister . . ."

"And I assume you have a backup plan for her job also?" Bettina said dryly.

"No, I don't," Nolan replied stiffly. "I'm just—"

"Thinking out loud," she finished for him. "Well, keep me posted. And, Michael?"

"Yes, Bettina?"

"Try not to think with your prick, okay?"

Nolan turned a deep scarlet. How dare she? "I'm only thinking of the good of the company," he said, fighting desperately to control his temper. "Besides, Kate Martin is not my type at all."

"Oh? Who *is* your type, Michael? I've often wondered. I wonder whether any woman is your type." Her bantering tone had a hard, cruel edge.

"Damn you, Bettina!" he exploded. "*You're* my type! I find you incredibly attractive."

The silence was deep and ominous. At last Bettina spoke. "Thank you, Michael dear," she said coolly. "That's terribly sweet, and a great compliment. Now I'm going to forget you ever said it, and I suggest you forget it, too. I'll call you when I return from Tokyo. Don't forget to fax me the new projections."

Nolan sat for a few minutes after she'd disconnected, wondering if he'd just blown his career. No, he decided at last. The Ice Lady was only concerned with the Genelife numbers; if they stayed strong, so would he. In fact, their worlds were so far apart, it probably amused her to think of him lusting after her untouchable body. For a moment he hated her intensely, and it pleased him to think of her left holding the bag after he'd collected his millions from the Genelife offering and disappeared.

He folded the phone and dropped it back into his briefcase. Then he signed the chit for the coffee and went through to the clubhouse entrance hall, shoving the case at the checkroom attendant on his way out the door. He hurried along the side path, his shoes kicking up the white gravel. It was ten past eleven, and the others would be waiting to tee off.

Bettina lowered the phone and sat thinking. So Michael found her attractive. That could be useful, sometime.

His hints about changing the staffing on Genelife were more disturbing. What sort of questions could the Mac-Allister Agency be asking to so upset Nolan, he'd actually consider firing them? Or were their budgets really getting way out of line? And why was Kate Martin no longer flavor of the month?

While it was certainly possible that the MacAllister situation really was about money, and the Martin thing was about sex, it was equally possible that both situations were connected, and had to do with something else entirely.

Did Michael have something to hide? Was Randall Webber dancing on the edge of illegality in some respect? Had a skeleton or two fallen out of the chairman's closet?

On the agenda in Tokyo next week was the finalization of the details of the Randall Webber spin-off. And there was serious talk of bringing the offering forward. The very last thing she wanted at the moment was even the faintest whiff of trouble. If Nolan had problems that could be solved by some short-term management changes, that was fine with her. She was all for preserving the status quo over the next twelve months.

And if, after the spin-off was completed, Nolan's problems were revealed to be more extensive, more . . . serious, well, she could honestly disclaim any knowledge of his activities.

According to all available information, both Genelife and the Randall Webber operation were profitable, legal, and trouble-free. She fervently hoped no one would feel it necessary to tell her anything different.

Avram had provided two house seats for *Love on the Moon,* a bit of musical fluff with a six-month waiting list for tickets. "You will excuse me if I do not join you at the theater," he had explained when Steve had called him from Kate's apartment to suggest they spend the afternoon together. "As the coproducer, I have seen that show too many times already. But I insist that you bring your girl to tea afterward."

He had smiled to himself when Steve hadn't protested

that Kate wasn't his girl. Progress, he thought, and congratulated himself on having chosen the perfect play for two people he hoped were on the edge of love.

Now the taxi drew up to the town house on East Sixty-fourth Street, and Steve gave Kate's hand a squeeze before reaching over to pay the driver. Kate smiled at him happily. The tension of the past weeks had drained away, and she was feeling wonderful. Looking at Steve, she knew he felt the same.

Avram welcomed them inside with obvious delight. "I cannot tell you how pleased I am to meet you," he exclaimed, kissing Kate's hand while raising an eye to judge the effect of his consciously *Mittel* European gesture. "I hope you enjoyed the play?"

"I loved it," Kate told him warmly. "Thank you so much for the tickets." Avram was still holding her hand and smiling at her. On impulse, she leaned forward and kissed him lightly on the cheek. He beamed at Steve.

"Be careful, my nephew," he warned Steve, "I might steal this magnificent woman away from you! Now come and have some tea." He turned and led them through the house, Kate's hand still tightly wrapped in his. Glancing back, Kate gave Steve an amused look. He grinned and shrugged his shoulders, pleased that Kate had made such an obvious hit with Avram.

"Victor is off today," Avram told Steve over his shoulder, "so it is just family."

"Who's Victor?" asked Kate.

"My houseboy. He cleans, he cooks. And despite the rumors, that is all he does." Steve raised his eyes heavenward, but Kate laughed.

Avram led them to the two-story atrium that had always been Steve's favorite room. It was filled with trees and flowering plants, and water spouted from an old terra-cotta fountain set in one corner.

"What an amazing place!" Kate exclaimed. "It's as though you cut a circle right through the center of the house!"

"Actually, we're standing in the backyard," Steve explained. "Avram enclosed the front half of the garden and then built a two-story extension beyond it."

"A garden in New York City is a stupidity," Avram declared. "You stroll outside for two minutes only, and you find pieces of black soot floating in your champagne. So I moved the outside inside."

"Amazing!" Kate repeated.

'What is really amazing," said Avram, "is that I got it past the zoning board. Of course it was many years ago. Please. Sit." An ornate silver tea service was set out on an antique stone table. "Shall I be mother?" Steve smiled at the aptness of the British expression, as Avram busied himself with the teapot. "Cream? Lemon? Sugar? Steve, pass Kate the scones."

They spoke of the play, the theater, Avram's new production, their conversation as light as the pastries and cream cakes they consumed.

"And how did you two meet?" Avram asked at last. "Last time you visited me, Steve, you went to the theater alone, as I recall. All he told me when he called," Avram continued, turning toward Kate, "is that you're a doctor."

"I'm Randall Webber's medical consultant," Kate explained. "Steve didn't tell you? He saw me on television, talking about Tucker, and called me. We decided to get together and share information."

"Tucker? You knew Tucker Boone?"

"No, he left before I joined the company. But we've been seeing some problems with Genelife, and I think maybe Tucker can clarify a few things. And of course Steve has his own reasons for wanting to find Tucker. If we *can* find him."

"Steve knows what I think," Avram said darkly. "I think he was the victim of foul play." He studied her face. "Usually people laugh when I say that."

"Not me," Kate said softly. "Something strange *is* going on at Randall Webber, if only I could—"

"Hey, no shop talk!" Steve interrupted, giving Kate a cautionary look. "This is the weekend!" He didn't want to get Avram wound up, nor did he want the afternoon to turn into a rehash of Friday's discussion. Such talk would only worry Avram without adding anything to their current fund of knowledge.

"Of course, of course," Avram agreed quickly. Stupid of me to break the romantic mood I tried so hard to create. "Never mind all that. Have another cake and tell me what you two have planned for tomorrow. They are calling for showers, I believe. A movie, perhaps? There are several good ones playing at the moment."

Steve and Kate exchanged slightly embarrassed glances; it had suddenly occurred to each of them quite separately that it would be nice to spend the entire day snuggled in bed together, listening to the rain. Avram grinned like a naughty boy at their discomfiture. "I'm sure you'll think of something," he said. "And when do you return to Boston, Steve?"

"Er, late Monday afternoon; I have a departmental dinner at seven. Marianne's due back from Minneapolis around three, and we're going to talk to her before I go."

"Ah, meeting all the family at once," Avram said, looking pleased. "You'll like Marianne. She's a little fragile at the moment ... maybe a little defensive. But nice."

"I'm sure I'll like her," Kate said hopefully.

"And I'm sure she'll like *you*." Avram glanced at his watch. "Have you made dinner plans?" he asked.

"After all these cakes, I don't know if I can actually manage dinner," Kate said with a smile, "but we're hoping you'll join us."

"Absolutely," Steve said. "Please come."

"I'd love to," Avram said, "but I'm going to say no. I have several scripts I simply must get through this weekend." And you two should be alone.

Steve caught his thought and smiled gratefully. He'd been sincere in his invitation, but he suddenly found the idea of being alone with Kate extremely appealing.

Avram studied the two young people benevolently over his teacup. "Well, since you're not rushing away just yet, how would you feel about my opening a bottle of champagne?"

It was nearly seven when Kate and Steve said their goodbyes and, happily tipsy, began wandering down Sixty-fourth Street toward Lexington Avenue, having decided that the twelve-block walk to Kate's apartment would do them good.

"Uncle Avram is a real charmer," Kate told him. "I like him very much."

"And he obviously likes you."

"I'm glad."

"Look, there's something you should know about Avram ..." Kate looked over at Steve questioningly. "Not that it makes any difference," he continued haltingly. "It's just ... How can I put this?"

Kate stopped walking. "Are you trying to tell me your uncle is gay?" she asked lightly. She sounded amused.

"You knew?"

Kate smiled. "I thought it was a possibility."

"It doesn't bother you?"

"Does it bother *you*?"

"No, of course not."

"Then why should you think it would bother me?"

Avram watched contentedly from the living room as Steve took Kate's hand and she smiled up at him. He watched them kiss deeply, then continue along the street. He drew the curtains across the high windows and toasted himself with the last of the champagne.

No one noticed the tall, solidly built man in the jeans and brown leather jacket slip quietly out of a dark blue car with Connecticut plates and amble up the street at a discreet distance behind the two lovers.

Chapter 22

April 15

Kate swerved jauntily onto the off ramp and headed north toward the Randall Webber complex. She'd left Steve asleep in her bed, with Cheerio curled around his feet, eyeing the tennis ball clock with happy anticipation. The day was fresh and clear, the sky an unbroken blue. It matched her mood precisely, and even the tie-up at the Triborough Bridge had failed to dampen her spirits.

Although she hadn't had much sleep the past few nights, she felt alert and energetic. First thing this morning, she'd have another chat with Jerry, she decided. Only two working days had passed since Nolan had mentioned firing him in the bar last Wednesday. Even if Nolan had made good his threat, Kate figured Jerry would still be around for another day or two. And now he'd have even more reason to cooperate with her.

The road that ran past the entrance to Randall Webber fed into a major route farther along. Traffic was always heavy at this time of day, and Kate didn't notice the dark blue sedan slow down behind her as she turned onto the company road, then accelerate past.

She parked the Toyota and headed for the executive building and her office. Her office; for how much longer would it be hers? She knew she couldn't remain here. Talking with Steve this weekend had brought it all into sharp focus: something was wrong at Randall Webber. But even if it hadn't been, she couldn't have stayed. Apart from her public relations appearances, the job had become a boring paper-heavy routine, unchallenging, unexciting, and unrelated to her professional training and talents. She'd call Dr. Gould this week; perhaps she could go back to New York General in July. But that didn't feel right, either. Surely there was some way she could practice medicine, the kind of medicine she loved—fast, meaningful, make-a-difference-right-now medicine—in an environment in which she felt more ... connected. No, she wouldn't call Gould just yet.

Besides, she still had work to finish here. Not Nolan's work; her own. First things first.

The phone was ringing as she entered her office and tossed her handbag on the side chair. Probably Michael, wanting to know where I was on Friday, she thought. But it was Victoria.

"Damnit, Kate, you promised!" Victoria said without preamble.

"What? What are you talking about?"

"My opening party. Last night at the Chamberlin Gallery."

"Shit! Was that yesterday?"

"It was. And you had better have an unbelievably good excuse!"

"God, I'm sorry, Victoria! I ... I got involved, and ..." Victoria maintained a stony silence.

"Listen, something rather weird and completely wonderful happened this weekend. I ... I've never done anything like this before, but, well, I met this man on Friday, and we spent the entire weekend together and I met his uncle and ..."

"You could have brought him."

"Victoria, we didn't get out of *bed* yesterday!"

"You didn't? Why, Kate! Good for you!" Victoria sounded surprised but delighted. "It's about time!"

"Hi, Kate! What's about time?" said a male voice.

"That's Mac on the desk extension," Victoria said. "He just walked in."

"You can't sit there on my sofa in my office and talk to my client and leave me out of it!" Mac said. "How're you doing, Kate?"

"Extremely well, apparently," Victoria said, laughing. "She fell in love over the weekend. Talk about using your free time wisely!"

"I know it sounds bizarre," said Kate, "but I guess these things do happen ..."

"Yes, they do. And I'm glad it happened to you," Victoria told her. "You needed a little romance in your life."

"So who is he?" Mac asked. "Names! I need names!"

Kate laughed and explained how she and Steve had met and that they had decided to try to solve the Genelife puzzle together.

"Well, that's good news," Mac told her. "The sooner, the better."

"Mac is really torn up about this Genelife business," Victoria said. "He'd like to keep the account, but he's a decent fellow and he really wants to do the right thing."

"I just don't know what the right thing is," Mac said. "Please keep me in the picture."

"I will."

"So when do we get to meet the lad?" asked Victoria. "Can you bring him to dinner this evening?"

"I'm afraid not. We're seeing his sister this afternoon, and then he's catching the Boston shuttle. But he'll be back next week. Can we do it then?"

"Of course. Is it love?"

"Do you think it could be, this soon?"

Victoria laughed. "How does it feel?"

"Wonderful! Just being with him feels so different from being with someone like Richard Day. Things never felt right with Richard, you know? But with Steve—"

"Richard Day?" Mac's voice came booming over the extension. "You've been dating Richard *Day*?"

Shit! Kate thought. She'd studiously avoided mentioning Richard's last name whenever she'd spoken of him before. "Er, yes," she said. "But believe me, I've never told him anything about MacAllister or ..." No, that wasn't quite true. She trailed off, feeling herself blush with embarrassment and guilt.

There was a brief, angry silence on Mac's end, followed by a crash as he slammed down the receiver. Kate jumped. "What the hell was that?"

"Hang on," Victoria said tightly. She pushed the hold button, then went outside to Mac's secretary's desk and picked up the phone there.

When she spoke again, she sounded troubled. "I'm sure you haven't betrayed any confidences," she said. "But Mac's very upset."

Kate's guilt turned to anger. "It's none of Mac's business whom I date!"

"Of course it isn't," Victoria agreed soothingly. "But he's going through a difficult time right now ... He's fighting for business, and Day is one of his hottest competitors. I don't think he honestly misinterpreted your relationship with Richard. But ... he's never liked him, and—"

"He doesn't have to like him. He wasn't dating him!"

"Come on, Kate! Richard never meant anything to you. I remember how you used to talk about him. Besides, you're involved with someone else now. You won't be seeing Richard anymore."

"I will if I want to!"

Victoria took a deep breath. "Mac was out of line, and you're right to be angry. But try to understand. He's pitching a couple of big accounts, and right now he's seeing spies under the goddamn bed, he's so jumpy. And then he's got the Genelife decision hanging fire, too. I really meant it before when I said he was a decent guy. He's suffering, just like you are. Is the drug safe or is it not? Should he resign the account right this minute? Or can he hang on a little longer and collect a little more of the Genelife money that's keeping the agency going?"

"Victoria, we're all under a lot of tension right now. He had no right to hang up on me like that."

"I already said you were right. I hereby apologize for him. Forgive him, okay?"

Kate paused. "Yes, all right. I forgive him. Frankly, I've always felt a little guilty, seeing Richard. So I guess I can't say I was completely surprised by his reaction." She sighed. "And you're right. I won't be seeing Richard again."

"Problem solved!" Victoria said brightly. "And now I must dash. I'm being interviewed by the *Village Voice*!"

"That's great!"

"Isn't it? Anyway, I really do want to meet your Steve. Let me know when he's back in town and we'll plan something special."

"I will."

"We'll talk soon, then."

"Yes. Bye."

Victoria stood by the secretary's desk, a troubled frown creasing her forehead.

She was glad she'd convinced Kate to forgive Mac. But she knew that in his current vulnerable state, Mac would find it hard to do the same. How could he accept that he himself had been out of line, when his intense sense of loyalty was obviously outraged by what he saw as Kate's betrayal? Victoria felt sure that in his heart of hearts, Mac couldn't really believe Kate would compromise him. But getting some perspective on the situation would be difficult for him, especially given the fierce competition between MacAllister and Imagemakers these days, and the vital importance of any new piece of business to Mac's bottom line.

Best to postpone that dinner with Kate and Steve next week, she thought. Getting Mac to forgive Kate for dating Richard could take some time.

Kate leaned back in her chair and sighed deeply. She'd felt so good before Victoria had called, and now she felt so rotten. And all for what? Someone she didn't even care for. She picked up the phone again and dialed Richard's number.

When he came on the line, she took a deep breath and jumped right in, explaining that she'd enjoyed their times together, that she liked and respected him, but that she'd recently met someone and had fallen in love rather suddenly. She hoped he would forgive her, but she couldn't continue to see him anymore.

He took it very well, which she found rather annoying. Then she chided herself for her vanity. Why shouldn't she have been a stop-gap for him, just as he had been for her?

"There's no reason we can't still see each other now and then," Richard was saying. "Just as friends, of course. After all, we *are* friends." He paused. "I'm glad you've found someone you really care about, Kate. But that doesn't mean we can't continue to care about each other, too. As friends."

"What a lovely thing to say!" Kate told him. "Of course we can—" She broke off. Of course they couldn't, not really. Not if she wanted to retain Mac as a friend. And yet, why should one friendship require the cessation of another? Because it's not just friendship, she thought. It's business.

"Lunch?" Richard asked. "Thursday?"

"Actually, I'm, uh, we've gotten awfully busy at the office," Kate replied awkwardly. "Why don't I call you in a few weeks?"

"Of course. I understand. By the way, how are you doing with Nolan and the side effects?" Kate didn't answer. "Look, I know it's none of my business, but I'm worried about you, and what you might be caught up in. You have to press him harder, Kate."

"Maybe," Kate said noncommittally.

"Well, how about the guy you replaced? He might help you put pressure on Nolan."

"Nicholas Butler? I never thought of him!" Kate explained. "Good idea!"

"I'm here to help. By the way, do you think you could give me a copy of MacAllister's research results?"

"Of course not!" Kate gasped. "That's privileged information. Besides, what on earth for?"

"A friend of mine works for the FDA," Richard said slowly. "I was thinking . . . maybe I can start a little something from my end."

"Don't you dare!" Kate exploded. "Whatever I've told you was in confidence! When, *if*, I have anything definitive, *I'll* go to the FDA! Please, Richard. Stay out of this."

"Okay, okay, just trying to help. I mean, I realize Mac needs the business pretty badly, so you can't expect him to push too hard with Nolan."

"That's a shitty thing to say! Mac's just as concerned as I am! He wants to get to the bottom of all this, too!" Defending Mac to Richard made Kate feel slightly less guilty about having dated his competitor.

"What makes you so sure?" Richard challenged.

"Because he says so. He's always saying so. He keeps asking me . . ." Kate trailed off. I'm talking too much again, she thought. Why does Richard always seem to make me go two sentences further than I should? "I, uh, really can't talk anymore," she continued. "Thanks for understanding about . . . us. And I'll call you soon."

"Promise?"

"Promise," Kate said mendaciously, and hung up quickly. A friend at the FDA indeed! How dare Richard even contemplate such a thing? Still, his suggestion that she talk to Nick Butler was a good one. Nolan's secretary would have his office number. She lifted the receiver and punched Jenny's extension, then hung up quickly as it began to ring. The less Nolan knew of her activities at this point, the better. She'd get the number from the phone book.

Dr. Butler's office hours were afternoons only, but his receptionist was in, and very accommodating. The doctor had a full schedule, but she'd fit Kate in around four; would that suit her? It would indeed. Don't be late, the woman warned; Butler had another appointment at four-twenty.

Kate scribbled the address on a message slip and crammed it into her purse.

Now for Jerry. Should she call him? No, better to simply appear at R&D; it would be harder for him to dodge her that way.

She drove to the R&D building, nodding at the guard standing just inside the outer door. But the man didn't nod back. Stone-faced, he watched intently as she used her pass-card to open the locked interior door. He must be new, she thought as she slipped inside. I don't believe I've seen him here before.

The frosted glass panel of Jerry's office door was dark, and the door itself was locked. It was hard to see through the glass, but it looked to Kate as though the room had been cleaned up; stacks of papers and reports no longer littered the floor.

"He's gone."

Startled, Kate whirled around. A matronly woman in a white lab coat stood behind her, a clipboard thick with reports in her hand. "Gone where?" Kate asked.

"Reassigned," the woman said. "To Puerto Rico, lucky devil!" She continued down the hall, but Kate caught up with her.

"I don't understand!" Kate said.

"It's simple enough," the woman told her. "They're sending him to the manufacturing facility in Barcelonetta. Assistant manager or something. Not exactly tough duty. Unless the government repeals Section 936. You know, the federal tax break," she continued, seeing Kate's confusion. "Kill 936 and everybody'll leave. Merck, Abbott, Pfizer ... we're all there for the tax credit. It's a cushy deal for Jerry while it lasts."

"But I thought all we did in Barcelonetta was assemble. We ship everything down and they put it together and ship it out."

"Exactly. Purely mechanical. Don't know why they need Jerry, but what the hell! Good money, nice climate. Boon-doggle City for a guy like Lim."

"When did this happen?" Kate asked weakly.

"Last week, apparently. Jerry's taking a little vacation—drying out, if you ask me!—before he heads down to PR for good." The woman hurried away, leaving Kate staring after her, openmouthed. Last week Nolan had told her he was planning to fire Lim. Instead, he'd given him a plum assignment. What the hell was going on?

Back in her office, a message from Steve confirmed their meeting with Marianne at three-thirty. Presumably that was the soonest Marianne was expected back from Minneapolis, but it didn't leave much time between meetings. She dialed her home number, hoping Steve might be able to move things up a little or delay his flight back to Boston, but reached only her message machine.

She got Jerry Lim's home phone number and address from the local phone directory, but he didn't answer, either.

She sighed and reached for the stack of papers in her in box, her mind whirling. Why had Jerry been reassigned instead of fired? Why had the guard chased her away from the cinder-block truck depot in the woods? Why hadn't Nolan told Tucker about the successful synthetization of Genelife? Tucker. If only they could find Tucker. Or find out what had happened to him. More and more, Tucker seemed to hold the key to the riddle.

Meanwhile, people everywhere were taking Genelife, believing it to be safe. Was Richard right? Was it time to go to the FDA? But with what? One small research study by an advertising agency? Nolan had FDA approval; the burden of proving Genelife dangerous would be on her. And she had no real proof. Furthermore, if she showed her hand too soon, it would be easy for Nolan to devise a cover-up, if one were needed. No, she had to maintain a low profile and keep digging from within.

She worked through lunch, making a point of wandering by Nolan's office and exchanging a few words on the weather, the weekend. She'd need to leave by two-thirty at the latest to make the meeting with Marianne, and she wanted to establish her presence in the office before that.

Promptly at two twenty-five, Kate filled her mug with steaming hot coffee and placed it on her desk next to an open report and a pencil. She left her jacket slung over her chair, enhancing the effect. To a casual passerby, this busy worker had left her desk for just a moment and would soon return. Then she slung her handbag over her shoulder and sidled out into the corridor, half closing her office door behind her.

She left via the rear exit and walked quickly around to the parking lot, sliding in behind the wheel of her Toyota and turning the ignition key in one smooth movement. Soon she was on the I–95 feeder road, relatively free of traffic at this hour. As she drove, she made a mental list of next steps. Talk to Marianne . . . talk to Butler . . . talk to Jerry, if she could catch him before he left for Puerto Rico. Have a closer look at that cinder-block truck depot or whatever it is. A thrill of fear shot through her at the thought of going back to that lonely spot. Perhaps she'd learn something from Butler today that would make it unnecessary.

Two cars behind her, the driver of the dark blue sedan tore the wrapper from a chocolate bar with his teeth. Then he shoved the candy into his mouth and began to chew.

"Kate, this is Marianne. Marianne, Kate."

The two women eyed each other tentatively. Marianne knew from her phone conversation with Steve that morning that he and Kate were becoming deeply involved. She also knew that Kate was committed to solving the mystery of Tucker's disappearance. Still, her little brother had been a loner for a long time; Marianne wasn't quite sure how she felt about a serious love interest for him, at his age. All during the plane ride home, she'd tried to imagine what sort of woman Steve could have fallen so hard for, so quickly. Was she cold and brilliant, the kind who would sneer at Marianne's low-profile teaching career? Or worse, was she a bimbo twenty years Steve's junior? Bimbos weren't really Steve's style, but he'd been spending a lot of time in the jungle lately.

Kate, too, had worried. Would Marianne, still suffering from Tucker's seeming desertion, resent her relationship with Steve? Would she feel Kate was being intrusive in trying to unravel the mystery of Tucker's disappearance?

But as they studied each other now, each felt reassured. Marianne had been hurt, but Kate could see in her eyes her determination to be strong and independent. Any resistance she might have to the match would be for Steve's sake, not her own. For her part, Marianne was relieved that Kate was no bimbo, nor was she as young as Marianne had feared. And the light of intelligence that shone in Kate's eyes was kindly.

"I'm so sorry," Kate said sincerely.

Marianne nodded, then glanced at Steve. "And I'm so glad," she told Kate warmly.

Steve let out a silent sigh. It was going to be all right.

Marianne led them into the living room, where her suit-case, still closed, leaned against a bookcase. "I literally walked in the door about five minutes ago," she explained. "Anything in the fridge will be poisonous by now. But if you can drink it without milk, I'll make us all a cup of tea."

"I'll help," Kate offered, and followed Marianne into the small kitchen. Marianne filled the kettle and Kate got down the cups and saucers, and they chatted easily about Marianne's trip and Uncle Avram. It wasn't until they were all settled in the living room, teacups in hand, that Steve mentioned Tucker.

"Did Steve tell you the police think he ran off with another woman?" Marianne asked Kate.

She nodded. "Of course, they could be wrong. I understand Tucker had a terrible fight with Michael Nolan the day he came back from the rain forest."

Marianne shook her head. "I never knew he went back," she said. "Not until Steve called and told me so, after he'd talked to you. Tucker was so secretive. Who knows? Maybe he did run off with someone."

"Steve said Tucker disappeared a couple of other times last year."

Marianne shot Steve a look. Uh-oh, Kate thought.

"Come on, Marianne!" Steve said. "We're all on the same side."

Marianne sighed. "You're right." She turned to Kate. "He did go off a few times last year. But I don't know where."

"Might he have gone to the rain forest those times, too?"

Marianne shook her head. "No," she declared. "I'm sure he didn't."

Steve looked surprised. "How can you be so sure?"

"I just am."

They talked some more about Marianne's marriage and Tucker's mood swings, and Marianne showed them some photos of Tucker. They all remarked on how young he looked, and Marianne repeated what she'd said to Steve, months before: Tucker was one of those people who never seemed to age. Kate had her own theory about that, but said nothing.

Aside from the photos, Kate learned nothing that Steve hadn't already told her, yet she felt Marianne knew more than she was saying. Could it be that Steve's presence somehow inhibited his sister? Those other disappearances of Tucker's last year were intriguing, as was Marianne's insistence that he hadn't left the country. Suddenly Kate looked at her watch: nearly four. She set down her teacup and stood. "I'm really sorry to have to run," she said, "but I've got an appointment with the man I replaced at Randall Webber, a Dr. Butler. I'm hoping he might be able to shed some light on all this. And of course, he will have known Tucker."

Marianne nodded. "I understand. It was nice to meet you."

"You, too. Look, Marianne ... could we get together again tomorrow? I know Steve won't be here, but ... maybe we can meet somewhere for breakfast, and talk? Would that be all right?"

"I guess so, sure. Uh, there's a coffee shop just down the block. Will that do?"

"Sure. Around eight? Or is that too early for you?"

"Eight's fine. I have an early class."

"Good. I'll see you tomorrow morning, then." Kate headed for the door, and Steve followed. "I'll call you later," he said as she stepped into the corridor. "I want to hear what Butler has to say. That damn dinner should be over by ten-thirty or so."

"All right." She pushed the elevator button, then turned back to him. "I think your sister's very nice."

"She likes you, too. But not as much as I do." He took her in his arms and kissed her and she felt herself melt as she pressed her body against his. Behind them, the elevator door wheezed open.

"You'd better go," he whispered. "You'll be late." Reluctantly, they drew apart. "I'll be back Wednesday morning."

"I'll miss you."

"Me, too."

She stepped back into the elevator and the door slid shut. Slowly the cage descended, taking her away from him.

Out on the street, the air had turned cooler, and Kate regretted having left her jacket in the office as camouflage. Fortunately, taxis were plentiful on West End Avenue.

"Park and Seventy-first," she told the driver. "And step on it."

The chunky man in the brown leather jacket, having noted the address of the building Kate had entered, had spent the past fifteen minutes searching for a parking place. He arrived back at the building just in time to see her flag down a cab. Shit! Who would have thought she'd be on the move again so soon? No time to retrieve the car; he raised his hand and a taxi cut across two lanes of traffic and screeched to a stop in front of him. He jumped in and pointed at Kate's taxi, which was rapidly disappearing southward. "Follow that cab," he shouted.

The driver turned around and gave him a tired smile. "Very funny, Mac, very funny. Now, where ya wanna go?"

Chapter 23

The suite of offices Dr. Nicholas Butler shared was housed in a rather elegant Park Avenue residential building. The bronze plaque beside the private street entrance listed three other doctors; either the offices were large or the practices small, Kate reflected as she descended the carpeted stairs.

Although below street level, the waiting room felt bright and airy, thanks to creative lighting and interior design. A wall of false windows gave the appearance of sunlight. The beige wallpaper, mushroom carpet, and pale leather furniture looked new. The rather bland color scheme was accented with a red and blue kelim rug, some good, bold prints, and several fresh floral arrangements. Four well-dressed patients sat reading magazines. At least one of the doctors sharing these quarters has a lucrative practice, Kate thought.

She introduced herself to the attractive receptionist, and was immediately led down a short hallway and into a small, attractive office. Dr. Butler rose as she entered, and extended his hand in greeting. "Dr. Martin! May I call you Kate? How delightful to see you. Please sit down. Some coffee? A soft drink?"

"No, thank you."

"Well, well! And how are things in the world of corporate medicine? I was quite surprised when Ellen—that's our receptionist—told me you were coming in for a chat."

"Really? Why?"

"Well, we haven't seen each other since your job interview ... what? Ten months ago? Not even a phone call. Of course, Michael explained your feelings to me when you joined the company, and I had to respect—"

"Wait a second. What did Michael tell you?"

"Why, that you felt you had to find your own feet, so to speak. That you'd prefer I not brief you or try to guide you in any way. That you wanted this to be a pristine experience. Pristine experience, those were the words he used. As I say, I felt I had to respect your decision, although I would have been happy to—"

"Dr. Butler—"

"Nicholas. Please."

"Nicholas. I never told Michael Nolan any such thing."

Butler stared at her in puzzlement. "You didn't? But Michael said . . . How very curious."

"Isn't it?" Kate said dryly.

Butler ran a hand through his salt-and-pepper hair. There was far more salt than pepper these days, Kate noticed. Semi-retirement obviously agreed with the man; he seemed calm and well rested, and the stress lines around his eyes seemed to have smoothed out. "I must have misunderstood Michael," he said apologetically. "Or perhaps he misunderstood you. How embarrassing."

"Never mind. Maybe we can make up for lost time. Would you mind if I asked you some questions?"

"No, not at all. Ask away!"

Knowing her time with Butler was limited by his patient appointments, Kate had jotted down the key questions she wanted answered. Now she drew the small pad from her handbag. "Nicholas, the advertising agency has done some research that seems to indicate a higher incidence of side effects than the FDA topline report shows. Can you think of any reason for this?"

"A higher incidence? That's not possible."

"Are you sure?"

"Absolutely. The clinical tests that were sent to the FDA were well within the FDA limits. Government regulation of prescriptive drugs is very tight, and there is absolutely no way Genelife would have been approved if there had been any doubt—"

"Excuse me, but did you actually review the clinical trial data? Did you see it yourself?"

"Yes, of course I did. Chemstra sent me reams of material, the same stuff that went to the FDA. Perhaps the advertising agency sample was too small."

"It was small, yes," Kate admitted. "But there are other things that . . ." She broke off; Butler was looking at her strangely. Careful, she thought. "What can you tell me about Chemstra?" she asked. "I understand their involvement in the project was kept, uh, secret from everyone at Randall Webber until fairly recently."

"Well, nearly everyone," Butler said. "I knew about them from the beginning. But Michael wanted to keep it from Tucker, so we had to restrict, er, access to the information."

"Why not tell Tucker? It was his project, after all."

"At the Randall Foundation, it was his project. At Randall Webber, it was a company project. Tucker was not a team player. He was also somewhat ... I believe the medical term is 'nutty as a fruitcake.'" He gave Kate a smile of complicity. "But you were asking about Chemstra ..."

"Yes. What was your involvement with them?"

"Actually, I had very little contact with Chemstra directly. Michael handled it all."

"Was that unusual?"

"I suppose it was, to some extent. But it was a special situation. You see, Michael set up Chemstra."

"He what?"

"He started it with Randall Webber money, back before Omni took over. We kept it quiet, since it would have been hard for Chemstra to solicit business from other drug companies if it were known who their backer was. Oh, there was nothing illegal about it," he added quickly, seeing Kate's expression. "And it paid off. They solved the problem Tucker couldn't."

"What problem was that?"

"The synthetization problem, of course. See, the first tests were done with the plant-derived enzyme, and the side effects were too high for the FDA. Tucker and Jerry Lim spent several years trying to reduce them, without success. So Nolan thought maybe a synthetic would be more controllable. He put Tucker on it, but the synthetization Tucker came up with was too erratic. Worse, it didn't produce nearly as dramatic a cosmetic effect as the plant derivative. Michael kept prodding Tucker to keep at it, but Tucker ... well, he wasn't the easiest guy to work with. He kept insisting he wanted to use the plant derivative, that the synthetic would never work as well ..." Butler sighed and shook his head. "He was a brilliant scientist, brilliant. But emotionally unstable, I'm afraid. The classic definition of genius."

"So Michael brought in Chemstra."

"Exactly. He couldn't be sure Tucker would be able to solve the problems of the plant derivative. And he couldn't trust Tucker to keep trying to find a workable synthetic. So he put Chemstra in business with the assignment to produce and test a synthetic version of Genelife. The deal was, they couldn't talk about it, not until the drug had been approved for market."

"And Chemstra delivered, where Tucker failed?"

"Precisely. Building on Tucker's work, Chemstra quietly came up with a synthetic that they tested extensively, and secretly, in Europe. It tested well within the FDA guidelines."

"And that's when Michael told everyone about it."

"Yes. After all, until the research had been completed and the FDA had approved, he didn't know whether there was anything to announce."

"But he told you."

"Of course. I'm—I was—his medical consultant. Are you sure you won't have a Coke or something?"

"No, thanks. So you can't think of any reason we could be seeing a higher incidence of side effects?"

"I just told you. The sample must have been too small." Butler thought for a moment. "It's also possible some people are taking too much. You know, not waiting the full week before reapplying the patch. I explain it very carefully each time I prescribe it, but there are always some people who think they know better." He shook his head.

"You prescribe Genelife yourself?"

"Of course. Why not? It's perfectly safe." He looked at her severely. "I hope you understand that, Kate. A doctor's reputation rides on every prescription he or she writes. I wouldn't jeopardize mine, believe me. And neither would my colleagues. Or any doctor I know, for that matter."

Kate nodded tiredly. Butler was obviously a believer, and she had no real information that would change his mind. "Tell me about Tucker's trip to the rain forest last May," she said. "Why did he go back?"

Butler stared at her, openmouthed. "Tucker went back? What on earth for?"

"That's what I'm asking you."

"But I have no idea. I had one foot out the door last May. No one told me he'd gone back." He shook his head. "I can't imagine why he would. I mean, even if he had some strange idea about finding a way to reduce the side effects of the plant derivative by going back to the jungle, it wasn't necessary anymore. Chemstra had the synthetic tested and ready."

"But Tucker didn't know that."

"Sure he did. Michael told him."

"You know that for a fact?"

Butler hesitated. "Well, I naturally assumed ... Why wouldn't he?"

But Kate ignored the question. Obviously, Butler knew less about that particular situation than she did herself, and she had no desire to enlighten him. "Whatever happened to Tucker, anyway?" she asked instead. "I know he fought with Michael when he came back; the next day, he was gone. Any ideas?"

"As I said, I was pretty much out of Randall Webber by then," Butler told her. "But I did hear that he went rogue one night, just before he left the company. He broke into the lab or something. Security got to him before he could do much damage. I understand he had a substance abuse problem. I've always assumed he'd gone into a detox facility somewhere. Perhaps you should ask Michael."

"Perhaps I should." Kate checked her notes. "By the way, where did they get the plant derivative Tucker was working with originally?"

Butler looked blank. "I assumed they had it flown in from the Amazon," he said. "Frankly, I never asked. Why?"

"Just curious." She put the pad back in her handbag. "One last question. Do you know that building where they kept the trucks?"

"Trucks? What trucks?"

"It's over past the gym, on a wide dirt road ... a clearing in the woods with a gray cinder-block building."

"I have no idea where you mean," Butler protested, his face open and innocent. "A cinder-block building, you say?"

"Never mind," Kate said quickly. "It doesn't matter." She stood and extended her hand. "Thank you so much for seeing me. I know you have patients to see ..."

"A pleasure, really," Butler told her. He grasped her hand firmly and beamed at her. "I'm only sorry we didn't do this sooner. But Michael distinctly said—"

"A misunderstanding," Kate assured him. Was there any credible way she could ask Butler not to tell Michael she'd been to see him? "But perhaps you'd better not mention I've been here. We wouldn't want to embarrass him."

"Oh, I don't think it would embarrass him," Butler said jovially. "No, he'd probably have a good laugh over it. A fine man, Michael. Known him for years."

"Really?"

"Oh, yes," Butler said, walking with her toward the open office door. "He brought me in to Randall Webber eight years ago. And when I retired last summer—that was Michael's idea, too, such a thoughtful man—he was very generous. Very generous indeed."

That explained the carpeting and the prints and the flowers, Kate thought. But why would Nolan urge Butler to retire, just before the launch of a major new product? It was a strange time to change horses. "Michael's a very unusual person," she said.

"He is, he is! You know, he actually gave me a seat on the Randall Foundation board when I retired. With a nice little stipend attached. And look what he did for Henri Koch!"

"Henri Koch?"

"Chemstra's managing director. Yes, we all think the world of Michael." Butler glanced at his watch in some dismay. "Why, it's nearly a quarter to five! You'll excuse me if I don't walk you back to reception."

"Of course."

"I've enjoyed our talk. So glad I could reassure you about Genelife."

"Oh, you have!"

"Good. Come and see me again."

"I just may do that," Kate told him, and headed back along the corridor, passing the receptionist, who smiled at her. The patient she was leading, presumably Butler's four-twenty appointment, scowled.

Butler stood for a moment at his office door, then re-treated behind his desk in readiness for his patient. Such an attractive young woman, that Dr. Martin. Instinctively, he brushed his longish hair back from his forehead and smoothed it down over the patch on the back of his neck.

Outside, the man in the brown leather jacket stood wait-ing a few paces to the side of the door into which he'd watched Kate disappear some forty minutes earlier. He was feeling conspicuous, and wished he had the car. A double-parked car was far less noticeable than a loitering man.

He saw the door start to open and quickly turned away and began sauntering down the street. He gave her fifteen seconds to get through the door, then dropped his keys and bent to retrieve them. Peering backward past his leg, he saw her turn and walk away from him, ignoring several cruising taxis. Excellent. He straightened up and turned back, following slowly.

Kate walked uptown along Park Avenue for several blocks, then headed over toward Lexington Avenue. There was a good chicken take-out place a few blocks up. She turned left onto Lexington, passing a dry cleaners, a fruit and vegetable store, a video rental place, then suddenly stopped and retraced her steps. Those asparagus looked good.

A man in a brown leather jacket was selecting apples. She couldn't see his face, but something about him seemed familiar. She chose her asparagus, went inside, and paid. She was just stepping out onto the street when the Korean owner approached the man in the leather jacket to offer assistance. The man looked up and Kate gasped and stepped back into the shadowy interior of the store.

She'd only seen his face for an instant, but it had been long enough to recognize the guard who had assaulted her on the dirt road at Randall Webber.

Chapter 24

"Does the name Nicholas Butler mean anything to you?"

Nolan exhaled forcefully. The trouble with giving people the number of your direct phone line was that they used it at the most inappropriate times. Here it was, nearly five o'clock, and he still had a good four hours of work ahead of him.

"Yes, of course," he said tiredly. "Dr. Butler was our medical consultant until last year. Why?" This guy hasn't even come on board yet; why is he bothering me about Butler?

"Well, I thought you might be interested to know that Dr. Martin is planning to question him about the safety of Genelife," the caller said. "She may have already done so."

Nolan gripped the receiver tightly. "It's perfectly natural for Dr. Martin to consult with Dr. Butler." Nolan spoke calmly, but his mind raced.

"Of course it is," the caller agreed. "But in the interests of full disclosure and cooperation, I thought I should let you know. Oh, and there's something else."

"Yes?"

"Mac MacAllister has stepped up his campaign against Genelife. He keeps pushing Kate, uh, Dr. Martin, to 'get to the bottom of all this,' as he puts it. He's the one who put her up to calling Butler, and God knows who else."

Shit! "Well, he won't be pressuring her much longer. I'm getting rid of both of them."

"It's definite? Martin too?"

"Martin especially."

"Good. That'll make everything a lot easier."

"For me, too, my friend. For me, too."

"And, uh, when . . ."

"When I'm ready!" Nolan said firmly. He checked his calendar; the conference and awards dinner dates were circled in blue ink. "A month or so should see us clear of media interest," he said. "Will you be ready?"

"We're all set. Uh, and you'll have a check for me, right?"

"I told you I would," Nolan said impatiently. Was money all this guy ever thought about?

"I'm sorry to bring it up again, but I've personally put myself on the line for some very big bucks, and I'm hanging out here in the breeze until you—"

"I told you it would be okay. Anything else?"

"No, just ... No."

"Okay. I'll talk to you soon. And thanks for the tip."

Nolan hung up and stared, unseeing, at the paperwork that littered his desk. So Kate was escalating her investigation. Staying his hand until after the media spotlight had moved away from Genelife might no longer be possible.

"You're *where*?"

"In a vegetable store on Lexington and Seventy-fifth. Actually, I'm at a pay phone just down the street." Kate looked around fearfully. The security guard had pulled a red-wrapped candy bar from his pocket, tearing it open with his teeth as he'd watched her head for the phone. Now he chewed slowly as he fussed with the fruit, the wrapper bright in his hand. "Someone's following me!"

"My God!" Victoria exclaimed. "Do you know who he is?"

"A security guard from Randall Webber, who—it's a long story. Look, I don't want to call the police, for reasons I'll explain later." The guard was strolling toward the pay phone. "I need your help, Victoria! Right now!"

"Of course, of course! You go back inside the store. I'll grab a cab and be right there."

"Good. But listen: when you get here, tell the taxi to wait. Tell him you're picking up a friend. Get out and look over the produce so I can see you through the door. Then go distract the guard, ask him what time it is or something ... He won't be far away. He's about five feet ten, solid-looking ... brown hair, brown leather jacket ... I'll jump in the cab and go home. Okay?"

"Not okay. If he's from Randall Webber, he'll know where you live. Better go to my place. I'll leave a key on the seat of the taxi."

"What about Cheerio?"

"Get a neighbor to feed him, or I'll do it later. Now go buy some oranges or something. I'll be there as fast as I can."

Kate hung up and pasted a smile on her face as she turned back toward the vegetable store. Heart pounding, she walked past the guard and into the store, and began sorting through the bananas. The guard continued to the phone Kate had just vacated, picked up the receiver, and began a long conversation with the dial tone.

It was now rush hour; although Victoria left her house within minutes of Kate's call, it took nearly half an hour to get uptown. Watching anxiously from behind the salad bar, Kate spotted her instantly and waved. Victoria nodded and disappeared from view. Kate paid for six oranges and a melon and peeked out onto the street. Victoria had managed to turn the guard around so that his back was to the store; she held a piece of paper in front of his face, obviously asking for directions. The guard was shaking his head, visibly annoyed.

Kate ran to the double-parked taxi, leapt in, and slammed the door. On the seat was the key, wrapped in a twenty-dollar bill. The driver turned around. "Where's your friend?"

"She changed her plans. She said to give you this." Kate held out the twenty. The meter read eleven twenty-five.

The driver smiled. "Nice lady," he said. "Where to?"

Victoria arrived back at the brownstone ten minutes after Kate. "Okay," she said, flopping down on the plush Edwardian sofa. "Give."

Kate described her initial encounter with the guard, and the mystery of the truck depot. "He saw my name on my ID badge," she said. "He must have gotten my address from Personnel. God knows how long he's been following me."

"So why not call the police?"

"To do what? It's his word against mine. He hasn't even attempted to speak to me. Unless he attacks me or something, there's not much they can do."

"That's crazy!"

"No, it's true. If I report it and they come over and catch the guy hanging around on the street, he'll deny he's following me and they'll warn him and run him off. For now. But then he'll know that I know about him and he'll be more careful. At least this way, I can see him coming."

"Then report it to Personnel at work."

Kate shook her head. "I don't think Michael Nolan is too pleased with me at the moment," she said. "He wasn't very friendly when I stopped by his office this morning. I don't think he'll take it seriously."

"But he has to!"

"Oh, right! He'll warn the guard, but I bet he won't fire him. And then the guy will know that I know about him." Kate sighed. "There's something else, too. Frankly, I don't want to call attention to myself at Randall Webber just now. I need to keep a low profile."

"That's crazy! That guard should be fired!"

"He still knows where I live."

"Arrested, then."

"On what charge? It's scary as hell, but . . . No police."

"But you're in danger!"

"Not if you help. And Steve will be back on Wednesday; he'll help, too." Kate thought of her meeting with Marianne the next morning. "This guy could have been following me all day," she said thoughtfully. "He certainly trailed me from Butler's office; it would be absurd to think he just happened to find me at the vegetable store. And he may have seen me at Marianne's. We're supposed to have breakfast tomorrow, but . . . I don't want to put her at risk."

"Cancel the meeting."

"I can't. I have a strong feeling she knows something she isn't saying. I need to talk to her." Kate paused, thinking. "But I know how to do it . . . if you'll help."

"Count on it."

"Good. It's really very simple."

Victoria nodded as Kate explained what she wanted her to do, and proclaimed the plan a piece of cake.

"And now let me see if the O'Neills are home," Kate said. "We keep each other's apartment keys for emergencies. They have a fourteen-year-old who loves Cheerio. He won't mind feeding and walking her."

Later, Victoria fixed brown rice and Chinese vegetables, and Kate spoke about her feelings for Steve.

"I must meet this paragon," Victoria told her with a smile.

"You will. In fact, you can say hello to him this evening. He was going to call me tonight for an update on my Butler meeting. I'd better leave a message on his machine telling him I'm here." Kate looked over at her friend. "You're very nice to let me involve you in all this stuff," she said.

"At the risk of being soppy, what are friends for?"

Chapter 25

April 16

Kate's white Toyota moved slowly out of the parking garage and turned sharply onto the street, where it paused for a moment despite the lack of traffic. Then it pulled out into the traffic lane, heading east. Some distance behind it, a dark blue sedan pulled out from the curb and followed.

The early morning was dark and drizzly and traffic on the interstate was heavy and slow. The driver of the blue sedan was forced to hang back farther than he'd have liked, but he was pretty sure where she was going. It had been a close call yesterday, he thought; he'd been afraid she would recognize him, but she'd walked right past him after her phone call, never noticed him at all. He felt bad about losing her at the vegetable store, though. That damn black woman had been all over him with her paper and that crazy West Indian accent he couldn't understand. Some looker, though. Well, the Martin woman must have gone home to make dinner; she'd been in that store long enough to buy a hundred vegetables. That's what he'd put in his report, he decided. Followed Martin to her home. Picked her up again this morning, coming out of her garage.

An hour and a half after leaving Manhattan, the white Toyota turned off I–95 and onto the busy county road leading to Randall Webber. The blue sedan followed at a distance, now certain of her destination. The last few days, he'd seen her safely into the company entrance and then driven past, turning in at the small back entrance three miles along. Now, feeling guilty about losing her yesterday, he stayed with her right into the parking lot. What the hell, he thought. I could be a coworker, for all she knows. She has no idea I'm tailing her.

She had just pulled into her numbered parking space as he entered the lot. He slid into a spot behind and to one side of the Toyota and watched her open the door and get out. Funny; she looked taller. He got out of his car and took a few tentative steps forward. Yes, she was definitely taller. And what had looked, from a distance, like her hair was actually a rust-colored headscarf.

Now the woman turned around, pulling off the scarf and shaking her hair loose, and he realized he'd been had.

Shit! He kicked his car in frustration.

Victoria waved to him cheerfully, got back into the Toyota, and drove away.

The eggs had been eaten, the coffee drunk, and still Kate hadn't been able to break through Marianne's reticence about Tucker's earlier disappearances. She felt sure the woman wanted to tell her something, something important. Otherwise, why agree to meet today? Kate decided to try another approach.

"How much did Steve tell you about me?" she asked Marianne.

"You're a doctor ... you're committed to finding out what happened to Tucker, what's going on with Genelife. You ... he ..." She smiled shyly.

"Yes," Kate said. "We are. But did he tell you I've been divorced?"

"No, he didn't."

"Well, it's true. I know it's not exactly the same thing you're going through, but I remember the pain, the anxiety. Our problems were different, but the symptoms were similar. Jon never actually disappeared, like Tucker, but I remember those nights toward the end when he didn't come home. First you're worried, then you're mad, then you're scared ... when he finally shows up, you don't know whether to kiss him or kill him!"

"That's it!" Marianne agreed. "I know exactly what you mean! It makes you crazy!"

"And it makes you do crazy things, things you never imagined you were capable of. I remember actually going through Jon's wallet when he was asleep, trying to figure out if there was another woman! I can't believe I actually—" Kate broke off. Marianne was looking at her so strangely. "Marianne? What is it?"

"I did that, too," she said softly. "God, I'm so embarrassed."

"Don't be," Kate told her. But Marianne lowered her eyes and drained her coffee cup. "Please don't tell him," she said.

Kate reached out and touched her hand. "Tell who?"

"Steve," Marianne said. "Don't tell Steve what I did. I don't want him to know that I could be like that."

"Come on, Marianne! So you went through his wallet. It's not so terrible."

Marianne shook her head, her eyes on her coffee cup. "I went through his wallet, his pockets, his briefcase ... I even listened in on his phone calls sometimes, not that there were many. I was sure he was seeing someone, and I was like a crazy woman, I really was." The dam had burst, and Kate was smart enough to keep quiet and listen. "I was half out of my mind," Marianne continued wretchedly. "I'd actually talked to a divorce lawyer, months before the disappearances started. I mean, it's not as if I really believed the marriage had a future. But to lose him to another woman! That seemed to say that he was capable of maintaining a relationship with someone else but not with me, his wife. It wasn't fair! Not after everything I'd been through with him. I had to know. I had to!"

"So you spied on him. Don't be embarrassed," Kate told her firmly. "It was a perfectly natural thing to do. I understand how you felt."

"No, you don't. It was all I thought about. I checked his pockets every night. I looked in his briefcase. I even sneaked into his office once, and looked through his desk drawers. Isn't that nuts?" Marianne had begun to sob softly. "I did all that, and I didn't even love him anymore!"

"It's okay," Kate told her. "It's over."

"No, it's not! That's the point! It's not over! And when you tell Steve, he'll think I'm—"

"First of all, I have no intention of telling Steve. Secondly, even if I did, I'm sure he'd understand. He's on your side, Marianne!"

"Promise you won't tell him!"

"I already said I wouldn't."

Marianne looked up at Kate and seemed to find reassurance in her eyes. She pulled a tissue from her handbag and dabbed at her nose. "You know the really stupid thing?" Kate smiled and shook her head. "I never even had the nerve to ask him about what I found."

Kate felt her pulse quicken. "What did you find?" she asked softly. "Marianne, you must tell me what you know. We'll think of a way to present it to Steve so he'll never know how you found it out. but you must tell me right now."

Marianne sighed. "Receipts," she said. "From motels."

Kate slumped back, disappointed. So Marianne had been right after all; Tucker had been seeing another woman. Mystery solved.

"And he didn't just have one woman," Marianne was saying. "He had them all over."

"What?"

"There were receipts from Georgia, from Florida, from Louisiana . . ."

"That's great!" Kate exclaimed. "That's wonderful!"

"Oh, yeah, safety in numbers. I feel so much better."

"No, Marianne. It means there wasn't any woman at all! Look, did you find any receipts from New York? Or Connecticut? Or New Jersey? Anywhere nearby?"

"No . . . I don't think so. We can check them."

"Check them? You mean, you kept them? Marianne, you're wonderful! Now listen: if Tucker was catting around, why would he go to Florida or Georgia to do it? Why not closer to home? It doesn't make sense."

"Well, maybe he met a woman from Florida. You know, at the lab, or a convention or something . . ."

"*And* a woman from Georgia? *And* a woman from Louisiana? Forget it! Tucker was obsessed all right, but it wasn't with women. It was with his work, and you know that better than anyone."

"So all my spying was for nothing," Marianne said. "I feel like such an idiot!"

But Kate shook her head impatiently. "Those receipts are pure gold! They'll tell us where Tucker disappeared to before. If we check out those places, we might get a lead on what happened to Tucker last May." And maybe what happened to Genelife, too, she thought.

"But what will we tell Steve?"

Jesus, such a to-do over some pieces of paper! "We'll tell him we went back to the apartment this morning and did a thorough search, and you found them shoved in the back of a drawer. If it'll make you feel any better, we can tell him *I* found them, okay?"

"Okay." Marianne smiled tremulously. "I feel much better, Kate. I wanted to tell someone, but I was afraid you and Steve would think I was an awful person."

"I could never think that. And neither could Steve. He thinks the world of you."

"I know. That's why I was afraid to disappoint him. Anyhow, thanks for listening. I feel like I've found a new friend."

"You have," Kate told her with a smile. "And so have I. Now let's go get those receipts."

The shiny aluminum mail cart rattled its way down the carpeted hallway, pausing briefly here and there while the shirt-sleeved young man identified by his corporate badge as a Mail Person ("mailboy" having been declared a no-no by Personnel on counts of both gender and age) distributed the morning's take. The stop at Jenny's desk was longer; Michael Nolan received a lot of mail. Then, emptier and lighter, the cart continued on its appointed rounds, leaving Jenny with a jumble of letters, business magazines, interoffice envelopes, and manila mailers in a variety of colors and sizes.

She sorted through the pile, opening some and leaving others sealed, and attempting to prioritize things. Then she gathered it all up, knocked softly at Nolan's door, and deposited it on the appropriate corner of his desk.

Nolan, deep in a report, merely nodded. "More coffee?" He shook his head without looking up, and she left as quietly as she had entered.

Another few minutes and he'd finished the document and initialed the pass-along list clipped to the top. Chucking it into his out box, he leaned forward and turned his attention to the 11:00 A.M. mail drop. Four minutes later, a shout of rage brought Jenny running.

"Get me MacAllister!" Nolan snarled. "Now!" Jenny rushed to comply. In moments, one of his phone buttons was blinking and Jenny's voice informed him via the intercom that Mac awaited his pleasure on line two.

"What the hell is this?" Nolan demanded, waving the papers he'd just extracted from a large manila envelope bearing the MacAllister Agency label.

"What the hell is *what*?" Mac replied evenly.

"This stuff you sent me," Nolan barked. "These damn

research tabulations. I thought we'd settled all that. I thought I told you—"

"You told me not to concern myself with them, yes," Mac agreed as pleasantly as he could manage. "You also said you hadn't actually seen them. Now that you have, my hands are clean."

"And who the fuck are you, Pontius Pilate? 'My hands are clean.' " Nolan breathed deeply several times. Mac remained silent. "Look, I need a strong, positive team working with me. *With* me, not against me. If you don't believe in the product, you shouldn't be advertising it."

He's absolutely right, Mac thought. He opened his mouth to speak. Then he thought of his secretary, and Dave's secretary, and the studio people, and the copywriters, and the art directors, and all the others who'd go down with the MacAllister ship. He closed it again.

"You still there?" Nolan growled.

Mac sighed. "I'm still here," he said.

"Despite your negative attitude," Nolan told him sternly, "your people have done a helluva job for us. And that's the only reason I'm prepared to give your agency one last chance. But this is it. Shape up or ship out. Understand me?"

"Yes, I understand. But I just can't understand why you—"

"You weren't listening! I said, drop it!"

I'd like to drop your account, Mac thought angrily. Drop it right in the sewer where it belongs, and you along with it. "Consider it dropped," he said quietly. He who fights and runs away lives to fight another day, he told himself. Discretion is the better part of valor. What goes around, comes around. Right. Sure.

"Good. I'm sure Kate Martin will be very glad to hear it." Divide and conquer, Nolan thought. Best motto ever invented.

"Kate? Why?"

"You're confusing the hell out of her with your constant pressure, egging her on all the time. I think she'd be glad to work with a different agency, one which is more supportive—"

Yeah. Like Imagemakers and that fucking Richard Day. "Michael, I have not been pressuring—"

"Don't try to con me," Nolan told him. "I know all about

it. Now. Do we understand each other? Or do I have to look for a new advertising agency?"

You won't have to look very far, Mac thought. Day's probably sitting in Kate's office right now. "We understand each other," he said.

"Good. Don't let me hear any more of this, or I'll be on the phone to your competition, make no mistake about that!" Nolan disconnected abruptly.

Mac slowly lowered the receiver, feeling like scum. But what should I have done? he asked himself. Resigned the account and put two hundred people out of work? We're damned lucky Nolan didn't fire us.

He got up and wandered over to the window and looked out on Third Avenue. Just what the hell was he supposed to do? Dump Genelife and watch the agency go under, taking some two hundred people with it, people he liked and respected and valued? Keep the account and possibly risk encouraging a lot more than two hundred people to gamble with their health, maybe even their lives?

Whatever he decided, he was going to end up hurting people.

If only Kate would assure him Genelife was safe. Or assure him it wasn't. How the fuck was he supposed to make an informed decision without information? He banged his fist on the windowsill in frustration. It was all so damned unfair!

He wandered back to his desk and tossed a few pencils at the ceiling, but his heart wasn't in it. Three more weeks, he temporized. Just three more weeks. The meeting with General Foods was three weeks away. GF had some loose business; maybe they'd give MacAllister a piece of it. Then he could afford to tell Nolan to go screw himself.

Behind the wheel of the rented green Ford, the folder of receipts locked in the trunk, Kate was thinking hard. What did Georgia, Louisiana, and Florida have in common? And what connection could they have with Randall Webber and Genelife? Maybe Steve would have some ideas; they'd arranged to talk again by phone that evening. In any event, one of them would have to check out the small towns listed on Marianne's receipts immediately.

Having made this trip so often during the past year, Kate drove automatically, her mind on other things. It was raining now, a fine light mist, but she barely noticed. Georgia. Louisiana. Florida. She'd been surprised and a little disappointed at the destinations listed on Marianne's receipts. Switzerland would have indicated that Tucker had had some contact with Chemstra; Puerto Rico would have suggested involvement with the manufacturing plant. But Louisiana? Florida? Randall Webber didn't have any facilities there.

Pondering this puzzle, Kate suddenly realized she'd overshot the Randall Webber entrance. Damn! Where could she turn around? The county road was heavily traveled, with few side crossings; a solid double line ran down the center of the black macadam. She drove for nearly a mile before spotting a small turnoff up ahead on the right.

She slowed and turned onto the narrow paved road. The main road had no shoulder along this stretch, so she'd need to turn right around again and approach it at a right angle, turning left onto it to get back to Randall Webber. She drove slowly along the tree-lined turnoff for fifty yards or so, looking for a place wide enough to make a U-turn. As she rounded a small curve, she was surprised to feel the asphalt turn to dirt beneath her wheels. Probably a construction road, she thought. There was always some building going on in the area. No doubt the road would soon dead end at a clearing and a half-built house. But as she continued along it, the muddy road began to narrow. Damn! Impossible to turn around now. She had two choices: back up the half mile she'd come or go forward. With a certain amount of trepidation, she went forward.

It was so well hidden by the surrounding trees, she nearly drove right into the steel barrier. She pulled up sharply and looked around. Beyond the metal gate, the dirt road continued into the woods. Barbed wire was strung among the trees along each side of the barrier.

That's that, Kate thought despondently, putting the gearshift into reverse. Strange place for a barrier, though. Suddenly a flutter of color on the side of the road caught her eye. A bright red candy wrapper.

She stopped short, shoved the gearshift forward into park, and pulled up the hand brake. She found she was trembling. She pictured the guard with the mirrored sunglasses tossing a red candy wrapper into the ditch six days before. She pictured him chewing on a red-wrapped candy bar as he watched her at the phone on Lexington Avenue.

Calm down, she told herself. Anyone could have dropped the wrapper. And yet, if it actually had been the guard, the significance was unmistakable.

She tried to visualize the Randall Webber property in respect to the distance and direction she'd driven to get here. Could this unmarked road be some sort of back entrance? If it was, that would explain why no one at Randall Webber knew anything about the truck depot. But it also raised more questions than it answered. A service road such as this seemed to be would only make sense if Randall Webber were in the business of trucking things in and out all the time. But they weren't. Furthermore, she herself had seen UPS and Federal Express trucks drive right up to the front of the executive building to make their deliveries, so there was obviously no dictum against trucks using the front entrance.

Therefore, why this hidden, unmarked road? And why a steel barrier and barbed wire? Leaving the engine running, Kate got out of the car and went to the gate. A metal post with a slot in the top was positioned about six feet in front of the barrier on the driver's side; a corresponding post stood on the other side of the gate. She went back to the car and dug out her passcard. She'd used it not only to get into the R&D building, but also to enter the executive building through the rear door. If it opened two doors, it might open more. She put the car in gear and moved slowly up to the post. Gingerly, she pushed the card down into the slot. Nothing happened, and Kate shrugged and leaned out to retrieve her card from the post. When she looked up again, the barrier was silently swinging open. Taking a deep breath, she drove through the gate, which immediately clanged shut behind her.

Why did you do that? she asked herself. You must be crazy! Well, at least she was driving a rental car; the guard who'd been following her had only seen the Toyota. If she were stopped, she could show her passcard and pretend she used the rear entrance all the time. Or she could simply hit the gas and head for the executive building. At any rate, being in a vehicle instead of on foot made her feel a little safer.

The road descended through the woods in a series of wet

curves, then broadened out; a short distance ahead, she could see the clearing and an edge of the cinder-block depot. She stopped and turned the car around so it was facing back in the direction of the steel gate. Then she tucked it into the trees at the edge of the widened road and turned off the ignition. Hoping she was sufficiently far from the clearing for the trees to have muffled the sound of her arrival, she sat for a few moments and listened. Sounds of activity filtered through the woods. Cautiously, she got out of the car and pulled her old army-green raincoat from the back seat. She shrugged it on, pulling the hood over her head, then softly closed the front and rear doors. Stepping onto the wet pine needles that carpeted the woods, she began to work her way through the trees in the direction of the clearing.

The sounds were louder now; banging, thumping, cursing, laughing. She pressed forward until she was no more than ten feet from the perimeter of the clearing, her eyes widening in surprise. No fewer than six large refrigerated trucks were clustered around the squat gray building. Men were unloading cartons, working fast. The cold boxes steamed in the warm, humid air.

Kate moved closer; what was inside the boxes? All she could see from where she stood was that each bore a bright blue label. Now a yellow forklift appeared from around the corner of the building, and the men began loading the cartons onto it. The forklift raised its filled platform and trundled off, presumably to deposit its load inside the building, while the men pulled still more cartons out of the trucks' cold innards.

She circled around through the woods to the other side of the clearing. From here it seemed as if one side of the depot had been somehow carved away, but on closer inspection she realized that a whole section, painted to look like cinder block, had been raised and partially drawn up into the building on huge hydraulic rollers. If she hadn't seen it, she'd never have realized that this side of the depot wasn't as solid as the rest. The forklift, empty now, moved slowly out of the dimly lit interior and back toward the trucks.

God, how I'd love a peek inside one of those cartons, Kate thought. But there was nothing she could do about it, not with this crowd. She began to back away, her eyes still fixed on the yawning interior of the depot. How can I get inside? she wondered. Somehow she doubted that her passcard would work here. She was deep in thought when her left shoulder blade connected with something metallic and hard, and she only half stifled a cry of pain.

Expecting the worst, she turned to face her captor. But instead of a man with a large gun, she found herself staring into the metallic hood ornament of a truck. At least it looked like a truck. It was hard to tell at first, because it was covered with leafy branches. She walked around to the side of the camouflaged vehicle; behind it, similarly bedecked, were two more. She peered between the vegetation at each in turn. Any identification the trucks might once have carried on their doors or sides had been painted over. Like the truck that had stopped for her on the dirt road last week, they were painted a flat, solid blue.

She went around to the back of the first truck and pushed aside the foliage to reveal the license plate, which proved, disappointingly, to be from Connecticut. Georgia, say, would have been a lot more helpful, Kate reflected. Water dripped from the brim of her hood; it was raining harder now. She was heading for the plate of the second truck when the sudden loud revving of a diesel engine made her jump. Apparently the refrigerated trucks had finished unloading; any minute, they'd be heading down the dirt road on which her car was parked.

Turning again toward the clearing to get her bearings, she whirled around and tore through the woods on an angle, hoping to bisect the road just above the green Ford. Panting with fear, she overshot the car by nearly fifty yards. Her shoes, already sodden, kicked up brown water as she ran to the mud-spattered vehicle through the pooling rain, yanked open the door, fell inside, and twisted the ignition key. The engine sprang to life, and flooring the accelerator, she raced out of the protection of the overhanging trees and along the rising, twisting road toward the steel gate. She shoved her passcard into the metal post, praying it worked as well leaving as arriving. It did. She barreled along the half mile to the main road, then paused, waiting for a break in the traffic stream. Come on! Come on! She saw an opportunity and took it, charging across the eastbound lane of traffic and swinging onto the westbound side.

Three miles along, she again crossed the traffic stream and shot up the entrance road to Randall Webber.

A scant five minutes later, a fleet of large refrigerated trucks, belching black diesel smoke and going too fast for the road conditions, thundered past the Randall Webber entrance and disappeared toward the west.

Chapter 26

April 17

Kate was awakened by a loud, unfamiliar ringing. Instinctively she reached out for the tennis ball alarm clock, but her fingers closed on air. Still half-asleep, she patted the side table for a few seconds. Where was the damn thing? Then, eyes open at last, she sat up and looked around. The ringing stopped, hiccuped, and started up again, but the clock was nowhere to be seen. She got out of bed and shuffled over to the dresser where her wristwatch lay. Damn car alarms, she thought, then realized with a start that the noise was inside, not outside; it was coming from the hallway. The building intercom! But who could be here at this hour? Steve wasn't expected until—Kate glanced at the wristwatch and saw with shock that it was nearly nine. She hurried to the intercom and instructed the doorman to admit Steve, then hurried to the bathroom to splash some water on her face and brush her teeth. She inspected herself critically in the mirror as she quickly ran a brush through her hair. Not great, but it would have to do. Where in God's name was that alarm clock?

Her doorbell rang and as she went to answer it, she spied Cheerio curled up in the living room, chewing on something that looked suspiciously like a tennis ball. The dog eyed her guiltily.

"And so you should be!" she told her sternly, opening the door to admit Steve.

"So you should be what?" he asked, taking her in his arms. "You look beautiful in the morning."

"Cheerio ate my alarm clock," Kate said. "You look beautiful, too."

His face was cool from the morning air, but his mouth was warm as he kissed her. He began to caress her with his lips, tenderly tasting her face, her hair, her neck, her breasts. It had only been a few days, but he'd missed her with a deep visceral need he'd never felt before. Kate moaned with pleasure as she unbuttoned his shirt, then pressed herself against his naked chest, inhaling the smell of his skin. She'd never felt this way with Jon, although she'd truly believed she'd love him when she'd married him. The depth of her feelings for Steve was entirely new to her, and a source of continual wonder. Kissing and touching, they stumbled to the bedroom and fell upon the bed, and upon each other.

Sometime later, a muffled yet insistent ringing brought them out of the daze of satiety into which they'd eventually fallen. Instinctively, Kate's hand reached across Steve to the night table and closed upon a disgustingly soggy, spongy, misshapen object.

"Yechhh!" It fell from her hand onto Steve's back. Startled by the feel of the cold, wet object, he jerked to one side. "What the hell was that?" he exclaimed.

"I believe it was an ex-alarm clock," Kate told him as the well-gnawed orb rolled onto the floor beside the bed, coughed twice, and expired. Cheerio quickly scooped it up in her mouth and deposited it carefully back on the night table.

"Good dog," Steve said.

" 'Good dog' my ass! Look what she's done to my clock!"

"Speaking of your ass ..."

"Actually, it was the clock we were speaking of." Kate smiled.

"Screw the clock," Steve told her. "And while we're on the subject ..." He rolled over and took her in his arms again.

"Oh, talk, talk, talk!" Kate teased. "Is that all you ever do?"

"No, I can also do this," Steve said. "If you care for that sort of thing."

"Oh, I do."

"And this."

"Mmmm ..."

"And this ..."

Cheerio stood by the bed and watched them for a few minutes. I suppose breakfast would be out of the question, she thought, and wandered away to the living room.

Eventually the two humans emerged dewy-eyed and hungry, and Cheerio padded after them into the kitchen, seated herself in front of her bowl, and looked up at Kate hopefully.

"Poor old thing!" Kate exclaimed, the fate of her clock now forgotten. She spooned a hefty helping of Chow-Down into Cheerio's plate and washed out and refilled her water bowl. Then she squeezed some of the oranges she'd bought while hiding in the Korean produce store, and made coffee, while Steve toasted bread and fried eggs. Over breakfast, Kate showed him the receipts Marianne had given her. "Georgia, Louisiana, Florida. Any ideas?"

"Not really. I mean, we don't exactly know what we're looking for. But I checked these names in the atlas yesterday when you called me. They're all small towns in rural areas. Anything unusual will have been noticed and remembered."

"Where will you start?"

"Louisiana. I've booked myself on a one-thirty flight today."

Kate glanced at her watch; it was nearly eleven. She sighed. "I know it was my idea, but I wish you didn't have to leave again so soon."

"Me, too. But you're right to want to move on this fast. And even professors with a reputation for erratic timetables need to teach a class now and then." Steve swallowed the last of his orange juice. "I wish you were coming with me."

"So do I. But I have to be a good little medical consultant, at least for a while, and keep the lines of information open." Kate sighed. "I remember my first day at Randall Webber. I was so eager, so happy!"

Steve smiled. "Well, you know what they say about the two happiest days of any job."

"No, what?"

"They're the day you start and the day you quit."

"Well, I've had the first, and I'm ready for the second, even if it turns out that Genelife is safe after all."

"Do you really believe that's possible?"

Kate thought for a moment. "As a scientist, I'm supposed to keep an open mind until all the evidence is in. But in my gut . . . no, I don't believe it's safe."

"All the more reason for me to head south right away.

The sooner we can figure this thing out, the sooner you can make some serious decisions." He ate a forkful of fried egg. "Have you thought any more about what you're going to do when you leave Randall Webber?" He spoke casually, but his stomach muscles tightened. Don't say you've applied for a job in Seattle, he prayed.

"No, not really. I'm pretty sure New York General will take me back, but ..." Kate trailed off. She hadn't been happy at New York General before; why should she think she'd be happy there now? She sipped her coffee glumly. It was so depressing to think about having to call her parents and tell them that once again she had changed her mind about her future.

Steve reached over and touched her face. "Boston is a nice place to work," he said with a smile. "We have hospitals and clinics and doctors in private practice ... Or you could get involved with Doctors Without Borders. Ever hear of them?" Kate nodded; she'd read about the group, founded in France, which sent professional medical personnel into emergency situations all over the world. "I ran into a few of them several years ago in Africa. Interesting people."

"It's my kind of medicine, all right," Kate agreed thoughtfully. "And a lot more meaningful work than I'm doing now."

"More meaningful than what you signed on for originally. But getting the real scoop on Genelife is meaningful, too, and big time. How many millions of people are using the stuff?"

"Too many," Kate said. She got up and refilled Steve's coffee cup and her own. "Steve, I saw something really weird yesterday."

"At the office, you mean?"

"Well, nearby. Remember that cinder-block building I told you about, the one hidden away in the back of the company property?"

"Where that guard tried to ... God, Kate, don't tell me you went back there!"

She waved away his objection. "I was thinking about the receipts and stuff and I missed the main entrance, and by accident I found a little road that led back into the complex. There was a steel gate, but my passcard opened it. Anyway, I saw a bunch of guys unloading refrigerated cartons, lots and lots of them, and moving them inside the cinder-block building."

Steve stared at her, his expression half fearful, half admiring. "You saw them? Did they see you?"

"No, I stayed back in the trees. Then I found some other trucks, all covered over with branches. Now, this is the really weird part. From where I was standing, I could see that each carton had a bright blue label or sticker or something. When I got back to the office, I checked. Guess who uses a bright blue label?"

"I have no idea."

"Chemstra!" Kate proclaimed triumphantly. "Now why is Chemstra shipping refrigerated cartons to Randall Webber in Connecticut, when all our manufacturing is done in Puerto Rico?"

"I give up. Why?"

"I have no idea! Steve, we have *got* to get inside that building!"

"The operative word there is 'we,' " Steve said firmly. "As soon as I get back, we'll—"

"I'm not sure we can afford to wait. Whatever's happening there is happening now."

"I'll cancel my flight."

"No, you mustn't! The Chemstra shipment is only one part of the puzzle. We need to find Tucker, too. Or at least figure out what happened to him, and why. Anyhow, we agreed that you'd do the legwork and I'd burrow from within." She smiled at him. "It'll be okay. More coffee?" But Steve only shook his head and looked worried. "Hey, I'm a company executive. Technically, I have the right to be anywhere in the complex."

"Try explaining that to the guy in the shades, the next time he stops you."

Kate shivered. She hadn't told Steve that the guard had been following her; it would only upset him, she reasoned, and possibly prevent him from going south to check out the receipts. And it was vital that he check them out as soon as possible. She sipped her coffee, reluctant to lie to Steve about her intentions regarding the depot, and unwilling to let him make her decisions, even out of love.

Steve studied her wordlessly. The wash of morning sun illuminated the fine laugh lines around her warm, intelligent eyes, and picked out three or four strands of gray in the luxuriant fullness of her copper hair. In the cold light of day, she looked every one of her nearly thirty-five years, and very beautiful indeed. He reached out a finger and traced the outline of her strong, determined mouth. Their eyes met and her gaze went deep; he felt a stiffening in his groin. She was one of the sexiest women he'd ever met, and one of the strongest.

"I know what you're thinking," he said slowly. "And you're right. You have to be free to make your own decisions. If you feel it necessary to do something that could be dangerous, I have no right to try and stop you, even though I might want to." He reached over and took her hand. "I trust your instincts and your brain, and I should be encouraging you, not getting in your way, encumbering you with emotional pressure." He paused. "But I can say 'Be careful.'"

Kate nodded. "I will," she said.

"We haven't known each other very long, but ... you mean a lot to me, Kate."

"And you to me."

"I don't want to lose you."

Kate smiled. "I'm not going anywhere."

The shrilling of the telephone made them jump. Kate rose and picked up the extension that hung on the kitchen wall. "Kate Martin."

"Kate, it's Jenny. Mr. Nolan's looking for you. He's furious!"

"But I told you I was taking a personal day today. Didn't you give him my message?"

"Yes, of course I did. But he says you needed his permission for that."

"His permission?" Kate exclaimed. The gall of the man! "What am I, a child?"

"Listen, don't shoot the messenger, okay? Just get in here right away. The sooner the better."

"Tell him I'm on my way," Kate said grumpily, and disconnected. His permission indeed! "Nolan's on the warpath about something," she told Steve. "I need to go to the office."

"Maybe he's talked to Butler."

"Very possibly, although I'd like to see him make a case against one of the company's medical consultants talking to the other one." She began stacking their dirty dishes in the sink.

"I'll do that," Steve told her. "You'd better get going. Although you might want to put on a few clothes, first."

"Good idea."

"On the other hand, maybe you should take a few off, instead ..." He went and put his arms around her from behind, cupping her breasts in his hands. "Nolan's waited this long; let him wait a little longer."

Too close for comfort, Nolan thought angrily. Much, much too close. How had he allowed it to happen? He'd been so careful. He'd retired Butler with a golden handshake, and replaced him with a too young doctor with no corperate experience whom he'd dazzled with a fancy office and a large salary. Hell, he'd even made her a television star! So why wasn't she sticking to lunches with the ad agency, tickets to the ballet, and clothes from Bergdorf's, instead of stirring up Lim and Butler with embarrassing questions about Chemstra and Genelife? Mac was behind it, obviously. And now there was someone else helping her, a mystery man who apparently lived in a town house on East Sixty-fourth Street, or so Ronnie had reported.

Well, it couldn't be allowed to continue. He still had hopes of keeping Mac dangling until after the media coverage that the pharmaceutical conference and the advertising awards dinner would bring. Cutting the MacAllister Agency loose after that wouldn't be so noticeable. But he'd have to get rid of Kate right now. He couldn't afford to have her snooping around, especially with the Chemstra shipment still on the premises. Ronnie had put a scare into her last week, but what if she wandered back that way again? No, he couldn't risk it.

His intercom buzzed. "Yes?"

"Dr. Martin has arrived," Jenny told him.

"She's in her office? Well, tell her to get—"

"Uh, she's standing right here by my desk, Mr. Nolan. Oh, and I have your travel documents for the conference. They switched you to the seven-fifteen flight tonight as you requested, and there'll be a car to meet you at the Scottsdale Airport—"

"Later!" he ordered. "Send Martin in."

Kate entered the office with a feeling of foreboding.

Jenny had avoided her eye, and others nearby seemed embarrassed. Still, she thought, how bad can it be? He might bawl her out, but he certainly wouldn't fire her; he still needed a medical consultant. But his first words were not reassuring.

"You're not going to like what I have to say," Nolan told her sternly. "But you can't say you weren't warned."

"May I sit down?" Kate asked stiffly. She'd be damned if she'd stand there in front of his desk while he scolded her like a naughty child. Without waiting for his answer, she seated herself on the leather sofa across the room. You want to talk, you come to me, she thought angrily.

Nolan hesitated, then walked around his desk and sat down in the wing chair to the right of the sofa. She's got gumption, he reflected. Which is precisely the trouble.

They stared at each other for a moment, Nolan with repressed fury, Kate with a blandness that fueled his anger. At last he spoke. "You have been guilty of grossly unprofessional behavior," he said. "Misplaced loyalties. Rumor-mongering. Such behavior cannot, and will not, be tolerated."

"Just what behavior do you mean, Michael?" Kate replied. Her heart was pounding, but her manner was cool and detached.

"You know damned well what I—"

"If you're referring to my conversations with Jerry Lim, they are well within the scope of my job. As was my conversation with Nicholas Butler."

"Bullshit! You're looking for ways to validate MacAllister's faulty research results, and sabotage my business, although I can't understand why. You and Mac are in it together! I don't know what there is between you, maybe you're sleeping with him, but—"

"How dare you?" Kate was on her feet at once. "Talk about unprofessional behavior!"

"Well, I can't think of any other reason you'd support him against the company that pays your salary!"

"I'm trying to support Randall Webber, Michael, but you won't let me! If there really is a problem with Genelife, and we don't find it and correct it, we'll kill this company! Don't you understand?"

I understand better than you do, he thought. "Fine words," he said instead. "Everything you're doing is for the good of the company, is it? Including upsetting Jerry Lim so much he asks for a transfer? And snooping around in the woods last week, when you were supposed to be reviewing those press releases?"

Kate gasped. There were only two ways he could have learned about the incident near the truck depot: from Freda or from the guard who had stopped her. Freda might have mentioned the incident to Personnel, she thought quickly, but she'd never have gone straight to Nolan. Most people in the company were rather afraid of him. And if the personnel director had felt it necessary to go to Michael, she'd have first asked Kate about the incident.

No, it must have been the guard. The same guard who'd been following her ever since. Not for her body, as she'd feared, but for money. Nolan's money. The man in the brown leather jacket wasn't a nutcase who'd wangled her address from the personnel office, but a hireling of Michael's. She found this new prospect equally chilling.

"I took a break and went for a walk, Michael, that's all. Why should that upset you?" She paused. "Is there something going on back there you don't want me to know about?"

Nolan went red in the face. "That's exactly what I mean!" he exclaimed hotly. "Innuendos! Nasty little suggestions! One of our guards offers you a perfectly innocent ride back to your office and you go running off through the woods like the hounds of hell are after you, scaring the poor man half to death. And now you have the nerve to accuse me of trying to prevent you from finding out God knows what!" What had she seen? he wondered, then reminded himself that the Chemstra shipment had only arrived the day before. Nothing had been going on last week. "It's no good, Kate. It's just no good."

Kate took a deep breath, aware she'd gone too far. "Michael, I'm sorry. But everything I've done, I've done for you, for Randall Webber, for Genelife. You hired a doctor, and that's what you got, a medical professional trained to care about other human beings." Don't let him fire me, she prayed. I need to keep a toehold here. There's so much more I need to find out. "If I've overstepped the line, I'm sorry. Just tell me what you—"

But Nolan wasn't buying it. "We've already had that

song, Kate," he said. He rose and stood over her. "Your identification badge and passcard, please."

Shit! "I left in a hurry this morning," she said at once. "I don't have them with me."

Nolan reached for the handbag she'd put down next to her. Pulling open the zipper, he upended it. Kate stared aghast as makeup, wallet, hairbrush, a silver pen, breath mints, all tumbled onto the sofa cushion. "You have no right—" she spluttered, but Nolan ignored her as he stuck his hand inside the empty purse, feeling around to see if anything had been left within, then tossed the bag back onto the sofa.

"Let's have your jacket," he demanded.

"You bastard!" But she shrugged out of it and handed it over, thankful that she'd slipped the half-forgotten badge and passcard into her trouser pockets as she'd left the apartment. If he tries to search me, I'll scream rape, she decided coldly.

Seeing the set of her jaw, Nolan rejected the idea of a body search. Instead he threw the jacket back at her, fixing her with a baleful eye. "Your passcard will be deactivated," he said.

Fat chance, Kate thought. Without the card itself, the only way they could lock her out would be to reset all the locks and issue new cards to every employee in the place. "I understand," she told him.

"And your final paycheck will be held until you return both the passcard and the badge."

"Why do you want the passcard if you're planning to— uh, right. I'll bring them in tomorrow."

"You will not bring them in tomorrow or any other day. You will mail them to me, and I will then have Personnel mail you your check. You are no longer allowed on the company grounds. If I see you anywhere in the complex, I'll have you arrested!"

"Come on, Michael. So you fired me. Okay, fine. But threatening me with arrest . . . isn't that a little dramatic?"

Nolan started to reply, then thought better of it. "I am through bandying words with you, Dr. Martin," he said. "I will now call a guard and have you escorted to your car."

"The same guard you've had following me for the past few days?" Kate asked innocently. "About five-ten, dark hair, leather jacket . . . ?"

For a moment Nolan seemed about to choke. "More innuendos, Kate?" he managed at last. "More accusations? You never stop, do you?"

Kate decided she too was through bandying words. "If you're serious about having me escorted off the premises, your ... henchman will find me in my office, packing my stuff. With or without him, I'll be out of here in twenty minutes, and believe me, it won't be a second too soon." She turned on her heel and marched to the door, shoving it open so it banged against the outside wall.

Back in her office, her bravado fading, she tried to formulate her next move. Obviously Nolan wouldn't let her leave with any reports or documents. She'd have to find a way to get them out later or through someone else. Jerry, perhaps, if he was still around.

A light knock on her half-closed door swung her around, ready for a fight, but it was only Jenny, holding out a Saks shopping bag. "I'm sorry," Jenny said. "I thought maybe you could use this."

Kate smiled and took the bag. "I appreciate it."

Jenny looked furtively up and down the hall. "We'll miss you," she whispered.

"Don't tell Michael that. He'll fire you, too."

Jenny gave her a weak half smile and retreated back down the corridor.

Kate quickly went through the drawers of her desk, tossing personal items into the bag and thinking furiously.

It has to be tonight, she decided. Before everyone hears that I've been canned. People over here probably know already, but it'll take some time for the news to filter over to R&D and beyond. She took her beige folding umbrella from the closet and threw it into the shopping bag.

She still had her badge and her passcard. If anyone stopped her, she could claim that her being fired was just an unfounded rumor. She might get away with it tonight, but by tomorrow, the word would be out. Tomorrow ... what were those travel arrangements she'd overheard Jenny reciting? Of course, the yearly pharmaceutical conference in Scottsdale. The conference brochure had passed her desk back in March, and she'd considered going herself. Then she'd seen Mac's research report and changed her mind. Whatever might be going on at the depot right now, Nolan wouldn't be able to resist such a prestigious, media-heavy

gathering, especially with his Genelife presentation a fea-
tured event. Not that she deluded herself that his three-day
absence would make it any easier for her to get access to
Randall Webber; Nolan would be sure to leave specific orders about her.

With a fast look around to make sure there was nothing
she'd missed, she grabbed the shopping bag and her purse
and strode out into the corridor. Barely five minutes had
passed since she'd left Nolan's office. Several people
watched her go, and a few smiled tentatively, but no one
said anything. She waved jauntily to the receptionist who
gave her a big smile and a nod—apparently, she hadn't
heard yet—and walked quickly to the green rental car.
Slinging the shopping bag into the back seat, she got in and
turned the key. She looked over toward the executive building and around the parking lot, but she didn't spot the
guard. Well, no doubt the bastard was somewhere nearby.

Fired for doing my job, she thought. That's a new one.
She gunned the engine and roared out of the parking lot.

It was still early, not yet two o'clock. She didn't want to
approach the cinder-block depot before dusk, so she had
plenty of time. The first thing she'd do would be to trade
in the car for something that looked a lot different.

She was very angry, and her anger gave her strength.
Millions of people were using a drug that Kate was now
certain would do them harm. A drug she herself had promoted and recommended. You screwed me, Michael Nolan,
she thought. You brought me in there as a rubber stamp,
not a scientist; a Barbie doll you could put on television to
help you sell a product that shouldn't be on the market in
the first place. You demeaned me and my profession.

She checked her rearview mirror as she turned onto the
feeder road. No one. Maybe her quick departure had
caught them unprepared.

You screwed me, Michael, she thought. Now it's my turn.

Chapter 27

The first-class lounge was starting to fill up, but Nicholas Butler had arrived early as instructed and commandeered the corner seating area farthest from the door. Nolan had requested privacy. Now he sat, a vodka and tonic on the low table in front of him, reading a medical journal and looking up each time the door buzzer sounded.

Nolan arrived precisely at six-thirty as agreed, and Butler rose from his seat and waved to him. Michael nodded and, stashing his carryon suitcase in the luggage area across from the reception desk, presented his ticket to the attendant for processing, then walked the length of the room to where Butler stood. Outside the floor-to-ceiling window, a silver 727 rose silently into the calm evening air.

"I appreciate your coming out here, Nick," Nolan told him, checking his watch. "I didn't want to do this on the phone, and I'm really pressed for time."

"No problem," Butler assured him. With the stretch limo Nolan had sent to fetch him here and drive him back to the city, champagne included, it had indeed been no problem. Once again, he reflected on Michael's thoughtfulness and generosity.

Nolan smiled. "That's what I like about you, Nick," he said. "You're always so cooperative. A man I can count on."

Butler beamed at the compliment. "High praise, coming from you," he replied graciously.

Nolan studied him. "You know, I've been thinking maybe you retired too soon."

"Oh?"

"Yes. I've been missing your ... unique perspective. After all, you bring years of valuable experience to the table. Hard-won experience."

Butler was puzzled. He hadn't been ready to retire last

year, but Nolan had made him an offer he couldn't refuse. Was Michael going to give him his job back? He sincerely hoped not; he'd gotten used to a slower pace and golf on Tuesdays. Yet how could he refuse Michael?

A steward came over and Nolan ordered coffee, then waved him away, "How would you feel about getting into harness again?"

Shit, Butler thought. "I'm not sure I understand you, Michael. You already have a medical consultant, that nice Dr. Martin. Such a charming woman, and genuinely interested in the—"

"To tell you the truth, I'm not really happy with Dr. Martin. I haven't been for some time."

"You'll recall that I warned you she lacked experience," Butler said quickly. "She came across very well in those television pieces, but from a professional point of view, she isn't really seasoned. I did tell you that."

"I should have listened," Nolan said, his voice dripping with regret. "You were right and I was wrong." He shook his head. "I had to let her go today."

"You did? That was fast!"

"Well, I knew I could count on you, Nick. That made the decision easier." Nolan's eyes bored into Butler's. "I can count on you, can't I?"

"Oh, of course! Of course! Only . . ."

"Only you're rather enjoying retirement, is that it?"

Butler smiled gratefully. "Yes, yes I am. But, Michael, you know I'll do whatever you need me to."

Nolan nodded. "You're a good man, Nick. And you deserve a little fun after a lifetime of hard work. So here's what I had in mind. You come back as our temporary medical consultant, for six, eight months or so. Just until we find a permanent person. We'll pay you a hundred percent of your old salary with one year guaranteed, but we won't require you to come into the office more than, oh, say two days a week. You'll still retain your seat on the board, and the stipend that goes with it. And to sweeten the pot even further, we'll send a limo to take you to and from the office. How's that?"

"It's . . . munificent! Munificent!" Butler was babbling in gratitude. "I . . . I'm quite overwhelmed!" Ninety thousand dollars a year for a hundred working days, he thought. And a limo. He could change his golf game for that.

Getting Butler back would cost the company some twenty thousand a year more than he'd been paying Kate, Nolan reflected. Plus the limo. But it would be worth every penny.

"You'll have to brief me on the daily nitty-gritty," Butler said. "I've been out of the loop for nearly a year."

"No problem."

"And I guess I should meet the ad agency sometime."

"Oh, I don't think that will be necessary. Actually, I may be replacing them."

"Really? I thought they were doing an excellent—"

"I'll tell you all about it next week."

Butler nodded. "Whatever you say." He sipped his drink happily. Ninety thousand buckerinos. "Well, well! It'll be like old times, working with you, and Jerry Lim and the gang at R&D ..."

"Nick, you should know that I'm replacing Jerry Lim, too."

Butler stared at him. "Good God, Michael. Do you really think it's wise to make so many changes all at once?"

"That's why I need *you,* Nick," Nolan said earnestly.

"It's awfully nice of you to say that, Michael, but Jerry is our last remaining continuity with Genelife now that Tucker—"

"American flight 906, now boarding, gate number seventeen ..."

"That's me," Nolan said, rising from the sofa. "Just trust me, Nick, okay?" Somewhat bemused, Butler nodded. "I'll brief you more fully when I get back from the conference." Nolan extended his hand, and Butler stood and grasped it firmly. "Glad to have you back aboard."

"Glad to be back," Butler said. "Have a good trip."

"Thanks." Nolan turned and started toward the luggage room, but Butler's next words swung him back around again.

"Uh, Michael, I've always wondered. What ever happened to Tucker, anyway?"

Nolan stared at him for a moment, then shrugged his shoulders. "God knows," he said softly. "God only knows."

Dusk was falling, and long shadows stretched across the scrubby clearing as Kate positioned herself just inside the tree line. She'd changed into jeans and sneakers, with a light sweater under a quilted jacket, and her bright hair hidden under a dark knitted watch cap. A cool fluorescent light leaked from the small high windows and spilled from the open side of the cinder-block building where the huge slab of a door had been rolled back. The voices of several men floated out on the quiet air.

She'd left the newly rented black Oldsmobile tucked into the sparse woods bordering the back road, and hiked to the clearing; just as she'd suspected, her passcard still opened the steel barrier. Now she edged along under the cover of the trees until she was looking into the interior of the building.

The depot consisted of one large open space, with a cement floor and exposed cinder-block walls. This interior space seemed shorter than the building itself, and Kate realized that a deep storage area of some sort had been built against the back end.

A wall of cartons stretched halfway along one side. Against the opposite wall stood what appeared to be two large commercial oil drums. More boxes, lighter in color, were piled high near the entranceway, and cartons of both colors were scattered here and there on the floor. Set on the two long makeshift tables in the center of the room were more light-colored cartons bearing bright blue Chemstra stickers.

Five men were working at the tables, while a sixth was loading one of several hand trucks that stood nearby. As Kate watched, one of the men carefully peeled off a Chemstra sticker and tossed it on a pile of others beneath the table.

What the hell are they doing? she thought. I have to get closer. She glanced around the clearing again; once she left the trees, there was no cover between the woods and the building. As long as everyone was inside the depot, that wasn't a problem; she could approach from the side. But if she came around the corner of the building into the light, she'd be highly visible to anyone who happened to turn around.

The men joked, argued, and ragged each other as they worked. Two were smoking, flicking their ashes on the cement floor. Because the tables ran lengthwise down the room, the men stood sideways to the entrance. Only the hand truck man turned toward the open flap as he stacked his cartons. Perhaps when he turned away for more cartons . . . But from the side of the building, how would she know when he did?

Well, she wasn't doing any good just standing here. At least she'd be able to hear better from closer in. She circled around until she was facing the right side of the building. The sun was well below the horizon now, and it was much darker than when she'd arrived. Taking a deep breath, she ran lightly across the open clearing and flattened herself against the cinder-block wall, then edged slowly up toward the spill of light from the open roller door. At the corner of the building, she found that the bulky metal frame of the door mechanism formed a right angle with the end of the side wall, offering some twelve inches of shadowy concealment. Kate tucked herself in and listened.

Beneath the casual conversation of sports and women, Kate could hear the ripping of labels, the rutch of a knife cutting through cardboard, the soft thud of a carton . . . and a sound that she couldn't define, a series of small metallic crashes that echoed away nearly as quickly as they had started.

"Are we nearly finished?"

"Yeah, we're gettin' there. Whatsamatta, kid, can't take the pace?" General laughter.

"The boy's only sixteen, Al. Cut him some slack!"

"Slack, shit! He's getting paid the same as us."

"Yeah, and aren't *you* tired? Hell, we've been up almost forty hours straight!"

"Big deal. This part's easy. You didn't have to go get the stuff! I drove round trip in two and a half days, but you don't hear me bitching."

"What a hero!"

"Screw you!"

"Come on, guys. Cool it. We're all tired."

"So have another beer." Sound of a can top being popped.

"Beer, hell! I need some coffee."

"All gone. Want a candy bar?" Rustle of candy wrapper.

"Hey, fellas, you ever see a guy eat so much candy? Guess that makes you a candy-ass, huh, Ronnie?" General laughter. "Whoa, just kidding, man! Let go of me!" Sound of a scuffle.

"Yo, Pete, get some of these cartons outta my way here, will ya? I got no room to—shit! Goddamn shit!"

"What's the matter?"

"What happened?"

"He's bleeding!"

"Don't bleed on the cartons, Al!"

"Fuck the goddamn cartons and fuck you, too! Goddamn fucking hell!"

"Wrap it in something!"

"Anybody got a handkerchief?"

Kate chanced a quick peek around the corner of the metal strut; inside, all was confusion as the men clustered around Al, who was wrapping his bloody hand in a rag and moaning.

You'll never get a better chance, she told herself. She quickly slipped around the end of the stanchion and into the depot, ducking behind the light cartons stacked at the entranceway. Though identical with the boxes on the worktables, these no longer carried Chemstra labels. Instead they were marked with the green and white labels of Randall Webber. She glanced at the destination: Barcelonetta.

"You okay, Al?"

"Yeah, I'm just dandy!"

"Lemme see it ... whoops, better keep it wrapped up tight."

"Who the fuck are you, Dr. Kildare?"

"Okay, okay! Show's over! Let's finish up and go get a cold one."

"Sounds good to me."

"Oh, sure! You don't have to drive the stuff to the docks tonight. Listen, you guys finish up here. Scotty, Al, and me, we'll go get the trucks. Can you drive, Al?"

"Yeah, I guess."

Apparently the cartons behind which Kate now hid were going to be moved out. She couldn't stay here; she'd have to get over to the low wall of darker cartons and duck down behind them. Some eight feet of open space separated her from those cartons. Her heart was beating fast; could she get across without being seen?

Peeking around the corner of the cartons, she saw three men leave the building. Of the three who remained at the worktables, two had their backs to her, but the third stood facing her. Turn around! she prayed. Go get another carton! Do something! She watched the man pull the Chem-stra label off the carton in front of him and throw it under the table. Then he took up a matt knife and carefully cut through the heavy packing tape. He set down the knife and pulled up the flaps.

"My last one," he told his companions, who, busy with their own boxes, merely grunted.

He lifted the carton and turned away, and Kate was off in a flash, flying across the open space and dropping to a squat as she squeezed into the narrow space between the cartons and the cinder-block wall. Curiously, it seemed colder in here than it had been out in the woods. Using the stacked boxes as cover, she began to work her way slowly up the side of the room on her hands and knees.

And there it came again, a series of echoey metallic pings, culminating in a muffled crash. As she worked her way up the room, peering between breaks in the cartons, one of the industrial drums came into view and she suddenly realized what she'd been hearing. Something was being dumped into the drums.

She looked more closely at the cartons behind which she was hiding. They were closed but not sealed, and bore no labels. The line of cartons was ragged, and several piles of only two or three sat just this side of higher stacks. Cautiously she took one down and opened the top flaps; the carton was empty. She checked several others. They were all empty.

The roar of the approaching trucks sounded suddenly loud in the quiet clearing. Her back to the cinder-block wall, Kate shuffled back down toward the doorway, searching for a chink in the wall of cartons. On the chance that these boxes were empty, too, she pushed gently at several near the top of the pile in front of her. They shifted easily, giving her a partial view of the clearing in front of the depot.

A ghostly luminance weaving among the trees suddenly resolved itself into flaring headlights as three trucks burst out of the woods, still draped with foliage. The drivers turned and backed up to the depot entrance. They pulled off the branches and tossed them aside, then went around and opened the tailgates in preparation for loading.

The light from the depot reached only partway into the trucks' interiors, but from Kate's cramped perspective, it appeared that the walls had been lined with some sort of insulation.

"You guys done yet?"

"Yeah. Want us to help you load?"

"What the fuck do you think?"

Kate shrank back as the men loaded the hand trucks and pushed them out to the waiting vehicles. They worked fast, but nearly an hour had passed by the time all the cartons with Randall Webber labels were loaded. Unable to move around, Kate found herself shivering with cold.

"We got everything? Oh, shit! Al? Where is that bastard? Hey, Al! You forgot the drums!"

"*I* gotta dump the drums? With *my* hand?"

"Joey here'll help you."

"Some goddamn help he'll be."

"Hey! I said Joey'll help you. Now shut the fuck up and load the goddamn drums."

Pressed against the side wall, Kate heard the scrape of metal on cement as the men hauled the oil drums out to Al's truck and, grunting and complaining, shoved them inside.

Kate shifted her position to get a better look. Should she try to slip out, once the trucks were gone? But with the Randall Webber cartons loaded, a wide empty space now gaped between her hiding place and the entrance. They'd be sure to see her.

"You two guys clean this place up good, understand. Don't go sneaking off for a brewski."

"Don't worry."

"Yeah, we'll take care of it, Ronnie."

"You better."

"We said we would. Jesus!"

So two of the men would stay behind for a while. Good, Kate thought; it would buy her a little more time to figure out her next move. She sat, stretching her cramped legs out in front of her, and leaned sideways against the wall. Outside, the trucks fired up and drove off, but Kate barely heard them. She was concentrating on what she'd heard and seen tonight, trying to fit it in with what she already knew.

The boxes with the Chemstra labels had been brought to the depot in a fleet of refrigerated trucks; she'd seen that yesterday. But why would Chemstra ship the synthetic enzyme via Randall Webber in Connecticut, instead of directly to Barcelonetta? It didn't make sense. Unless, of course, someone wanted to ship something else to Barcelonetta. For the past twenty-four hours, these men had been removing the Chemstra labels, dumping the contents, then refilling the cartons with—what?

She glanced at the low, short wall of empty boxes behind which she sat. These must have held the "stuff" Ronnie had bragged about having driven two and a half days to bring back, she decided. And she had a pretty good idea what that "stuff" was.

Georgia. Louisiana. Florida. She'd been right, so right, to urge Steve to check out those receipts immediately . . .

"What time you make it?"

"Nine-thirty. Getting late."

"Yeah. You thinking what I'm thinking?"

"Ronnie'll kill us."

"Ah, screw Ronnie. We'll do it early in the morning. We'll borrow the security key. He'll never know."

"What if he checks tonight, when they bring back the trucks?"

"At midnight? Get real!"

A profound depression washed over Kate as she sat there, her thoughts turned inward. She had come to believe that finding Tucker would provide an explanation of the Genelife puzzle. But she'd never imagined he himself would *be* the explanation. Was he unstable enough to actually . . . ? But no, he'd hated Nolan. He'd fought against the launch. It couldn't be Tucker. And yet . . .

A low rumble brought Kate suddenly alert. What the hell was that?

"Ronnie thinks he's such a hotshot driver. He makes me puke!"

"Yeah. Always bragging. Remember his story about outrunning two troopers on Alligator Alley? You believe that shit?"

Kate looked up. Above her, the massive slab of steel was rolling forward along the ceiling; as she watched, it curled over and began to drop. She had to get out! Crawling quickly toward the front of the depot on hands and knees, she half rose, ready to run, then froze. Two figures were silhouetted just beyond the rapidly descending door.

"Hey, you left the lights on!"

"Shit!"

"Hurry up! Once it's locked shut, only Ronnie or security can open it!"

One of the figures ran back in and hit a wall switch just inside the entrance. The fluorescent lights flickered and went out.

"Come on! Come on!"

The man bent low and scrambled out, the edge of the descending steel slab just scraping his back. Kate stood, stunned, as the huge door completed its inexorable drop, hitting the ground with a heavy clang and plunging her into total darkness.

Chapter 28

Steve sat on a bar stool just outside Tupaloosa, Louisiana, population 1056 excluding the alligators, peeling shrimp with his fingers and popping them into his mouth. The shrimp had been steamed in beer and cayenne pepper, then dumped unceremoniously on a tray that reminded him of his elementary school cafeteria. They were the best shrimp he had ever eaten. Between shrimp, he drank cold beer. He wondered if Tucker had ever come here. It was his kind of place.

The ramshackle wooden structure was set alongside a creek some two miles beyond the tiny, rather picturesque town, and the tree frogs were giving the rockabilly jukebox some serious competition. He finished the shrimp, then swiveled around and leaned back against the bar. This was his kind of place, too, and he was glad the receptionist at the Tupaloosa Inn had recommended it.

According to Marianne's receipts, Tucker had stayed at the Tupaloosa Inn four times during the last three years, which was as far back as the receipts went. The receptionist couldn't quite place the name, but when Steve showed her Tucker's photo, her face brightened.

"I remember him now," she declared. "No, I can't exactly say what his business was, but I recollect it had something to do with Sheriff Lucknell's land out to Brady Swamp." It was common knowledge that the good-looking young man from Kentucky worked for some Yankees who had bought the worthless acreage for an exorbitant price, but she wasn't about to tell that to a stranger. The sheriff would decide what to say.

"And where do I find Sheriff Lucknell?" Steve had asked.

"Why, honey, you'll find him the same place you find those shrimp I told you about. Matt Lucknell just loves those shrimp! You go along there and set a spell. Sheriff'll show up sooner or later."

"Thanks, I will. By the way, does the name Randall Webber ring a bell?"

"No, honey, I never heard tell of no Randall Webber around here. We had a Randall Peachtree once, but he died."

Steve waggled his empty beer bottle at the bartender, a tall blonde in jeans and a tight red T-shirt that said "Bayou all come back, y'hear?" She nodded and reached into the cooler behind her. The place was half-full, which he imagined was pretty good for nine o'clock on a Wednesday night. The blonde, having fished out his beer, uncapped the dripping brown bottle and sent it sliding down the short bar. He grabbed it before it went over the side, and she winked at him.

Steve took a swallow of beer and put the bottle back on the counter behind him. Should he try Kate again? When he'd called from the inn, he'd gotten her answering machine. No, he decided; he'd have more to tell her once he'd spoken with Lucknell. Hopefully, a lot more. This sounded like a strong lead.

The sound of an approaching siren cut through the night, increasing in volume until revolving red and blue lights flashed through the windows and bounced off the ceiling. The lights and noise faded together and a car door slammed shut. *I do believe that's my man,* Steve thought hopefully. He glanced at the bartender, who smiled and nodded and yelled to the kitchen for a double order of shrimp.

The man who strode through the door was short and broad, muscle running to fat, but still strong for his fifty-odd years. He was dressed in khaki shirt and pants, and well-worn tooled leather boots; his thinning hair was cut short. He bellied up to the bar, acknowledging greetings from the crowd, as the bartender pushed a heaping tray of shrimp and a beer toward him. Then she leaned toward him and spoke quietly, her eyes shifting toward Steve as she explained that the beer he was drinking was courtesy of the tall dark stranger.

The sheriff nodded toward Steve and lifted the bottle, and Steve smiled and nodded back. *Now what?* He sipped more beer and waited. Eventually, the sheriff finished his shrimp and ordered another beer. When it came, he picked it up and walked down the bar to Steve.

"Thanks for the beer," he said. His voice was deep and well modulated. "You want to see me?"

Steve nodded. "Yes sir," he said. "I'm trying to find a man named Tucker Boone."

"Who?"

"He was involved in your land at Brandy Swamp. At least, that's what the woman at the Tupaloosa Inn said. He's—"

The sheriff held up a hand. "Hang on, son," he said. "Let's take us a little walk outside, shall we?"

Steve followed the sheriff out to the rough wooden deck behind the bar. They sat down at a rickety table and looked out over the creek. The night was clear and the stars were very bright.

"What do you want with Mr. Boone?"

"He's my brother-in-law. He disappeared almost a year ago, and the police have no leads. I'm trying to see what I can find out."

"I haven't heard from any police. Where'd he live?"

"New York City. But they're not pursuing the case. They think he ran off with some woman."

"And you don't?"

"It's possible, yes. But . . . I think it had something to do with his work. That's why I came down here. My sister had some old receipts that showed he'd spent some time in Tupaloosa, and then the woman at the inn said something about a piece of land you owned."

"Brandy Swamp, yes. Worthless piece of garbage, between you and me. But somebody up north thought it was just what they'd been looking for and offered me a lot of money for it. Wasn't going to say no, now was I?"

Steve smiled. "May I ask who bought it?"

"Some foundation, I think it was. Got the name in my file at home."

"Was it the Randall Foundation?"

"Mighta been . . . it sounds sorta familiar. But I never had anything to do with them. The deal was put together by a real estate agent out of Houma. My attorney drew up the papers, and I signed, and we took the money and ran."

"Was Tucker Boone involved at that point?"

"No. Guess they hired him later, after they built the big fence."

"Fence?"

"Electrified. Solid. Couldn't see in, couldn't climb over, and believe me, the kids tried. We all wondered what went on in there, but they didn't hire locals. They brought in their own staff, who lived there. Boone was the only one we ever saw. He came down three, four times, to do some consulting for them. Least that's what he said."

"What kind of consulting?"

"Beats the shit out of me, pardon my French. He never said much, your brother-in-law. Cherie in there"—the sheriff jerked a thumb toward the interior of the bar—"she had the hots for him. He used to come out here sometimes, sit right where you're sitting, drink himself a beer ... But he never talked to anyone. And he never would give old Cherie a tumble. Made her so mad!" The sheriff laughed. "She finally married Lyle Benning. Lyle looks a little like Boone, so she took a lot of ribbing."

"When was the last time he was down here?"

"Let's see ... Cherie got married last fall, so ... two years, at least. You could check the register at the inn. But I think it's something like two years."

"Any chance he could have come down again since then, say a year ago, and gone straight to the ... factory or whatever it is, without stopping in Tupaloosa? Maybe he's still inside ..." The sheriff was shaking his head. "Look, if you could just give me the directions, I'll drive out there and—"

"I'll be happy to, son," the sheriff said, "but it won't do you no good."

"Well then, maybe you could come with me. Hell, you're the sheriff. If you say you're trying to trace a missing person, don't they have to let you in?"

But Lucknell only smiled. "I can promise you he isn't there." He finished his beer and got to his feet. "Time to saddle up again. Catch me some drunk drivers."

"I'd still like to have a look around," Steve said stubbornly. He got up and followed the sheriff back toward the noisy bar.

"You don't understand, son," the sheriff told him over his shoulder. "About two years ago, they had themselves a big fire out there. Guess business wasn't so good, because the rumor is they set it themselves. Burned all night and smoldered for two days, but they wouldn't let the fire trucks inside. When we finally unwired the gate, everyone was gone."

He pushed through the screen door, then turned and looked back at Steve. "I sure do hope you find your friend," he said, not unkindly. "But you won't find him at Brandy Swamp. There's nothing there, son. Nothing at all."

Don't panic, Kate kept telling herself. Don't panic. But she couldn't stop shaking. She heard their cars start up behind the depot. Once the sound of their departure had faded, she reached into her shoulder bag and withdrew a sturdy orange plastic flashlight. Its trembling beam cut through the darkness. Get a grip! she thought.

It was very spooky in the darkness. Cautiously, Kate stepped out from behind the cartons and went toward the worktable. *Ping!* She gasped in fright, then realized it was only the fluorescent light, beginning to cool. She slumped down in a chair, fighting for control.

It was frightening enough, being locked in. But the darkness made everything so much worse. Dare she turn on the lights? The men who'd been left to clean up had said Ronnie and the others wouldn't be back until midnight, and they themselves were gone till tomorrow. Why not turn them on? Who would see them?

She rose and went slowly toward the front of the building, playing the flashlight ahead of her to locate the switch. The fluorescent tubes flickered on with a buzz as she pulled the handle, flooding the room with cool blue light.

Standing before the closed entrance flap, she surveyed the room. Across the rear wall was a series of what appeared to be refrigerated cabinets. That must be where they'd stored the enzymes. It would be empty, now. To one side was a small door. I hope it's a bathroom, Kate thought.

It was. Kate used it and washed her hands in the grimy sink, then came out into the room again. Taking a small camera from her shoulder bag, she flicked on the flash and began taking photos: the worktable, the pile of discarded Chemstra labels on the floor, the stacks of cartons. She shot from different angles, to give a feeling of the building itself, and even photographed the interior of the massive steel slab that served as a door. She went across the room for a wide shot of the cartons she'd hid behind and took several pictures. As she walked forward to change the angle, she felt something hard under her shoe. She stepped back and looked down; a small glass ampule glittered in the bluish light.

Leaning down to pick it up, she realized she was standing about where the large metal drums had been set. The ampule must have bounced out. She took it to the worktable and examined it. She could just make out the thin faint lettering along the side: "Chemstra NA, Switzerland," and under that in smaller print, "SOD–2000." She wrapped the vial carefully in several discarded Chemstra labels and placed it carefully in an inner compartment of her bag. Now if only she had a sample of what they'd replaced the Chemstra ampules with.

It was too much to hope for, but she spent the next forty-five minutes opening and restacking the dark cartons, and checking the refrigerated cabinets. Nothing.

Her watch read nearly eleven; an hour before Ronnie and the other drivers came back with the trucks. Would he check to make sure that the cleanup had been completed? The men certainly hadn't thought so. If they were right, she'd be safe until daybreak. But what then? With the rising of the sun, she'd not only be at risk in here when the men returned, but outside as well.

The men had said only Ronnie or security could open the massive door. Was there any way to call security? Was there a phone? And what would she tell them? Never mind, she'd think of something. She still had her ID badge. But an exhaustive search revealed no phone.

She turned off the lights and, with the flashlight to guide her, went back to the worktable and sat down. Think! she urged herself. There has to be a way out! The air was stale with cigarette smoke, and butts were scattered on the floor under her feet. As she moved her arm, something fell to the ground. Looking down, she saw a book of half-used matches. She stared at them for a moment, an idea forming. Then she reached down and picked them up.

"Shit! Are those bozos still at it?" Ronnie exclaimed as he roared into the clearing. He stared at the light spilling from underneath the entrance door and through the high small windows. "How long does it take to flatten some cartons and sweep up?"

The other trucks had rolled to a stop behind him. "Anything wrong, boss?" one of the drivers called.

"Nah. Go get your vehicles under cover. I'll see what's holding them up."

Leaving the engine idling, Ronnie jumped out of the cab, reaching in his pocket for the master key.

Inside, Kate was lighting matches. Already the cartons she'd piled up in a line just inside the massive door were beginning to flame.

Ronnie hesitated. Hell, they'd probably just left the lights on. He yawned. God, he was beat. So what if the lights were on all night? He didn't have to pay the bill.

Kate squeezed back against the side wall, holding a wet scarf to her mouth. The building was filling with smoke, and she could feel the heat of the flames. Open the door, Ronnie!

Ronnie climbed back into the truck and let in the clutch. No skin off his ass, he thought. Turn 'em off tomorrow.

The smoke was thick now, and Kate began to cough. She'd heard him arrive and talk to the others. What was taking him so damn long?

Ronnie got to the edge of the clearing, then jammed on the brakes. If those two assholes skipped out for a beer and never came back, he thought, I'll kill them! Reversing quickly, he backed up to the depot, shoved the clutch into neutral, and leapt out. Those bastards! That's just what they would do! Figured he'd be too tired to check. He'd show them!

He pulled out the key and inserted it in the lock at the side of the entranceway, turning it hard. With a shudder, the huge door began to lift. Smoke rolled out from beneath it.

What the hell . . . ? He stepped back as the smoke billowed around him. Holy Mother of God! Fire! His eyes began to smart. Those assholes and their cigarettes! The smoke thickened as the flames, fanned by fresh oxygen, leapt higher.

He tore back to the truck and scrambled in, his first instinct to go find security and have them call in the alarm. He'd told them they should put in a phone! The others came running from the woods. "Get out of here!" he yelled. "Go on! Go home!" For a moment they stood mesmerized by the smoke and flames, then they scattered.

Ronnie hesitated. Now that the initial shock was wearing off, he began to reconsider. Maybe he should just let the fire burn itself out; no one would want the fire department poking around in there. But what if it spread to the woods? Then he had another thought. The building was made of stone and steel and concrete. There was nothing in there except some cardboard and a couple of tables. Maybe he could afford to let it burn itself out, after all. A fire like that wouldn't burn very long. Especially if he closed the door again.

He jumped out of the cab and went back to the building, approaching from the side to avoid the flames that were licking out at him. Coughing and feeling around in the smoke, he quickly located the control panel and inserted his key; the huge door rolled forward, locking the fire inside.

Back in the truck, he jammed the gear lever down and floored the pedal. I don't know nothing about this! he told himself. I don't know nothing! Hauling hard on the wheel, he skidded the truck around in a tight circle and headed down the road.

In the woods, a small figure rose to her knees and retched. Then, using a nearby tree for support, she pulled herself erect and stood trembling, drawing the cool night air into her lungs in great raw gasps.

Chapter 29

April 18

"You sound terrible! Are you sick?"

"It's a long story," Kate croaked. "Can't talk too well. You go first. Find anything?"

"Tucker was down here all right," Steve told her, "but not lately. The Randall Foundation bought a piece of marginal land and set up an operation, very hush-hush, but it burned to the ground a couple of years ago."

"That's great!"

"It is?"

"All fits. On the right track."

"God, you really sound awful! By the way, I tried calling you up until midnight last night."

"Got trapped in the depot. Had to start a fire to get out. Inhaled a lot of smoke. Be all right soon."

"Jesus! Don't try to talk. Look, I'm sorry to call so early, but I've got a nine-twenty flight out of Baton Rouge for Atlanta. Why don't you get some rest and I'll call you from Okefenokee when I get—"

"Not Okefenokee. Alligator Alley."

"What?"

"Nolan's men are dumping Chemstra's SOD-2000. They're replacing it with something else. Ronnie drives it up." Kate was forcing the words out painfully. "They said 'Alligator Alley.' Ever hear of it?"

"Sure. It's the main east-west road through the Florida Everglades."

"Then that's where it'll be."

"It? You mean, you know—?"

"Yes. Wait." She leaned forward and sipped some water from the glass by the bed. She hadn't slept much. In addition to her raspy throat and lungs, she'd been tormented by her thoughts. How could she have been so naive, so easily dazzled? She'd taken far too much on faith. "Steve, I don't know for sure, but ... Tucker may be involved."

"Well, we always knew he—"

"No, I mean actively involved."

Steve was silent. When he spoke at last, it was with deep conviction. "I can't believe Tucker would knowingly do anything to hurt people. I admit he was a crazy bastard, but he wouldn't do that."

"I hope you're right," Kate said. "Now let me tell you what to look for."

"... or I can recommend the California salad, sir," the waiter said. "Avocado, sundried tomatoes, white meat chicken ..."

"That does sound good," Nolan agreed. "Nice and light. And for you?" He turned toward his lunch companion.

"The California salad for me, too. Much too hot for anything heavy." He sipped his iced tea and admired the view of the pool and gardens beyond. He hated iced tea. But Nolan apparently didn't drink alcohol, so he wouldn't either.

The dining terrace was filled with cheerful-looking business people, enjoying their three-day respite from neckties and spouses and the daily grind. The sun was warm and the turquoise pool sparkled invitingly, but both men's thoughts were centered on the Genelife presentation Nolan would give that afternoon.

"I'm really looking forward to your speech," his companion said. "You'll dazzle them!"

Nolan looked pleased. "Yes, I believe I will," he agreed. "So nice to have your support."

"Happy to give it."

"I was quite impressed that you decided to spend your own time—and money—to come out here for the conference. You'll notice," Nolan remarked darkly, "that others are conspicuous by their absence."

"You mean Kate Martin? Actually, it's just as well she—"

"No, I meant MacAllister. Frankly, I wouldn't have allowed Kate to come at this point, even if I hadn't fired her."

"You fired Dr. Martin? When was that?"

"Oh, a few days ago. That'll put a stop to her smart-ass

prying." Nolan squeezed lemon into his iced tea and took a long draught. "I'm really grateful to you for alerting me to the situation. I had no idea she and Mac had gone so far in their efforts to discredit Randall Webber. Imagine her planning to show our confidential reports to a friend at the FDA! Thanks for alerting me."

His companion shrugged modestly. "I felt it was the least I could do. I've always believed Genelife was one helluva product. It deserves better."

"Well, now it'll get it," Nolan assured him.

"Do you have a replacement for Martin yet?"

Nolan nodded. "Our previous medical consultant, Nick Butler, is coming back on a temporary basis."

"I'd like to meet him. Is he out here?"

"No, I didn't feel his attendance at the conference was necessary," Nolan said quickly.

Didn't feel it necessary to share the credit, his companion thought cynically. Well, no skin off my nose. "And Mac-Allister? How did you discourage him from coming?"

"Didn't have to. He never suggested it, and frankly, neither did I. After what you've told me ... well, never mind all that. I'll soon have the pleasure of firing him."

The pleasure will be all mine, his companion thought. "Have you decided when?"

The waiter appeared with their salads. "More iced tea? No? Enjoy your meal."

"Looks good," Nolan said, spearing a chunk of avocado.

"Uh, have you decided when you'll fire him?" the man repeated.

"Oh, sometime after the Clio Awards dinner next week," Nolan told him casually. The prestigious Clio advertising awards were given out yearly at a gala event in New York. "We've been told that Genelife has won in a number of categories. I want to give the press coverage a little time to die down before announcing an agency switch. Are you going?"

"Certainly. We're slated to pick up a few advertising awards ourselves."

"Glad to hear it. Do your people know yet?"

"No, not officially. But you must realize that in the course of setting up—office space, staffing, making the media buys you wanted—I've had to take a few people into my confidence."

"Well, make sure they keep it quiet. I don't want to open the business section tomorrow and find an article about myself."

"No, of course not. Uh, Michael, I hate to keep coming back to money, but now that we're so close to announcing, I wonder whether you could advance me the first quarter's fee. I'm sure you can understand my position. I've committed a great deal of my own money, not to mention my bank's, and—"

"We've been over this before," Nolan said testily, stabbing at a piece of chicken. "It is simply not possible for me to do that, not while I still have MacAllister on the payroll. Once he's no longer agency of record—and believe me, that day can't come too soon for me—you'll have your money. Until then, you'll just have to do the best you can."

Richard Day sighed deeply. "Sure, I understand," he said. His armpits were damp and it wasn't just the heat of the Arizona sun.

"I felt sure you would." Nolan set down his fork. "I'm really looking forward to working with you, Richard."

"Me, too."

"Well, I'd better get in there," Nolan said, checking his watch. "I want to run through the slides before we get started." He stood, drained his iced tea, and set the glass down on the table. Then, waving to acquaintances at other tables, he headed for the entrance to the auditorium, leaving the president of the newly formed Richard Day Agency to pick up the lunch tab.

It had taken Steve six hours, with stops in Jackson and Atlanta, to fly from Baton Rouge to Miami. Now, as he drove west along Alligator Alley past small roads leading to remote, unseen ranches, he was decidedly tired. He blinked in the late-afternoon sun and rubbed the bridge of his nose, sweaty under his sunglasses, as he scanned the side of the road for the entrance to the Randall Foundation's land.

From conversations with people at two of the properties along the Alley, he'd confirmed that several landowners had unexpectedly sold their holdings about eighteen months back to some sort of research foundation. Yes, the pieces of land were contiguous. One man Steve had questioned thought the research had something to do with cattle; another remembered pineapples.

The road into the newly created property had been shifted and was now unmarked, the pineapple man had told him. He'd provided some vague landmarks and approximate distances, but Steve had already wasted nearly half an hour on a wrong turning.

Back on the main road, his rental car spattered with mud, Steve drove slowly, peering anxiously ahead. White egrets and small blue herons fished in the swampy creeks that lined the road. Above, a hawk was circling lazily. His thoughts drifted, and he realized with a start that he'd actually just driven past the tall, lightning-struck tree that the man had described. He pulled off the road and backed up along the shoulder until he was even with the tree, which stood a good distance off in the middle of a rough field. Some two hundred yards behind him, a chain-link fence stretched across the property's frontage. A metal gate, chained securely shut, blocked access to a winding track that led past the burned tree and disappeared into the scrub beyond. The only sign read "No Trespassing" in bold red lettering.

The sun was lower now, the shadows lengthening. Steve had no idea how far the road meandered before it reached the research station. A quarter of a mile? Five? The men had agreed that the combined parcels of land now comprised substantial acreage. Well, there was no choice; he'd have to walk in.

Killing the engine, Steve got out and locked the car, hoping it would be there when he returned. Did it look abandoned? He went to the trunk and removed a denim jacket from his bag. A small creek ran alongside the fenced-in land, and he walked up the soggy bank, mud squelching under his well-worn Timberland boots, until he found a spot where it dipped slightly. He hung his denim jacket over some stiff reeds, and stepped back to study the effect. Yes, he decided, viewed from the road the jacket might indicate the presence of someone fishing in the creek. Not great, but the best he could do.

He went back to the chain-link fence and padlocked gate. It would be easy to climb, but was it electrified? A close inspection seemed to indicate that it was not, but just in case, Steve threw a handful of reeds onto the top wires. Nothing sparked, hissed, or burned. He kicked it with the steel toe of his boot. Nothing. Here goes, he thought, and grabbing hold of the fence, began to climb. The fence was only about ten feet high, and he was soon up and over. Obviously, no one was worried about walk-in guests.

He turned and followed the road back into the property. It wandered through marshland and scrub, then ducked under a tangle of trees that admitted only a spotting of late-afternoon sun. The track was completely unmarked, even at the crossroads Steve came upon some two miles along.

Which way? Steve asked himself urgently. It was darker now under cover of the trees; no time to choose wrong and double back, not if he hoped to reach whatever was hidden away back here before nightfall. He studied the surfaces of both roads in the fading light. One seemed better traveled, and he set off on it hopefully.

Half a mile along, the road left the tangle of live oak and cottonwood, crossing a wide marsh and then more scrubby grassland. Looking around him, Steve saw nothing but more of the same, stretching in all directions. Swatting at the no-see-ums that had begun to gather, he trekked on.

Without warning, the road turned sharply left and entered a small copse of tortured trees shrouded with Spanish moss, then hurried out again, crossed a canal, and stopped. Steve gasped.

In front of him, glowing bloodred in the light of the setting sun, stood a huge glass pyramid. Steve moved forward, drawn toward the luminance like a moth to a flame.

Was Kate right about what it held? Reflected sunlight made the glass opaque, so he circled around to one side in an effort to eliminate the glare. From here he could see that the huge glass structure extended for at least a mile across the open scrubland. He stared into the hazy interior trying to decipher the vague forms he could just make out in the dimming light.

Clouds of mist filled the pyramid, and the inner surfaces of the glass panels were lightly fogged with moisture. Steve looked around quickly. Seeing no one, he ran toward the glass building, then stopped, awestruck. Kate had been right on the money, he thought.

Beyond the misted panels he could clearly see, pushing against the glass and twisting around each other in their struggle toward the light, the shadowy shapes of a thousand giant plants.

Chapter 30

Kate sat staring out the window of the 727 at the clouds that shrouded the Florida coast. No wonder the research had turned up a higher incidence of side effects. The plant derivative had been systematically substituted for Chemstra's synthetic, and the huge greenhouse Steve had discovered, hidden deep in the Everglades, was its source. Soon she would see for herself what Tucker Boone had brought back from the rain forest.

"But why substitute the plant derivative, with its side effects?" Steve asked, when she'd explained it to him on the phone last night.

"Because the synthetic didn't deliver a dramatic enough cosmetic effect," she told him. "That guy Fannon actually told me so, but I didn't realize the significance of it. You see—"

"Your voice still sounds lousy," Steve told her. "Get some rest and tell me about it tomorrow."

"Please fasten your seat belts and bring your tray tables to their upright position for our landing in Miami." The 727 began to descend through the thin cloud layer. Now the ocean was visible below.

Soon she and Steve would be ready to talk to the FDA, and to warn Mac as she'd promised. She felt a pang of guilt about Mac; aside from reassuring Victoria that she was okay, she had pleaded illness to avoid a long conversation with her. She trusted Victoria's discretion in most things, but Mac was very dear to her. If Kate told her all she knew, Victoria would tell Mac and he'd resign the business and the whole thing would suddenly become public knowledge. And Kate didn't want the Genelife fiasco to go public just yet. There were still vital questions that needed answers. And the fewer people who knew what she and Steve knew, at least for a few more days, the better her chances of ferreting out those answers, and getting the evidence needed to make her accusations stick.

The plane slid onto the runway, braked, and turned onto a taxiway. Around her, passengers immediately stood up and began rummaging in the overhead compartments, while flight attendants begged them to remain seated. Kate sighed. People were so stupid, sometimes. A man pulled her black and gray overnighter out of the bin and dropped it on the floor.

"Hey! That's mine!"

"Sorry." He picked it up and slung it over into her lap, then retrieved his jacket from the bin. Annoyed, Kate shoved it onto the floor in front of her, then gazed out of the window in an attempt to ignore the noisy men and women who now crowded the aisles.

How many of them used Genelife? she wondered. How many of them, despite its potential side effects, would be happy to see it removed from the market? Even after years of serious medical controversy surrounding silicone breast implants, women continued to request them, and some doctors continued to supply them.

The crowd in the aisles continued to press forward as they taxied to the terminal, where at last the jetway was connected, the doors opened, and the pent-up flood of humanity released. Kate waited for the crowd to thin, then gathered up her belongings and made her way out of the plane.

As planned, Steve was waiting for her at the gate. His eyes lit up when he saw her, and she could feel herself grinning a loopy grin. Well, something good has come out of all the Randall Webber shit, she thought as they embraced.

"Any luggage?" he asked. God, she looks great in jeans, he thought as they separated at last.

"Only this stuff," she told him, swinging her black and gray soft suitcase in one hand and her medical bag in the other.

He eyed the small black bag with interest. "Ready for any emergency, huh?"

"You never know," she said. In fact, she rarely traveled without it.

Soon they were heading out of the airport in Steve's

rental car. The thin cloud cover had dissipated, and the sky was a clear light blue. Although it was only ten in the morning, the sun was already hot, the air humid.

"I love this weather," Kate said. "Steamy and sticky."

"Me, too," Steve said. "Although most people wouldn't agree with us."

"Is that why you live in Boston?" she teased.

"Boston's my base," he said. "I travel a good part of the year. What's your excuse?"

Kate smiled. "Guilty as charged," she said. "Maybe I should start traveling, too."

"Maybe you should. Start with Boston."

"Not exactly steamy and sticky."

"We can work on that."

The day grew hotter. Reluctant to stop, they drank from the bottles of juice Steve had packed in a cooler of ice. "I made some sandwiches, too," he told her. "Chicken. Are you hungry?"

"Ravenous." Kate unwrapped one of the thick square packets. "You want half?"

"Sure." He took a large bite, then glanced over at Kate. "You sound a lot better than you did yesterday."

"I feel a lot better."

"Good. Are you well enough to tell me what I wouldn't let you tell me last night?"

"Sure. Where were we?"

"You were saying that Fannon told you the synthetic didn't pack the same cosmetic wallop as the plant derivative."

"Right."

"But that means that Chemstra didn't actually do any better than Tucker at synthesizing the SOD."

"No, they didn't, but nobody realizes it except Nolan."

"How do you mean?"

"Look, Tucker had been trying to develop a synthetic that combined low side effects with a dramatic cosmetic result. He couldn't do it, but Nolan thought he was holding out on him. Remember, Nolan and Tucker hated each other. Nolan probably figured this was Tucker's way of paying him back for ousting Clark Randall. Chemstra had tested the original plant-derived drug, turning up side effects outside the acceptability range. So Nolan put Chemstra on the synthetization, figuring they'd solve it where Tucker had claimed to have failed."

"But they didn't."

"No. Nolan must have realized, after Chemstra had worked on the synthetic for a while, that Tucker had been right; the cosmetic and side effects were linked; you couldn't have one without the other. Still, Chemstra's synthetic had side effects that fell within acceptable levels, there *was* some degree of cosmetic change, and the FDA said okay. So everybody started celebrating."

"But without a dramatic cosmetic effect, there was no product," Steve said.

"Right. And Nolan needed a major product launch to cement his position with Omni. After all, that's what he'd promised them before he realized the side effects issue was unsolvable. So he decided to use Chemstra's synthetic in the clinical trials for the FDA, but secretly substitute the plant derivative in the real product." Kate took a bite of sandwich and chewed thoughtfully. "I'll bet you," she said, "that Genelife's cosmetic effect is a lot lower in the research the FDA saw than what's being experienced by consumers of the marketed drug."

"And nobody at the FDA has noticed?"

"After the fact? Why should they? Besides, Genelife is a cosmetic, not a medicine per se. Proof of efficacy would have been required of the clinical trials, and the synthetic would have delivered it to some extent. But the emphasis would have been on consumer safety. Now that the stuff's on the market, as long as no one's complaining that the cosmetic results are *less* than what was promised, who's going to worry about that part of it?"

"And where does Tucker come into all this? You said you thought he—"

Kate nodded. "When I realized the plant derivative was being used, I immediately thought of Tucker. After all, he'd disappeared just about the time Genelife went into large-scale production. I wondered ..."

"What?"

"Well, I wondered whether Nolan might have told Tucker he'd found a way to eliminate the side effects of the plant derivative. If he did, isn't it possible Tucker's working away in the giant greenhouse this very minute, supervising the extraction of the real SOD-2000?"

"Surely, Tucker would know better," Steve said firmly. "You told me yourself that he argued with Nolan about the Genelife launch, just before he disappeared."

"That's true ..."

"Hell, anyone could have learned to extract the stuff," Steve said. "They had that place in Louisiana for a couple of years before it burned down. They didn't need Tucker anymore."

"But they did. They sent him back to the rain forest."

"We don't know that. He might have gone on his own."

"I don't think so. I worked out a time line yesterday. Tucker's rain forest trip came just after the Louisiana fire. I wonder when they set up the place in Florida."

"The locals say about eighteen months ago," Steve said. "After Louisiana burned to the ground."

"And before Tucker went back to the rain forest."

"Before he was *sent* back," Kate said softly. "Before Nolan sent him back to get new root stock to replace what they'd lost in Louisiana."

They drove in silence for a while. Finally Steve spoke. "How could Nolan risk substituting the plant derivative in secret? Surely the side effects would have come to light."

"Yes, but maybe not for years. Don't forget that Mac's research tabulations came about almost by accident, as an adjunct to an advertising campaign. Consumers don't seem to be complaining. Even the women on the focus group videos who'd experienced severe headaches and weight loss kept insisting Genelife was a miracle. Even Dave ..." Kate shook her head. "No, it could have been years before the full effects of the plant derivative were recognized."

"But eventually, it would come out, wouldn't it? And Nolan's career would go down the tubes. Hell, he'd go to jail! He had to know that sooner or later, he'd—"

"You know, there's been a rumor circulating around the office lately, about Omni spinning off Randall Webber. I wonder what Nolan's financial position would be if they did? You're right, of course; long-term, the side effects issue would have to surface and kill Genelife. But a year or two might have been all the time Nolan needed to cash in and get out ... And then there's Chemstra and Henri Koch. How much does Koch know?"

"Nolan placed him there," Steve reminded her. "Nolan funded him."

"Nolan's good at buying loyalty. You should have heard Nick Butler talk about what a prince Michael was. But would Koch actually sit still for fraud? Could Nolan pay him enough to risk prison? I'm not so sure ..." Kate thought of the men in the depot, dumping Chemstra's SOD-2000 into the empty oil drums and the small vial that lay hidden in her underwear drawer. "If Chemstra were part of the fraud," she said at last, "it would be a lot simpler for Nolan to send them the plant derivative in bulk and have them ship the SOD-2000 vials direct to the manufacturing plant in Puerto Rico. Better still, he could simply have Chemstra ship empty vials to Florida for filling. Why make the switch at the depot? No, I think Chemstra is clean."

"Then why was Fannon so upset when you implied that Randall Webber owned Chemstra?"

"Well, the Randall Webber financial connection could make it difficult to do business with other pharmaceutical companies if it were known," Kate said reasonably. "No, Chemstra believes the synthetic is being used; I'm sure of that. Shipping the vials of synthetic to Connecticut, dumping them, driving new SOD-2000 up from Florida, and refilling the boxes ... none of that would be necessary if Chemstra were in on the deception." Her muscles felt cramped from so much sitting; she rotated her shoulders and arms. "God, I hope we're doing the right thing," she said. "Not going to the FDA right away."

"Too late for second-guessing," Steve told her. "Alligator Alley's just up ahead. Besides, we *are* doing the right thing. Burrowing from within, I believe is how you put it." He slowed and signaled right. "Pit stop," he announced, pulling into a ramshackle service station. They gassed up the car and took turns using the very grimy toilets.

"How far away are we?" Kate asked.

"Only about an hour," Steve told her. "You really think this TV scam will work?"

"You'll be fine," she reassured him. "Just keep muttering about camera angles and how bad the light is." She climbed back into the passenger seat and he slid behind the wheel. Soon they were barreling along the strip of straight, rather boring road that ran across southern Florida.

Steve looked over at Kate, who had gone quiet, her forehead creased with concern. "You're still worrying about whether we're doing the right thing, aren't you?" he asked gently.

Kate sighed. "Yes, I am. As a doctor, I have a responsibility to blow the whistle on anything that could hurt people. But without some hard evidence, it's my word against Michael's. Going to the FDA without tangible proof would give him time to protect himself. He had a fire in Louisiana; he could have another one down here."

Steve nodded. "At least you have that Chemstra vial."

"Yeah. And it contains precisely what the FDA approved: the synthetic. What we need is a vial of the plant derivative."

"And we need to find Tucker."

"Yes . . ."

They both fell silent then, unwilling to voice the thought they shared: Was Tucker still alive?

At last Steve pulled over to the shoulder. "See that burned tree? We're here." Clouds were gathering again, and the light was dull and flat.

Kate got out and inspected the heavy chain and padlock that secured the gate. "You sure you can get through this?"

Steve had gone around to the back of the car. Now he lifted a heavy bolt cutter from the trunk. "They promised me this would do it," he said. Together they positioned the bolt cutter, and after several tries, Steve managed to snap off the padlock. They unwrapped the heavy chain and the gate swung open invitingly.

"And what will we say when they ask us how we drove our car through a heavily chained gate?" Kate asked.

Steve dragged the chain over to the bank of the muddy creek. Then, laying it out carefully in a long snakelike line, he kicked it in and watched it sink out of sight. He tossed in the padlock, then looked back at Kate and smiled. "Chain?" he asked. "What chain?"

They got back into the car and drove through the gate. In daylight, the terrain seemed even bleaker than it had the night before. They bumped along the hard-packed dirt road, blinking in the occasional ray of sun escaping from the thickening cloud cover and peering ahead in the sudden gloom of wooded swamp.

"Spooky in here," Kate observed, eyeing the dark twisted trees rising from the marsh. "What's that gray cobwebby stuff hanging off those branches?"

"Spanish moss."

"Looks like shrouds." Kate shuddered.

"You ain't seen nothing yet." They came out of the trees and crossed a canal. A long brown snake slid languidly across the planks of the makeshift bridge and disappeared among the reeds along the far bank. "Here we are."

Kate looked up as the huge glass pyramid loomed up in front of them. Knowing about it beforehand did nothing to lessen the effect, she thought. Through misty panels she could see huge tropical greenery. "How big did you say this thing was?"

"A mile each side would be my guess."

"Jesus." She dug her Randall Webber ID badge out of her handbag and clipped it to her shirt.

The pyramid stood in marshland surrounded by trees. A strip of asphalt paving ran along the perimeter of the building. Steve followed the path around to the right where it swelled into a small parking area. Just beyond, a boxy annex some three stories high had been affixed to one side of the pyramid. It appeared to be built of cement blocks, and was painted white. There were no windows. "Offices," Kate suggested. "And the lab."

"And security," Steve added. "Here they come."

Three men in gray uniforms had emerged through a door in the annex. They were wearing sidearms and didn't look happy.

"Guns," Steve said. "Get out of the car slowly and keep smiling."

"Hello," Kate called as she stepped out onto the road. "I'm Dr. Kate Martin. I work for Randall Webber." She pointed to her ID badge.

Two of the men took up positions in front and to either side of the car; the third approached Kate and inspected her badge. "What y'all doing here, Miss Martin?" he drawled.

"That's Dr. Martin," Kate told him sternly. "Who's in charge?"

"Who's he?" the guard asked, jerking a thumb at Steve.

"He's with me," she answered. "Where's your boss?"

The man shrugged. "In there," he said. "Guess y'all better come on in."

He turned and led them toward the annex, gesturing for one of the others to stay with the car.

The guard led them through an air-conditioned and carpeted waiting area decorated in primary colors, past an elevator and open stairway, and along a short corridor to a door marked Administration. He pushed it open and ushered them through.

Seated at the desk inside was the fattest man Kate had ever seen. His body overflowed his painted metal chair, and sweat beaded his forehead despite the cooled air. He wore brown polyester pants and a wrinkled khaki shirt open at the neck. His sparse brown hair was cut short, and his complexion was ruddy. A holstered gun was slung over the back of his chair. He put down his Dr Pepper and blinked at them, toadlike. Any moment, Kate thought, his tongue will dart out and catch his dinner.

"This here's Bobby Beach," the guard said. "He's in charge. Bobby, she says she works for Randall Webber. This here's her badge." He reached for Kate's shirt, but she shoved his hand away.

"Mr. Beach, I'm Dr. Martin," she said, taking a step toward him. "And this is Phil DeCherico. Perhaps you've heard of him."

"No," said Bobby slowly. "Should I have?" His voice was deep and rumbling, his expression sardonic.

"He's only the most famous commercial director working today!" Kate enthused. "Surely Michael told you?"

"And just who would Michael be?"

"Michael Nolan, of course!"

"Well, Miss Martin—"

"Doctor. I'm Dr. Martin."

"Oh, yeah, sorry, Dr. Martin. And Mr., ah, Cherco, was it?"

"DeCherico."

"Uh-huh. Why don't you sit down and tell me what you're doing way out here in the swamp? And while you're at it, why don't you tell me how you drove that car of yours through a chained-up gate."

"Chain?" Steve said. "What chain?"

Bobby flicked a cold blue eye at the guard who'd brought them in. "Wanna check that gate, Billy?" Billy nodded and left. "So you work for Randall Webber," he said, turning back to Kate.

"That's right. And—"

"And who do you work for, Mr. Dee Cherco?"

"DeCherico. I work for her."

"Well, not directly for me," Kate explained. "He was hired by the advertising agency, you know, MacAllister? The people who make the commercials for Genelife?"

"You mean the ads? Yeah, I like those ads," Bobby said. "You make those?"

"Well, I . . ."

"Yes," Kate jumped in. "Phil's a film director. He directed those ads."

"You're a director, huh? Know any stars?"

"Um, uh, Madonna. I know Madonna," Steve extemporized.

"Yeah? You ever sleep with her?" Bobby leaned as far forward as his huge belly would allow, which wasn't very far.

"No, we're just friends," Steve said blandly. "And I worked with Clint Eastwood, too."

Bobby's eyes lit up. "You know Eastwood?"

"Sure do. Wonderful man."

"Eastwood!" Bobby shook his head in admiration, blubber wobbling back and forth under his chin. "But I still don't understand what you two're doing way out here. Especially with that chain." He looked at Steve suspiciously.

"Chain?" Steve said. "What chain?"

"Mr. Nolan sent us here to make a movie!" Kate broke in quickly. "A movie for television. About *you*!"

"Me?" Bobby's brow furrowed.

"I mean, about all of you. What you do here. The greenhouse. The plants. The lab."

Bobby shook his head. "I don't think so," he said slowly. "Not this place."

"Oh, you're wrong!" Kate gushed. "It's so . . . so filmic."

"Very filmic," Steve chimed in. "Great angles. Although the light isn't very—"

Bobby was shaking his head. "I don't get it," he said. "Mr. Nolan always told me never to talk to nobody about this place."

"He's obviously changed his mind," Kate said. She opened her purse and took out a letter she'd typed on the company stationery she'd removed from her office along with her personal possessions. Nolan's signature was a little shaky, but then, how often had Bobby seen the real thing?

"They were supposed to send you a copy of this. Didn't you get it?"

Bobby took the letter in his pudgy fingers and read through it slowly. "They never sent me nothing like this," he said slowly. "Mind if I keep it?"

"Sure, no problem."

Bobby put the letter down on his desk and flattened it several times with his sweaty palm. "I just don't get it," he repeated, "but if that's what Mr. Nolan wants ... Where are your cameras?"

"Oh, we're not going to shoot the movie today," Steve explained. "We have to look around first, check out the camera angles, figure out the lighting ..."

"We're scouting," Kate told Bobby. "That's what they call it in the movie business."

"Yeah. So if you could just show us around ..."

But Bobby looked thoughtful. "Whyn't y'all just have a seat outside for a minute?" he suggested in his rumbly bass. "Let me see what I can organize. Billy Ray! Where the hell are ya, boy?"

A gangly young man with hair the color of straw stuck his head in the door and grinned at everybody. He too wore a gray uniform, but was unarmed. "Yes, boss?"

"Show our guests where the soda machine is at, will ya?"

"Sure will, boss." Kate and Steve rose and followed the young man out into the corridor. "We got Sprite," he announced proudly over his shoulder, "we got Fanta, we got Coke ..."

"And Billy Ray!" Bobby's voice boomed out in the corridor after them. "Bring me another Dr Pepper!"

Back in the waiting area, a cold can of Fanta in his hand, Steve looked appraisingly at Kate. "Think he bought it?"

"Sure. Everybody wants to be on television." Kate smiled ruefully. "Even me, I guess."

"So what's he doing in there?"

"Oh, I expect he's calling Nolan to check us out first."

"You don't seem very worried about it."

"Nolan's in Arizona."

The chair creaked as Bobby leaned forward and redialed the special number Mr. Nolan had given him. This time he let it ring fifteen times. Still no answer. Damn! What should he do? He'd received no orders from Mr. Nolan about this TV stuff. And he hated doing things without orders. He fumbled with the letter the doctor woman had given him. There was a number for Randall Webber up on top. Dare he use it? Mr. Nolan had forbidden him to use any number but the one he'd been given, the one that didn't answer. He thought for a long time, his toadlike face wrinkled with indecision. At last, he picked up the phone and dialed.

"Randall Webber, good afternoon."

"Uh, is Mr. Nolan there?"

"I'll connect you with his secretary."

Bobby almost hung up when the secretary answered; what if Mr. Nolan found out he'd called? Then he thought, I don't have to give my name. "Lemme talk to Mr. Nolan, please," he told her.

"Mr. Nolan's out of town," the woman said. "May I ask who's calling him?"

"Uh, no, I . . . uh, you know anything about a TV shoot down here in Florida?" Shit! he thought. I shouldn't never have said that. He felt the sweat coursing down his cheeks.

"You're calling about a TV shoot?" the woman said. "You would need to talk to the MacAllister Agency . . ."

MacAllister was the name the doctor woman had mentioned. So that part checked out. The secretary began reciting a phone number. "Listen," he interrupted her, wanting to end the conversation quickly before he made any other slips, "y'all know anything about a Dr. Kate Martin? Does she work there?"

"Kate Martin? Yes, of course. Dr. Martin is—that is, she used to be—hello? Hello?"

But Bobby, having received the confirmation he sought, had disconnected.

"It's . . . amazing!" Kate breathed as she followed Steve and Bobby through the glass door into another world. "It seems so . . . real!" A few tentative steps and she was surrounded by a vast artificial rain forest, the entrance and glass walls completely lost to view.

"Of course it's real!" Bobby snorted. He dragged his huge bulk after Kate reluctantly. "Hot, too." Sweat was pouring down his face and back. "Okay, let's go see the labs. Ready, Mr. Dee Cherco?"

But Steve had wandered some distance into the mock jungle and now stood gazing around with a slightly dazed expression.

Light filtered through the canopy of interlocking vegetation high above. The humidity and dense earthy smell were just as he remembered. Pushing the foliage aside, he moved deeper into the thick tangle of trees, the ground spongy beneath his feet. It was a very strange sensation, being back in the rain forest, and yet, not back. His heart jumped suddenly; was that thin line of green an eyelash viper? But of course there would be no such dangers here.

His shirt, already soaked with perspiration, clung to his back as he moved. Yes, these were the same strange leaves they'd seen growing in the sacred clearing. But unlike that place, many of these plants were not fully grown. A scattering of saplings and midheight plants struggled through the higher growth toward the light. Everything was slick with moisture.

He pushed farther into the interior, oblivious of Kate and Bobby Beach who had begun to pick their way through the foliage behind him. Accustomed to this kind of terrain, he was well ahead of them when he saw the faint trail to the right. Curious, he thought. A service track would be well defined. But this one . . . if he hadn't seen its like in the wild, he would have missed it. Who or what could have made it?

He bent down and examined the lightly packed soil, identifying the clear imprint of a bare heel. Behind him, voices filtered through the leaves as Kate asked how they cared for the plants and Bobby answered.

"We got ourselves some kinda plant expert living here in the annex with the science whizzes upstairs. Name's Thompson, real snotty fella. He supervises the team a' colored boys who live out beyond the marsh."

Steve crept silently along the narrow trail. He had a strong feeling of déjà vu; in a minute he would come upon a small roughly woven basket with three purple fruit.

"Hey!" Bobby's voice boomed. "You there! Dee Cherco! Wait up!" Steve could hear his huge body crashing through the foliage. Sweat dripped into Steve's eyes; he wiped an arm across his forehead and continued along the trail.

Here, deep inside the artificial rain forest, the feeling of displacement was almost dizzying. Breaking through a particularly dense patch of growth, he found himself reaching for his machete, then realized where he was. God, it was strange, everything familiar, yet different. Distant thunder growled as he stepped through a natural arch of trees and found himself in a tiny clearing. An old man was seated on a piece of fallen log, gnawing at a piece of fruit. Its juices ran over his gray beard and onto his naked chest. Steve rubbed his eyes; was he hallucinating? The old man raised his palm in greeting, then reached into a small basket beside him. Rising with some difficulty, he extended a wrinkled and rather dirty hand in which nestled a round pink fruit. Wonderingly, Steve moved closer. It was a peach.

"Eat," the old man said. His voice was low and soft, his expression glassy. The thunder was louder now, the storm approaching fast.

Gingerly, Steve took the fruit, his eyes on the old man. Seen close up, he was even older than Steve had realized, his skin deeply wrinkled, his thin limbs flaccid and pale. What a strange character, he thought. Yet something about him seemed vaguely familiar.

"Who are you?" he asked. "What are you doing here?"

"I take care of the trees," the old man said dreamily. "I help them grow." Swaying slightly, he reached out and caressed a nearby sapling. Then without warning, he grabbed its top leaves in his bony fingers and crushed them to pulp. "I help them grow!" he repeated fiercely, pulling up on the slender trunk and shaking it from side to side. The roots came loose and he flung the plant away from him. Steve backed off fast as Bobby came crashing through the forest with Kate just behind. The two newcomers stood staring at the wraithlike figure whose attention was fixed on Steve, an expression of sudden surprise on his wrinkled face. Then his eyes clouded over with doubt and confusion, and he backed away, fading into the bush like a shadow.

"Who the hell was that?" Steve asked. There was something about the old man's eyes . . .

Bobby shook his head. "You don't want to film the old guy," he said nervously. "He's part of some drug program Mr. Nolan runs. For company employees."

"What's his name?" Steve asked, knowing the answer.

"I don't rightly remember . . ."

Steve looked at the wall of jungle through which the old man had disappeared. Finally he turned back to the two of them, Bobby impatient, Kate filled with dread. "It's Tucker Boone, isn't it?" he said softly.

Bobby looked surprised. "Yeah," he said. "How did you know?"

Chapter 31

"Billy Ray! Bring these folks some Fanta, ya hear? And get me another Dr Pepper!" Bobby turned his attention to the doctor and the film director, who had followed him reluctantly back to his office. They looked pale, almost ill. Yankees just couldn't take the heat.

"Are you sure it's Tucker?" Kate asked Steve. "He's ... so old."

"I'm sure. Ask *him*," and Steve jabbed a thumb at Bobby Beach.

"It's Mr. Boone all right," Bobby assured them.

"But if that's true ..." Kate broke off, her eyes deeply worried.

Steve looked at her in alarm. "What is it?"

"Never mind," she said quietly. "Not now."

Steve turned to Bobby. "What happened to him?"

"Happened? I don't know what you mean." Bobby opened his eyes wide and tried to look innocent.

"Sure you do. It must have happened down here." Steve leaned forward in his chair and looked intently at Bobby. "Tucker Boone's the same age I am. I've known him more than twenty years."

Bobby shook his head. "Mr. Boone the same age as you? I don't think so." He smirked; this director fella looked around forty. "Not a chance."

"Why?" Kate challenged. "Because Tuck—uh, Mr. Boone looks so old? Or because he used to look so young?"

Bobby blinked, suddenly nonplussed, but kept silent.

"They brought him down here last May, didn't they?" Steve said urgently. "Right around Memorial Day. He still looked young then, didn't he? Younger than me."

"I thought you were a film director," Bobby said suspiciously.

"He is. He was filming Mr. Boone for Genelife last year," Kate lied. "I saw him, too. He looked wonderful. What happened to him?" Bobby still seemed reluctant to talk, so Kate pressed on, making it up as she went along. "You're in big trouble, Bobby," she said. "We were sent down here to shoot commercials, and one of the most important things they want us to shoot is pictures of Tucker Boone. They know what he used to look like. Now, you seem like a real nice guy. Responsible. Cooperative. Maybe we can find a way around this thing, use old footage or something. Save your ass. But to do that, we need to know what really happened."

Billy Ray arrived and passed out the sodas. Bobby popped his open with a loud click, and sucked up nearly half the can before he looked over at Kate, and then at Steve. "You with her on this?" he asked cautiously.

"Every step of the way."

"I understand your reluctance to talk about it," Kate said. "So let me tell you what I think happened. You knew Tucker before. Not well, but you knew him. He consulted on the building of this place. He brought the root stock to plant that rain forest in there."

"He didn't bring it," Bobby interrupted. "He had it shipped up from Brazil last May."

"You were right," Steve said to Kate. "He *was* sent back to the rain forest for root stock, after the place in Louisiana burned down."

"Didn't burn," Bobby said. "We burned it. Some sorta disease hit the plants. We couldn't save nothin', had to burn it to the ground. The scientists were afraid the sickness could still be in the soil. Said we had to find a whole new place. Mr. Boone brought us here."

Kate nodded to herself, then looked up at Bobby appraisingly. "How much does he pay you?" she asked.

Bobby looked surprised. "Pay me? Mr. Boone?"

"Come on, Bobby! You know what I'm talking about!"

Bobby's little pig eyes narrowed. How did she know about the money?

"The drug recovery program, Bobby," Kate said. "Nolan's been paying you extra ever since they brought Mr. Boone down here, right?"

Bobby nodded sullenly. "I earned every penny," he said truculently.

"Of course you did," Kate agreed soothingly. "I'm sure you didn't mean to make Mr. Boone get old."

"Me?" Bobby squeaked. "I didn't do that!"

"Oh, but you did! I'm a doctor, Bobby. I know these things. Why don't you tell me what happened?"

Bobby downed the rest of his Dr Pepper. Why the hell should he tell her anything else? Why didn't he just throw them out? He started to rise, then reconsidered. She seemed to know most everything already. And she worked for Randall Webber; if he could convince her that it wasn't really his fault, maybe she would explain it to Mr. Nolan, get him off the hook.

"I don't rightly know what happened, exactly," Bobby began slowly. "I mean, I always gave him his medicine right on time, twice a day like they said. I felt sorry for the guy. They said to let him live in the rain forest, that it was part of the treatment. Re ... re-gretting? Something like that, Mr. Nolan called it ..."

"Regression?" Kate suggested.

"Yeah, I think that was it ... Anyhow, as long as he got his medicine regular, he wasn't much trouble. We left his food in the baskets like Mr. Nolan said, gave him a hammock ..."

"What happened when he came up against the glass?" Steve asked, curious.

"The first couple of times it happened, he got real confused, sort of backed off and shook his head ... we had to give him an extra injection. After that, it seemed like he tried to stay away from the sides of the building. Hell, it's a big place. He had plenty of room."

"And when did he start to change?"

"About three months ago, I think it was. One morning I sent the boys in to find him so I could medicate him, and when they brought him out, he had these gray streaks in his hair. Next day, the gray was worse, and so were the wrinkles. In a couple of weeks, you'd never know it was the same man." Bobby turned and tossed the empty soda can across the room toward an open trash bin. It hit the side of the bin, bounced off, and clattered across the floor. Bobby sighed hugely. "Don't know how you recognized him," he told Steve. "Anyhow, the boys were plenty scared. But I told them it was all part of the treatment."

"Why didn't you tell Mr. Nolan?"

Bobby looked at Kate belligerently. "Who says I didn't tell him?" he snorted.

"Come on, Bobby. I can't help you if you don't cooperate." Kate finished her Fanta and tossed the empty can at the trash bin. Bobby followed it with his eyes, clearly impressed when it went in cleanly, rattling around for a moment before settling on top of the other empties already in residence. "You didn't tell him," Kate said, "because you thought maybe it was something you did. Maybe you'd measured the medicine wrong, or maybe you hadn't fed him enough or something. You thought it was your fault Tucker suddenly got old. Wasn't that it?"

Bobby nodded. "Yeah, that and the money. If it was my fault, Mr. Nolan would take Tucker somewhere else and I wouldn't get the extra money."

"Perfectly understandable," Steve said. "Right, Kate?"

But Kate only shrugged.

"Was it really my fault, miss, uh, Doctor?" Bobby asked tentatively.

"I'm afraid it was," Kate told him sternly. She looked thoughtful. "On the other hand, you're not trained for this, are you?"

Bobby shook his head. "No, ma'am," he said.

Steve glanced at Kate curiously. What was she up to? "So even though it was technically your fault, it's really not fair to blame you." Kate sighed theatrically. "What a pity Mr. Nolan won't see it that way."

"He won't?"

"No. It's so unfair!"

"You could explain it to him. Tell him I didn't do it on purpose."

Kate shook her head. "He'd never listen," she said regretfully. "He'd be too mad to listen."

"Well, can you put Mr. Boone back the way he was?"

Kate appeared to consider the idea. "It's possible," she said. "But it'll take time, more time than you have." She reached over and patted his huge paw sympathetically. "I sure wouldn't want to be in your shoes when Mr. Nolan comes down here next week!"

"Next *week*?" Bobby half rose from his chair in alarm, catching his stomach painfully on the overhang of his desk and subsiding back into his chair.

"That's right. Tuesday or Wednesday, I think he said."

"But that's only four days away!"

Kate shook her head. "I really wish we could help you," she said. "And I just thought of a way we can." Bobby's face brightened. "The thing is ... I don't want to get in trouble with Mr. Nolan myself. He's a terrible man to cross. But I'm sure you know that."

Bobby gulped. "Well, I surely would appreciate it if you could help me, Doctor."

"As I said, I'd like to. But I don't know if we dare ... what do you think, uh, Phil?"

"I think we should take a chance and help Mr. Beach," Steve said firmly, picking up the cue. He wasn't quite sure where Kate was going with this, but he had faith in her. "You can see he's done the very best he can."

"I have! I have!" Bobby moaned. He massaged his sweaty cheeks and neck.

Kate pretended to think awhile. "Well, okay," she agreed. "I'll risk it. While you're showing us the lab area, tell your boys to bring Tucker out. We'll take him with us when we leave."

"No! I can't allow that!" Bobby shoved his chair away from the desk and pushed himself up on his feet. "Mr. Boone's never supposed to leave the facility! Mr. Nolan was very firm about that!" He performed an agitated little dance behind his desk.

Kate shrugged. "Have it your way," she said. "I was just trying to help, but if you want to show Nolan a doddering eighty-year-old savage instead of the brilliant scientist he entrusted to your care ..."

"You're a brave man, Bobby!" Steve told him dolorously.

"What I was thinking," Kate continued, "was that we could keep Mr. Boone out of sight for a couple of days, just till Mr. Nolan leaves. You could say that Mr. DeCherico here is filming him on location. Meanwhile, I'll give him some special medicine I have, try to get him back the way he was. As soon as Mr. Nolan's gone, we'll bring Mr. Boone right back to you. Mr. Nolan will never know."

"You really think you can change him back?"

"I'll give it a shot. Frankly, I'd like to help Mr. Boone if I can. He's a great man." She studied Bobby's face; the fact that Tucker was a great man obviously cut no ice with him. "And it'll solve your problem, too," she added quickly, "because Mr. Nolan won't find out what you've done, and take Mr. Boone away. Or worse."

"And you can keep collecting that money!" Steve chimed in.

Bobby shook his head; something didn't smell quite right here. Why should these two be so anxious to help him? Still, he'd checked the woman out with Randall Webber. And the more he thought about it, the more he liked the idea of getting Tucker Boone off his hands for a while. The old man seemed to be getting worse; what if he died on him? If the woman doctor took Boone for a few days and actually changed him back the way he had been, Bobby's problem was solved. If she didn't, he could blame her for Boone's sudden aging. "He was fine when he left here," he could hear himself telling Mr. Nolan. "Don't know what that doctor of yours did to him." Sure; let her take the fall.

He turned and beamed at them. "I sure do appreciate this," he said. "I'll just go tell the boys to find Mr. Boone and pull him outta there. Then we'll take a quick look at the lab." He waddled out of the office, calling for Billy Ray.

"Were you serious about changing him back?" Steve asked Kate, but she shook her head sadly. Her face was pale and drawn.

"Remember those photos of Tucker? The ones Marianne said were taken maybe a year before he disappeared?"

"Sure. I'd seen one of them before. I was really surprised at how young he looked, but Marianne said Tucker was one of those people who never seemed to age."

"You know why, don't you?"

"Genelife, obviously. But ... it wasn't on the market then. Tucker must have started a couple of years before, taking the experimental drug in the lab."

But Kate shook her head again. "I think he started way before that," she said. "He was in such bad shape when you two were rescued, you thought he'd die if he stayed. But he didn't; he stayed and he survived."

"Just barely. I saw him when he came out. He looked awful."

"Awful ... I know it was a long time ago, but can you remember *how* he looked awful?"

Steve closed his eyes and tried to conjure up a picture of Tucker, sitting in an armchair with an afghan thrown over his slight figure. "He looked exhausted . . . undernourished . . . shaky . . ."

"But young, right?"

"Well, he *was* young; we all were, then."

"Of course. But an experience like that is bound to take a certain toll. Didn't you notice new lines on your face, afterward?"

"Yes, I did . . . But Tucker . . .?" Steve shrugged. "It was a long time ago." Suddenly the implication of what she'd said hit him. "Hey, are you suggesting he started taking Genelife back in the rain forest?"

Kate nodded. "Of course it wasn't actually Genelife back then; he probably just chewed the leaves."

"But that was *years* ago . . ."

"Exactly. Tucker's the only long-term user anyone's ever seen."

"But he's old," Steve protested. "If he's been using Genelife all along, why didn't he stay young?" Then his expression changed. "Jesus! You don't think Genelife . . .?"

"What I think," said Kate slowly, "is that the terrible headaches, the lack of appetite, the low sperm count . . . all the side effects we've come to associate with Genelife . . . they're nothing compared to this one."

Richard Day took a shrimp ball from the waiter's tray, popped it into his mouth, and looked around. His was a slightly awkward position. He wasn't officially part of the Randall Webber party, nor did his agency handle any other pharmaceutical business at the moment. When people asked him, nicely, of course, why he was there, it was difficult to know what to tell them. Especially as they'd be seeing him here next year, and in a far more important position. So he'd settled for a white lie: his agency was pitching a drug account, but it had to be kept confidential. He was here to learn about the industry. Corporate types seemed to accept that, and the few agency people he'd identified—none from MacAllister, thank heaven—eyed him suspiciously and left him alone.

Now he scanned the crowd. Michael had promised to introduce him to the woman from Omni during the closing cocktail party, though he hadn't invited Richard to join them for dinner. Fuck him, Day thought. It's his business I'm after, not his company. But he was miffed.

Another waiter came by with chicken pieces on skewers, and Richard took two. He was hungry. He wandered over to the bar for a refill; he was drinking Scotch tonight, no longer caring whether Nolan approved. Maybe he'd just stay here and drink when the others went in to dinner. It would be boring to eat alone. Besides, the conference was just about over. Most people would skip the two-hour wrap-up the following morning and play golf instead or just head home. He himself was booked on a noon flight. He noticed a pretty, dark-haired woman smiling at him from down the bar, and he smiled back, then realized she was actually smiling at the couple next to him. Embarrassed, he downed half his drink and wandered out onto the terrace.

After the crush at the bar, the cool night air was refreshing. But few people were taking advantage of it, preferring to continue networking in the overheated interior.

Richard strolled to the edge of the flagged terrace and leaned his forearms on the broad stone balustrade separating him from the darkened garden below. It had been a good idea to come; Nolan had seemed impressed with his dedication, and Richard had cemented their friendship further by rising early each morning to jog with the man, much as he hated jogging. Well, once the papers had been signed and the Randall Webber check had cleared, he could send an account director to jog with Nolan at conferences. Hell, maybe a *female* account executive; Nolan would probably like that. Michael had never mentioned a wife, but from the way he'd eyed several of the younger women in the hotel pool, he obviously found the fair sex attractive.

Lost in such thoughts, it was some time before Richard became aware of the soft moaning coming from somewhere below him. He peered out into the garden, but could see nothing. Curious, he made his way around to one of the curved stone stairs that led down into the garden from each side of the terrace. As he started down the stairs, he heard it again: a gasp, followed by a soft drawn-out cry. Was someone in trouble? From where he stood, the central area just below the balustrade was now faintly visible, barely illuminated by spill from yellow lanternlike light fixtures at each end of the terrace above. A woman lay sprawled across a wooden bench, her dress hiked above her waist, legs splayed. But from the way she was clinging to the muscular body of the man above her, she didn't seem to be in trouble. No, far from it.

Richard moved closer; this was better than the movies in his hotel room. He watched as the man's mouth moved over her body; he saw her claw at his tight-fitting jeans; he heard the woman scream with pleasure as the man entered her at last, and they writhed together on the bench. His eyes had become adjusted to the light as he watched; now he could make out her features, distorted though they were by passion. She was older than he'd thought at first, and rather severe-looking. Not the sort of woman you'd expect to find having sex on a bench in a public garden. At last they finished, and the woman pushed the man away. He turned toward the light as he zipped up his jeans, and Richard recognized the tennis pro's good-looking young assistant. A kid, he thought in some surprise; can't be more than twenty or so. And not overly bright. An odd couple indeed. The young man scurried off, and the woman rearranged her blue cocktail dress and turned toward the stairs. Richard fled.

"There you are!" Michael greeted him as he stepped inside. "Been looking for you. What are you drinking?"

"Scotch," Richard told him firmly.

"Get me one too while you're at it, will you?" Nolan extended a glass containing half an inch of clear liquid and a wedge of lime. "Perrier. Don't know what's keeping Bettina."

Fuming, Richard elbowed his way to the bar and got the drinks. When he returned, Nolan was deep in conversation with an attractive blond woman in a pink suit. Handing Nolan his mineral water, he stood awkwardly by, waiting to be introduced. But Michael ignored him, chatting on about Section 936 of the federal tax law. Whatever in hell that is, Richard thought angrily. He felt very ill-used. At last the woman in pink moved on.

"Bettina's younger than I thought she'd be," Richard said with ill-concealed irritation. "Why didn't you introduce me?"

"Bett—Good Lord, that wasn't Bettina! Meredith's with Pfizer; I've known her for years." He studied Richard closely; how much Scotch had the man had? The last thing he needed was another Jerry Lim. But Richard, sensing Nolan's displeasure, smiled engagingly. "I'm just so anxious

to meet the woman," he said. "You've made her sound so
. . . unique. I'm fascinated."

"She *is* an unusual woman," Michael agreed forgivingly.
"She's so smart, it's scary, and a real risk-taker. Ah, there
she is!" Michael took a few steps toward the tall blond
woman making her way toward them through the crowd.
He waved, which the woman acknowledged with a faint
smile.

"That blue is a wonderful color for you, Bettina," Nolan
told her as she joined them. He reached for her hand and
then thought better of it. "And I see you've gotten a little sun."

Bettina touched a fingertip to her flushed face in a moment of confusion, then quickly recovered. "Yes, I had a
walk in the garden this afternoon, after the last
presentation."

That's not all you had in the garden, Richard thought. So
Bettina liked them young and stupid; that could be useful.

"I'd like you to meet Richard Day," Nolan was saying.
"He's the man I was telling you about. The new advertising agency."

Bettina gave Richard a cool appraising stare that would
have unnerved him, had he not seen her *en déshabillé* several minutes before. He recalled a public speaking class
he'd attended years ago, when he'd first gotten into the
business. "If you're nervous speaking to large groups," the
instructor had told them, "try picturing everyone naked."
He smiled to himself; this was much better.

"I can't say what an honor it is to meet you," Richard
said ingratiatingly. "Michael's been singing your praises."

"Why thank you, Mr. Day. And has this conference been
useful for you?"

"Definitely. I've picked up all sorts of information."
More than you could ever imagine.

"I'm so glad."

"Can I get you a drink?" Richard offered.

"Thank you, no. We'll be going in to dinner in a moment.
Will you be joining us?"

So she's not the one who decided to leave me out, Richard thought. He glanced over at Michael, who was gazing
worshipfully at Bettina.

"Actually, I thought we should dine alone," Michael was
telling her. "So much to discuss, and this is the last chance

we'll get, face-to-face, for a while." Richard noted Michael's expression with interest.

Bettina raised an impersonal eyebrow. "Really? You don't have bad news, I hope?"

"No, not at all! Business is wonderful! Omni can rest assured their recent decision in Tokyo to—uh, their confidence in Randall Webber is completely justified."

"Good." Bettina turned back to Richard. "So nice to have met you, Mr. Day," she said dismissively. "I'm looking forward to seeing your work. I hope it's as good as Michael assures me it will be."

Bitch, Richard thought. His cheeks hurt from smiling. "Oh, it will be," he assured her.

She gave him a regal, disinterested nod, then turned away. "Richard, shouldn't we be—"

"We'll want to feel our way at first," Richard continued, riding over her. Patronize me, will she, the slut? "Push a few buttons, see what excites you." Bettina swung around to stare at him. "And the consumer, of course. But I can promise you that once we've entered into it, the thrust of our work will be deeply satisfying." He glanced over at Nolan who was obviously trying to decide whether Richard's tasteless double entendres had been intentional, and if so, what to do about it.

But Bettina remained serene. "That sounds like an excellent approach," she told Richard, shooting him a look that went right through to his brain. "But I'd advise you not to get carried away. I understand you're out a great deal of money at the moment. We wouldn't want to see you get . . . I believe the expression is 'fucked'? Come, Michael."

She turned on her heel and headed for the dining room, and Nolan scurried after her.

Richard went to the bar for more Scotch. He was already half-drunk, but decided it didn't matter; he was through being pleasant for the evening. As for Bettina, her veiled threat didn't bother him. Nolan now hated Mac, couldn't wait to get rid of him. And Richard had made sure Nolan realized, early on, that he knew all about the side effects issue. Such knowledge could be dangerous. No, Genelife was locked in to the Richard Day Agency.

He sat at a table on the deserted terrace under a quarter moon, his glass and a dish of peanuts beside him. So Michael fancies Bettina, he thought. And Bettina fancies pretty boys. And Omni has just made an important decision concerning Genelife; he'd have to find out what it was. He sipped his Scotch and ate a handful of nuts. It was truly amazing the amount of valuable information you could pick up at a business conference.

Chapter 32

The rhythmic drumming increased in intensity as the young chief and his wife stepped into the ceremonial circle. The shamans lifted up the heavy calabash and the acrid smell wafted out over the clearing.

Tucker looked around him; the tribe seemed smaller than he remembered, and he recognized few faces. Fortunately the chief had remembered him.

How many years had gone by since he'd first suspected what the calabash held? Since he'd arranged with Kuna to slip away from Father Jim's rescue party and rejoin the tribe? Since he'd spied on the elders as they gathered the sacred leaves, then gathered the leaves himself?

Yet he'd instantly recognized Kuna, now seemingly a man in his middle twenties. And Kuna had remembered him, too. Well, that was one advantage of what was now known as Genelife.

The drumming was terribly loud now, the waves of sound almost palpable. Kuna was drinking from the calabash. Kuna, the chief. Tucker held his head and moaned.

"Is he awake?" Steve asked. The rain was torrential, and he didn't dare take his eyes off the road to look at the two figures in the back seat of the car.

"No, I think he's dreaming . . ." Tucker half lay across the seat, his head on Kate's shoulder. She spoke loudly to be heard over the drumming of the rain on the metal roof of the car. "Whatever they've been giving him is starting to wear off. But he'll have residual effects for some time."

Tucker moaned again and thrashed his arms. Kate mopped his forehead with a wet handkerchief and he mumbled raggedly before lapsing back into a fitful sleep.

"What's he saying?"

"I'm not sure. It sounded like . . . Kuna?"

"Kuna!" The ceremony was over, the calabash con-

taining the chief's supply of the Genelife-like drug tucked
carefully away in the makeshift shelter. Tucker had brought
a new machete for the former tribal leader, but now he
presented it to Kuna with a flourish. "This is the knife of
a chief," he said, surprised to find the strange words coming
back to him.

Kuna took the knife, his face wreathed in smiles, and
slashed at the air with energy. "You have come back to
live with us again?" he asked.

"Uh, no," Tucker stammered guiltily, thinking of the
men encamped less than a mile away who were standing
by to transport the root stock to San Jose, whence it would
eventually find its secret way to the new Florida compound.
Secrecy was important. Industrial spies, Nolan had assured
him, were everywhere.

"Uh, what happened to the old chief?" Tucker asked,
puzzled. Thanks to the tribe's primitive version of Genelife,
the chief should still be young and vital; surely, that was
the whole reason for the calabash ceremony. Why was
Kuna the chief now?

Kuna seemed perplexed; perhaps the words weren't right
after all. But then, Tucker had never been completely sure
of the meanings of the words he and the others had attempted to exchange.

"How did the old chief die?" Tucker tried again. Probably a hunting accident, he thought. The contents of the
calabash would have assured him perpetual youth. Tucker
grinned to himself; perpetual youth! You and me, Kuna,
we'll live forever!

But Kuna was shaking his head, confusion clouding his
face. "Not die," he said.

"Then why did they make you the chief?" Tucker asked,
cursing the vagaries of this language he would never really understand.

Again, Kuna shook his head; then his expression cleared.
He gestured for Tucker to follow him, and strode off across
the clearing. There, sitting on the ground, was an old man.
His face was wrinkled, his muscles withered and limp, his
sparse hair white. Tucker stared; he'd never seen a man as
old as this in the rain forest. He and Steve had actually
seen the tribe leave several sick and injured members along
the trail to die. Surely this man couldn't keep up on his
own.

An old woman approached. Pale, waxy grubs wriggled in her palm. Patiently, she fed them to the old man who mumbled them down, one at a time.

Kuna squatted and spoke rapidly to the old man, who looked up at Tucker with rheumy eyes. A faint smile hovered around his lips, as he pointed to Kuna's new machete, then whispered something that Tucker couldn't hear. Kuna turned back to Tucker and spoke. At first Tucker thought he'd misunderstood what Kuna had said: how could he have given such a knife to this old man, once? He and Steve had had only one spare machete, and they'd given it to the chief. Then he looked closer, and his blood ran cold. There on the man's left cheek was a faint, jagged scar in the shape of a W.

"He got old!" Tucker heard himself shout at Kuna. His words seemed to come from a long way away. "How could he get old?"

Kuna shrugged. "It is the way," he said.

"But the drink in the calabash ... ! And you, you are still young!"

" 'Young' or 'strong,' " he'd told Steve, that long-ago evening in the jungle. "I can't understand half of what they're saying." Now, too late, he realized why the word Kuna had used had meant both things.

"I am like him," Kuna said. "Strong for many years. Then old and die." With an abrupt hand movement, Kuna strode away from the old people. Seeing his own fate obviously made him uncomfortable.

Tucker squatted down in front of the old chief. "How long ..." he tried. "When ..." The old man shrugged tiredly, then lay down on the ground, drawing his knees up to his belly. Tucker turned to the old woman who was regarding him with a sympathetic eye. Taking up a stick, he drew a circle in the damp ground and pantomimed the tribe on the move around the circle. Next he marked an X on the circle and then pretended to gather leaves and drink from a calabash. He jabbed repeatedly at the mark and then at the clearing around them in an attempt to communicate that the mark on the dirt circle represented the place where they were now camped. Again and again, he traced along the circle the tribe's yearly journey through the jungle, each time coming back to the X. At last, she seemed to understand. Taking the stick from him, she traced the circle once. She pantomimed drinking, then pointed to her husband and herself. Turning, she surveyed the tribal members nearby, then indicated a young man. Again, she traced the circle, stopping about three quarters of the way to the calabash mark, then pointed at the old man and herself. Tucker nodded; the tribe had been about three months away from the leaf-gathering place when the chief and his wife had begun to change.

That would have been just three months ago, Tucker realized. In just three months, this young, vibrant man, leader of his people, had become the empty husk that lay before him. And Kuna, one of the two youths chosen years before to be tested and trained to succeed the chief, had been ready.

The old woman was pulling on his arm. He followed her into the jungle along a barely discernible path. Suddenly she stopped and pushed him forward. He took two steps and froze. Before him was a deep, wide pit festooned with creepers. The pit was filled with human bones.

He turned back to the old woman who was regarding him calmly. She bent and smoothed a tiny patch of earth with her hand, then drew a circle like the one Tucker had drawn earlier. She jabbed at the circle with a forefinger and pantomimed the tribe on the move, then patted her chest and shook her head. She rose and pointed to the pit.

A howl of anguish and deep despair rose from Tucker's throat. It filled the clearing and echoed through the trees.

"My God! What's going on back there?" The rain had slowed. Steve pulled off onto the soggy shoulder and turned around. Tucker howled again, twisting his body this way and that.

"Steady him," Kate directed, reaching for her medical bag. She began to fill a syringe. "I'm going to have to sedate him."

April 22

"I'm sorry, Marianne, so sorry . . . At least I never gave you Genelife . . . thank God for that. Marianne?"

"This is Kate," Steve told him. "Remember?"

"Kate? Where's Marianne?"

"She's not here," Kate said firmly. "But she understands. She forgives you."

Two dismally wet days and nights had passed since they'd brought Tucker out of the greenhouse and hidden themselves away in the tiny cabin deep in the Everglades. Tucker slept most of that time, fading in and out of consciousness. They took turns keeping watch over him while he slept, mopping his sweaty face with cool towels. When he woke, they fed him soup and sweet biscuits and tea, and tried to explain where he was and what had happened to him. He spoke to them of his second rain forest trip during one of his lucid periods, then lapsed back into a stupor before they could question him further.

"How much longer will he be like this?" Steve asked.

Kate sighed with frustration. It was so important that Tucker talk, and talk fast. Genelife would have to be pulled off the market immediately; that much was certain. But there were still enough gaps in their knowledge to allow Nolan a chance to slip through. "I thought we were over the worst last night," she said, "when he told us about Kuna and the old chief. But . . . he's been through a helluva lot." She shuddered. The image of the old chief's wife pointing to the pile of human bones was hard to forget.

But Monday morning brought bright yellow sunshine and a newly washed day, lifting their flagging spirits. Even Tucker seemed to respond to its healing rays. He seemed calmer and more lucid, though depressed and still somewhat confused.

"I didn't understand!" Tucker exclaimed suddenly. "You have to believe me! I didn't know!" He blinked up at the two faces studying him with concern, then looked around in confusion. "Steve?"

"Yes, it's me."

"What are you—where am I?"

"A cabin in the Everglades," Steve said. "Not far from the compound, remember? We talked about it before."

Tucker shook his head. "I'm not sure," he said. "I remember the trees . . ." Suddenly his body convulsed. "The trees! I hate the damn trees!"

"Think you should give him something?" Steve asked, but Kate shook her head. "Not unless we absolutely have to."

As they watched, Tucker unclenched his body and slowly

opened his eyes. "They made me take care of the trees,"
he said.

"I know," Steve said.

"Goddamn trees! I told him but he didn't believe me!"

Kate leaned in, alert now. "Who did you tell? Michael
Nolan?"

"Who's she?" Tucker asked, looking over at Kate with
suspicion.

"Her name is Kate. She's here to help you. She's my . . .
friend. Go ahead and answer her, Tucker."

But Tucker shook his head, following his own thoughts.
"I didn't mean to hurt anyone," he said. "I just didn't understand how it worked." He pushed himself up from his
semirecumbent position on the bed and dropped his feet
to the floor. He surveyed the small, stuffy cabin. "How'd I
get here?"

"We brought you here from the greenhouse two—no,
three days ago," Kate said. "You don't ever have to go
back."

"Oh, yes I do!" Tucker said softly. Then his eyes filled
with anger. "The discovery of the century! It kept the chief
young forever. That's what I thought. But I was wrong,
God was I wrong! The stuff works for twenty years or so,
and then suddenly everything falls apart. You get old . . .
fast and painfully . . . way beyond your actual age." He
looked down at his wrinkled hands. " 'The Wonderful One-
Hoss Shay!' That's what I told him, but he didn't believe
me. He thought I was trying to sabotage his sweet little
deal with Omni. Not that I wouldn't have liked to." He
stopped suddenly and shook his head, then looked up at
Kate like a child. "I'm hungry."

A pot of soup was simmering on the stove of the tiny
kitchenette. Steve poured some into a cracked bowl and
held it up in front of Tucker who grasped the spoon with
shaking fingers and began to eat. Kate leaned over and
wiped his face between spoonfuls. He'd finished nearly all
the soup when he suddenly pushed the bowl away, then
stared at his hands again. "I wanted to live forever," he
said bitterly. "Doesn't look likely, does it?"

Kate blinked away a tear. Steve set the soup bowl on
the dresser with a bang, overcome by deep sadness and a
terrible feeling of futility.

Tucker stretched out on the bed again and closed his

eyes, and Kate spread the tattered coverlet over him, then turned to Steve. "I still don't understand," she said. "Couldn't the chief be expected to lead the tribe for years, without Genelife? Why do this to him?"

"It was different for them," Tucker said, startling them both. He opened his eyes and looked around for Steve. "Remember when they chose Kuna and that other guy?" he asked softly.

Gravely, Steve nodded. "The chief and his wife couldn't have children; Genelife prevented it. So they chose two possible successors. Am I right?" Tucker nodded. "But . . . that was years ago. Why choose successors so long before they'd be needed?"

"Because the tribe had to be prepared," Tucker explained slowly, his voice thin and tired. "See, they couldn't be sure exactly when the aging would happen; some people lasted longer than others. But they must have gotten a good twenty years out of it. Imagine having a leader who stayed strong and young and able to lead the hunt for twenty years straight. They figured it was worth it."

"The tribe was very small," Steve explained to Kate. "And a true stone-age people. Did I tell you they'd lost the knowledge of making fire?" Kate nodded. "Their nutritional intake was very poor, their environment incredibly hard. They aged so much faster and younger, and their average life expectancy was so short, Genelife made sense to them. Twenty years of youth and strength for their chief seemed a pretty good trade for his sudden aging and death."

"But why did Tucker age so much sooner?" Kate asked. "Tucker? What happened to you?"

Tucker shrugged, but his eyes were dark and brooding. "Who knows? Their diet, their life-style, it was so different from ours . . . they probably metabolized the drug differently." He pushed himself up against the pillows. "And who the hell knew how much was too much? Not me, that's for damn sure!"

"Then how did you decide how much to put into the Genelife patch?" Kate asked.

"Basically, I experimented on myself. I started taking the stuff years ago, in the rain forest that first time, chewing the leaves. I brought root stock out with me, grew some on the balcony of our apartment, kept chewing the damn leaves. Then, when I got that grant to work at the Randall Foundation, I made extracts for myself. I kept notes of how much I took, and kept increasing the dosage until I could really see it working. The leaves on their own didn't smell anything like the disgusting mess in the calabash. I think the shamans must have put something into the mash to keep the rest of the tribe from being tempted to drink. Anyhow, I just kept on taking it. I didn't know what the hell I was doing, but I didn't get any real bad side effects, just some headaches and appetite loss, so I figured it didn't really matter, at least as far as I was concerned."

Steve and Kate exchanged glances; obviously, Tucker hadn't recognized his own adverse reactions to the drug; the personality shifts and paranoia, the lowered sperm count. No wonder Marianne had never been able to have a child.

"Of course we had to lick the side effects for the FDA ..." Tucker continued, his voice fainter now, like a spring winding down. "We couldn't release it like that. I couldn't get anywhere, but Jerry Lim fixed it while I was away in the rain forest."

"Jerry Lim?"

"Yeah, that's what Michael said when I tried to tell him about the time bomb ... He refused to understand that those side effects were nothing to the one I'd just found out about." Tucker's fists were clenched in frustration.

"Tell us about it," Kate said softly. "Tell us what happened ..."

"So you're Tucker Boone!" Father Jim's young successor stared in amazement. "You're a legend in these parts, man! Funny ... you look a lot younger than I expected."

"I really appreciate your assistance," Tucker said gruffly, embarrassed and irritated by Father Larry's obvious hero worship as well as the comment about his youthful appearance. Still, the missionary's help was more than welcome; it was essential.

Despite the disaster in Louisiana, Tucker had returned to Brazil with high hopes. The Florida facility, built under the Randall Foundation name, was ready to receive and nurture the new root stock. Meanwhile, they had plenty of stockpiled plant extract to work with.

He'd heard rumors that Michael was preparing to launch

Genelife nationally, and had argued against moving too fast, but he knew the FDA would never allow the drug on the market without proper testing. No, once he got Florida up and running, he'd have to find a way to reduce those side effects. He was hoping this trip might provide some answers.

But his positive mood was tinged with trepidation; May was the month the tribe's year-long trek led them back to the sacred collection place. Would he meet them there? If so, how would he be received?

"Father Jim left me his notebooks," Larry said. "And five of our boys claim to know the area where you and Steve Kavett were found."

"Boys?"

"Local Indians who work with us. Heck of a nice bunch of guys. Anyway, they've agreed to guide you in, and work with you. There's a new lumber camp not far away, and their helicopter'll take your medical plants to San Jose. You've got a courier standing by there, you said in your letter?"

Tucker nodded. "There'll be a lot of plant material. It'll probably take three or four trips."

"No problem. The camp pilot's happy to make the extra bucks."

"Thanks. It was nice of you to set it all up."

"Glad to do it. Your research project sounds interesting." Tucker had told the missionary that he was collecting a variety of plants for possible medical development. "And frankly, I'm delighted to have a chance to try and contact that particular tribe again. I know Father Jim did a little trading with them a couple of times, after you left. And some of the boys have spotted them now and then, but I haven't had much luck." Larry shook his head. "I understand they've fallen on hard times," he said. "Sure wish they'd let us help them."

Tucker wasn't surprised; in fact, the one fear he'd had when he'd first written to the mission explaining his trip was that, thanks to the unstoppable encroachment of slash-and-burn agriculture and the logging industry, the collection place had already been destroyed. Fortunately, the mission Indians believed the area was still intact, although how long it would remain so seemed questionable.

Recent development, Father Larry explained, had brought

what passed for civilization these days much closer to parts
of the tribe's traditional yearly route, making encounters
with outsiders a lot more common. Not only had this
brought the tribe into contact with new diseases, it had
made the collection of sufficient food more difficult. The
tribe had shrunk in size, several families having defected
to a larger, better-contacted tribe in the area. A larger tribe
meant better hunting and gathering, and more nourishment
for all, while contact with the outside world meant an abun-
dance of exciting trade goods.

It was Father Larry's fond hope, he told Tucker wistfully,
that the remaining tribal members could be persuaded to
come in to the mission, from where they would be flown
to a large evangelical complex some twenty miles distant.
There they would join Indians from other tribes and learn
slash-and-burn farming. They would grow bananas and take
baths and be saved. He showed Tucker photos of the rickety huts. The whole idea turned Tucker's stomach, but he
said nothing.

Tucker and his Indian escorts flew out early the next
morning. Within five days, they'd located the sacred collection grove and set to work. It was a strange feeling, being
back after so many years; so much was familiar, but there
were subtle differences. The clearing seemed smaller, the
trees denser. And it wasn't until the morning of the second
day, eating his breakfast of biscuits and tea, that he realized
the neon bees were gone for good.

He gathered his root stock, packed it with care, and sent
three loads to the logging camp. Two more days, he
thought as he slung his hammock that night. He awoke at
dawn to find himself surrounded: the tribe had returned to
the gathering place.

The shamans in their conical leaf hats hissed threateningly at the intruders, and the children screamed in fear.
The mission Indians melted into the forest, but Tucker
stood his ground, searching for a familiar face. A tall young
man strode toward the hammock, and the crowd made way
for him respectfully. Tucker recognized him instantly and
held up a hand in greeting: Kuna! Kuna remembered
Tucker as well, and made him welcome.

Tucker had pulled himself upright against the bed pillows
as he'd spoken. How his face contorted with pain as he

recalled what had happened next: his discovery of the aging chief and the pit of human bones.

"Here," Kate said, handing him a small glass of orange juice. "Drink this."

Tucker drank the juice, sighed deeply, and continued ...

"Good God, man! What happened to you?" Father Larry exclaimed as a wild, distraught Tucker burst into the mission late in the afternoon, barely a week later. "I didn't expect you for several more days, at least! Sit down, man. Let me get you something to—"

"Stop it!" Tucker croaked hoarsely. His throat was parched, his eyes feverish. "We have to stop it!"

"Stop what?" Larry looked questioningly at the Indians who had followed him to the door, but they shrugged their shoulders impassively.

"The plants! We must—"

"Don't worry about your root stock," Larry told him soothingly. "The camp pilot radioed me the other day. He's delivered it safely to San Jose, put it right in the hands of your courier. All taken care of."

"... my fault! I didn't understand!"

Father Larry looked bewildered. "Are you all right? You'd better sit down. You look terrible!"

"No time! Must get to San Jose, warn them—"

"You know we can't fly you out at this time of night. First thing tomorrow, I promise. Now calm down and let me get you something cold to drink ..."

By the time Tucker reached San Jose, the plants had cleared Sao Paulo; by the time he bulled his way onto the first available flight back to the States, one thousand new saplings were being pressed into the warm, damp earth beneath the giant glass pyramid, deep in the Florida Everglades.

"I told Michael! I told him, but he wouldn't believe me!" Tucker thrashed around on the bed. His face was slick with sweat, his eyes, unfocused. "Five years of testing weren't long enough!"

"Is he okay?" Steve asked Kate.

Kate sighed. "I can't sedate him," she said. "We need to hear the rest."

               *   *   *

"I don't believe you!"

"It's true! Genelife is no good! You have to destroy it!"

Michael Nolan regarded Tucker with alarm. Even allowing for the physical punishment a month in the rain forest could inflict, the man looked, and sounded, completely mad. Or was this a calculated attack? "You've always hated me," Michael hissed. "You've tried to destroy me ever since Omni took over. Well, I'm not buying it!"

Tucker pounded on the door of his office in frustration. He'd come straight to Randall Webber from the airport with news of his terrible discovery, nearly crazy with guilt and despair. And Nolan was refusing to listen.

"I know all about you and Bettina Hollis!" Tucker shouted. "You gave her inside information! You gave Omni the company right under Clark Randall's nose, and you got Clark's job and a lot of stock in return!"

"You're nuts!"

Nolan turned away, furious, but Tucker spun him around again. "You told them about Genelife, didn't you?" he demanded. "That's why they bought Randall Webber and made you chairman! You promised Omni a miracle drug that would make them millions. Well, you fucked yourself this time, Michael! Genelife's a bomb! It's worse than a bomb—it's a time bomb!"

Could it possibly be true? Nolan wondered. Had Tucker really discovered a horrible new side effect, back in the rain forest? No, of course not! Look at the man! Obviously crazy. He'd long been teetering on the edge, and this trip back in time had pushed him over. Sudden aging indeed! Tucker had taken the drug longer than anyone, and he hadn't aged.

"Your long-term research is clean," Nolan told him. "Aside from the normal side effects, that is."

Tucker seemed to visibly relax. "Thank goodness for them," he said. "You can't launch anyway. The FDA won't let you."

Nolan smiled. "Ah, that's where you're wrong, Tucker. We've solved that little problem. We're going ahead."

"You mustn't!" Tucker slammed Nolan against the corridor wall. "You can't launch Genelife!"

"I don't believe you! You want to destroy me, and you don't care if you take Randall Webber down, too!"

"Cancel the launch, Michael! You have no choice!"

Over Tucker's shoulder, Nolan saw Jerry Lim enter the hallway. "Get out of here!" he yelled.

"Stay!" Tucker called to Jerry. "You should hear this!"

"Go home!" Nolan shouted. "Now, Jerry! Move!"

Jerry scuttled out of sight and Nolan shoved Tucker away from him. "Get in here," he said roughly, pulling Tucker inside the office and slamming the door behind them.

For half an hour, a barely coherent Tucker tried to convince Nolan that Genelife was horribly flawed; for half an hour, Nolan insisted Tucker was trying to ruin both their careers. At last Nolan called for a taxi, pushed Tucker into it, and sent him home.

"Jerry Lim says you went back to R&D," Kate said.

Tucker nodded slowly. "Late that night," he said. "I . . . I was exhausted, and angry and confused—I hadn't slept in days—I was half out of my mind. I didn't know what to do. I mean, Michael had kept insisting he was going to launch, that I was lying to him about the aging . . ." Tucker looked down at his wizened body. "He should see me now."

Steve put his arm around Tucker's shoulders. Tucker had concealed important information from him, in the rain forest and afterward. He'd treated Marianne badly, and caused her great pain. But ultimately, Tucker had hurt himself most of all. And now he was dying.

Tucker leaned back into the pillows. "I'd better tell you the rest," he said.

"Mr. Nolan, this is Security. One of our men saw a light on over in the R&D building, and when he went to investigate, he found this crazy guy . . . well, he says he works there, but frankly, he looks like a bum to me. Anyhow, he wouldn't identify himself to the guard . . . actually threw stuff at him. He was tearing up papers, and he'd started a little fire in his wastebasket. We had to restrain him. You want I should call the police?"

"No. I know who he is. Just hold him there. I'll be right over."

This is no good, Nolan thought as he threw on some clothes. I can't have that nutcase running around spouting off about some mythical side effect. Not now, when we're

about to get FDA approval based on Chemstra's tests with
the synthetic. And Florida! Jesus! If Tucker starts talking
about Florida ...

He reached for the phone. "Ronnie, it's Michael Nolan.
Sorry to get you out of bed at this hour, but we've got an
emergency. Something you've got to deliver to Florida right
away. No, I can't talk about it on the phone. Bring the van
and meet me at R&D in fifteen minutes. I know you're not
supposed to go to the office compound! Just *be* there!"

From his medicine cabinet, Nolan took a vial of tranquil-
izers. Then he grabbed his car keys and headed out the
door, his mind churning. He didn't believe Tucker's story
about sudden aging, not for a minute! The man was obviously crazy, and dangerous as hell. He had to get him out
of the way, at least until after the Genelife launch. Hell,
maybe he could keep him down in Florida until after that
spin-off Bettina had promised him if Genelife were
successful.

He swung onto I-95, heading north at seventy-five and
watching for troopers. How much data had Tucker already destroyed?

He cursed softly. He'd take care of that bastard! There
was too much at stake here: his career, his reputation, and
most of all his stock options, worth millions if everything
played out the way he'd planned.

As he turned into the Randall Webber property, tires
squealing, an idea was already forming. He'd find a way to
get the drugs that would keep Tucker manageable. He'd
tell Bobby Beach it was part of a corporate substance abuse
program, pay him a nice little bonus not to ask any questions. Nolan smiled grimly. Bobby could always use help
with the plants.

Boone's always hated me, Nolan thought angrily. He
knows if Genelife goes bad it'll kill my career. But couldn't
he think of anything better than that ridiculous tale about
an aging time bomb, for chrissake? Who'd be stupid
enough to fall for a story like that?

Suddenly Tucker rose from the bed, his arms flailing. "A
time bomb!" he exclaimed agitatedly. "I thought I'd found
the fountain of youth but it was a goddamn time bomb! I
spent years developing a drug that's completely worthless!
I blew my marriage and my career and my goddamn life

for fuck-all!" He chuckled softly to himself. "That's really funny. Huh? Don't you think that's funny?" The chuckle turned into a manic laugh and he collapsed on the bed, rolling around and laughing hysterically.

"Hold him down, can you?" Kate said. "Don't let him hurt himself." Her face was pale, her expression bleak as she thought of the many millions of potential time bombs ticking away all over the country. And inside her own body.

Slowly Tucker quieted. "Someday they'll find it," he said. "Then they'll know."

"Find what?" Steve asked.

"I wrote it all up, when I went back to the lab that night. How I discovered Genelife . . . my work on the side effects . . . how I found out about the aging . . . It was sort of a confession. It's on a computer disk. I was going to send it to someone, but . . . as I wrote it, I got madder and madder . . . I went a little crazy and started burning stuff and the guards came. So I hid it."

"Then it's gone," Kate said. "Jerry had the office after you left, and when they transferred him to Puerto Rico, they cleaned it all out."

But Tucker shook his head and looked crafty. "I hid it," he said, "under the desk."

"Great place, Tuck," Steve said disconsolately. "No one would look in a desk."

"Not in the desk," Tucker said testily. "Under it. I bet it's still there."

"We'll find out soon enough," Steve told him. "When we get back to New York this afternoon, you can show us—"

But Tucker had half risen from the bed in panic. "No! I'm not going! I'm not leaving here!"

"We have to go back!" Kate told him firmly. "We have to stop them from selling any more Genelife!"

Tucker stared at her in disbelief. "They're actually selling it? They can't be! Clark Randall would never have allowed—"

"Randall retired, remember?"

"I know that!" Tucker exclaimed impatiently. "But he knew all about the trouble we were having with the side effects; I told him. I can't believe he'd keep quiet!"

"Clark Randall died back in January," Kate told him. "Right around the time Genelife was launched."

"But how could they launch in January? There wasn't time! The FDA—"

"The FDA approved a synthetic made by a company called Chemstra in Switzerland," Kate explained. "They'd been quietly testing it for years. It has no side effects and not much cosmetic effect, so Nolan's been secretly substituting the Florida plant derivative. Millions of people have been taking it. I took it, too, for a while."

Steve swung around to look at her. "My God!"

"I only took it for about ten months. I'll probably be okay."

Tucker was crying softly, and Kate hugged him. "It's all right, Tuck," she told him. "You didn't know." She turned to Steve. "You made the reservations?" He nodded.

"I'm not going," Tucker said through his tears.

"You need help, Tucker. A hospital. Maybe someone can—"

"There's no way to help me!" he insisted. "I'm staying here. I have to—"

"What?"

"Nothing," Tucker said quickly. "But I'm not going back."

Kate looked helplessly at Steve. "We have to go," she said. "We're out of time on this."

"I know," Steve agreed. "Why don't you go? Go now. I'll stay here with him for a few days ..."

Kate nodded. Steve was right. Tucker didn't have long, and Steve was all he had. "Where exactly did you hide that disk?" she asked Tucker, but his eyes were already closing. "Tuck! Wake up!" Tucker turned over and began to snore. "Shit! Well, I'll do my best. Leave a message on my answering machine if you find out anything more."

Steve nodded. "I'll try and get to a phone," he said. Their remote cabin had neither phone nor TV.

"I'll have to warn Mac," Kate said. "He'll need to resign the business, fast," She thought for a moment. "Mac and I should make a public statement about Genelife. Maybe he can arrange for TV and radio time."

"And the FDA?"

"They're my first call," she said, "as soon as I've got hold of that disk." She began tossing the few things she'd unpacked back into her carryall.

"Why wait? You have a leaf sample from the green-house. We know the whole story now."

"*We* do," Kate agreed, "but everyone else, including the FDA and Omni, thinks Genelife is just terrific. It's my word against Nolan's, and he's got all those clinical tests and approvals on his side. Not to mention Omni's power and money. And who am I? A youngish doctor with less than a year of experience in pharmaceutical marketing."

She drew Steve away from the bed and lowered her voice. "Look, everyone at Randall Webber thought Tucker was a flake. And they knew he hated Nolan. Michael can make this whole thing sound like a personal vendetta." She sighed. "He'll play on my lack of experience, make me sound like a credulous fool. He can delay and delay ... he might even try blaming the whole thing on Tucker. He might even make it stick."

"But the truth about Genelife will come out, sooner or later."

"Of course it will. But it'll take time. The FDA will con-tact Nolan, he'll deny everything, maybe even destroy the Florida facility. Meanwhile, the FDA will have to decide whether there's enough evidence to start an investigation. We just can't wait for all that! People are using Genelife right now! We have to find a way to focus attention on this thing, stop people now, even before the FDA steps in."

Her eyes flashed angrily. "Besides, I want to nail Nolan," she said. "Tucker's information was written before he aged—the computer clock will have automatically dated it—and that's great. It'll clear Tucker's name, in case Nolan tries to accuse him. The disk is the only real documentation we've got."

"There's Tucker. He's evidence."

Kate looked down at the shell of a man, tears drying on his old, tired face. "Yes," she said. "We have Tucker. But for how long? And without the disk, will anyone believe him?"

"How will you get into the lab?"

"I'll find a way."

"... in the bones."

"What?" Kate swung around.

"He said, 'The secret's in the bones,'" Steve told her. "At least that's what it sounded like." He looked down at Tucker's sleeping form. "He must be dreaming again."

Chapter 33

Because of Lincoln Center's peculiar layout, the limo was forced to drop them at the curb in front of the plaza in the pouring rain. Despite the filthy weather, people turned to stare as they got out. Mac was resplendent in black tie, and Victoria glowed in rich gold satin. Huddled together under a huge red umbrella with "MacAllister" stenciled boldly on it in white and black, they ran laughing toward the high, glittering entrance beyond the fountain. As they waited their turn at the coat check room, Mac smiled and nodded to acquaintances from other advertising agencies, here for the annual Clio Award presentations.

Wet umbrella disposed of at last, Mac took two glasses of champagne from a passing waiter, handed one to Victoria, and scanned the crowd for his people. Two bars and a lavish buffet had been set up for pre-gala partying; the actual awards ceremony was half an hour away. Mac smiled and glad-handed his way through the throng; a gathering like this was always good for picking up gossip about loose accounts and dissatisfied clients.

He turned to Victoria only to find her progress had been arrested by a somewhat recovered Dave in pressed jeans and a blue velvet jacket. He smiled back at her, waved to Dave, and continued on. Victoria was used to his working the crowd at such events.

"Glad to see him looking so happy," Dave said. "He's been in a terrible mood all week."

"He needs a night like this," Victoria said affectionately. "Awards, recognition, a little fun." She studied Dave for a moment. "You're looking better," she said. "And Mac says you told him you were off Genelife."

Dave looked guilty. "Uh, yeah," he said. "Any day now."

"Dave!" Victoria was genuinely angry. "After what happened to you—?"

Dave lowered his voice. "I love Mac, you know that. But I've been hearing some rumors that MacAllister's in trouble. If the agency goes under and I'm back on the market again, I can't afford to look old."

Victoria put a hand on his shoulder. "Listen, Dave, I promise you that won't happen."

Dave looked at her questioningly.

"Besides, rumors like that are bad for business," she told him, "and you know it. So you go over to that bar and tell everybody you know that MacAllister is as sound, financially, as it's ever been."

"But if we lose Genelife . . ."

Victoria took a deep breath. "This is confidential," she said softly, "so don't repeat it. But there's a new investor coming on board."

"Oh, shit! Someone who wants to play advertising? That's all we—"

"Shut up, Dave! This person's got no interest in being involved in the agency. It's purely a financial stopgap, until you guys land some of that new business you're going to be pitching over the next six months."

"Well, that's different!" Dave seemed considerably cheered. "You're sure about this?"

"Absolutely." Suddenly Victoria caught sight of Mac through the crowd; he looked perturbed. "Listen, don't say anything to Mac," she begged. "Just go spread the word that MacAllister is solid, okay?"

"Starting now!" Dave promised, and headed for the crowd around the buffet table.

"It's all coming together," Mac announced obscurely. "They're screwing me. Nolan and your buddy Kate."

"Kate? What are you on about?"

"I should have resigned the damn account when I had the chance," Mac said angrily. Several people nearby turned to look at him. Victoria took his hand and led him to a quiet corner. "Okay," she said. "Tell me."

"There's an interesting rumor circulating here tonight," he said. "Richard Day's forming his own agency, with Genelife as his first big client. Wanna guess who set that one up?"

"Not Kate, surely!" Victoria protested.

"Why not Kate?" Mac demanded.

"Because she's not like that. She wouldn't do it. Besides, why should she? What's in it for her?"

"My God, Victoria, she's been dating Richard Day! Probably sleeping with him!"

"That's not fair! Also, it's not true. Oh, she mentioned a guy named Richard to me a couple of times. She said he was fun, but she never really cared for him. And when Steve came along—"

But Mac brushed aside her protests. "Michael Nolan called me this afternoon. He asked why I was setting up a film shoot in Florida. I said I didn't know what he was talking about, but he accused me of lying. He said Jenny—that's his secretary—got a phone call asking about some film shoot at the Randall Foundation's research facility down in Florida. She told the guy to call us. Hell, I never even knew they *had* a facility in Florida! And I certainly never discussed it with Kate. I haven't even seen Kate for—"

"He said Kate was involved?"

"Yeah, apparently the caller mentioned her name. Which really got Nolan steamed, since he fired Kate last week."

"He fired her? I had no idea! I tried to call her a couple of times but I got her machine. Why's she involved in a film shoot if she's been fired?"

"How the hell should I know?" He shoved his hands in his pockets and glowered at the crowd. "Maybe she's working for Richard Day now."

"Oh, I can't believe that!"

Mac eyed her cynically. "I can. Anyhow, Nolan warned me that he'd already sent a fax to the Florida facility reminding them that no film shoots were allowed down there. He practically threatened me with arrest for trespassing, if I sent a crew down."

"Talk about overreacting," Victoria said thoughtfully. "What do you suppose that Florida facility is for, anyway?"

"I don't know!" Mac shot back angrily. "And frankly, I don't give a damn. What I *do* know is that Kate was supposed to warn me when things were getting hot, and instead, she gave my business away to Richard Day."

"You don't know that."

Mac was silent.

"Maybe she's still trying to find out the truth about Genelife."

The ringing of a musical chime signaled the beginning of the awards presentation. People began filing into the theater, but Mac held back.

"Come on, sweetie," Victoria said. "It's time to smile and say thank you to the nice people. We'll sort it all out later."

" 'I'd like to thank my client who's about to fire me ...' " Mac said morosely, " 'and my staff whose salaries I can't pay ...' "

"Lighten up," Victoria told him. "There is a very simple solution to the second of those problems. The bank will give me half a million on the house."

He shook his head. "No. I won't let you."

"You'll pay me back."

"What if I can't? How will you repay the bank loan? You'll lose the house."

"So I'll come live with you," she told him lightly. "You keep saying we should live together." She leaned over and kissed him. "I believe in you," she said. "You'll pick up so much new business this year, you'll have to move to bigger office space. All you need is six months. Let me give them to you."

Mac sighed deeply. "The house is your one real asset. If you lose that— No, I can't let you put yourself at risk for me."

"Then let me do it for Dave. For Larry. For all the people who'll be out on the street if MacAllister closes its doors." She saw the torment on his face. "Think about it," she said.

"I've *been* thinking about it," he said softly.

"Then think about it some more." She took his hand and led him into the theater.

April 23

The weather front that had stalled over Florida on Friday and Saturday had been making slow progress up the East Coast since then. By Monday afternoon, thunderstorms had closed the New York airports, and Kate's flight had been diverted to Atlanta. Seven hours and several dry cheese sandwiches and cups of stale coffee later, passengers had been allowed to reembark for the bumpy flight into La Guardia. By the time Kate finally reached Randall Webber's Connecticut offices, it was nearly six o'clock on a dreary, overcast morning.

The executive parking lot was empty but Kate skirted it, pulling up at the rear of the R&D building. The golf carts had been gathered under cover of the overhang, their plastic side curtains spattered with rain. She saw no one as she walked quickly to the door. She inserted her passcard confidently and waited impatiently for the *click* that would tell her the door had unlocked. But the click didn't come.

She tried reinserting the card, turning it around and jiggling the door handle, but with no luck. She was locked out. Nolan must have decided to change the locks after all.

Her shoulders drooped; had Bobby Beach reported their visit to the Florida facility? Did Nolan know they had Tucker?

She had to find a way in, and fast. Soon staff members would be arriving. She went back to her car. Who could she get to let her in? Freda? No, she'd have heard about Kate's being fired; everyone over at the executive building would have. Butler? Should she drive back to New York and tell him the whole story, tell him how important it was to find the disk? No, it would take too long. And what if he told Nolan, and Nolan found the disk first?

Her best bet was Jerry Lim, she decided. He lived close by. And he'd been cooperative when she'd questioned him in The Three Pheasants. She hoped he hadn't already left for Puerto Rico.

She drove out of the Randall Webber complex to an all-night gas station and looked up his address in the local phone book, then got directions from the sleepy attendant. Ten minutes later she was leaning on the bell beside the redwood door of Number 24, Owl Court.

She'd nearly given up when she saw a light come on behind the thin blue curtains that covered the glass door panel.

"Who is it? Who's there?" said a groggy voice Kate recognized.

"It's Kate," she told him. "Kate Martin. It's an emergency."

"Go away!"

"Open this door, Jerry! Something's happened and I need your help."

"No." The light behind the curtains was extinguished. Kate put her finger back on the doorbell and kept it there. After some minutes, the light switched on again. "Get out of here or I'll call the police," Jerry told her through the door.

"You do that, Jerry," Kate told him. "And I'll tell the FDA you're responsible for the new side effect that's going to kill everybody who's taking Genelife."

"What? Kill—?"

"That's right. I found out—" Careful, she thought. Better not tell him everything. "I found Tucker."

Slowly the door opened. "You'd better come in," Jerry told her. Kate followed him down the empty hallway and into the living room. A sweetish, musty smell—two parts stale alcohol, one part dust—assailed her nostrils. Furniture had been shoved against one wall, and boxes and crates were everywhere. "I've been packing," he said half apologetically. "The movers come tomorrow . . . uh, today. You want some coffee?"

Kate shook her head. "I need your help," she said. "You have to get me into R&D right away."

"Start from the beginning. What's this about Tucker? How'd you find him?"

"I just found him, that's all I can tell you."

"Is he okay?"

Kate nodded. "Tucker told me . . . there's something very wrong with Genelife."

"What? What is it?"

"I can't tell you, not yet. But it's bad, really bad. Tucker told Nolan last May, but Nolan wouldn't believe him. Remember when you saw them arguing?" Jerry nodded. "Well, when Tucker went back the next day, he wrote it all down on a computer disk and hid it in his office."

"They cleaned out my, uh, his office," Jerry said. "All the files, the reports, everything's gone."

"I know. But he seems to think it might still be there. Look, my passcard doesn't work anymore; Michael must have changed the locks. I need yours."

"If he changed the locks, mine won't work either," Jerry told her. "I haven't been to the office for over a week."

"Shit!"

Jerry studied her. "Tucker could be using you," he said at last. "Remember what I told you about how he hated Nolan? He could be lying."

"He's not!"

"How can you be sure?"

"Because . . . well, I just am," Kate said, reluctant to trust Jerry with any more information than she had to. "Are you sure your card won't work?"

"You can have it if you want," Jerry offered. "I won't need it in Puerto Rico. But I don't think it's any better than yours."

"There has to be a way in. Listen, you could come with me, and we can find a guard and tell him—"

Jerry shook his head. "Not a chance!" he said. "I've got a great job waiting for me in PR. I'm not about to mess it up."

"There *is* no job in PR, not if Genelife's a bomb! Don't you understand? They'll have to stop making it!"

"Randall Webber makes other products," Jerry said firmly.

"Randall Webber won't be in business anymore!" Calm down, Kate told herself. Think. Outside, it was growing light. She didn't have much time. "How about this?" she said, working it out in her mind as she spoke. "You call Randall Webber's night line and tell security you forgot something in your office . . . uh, something you need to take to Puerto Rico."

"Forget it. I told you, my office is packed up."

"They probably won't know that. You could say you left it in a closet or something. Tell them you lost your passcard and you need them to let you in."

"I told you! I'm not going!"

"Okay, okay. Uh, tell them you're sending someone over to pick it up for you . . . your girlfriend or something. We'll make up a name."

"What if they recognize you?"

"The night guys don't know me." I hope. "It's worth a try."

"I don't know . . . I mean, if there really is a problem with Genelife—"

"There is. A serious one."

"—it would be wrong of me not to do everything I can to help. But . . . what if Tucker's wrong?"

"What if he's right? Jerry, I *know* he's right! And the disk will prove it."

Jerry sighed. He'd certainly had his doubts about Genelife; he'd nearly lost his job because of them. But Michael had been so reassuring lately. He'd even forgiven his drinking, and set him up with a wonderful new job. And yet, Kate seemed so sure. And she'd actually talked to Tucker. If something was wrong with Genelife, he had a responsibility as a scientist to help Kate retrieve the disk that could prove it. How embarrassing it would be if the drug were recalled and it came out that he had refused to help!

But what if it turned out that nothing was wrong with Genelife? That Tucker was using Kate, as he'd suggested? Nolan would kill him for helping her! And yet, if the disk proved that Genelife was actually okay, wouldn't Nolan be grateful?

He'd have to hedge his bets, he decided. "Okay," he said at last. "I'll call security. What name do you want me to tell them?"

Kate sped back to R&D under a brightening sky. It was after seven; R&D staff tended to arrive early. She had perhaps an hour to get in and out.

She had no idea whether she'd need any tools to retrieve the disk. Would she have to unscrew a section of the desk? Slice through layers of duct tape? She couldn't do much about a screwdriver, but she'd taken several scalpels from her medical bag and jammed them into her purse.

A security guard was waiting for her at the rear door to the R&D building, as directed; he didn't look familiar. Kate had tied a patterned scarf around her braided hair, and in her grubby jeans and sweatshirt she looked decidedly un-executive.

The guard let her into the building, then led her to Jerry's old office and unlocked the door.

"This could take some time," she told the man. "You don't need to wait."

"I thought you were just picking up some stuff," he said, surprised.

"Yes, but Jerry asked me to go through it first. Really, I'll be fine. I'll let myself out when I'm through."

The guard shrugged. "Okay, but remember once you leave the building, you can't get back in again."

"I understand."

The guard looked around the barren room; everything but the desk and the stained sofa had been removed. "Okay," he said again, somewhat puzzled but happy to be let off the hook. He'd left a mug of hot coffee back in the security office, and it had been a long night. "Uh, shut this door when you leave, will ya?"

Kate waited until he'd disappeared down the corridor, then went over to the heavy steel desk. She knelt down and felt along the bottom edges, and inside the side supports, and along the undersides of all the drawers. She pulled out each drawer and checked it, then ran a careful hand over all the desk's undersurfaces again. Nothing. She went over it all a third time. Still nothing.

"Under the desk," she repeated to herself, getting to her feet. Had there been something else under the desk when Tucker had hidden the data, something that had since been removed?

The whole office had a sad air of disuse, and her jeans were grimy from contact with the rubber-tiled floor. She bent and began to brush the dust off them. How could they let this place get so dirty? she wondered. You'd think the cleaning staff would at least sweep—suddenly she stopped dead. The floor, she thought. The floor was under the desk.

Gathering her strength, she put her hands on the desk and began to shove it out of the way.

All the glasses had been packed except for the cracked one he was leaving behind. He carefully avoided the rough edge as he drank the Scotch, then set it down on a packing crate and refilled it. He'd made a terrible mistake.

She'd caught him half-asleep. If he'd been more alert, he never would have gone along with her crazy scheme. Hell, the woman had been fired. So what if she'd found Tucker? Everyone knew Tucker was nuts. He'd say anything to get back at Nolan.

Nolan, Jesus! Nolan would kill him. No nice cushy job in Barcelonetta. No piña coladas under the palm trees. The Scotch slopped out of the overfilled glass and onto the carton, where it seeped between the untaped flaps and soaked into the clothes below. Jerry swiped at it ineffectually, then mopped it up with the bottom of his pajama shirt. The damage was done, he thought mournfully. With the overly controlled movements of the almost-drunk, he carefully lifted the glass to his mouth, cutting his lip on the damaged rim. His hand jerked as the alcohol hit the wound, spilling liquor onto his knees. God, what a mess! He sucked his throbbing lip, feeling very sorry for himself.

Why had he allowed himself to be manipulated by that woman? Hadn't she gotten him in enough trouble with Nolan, that afternoon in The Three Pheasants? If Michael hadn't been such a kind, forgiving man, so understanding about how easily someone in Jerry's position might be maneuvered into saying more than he meant to, he'd never have given Jerry a second chance. And what a chance it was! He took a long draught of whiskey, eyes watering at the sudden pain.

Tucker was unstable, always had been. A brilliant scientist, but unhinged. Chances were, there was no terrible new side effect. Tucker was using Kate against Nolan. And now she'd drawn him into the plot. Well, Kate had nothing to lose; she'd already been fired. But he had to save himself.

Unsteadily, he rose to his feet and tottered over to the phone that sat on a wooden packing crate. It wasn't due to be disconnected until tomorrow. He began to dial, then hesitated and hung up. He'd had a lot to drink. He'd better take a few minutes to think about what he would say. He wanted to phrase it just right. Maybe he should make a few notes. He reached for the glass, then remembered his lip. No more! he told himself. Not until after you've talked to Nolan.

He sat quietly for some minutes, rehearsing his story, then went and dug into one of the open cartons for his address book. It was still pretty early. He'd better call Michael at home.

With the help of the scalpels, Kate had managed to pry up most of the tiles on which the desk had stood. It had been a filthy job, and aside from an aching back, she had nothing to show for it. She stood and arched her spine and shoulders in an attempt to stretch away the pain. She'd been so sure!

She went to the sofa, kicking at the loose tiles in passing, and collapsed onto the stained cushions. God, she was tired! It was after eight o'clock, and she was out of both time and ideas. Where could it be, if it wasn't under the floor tiles?

She looked around the grubby room. Less than a year ago, she'd come into this same office to talk to Jerry about Genelife. She'd sat right here on this sofa ... no, she hadn't. The sofa had been stacked with paper, she remembered. And it hadn't been here, it had been over there, closer to the desk— Of course! Everything had been moved in order to clear the glut of reports and printouts Jerry had collected!

Excited now, she leapt up and began examining the floor again. Sure enough, some distance across the room she found imprints in the tile that matched the shape of the desk legs. Yes! she thought triumphantly. Here's where the desk used to be! Retrieving her scalpel, she got down on her hands and knees and began to dig.

The glue was old, and progress was slow. The first four tiles revealed nothing. She cut through the fifth accidentally when removing it, cursing herself as she pulled it up. If it had contained the disk, she'd have ruined it. But it didn't. The sixth one did.

She turned the tile over and there it was: a neat black square encased in a clear protective wrapper. Carefully she sliced through the wrapper that was inextricably stuck to the tile glue, and gently pulled the disk free. She was just about to drop it into her handbag when the guards burst through the door.

Chapter 34

Nicholas Butler's driver was pulling into the parking lot when he heard the cry. Peering through the windshield, he saw three figures on the path that led from R&D to the executive building: two guards, and between them a woman in jeans. The woman was struggling. As he watched, the guard on the left clapped a hand over the woman's mouth and shoved her roughly forward.

The driver rolled down his window. "Hey!" he called. "Hey, you!" He twisted around in his seat. "You see that?" he asked.

Butler put down his newspaper. "See what?"

"Two security guys. They're roughing up some woman." The driver hit the gas and the Lincoln Town Car sped across the parking lot, pulling up just across from the path. The driver jumped out, and Butler followed more slowly.

"What's going on?" the driver called.

The guards turned. "A burglar. Nothing to worry about, sir."

But the woman used the opportunity to break free. "It's me!" she called out. "Dr. Butler? It's Kate Martin!" The guard turned back, grabbing her by the arm and hustling her along the path.

"Kate?" Dr. Butler hurried across the grass divide after the trio, closely followed by his driver. "You there! Stop!" He grabbed the nearest guard by the shoulder. "I'm Dr. Butler," he said angrily. "Tell me what happened. And let go of Dr. Martin."

"Caught her sneaking into R&D," the guard said without relaxing his grip on Kate's arm. "She stole that. Show them, Ken." The second guard held up a computer disk.

Butler eyed Kate suspiciously. "Michael warned me about you," he said. "He told me you were inexperienced.

Brash. Had some crazy ideas. But he never said you were a thief."

"I didn't steal it!" Kate gasped. "It's Tucker's. He hid it."

"What? Tucker Boone?"

Kate nodded. "It's very important," she said urgently. "Make them give it back!"

Butler looked at Kate carefully. A bruise was swelling on her cheek, and her sweatshirt was torn. "Why, you're hurt." Kate didn't reply. Her attention was fixed on the disk in the guard's hand.

"Please step aside, sir," said the guard who was holding Kate. She kicked him hard on the shin and he swung her around by the arm and slapped her hard.

"Stop that!" Butler cried, aghast. "Let her go." The driver had already moved in and was grappling with the other guard. The disk fell to the ground.

"Mr. Nolan said—" the first guard began to protest.

"I don't give a damn what Mr. Nolan said!" Butler replied, his face red with anger. "You can't treat a woman like that!" He turned to Kate. "Promise me you won't try to run away?" Kate nodded; she could barely stand. Butler stared fiercely at the guard, who reluctantly released his prisoner. Kate staggered slightly and rubbed her arm.

"Are you all right?" Butler asked.

"I guess," Kate said distractedly, her eyes searching the cement path. "What happened to the disk?"

Butler bent and retrieved it from the grass border. "Is this it?"

"You'd better give that to me, sir," the first guard said firmly, reaching for the disk.

"No!" Kate cried out. "Don't!"

Whatever Kate may have done, Butler thought, she's a physician and those two are goons. "I think I'll just hang on to this for the moment," he said.

"But Mr. Nolan said—" The guard moved toward Butler threateningly, but the driver stepped between them.

"You just tell Mr. Nolan it's safe with me," Butler said, sounding braver than he felt. The guard hesitated, then backed off with a shrug. Butler outranked him.

"What are you doing here?" Kate murmured softly.

"I took over your job," he explained with a puzzled air. "Didn't you know?"

Kate shrugged. "It doesn't matter," she said tiredly. "What matters is that disk."

"You said it was Tucker's disk. What did you mean?"

"Tucker made it just before he disappeared. It tells the truth about Genelife."

"The truth? What truth? My God, catch her!" Butler grabbed Kate's arm as she began to sink to the ground in exhaustion and pain. "Help me get her into my office!" he ordered his driver.

The lobby was deserted as they carried Kate into the executive building. They laid her gently on the sofa in the office that had once been her own, and Butler sponged her face with cold water until she opened her eyes. "The disk," she murmured. "Where's the disk?"

"I've got it," he said. "No, don't try to talk. Just rest."

But Kate struggled upright against the pale cushions. "Listen to me, Nick," she said urgently. "Genelife is a fraud."

"Nonsense," Butler said, unconsciously smoothing his hair over the patch on the back of his neck. "Brian, you can go now. And close the door behind you." The driver nodded and left the room, while Butler regarded Kate severely. Not in front of the help, his look said.

Kate sighed. There was no time for such niceties. "Michael Nolan told the FDA that Genelife uses a synthetic. But it doesn't. That's why the side effects are so high."

"That's impossible!" Butler exclaimed. "Besides, the side effects are not high. I've seen the reports myself."

"Those reports are based on clinical trials with Chemstra's synthetic. The real Genelife, the one on the market, is made with a plant derivative. They grow it at the Randall Foundation research facility in Florida, and substitute it for the Chemstra synthetic. I've seen them!"

"I don't believe you!" Butler protested. "Nolan's a well-respected professional! I've been involved with Genelife for years! No reputable company would be a party to such a scheme. It's simply not possible. Anyway, there's no need. The side effects are well within normal limits. You'll remember I told you so, when you came to my office." He looked at her sternly. "There was no excuse for the guards to treat you like that," he said. "But that doesn't mean you're justified in sneaking in here to pursue some destructive idea Nolan says you have about side effects that are well within—"

Kate laughed bitterly. "Those side effects are nothing compared to the real one."

"That's right. Compared to the real effect of Genelife—eternal youth—the side effects are indeed nothing. Of course, in this case, they are well within—"

"Eternal youth? Guess again!" Kate rubbed her head, which was beginning to throb. "Let me tell you about Tucker Boone. And then we'd better have a look at that disk."

Ursula, the new receptionist, dumped her handbag into the bottom right-hand drawer of her large marble-topped desk, then combed her hair and straightened her jacket. Several early birds drifted in through the large glass doors, and she greeted them by name. In fifteen minutes or so, the bulk of the staff would crowd through the doors, and a wave and a smile would have to suffice.

"Good morning, Mr. Barry ... Good morning, Mrs. Forrester ... Good morning, uh, I'm afraid I don't—"

"Richard Day ..."

"Good morning, Mr. Day. I'm new here, and—"

"... to see Mr. Nolan," Day said shortly.

"I'll ring his secretary ... No, she's not in, yet. Uh, could I get you some coffee while you wait?"

"How about Mr. Nolan?" Day said impatiently. "Is *he* in yet?"

Ursula blushed. "I'm so sorry! I'll just try that extension ... no, he doesn't seem to be answering. Did you have an appointment?"

But Day was looking out through the glass toward the parking lot, where a figure was approaching the building at a run. Ursula followed his look. "Oh, here he comes!" she said brightly.

Day scowled at her, then crossed the lobby to intercept Nolan as he bulled through the glass door. "Michael—" he began, but Nolan brushed by him. "Not now!" His face was stormy and his clothes disheveled.

"It's important," said Day, trotting alongside. "We have to talk!"

Nolan stopped and fixed Day with an angry stare. "Goddammit, Day!" he said. "I just told you—"

"I know, and I'm sorry. But my backers are getting restless. They're putting real pressure on me. I have to announce. Er, and I need some money."

Like a caged animal, Nolan swung his head from side to side. He didn't have time for this shit. "You'll get the money when I give you the money!" he exploded, shoving Day aside and heading toward the corridor.

"At least let me announce," Day called after him.

"How can you announce before Mac resigns?" Nolan barked over his shoulder. "Don't be an idiot, Richard!"

"Okay, okay. So when—?" But Nolan was already out of sight. Cursing under his breath, Day wandered back through the lobby. His financial position was worse than tenuous, it was a potential disaster. For a moment he regretted pushing Nolan so hard; without Randall Webber's funding, his agency would have to close before it opened, and he himself would be ruined. Then he thought: No, I was right to give Nolan a push. What is the man waiting for? The conference and the awards dinner are both over. There's no reason to delay. God, I can't survive much longer without that bastard's money.

As he passed the receptionist's desk, she gave him a big smile. "Good-bye, Mr. Richards," she said brightly. "Have a nice day!"

Butler put down the phone and turned to Kate. "Beach confirmed everything," he said. "I can't believe it." He shook his head as though to clear it of nightmares. "I never even knew we had a research facility in Florida. The thought of Tucker being kept prisoner there, all these months . . ."

Kate was silent, remembering.

"It's so hard to believe that Michael Nolan, a man I've worked with and admired, would do something so . . . immoral," Butler continued. "Not just Tucker. Genelife. The whole thing." He stood staring at the monitor, his face pale, his hands trembling.

Kate nodded. "I'd better keep the original disk," she told him. "You hold on to this copy." She shoved the disk deep down in her handbag.

Butler nodded. Making a copy had been a good idea. With something this hot, the original was best kept safely hidden. "What a password," he said, shivering. " 'Bones.' "

He turned to Kate. "I'd better call the FDA immediately. God, I can't believe this is happening! Poor Tucker."

"Poor everybody."

"How long did you take it?"

"Ten months or so. And you?"

"Nearly two years. I started early." He shuddered. The transdermal patch over which he'd smoothed his hair now lay discarded in the wastebasket. "Do you think I'll—?"

"I don't know," Kate said softly. "But two years isn't too bad ..."

Butler looked back at the poisonous green glow of the words on the computer screen. "Not too bad ..." he repeated despondently. Then a thought occurred to him and he brightened up a little. "Didn't the clinical tests indicate that the side effects disappeared when usage was discontinued? The appetite repression, the low sperm count ... ?"

"Yes, but those tests were done using the synthetic, remember?"

"Yes, I forgot. God, what a terrible thing!"

"I've got to call the advertising agency, warn them to resign before the news breaks. It's not fair that they should be caught in the middle. None of it was their fault. And of course we have to warn the public. MacAllister can arrange for press coverage. Will you stand up with us?"

"Of course, of course. And Tucker?"

"Tucker, too, if he can."

"Where is he?"

"I ... I'd rather not say."

Butler studied her. "I understand," he said. "Keep him safe."

"Look, I'd better get on the road. I have to talk to Mac, and frankly, I don't want to be here when you tell Nolan."

"Are you sure you're all right? You look kind of rocky."

"I feel kind of rocky. I'll be better after I get some sleep." Kate stood and gathered up her handbag and jacket, then extended her hand. Butler grasped it firmly.

"Have MacAllister call and tell me where to show up for the press conference," he said.

"I will," Kate told him. She opened the door and stepped into the corridor.

"Stop!" She swung around to see Nolan bearing down on her. "Give me that disk, you thief! How dare you show your face here!" Several people came out of their offices to see what was going on. "Butler!" Nolan shouted. "Where the hell are you?" Security had told him Nick had taken possession of Kate and the disk. "How dare you countermand my orders, Nick! How dare you meddle in company affairs that don't concern you!" Nolan's face was livid, his eyes blazing with fury and fear. What was on that disk? Could he get his hands on it before they saw it? He reached out to grab Kate, but Butler stepped into the corridor between them.

"It's too late, Michael," Butler said. "Get out of here, Kate. Go on!"

"How dare you? The woman's a thief, a liar—" But Kate was already running down the hallway. Nolan turned his attention to Butler. "You're fired! Get off these premises immediately! I will not stand for—"

"It's over, Michael," Butler told him angrily. "I know everything, and soon the FDA will, too." Nolan swung at him but Butler jerked aside and the blow landed on the doorjamb. Michael roared with pain and came at Butler again, but people were streaming out of their offices now, and several men restrained him.

"She's a liar!" Nolan repeated loudly.

"I've seen Tucker's disk."

"Tucker's crazy!"

Butler shook his head sadly. "I've talked to Bobby Beach in Florida." Nolan jerked as though he'd been shot. "That's right, I know all about the plants. And what you did to Tucker."

Nolan pulled free and looked around. "Let's go into your office," he said. "I don't want to talk out here."

Butler hesitated. "You won't take another swing at me? Okay. Go on in."

"You don't understand," Nolan said as soon as the door had closed behind them. "Those plants in Florida have nothing to do with Genelife. They're part of a Foundation research project. And Tucker had a drug problem. I sent him down there to recover."

"Bullshit!"

"It's true! Come on, Nick, you've known me for years! How can you take that woman's word against mine?"

"It's not just what she says. There's the disk."

"Tucker's disk?" Nolan allowed himself a sardonic laugh. "You know how he hated me. He'd do anything to discredit me. What does he care if he brings the company down, too?"

"No, Michael. Oh, Tucker hated you, all right. But he wasn't trying to hurt you when he told you what he'd found in the rain forest last year. He was telling you the truth."

"The truth? You mean that ridiculous story about sudden aging? You can't really believe—"

"I had a long conversation with Bobby Beach," Butler said. "You sent Tucker to Florida, kept him sedated so he wouldn't talk. You didn't believe him, but you couldn't afford to have him focus the FDA's attention on Genelife. Not when you were pulling that switch with the plant derivative." Nolan gasped; so they knew that, too. "He went down there a young man, thanks to Genelife," Butler continued. "But three months ago, he began to change."

"What do you mean, change?"

"Age. He began to age, Michael!"

"No!"

"Tucker's now a very old man. He's going to die soon. And so will everyone else, if we don't pull Genelife off the market immediately."

Nolan thought furiously. Genelife was gone, that was certain. But the company, and his career, might still be salvageable. He'd blame it all on Tucker, that's what he'd do! He could depend on the boys in Florida to say what he told them. And he'd take care of Kate, somehow. But first he had to get Tucker out of the way. If no one actually saw Tucker . . . "Maybe it's reversible," he said reasonably. "Or they're all exaggerating."

"I doubt—"

"After all, you don't really know. No one does. You haven't actually seen him! I've got to go and talk to him myself. Apologize to him. I really didn't believe him, you see; if only I had! God, how can I make it up to him?"

Butler eyed him cynically. "Can the histrionics, Michael. It's too late. Tucker's gone."

"Gone? You mean, he's dead?"

"No. He's gone. Escaped. Beach said—"

"God! No!" Nolan pounded the desktop with his fist, his features contorted with rage. "I'll go down there! I'll find him! I'll—"

"Michael, let it go!"

"Fuck you, Nick!" Nolan shouted. "Fuck you all!" With

a strength born of desperation and fury, he grabbed the computer monitor from the desk and smashed it to the floor. Then he yanked open the office door and ran from the room.

Chapter 35

The sun moved across the sky, slanting in through the uncurtained windows. It touched the car keys on the dresser, the orange peels on the counter in the kitchenette, the wallet lying open on the floor, and, finally, Steve's eyelids. He blinked, scratched, and came awake, thinking about coffee.

How long had he slept? he wondered as he stood and stretched. God, he'd been tired! He consulted his watch: ten past eleven. Not surprising, really. Tuck had woken several times during the night, wanting to talk. During his lucid periods, Steve had steered the conversation to the old days since this seemed less likely to set Tucker off. But inevitably, Tucker would slip into a shadow world, muttering and thrashing about.

How was he this morning? He glanced over at the rumpled bed across the room and was mildly surprised to find it empty.

"Tuck?" he called. No answer. Well, he'd probably wandered out to the small backyard that bordered the creek. Steve pulled on his jeans and started toward the back door that opened out of the small kitchenette. He was glad to see the orange peels on the counter; apparently, Tuck was eating again. That was good.

He nearly tripped on the wallet before he saw it. Now how had that gotten there? As he bent and picked it up, cards and bills scattered from his hand; someone had been going through it. He checked quickly; yes, he was definitely missing some money, though his credit cards and driver's license were still there. Strange that a sneak thief wouldn't take all—oh, shit!

He banged open the screen door and hurried out. "Tuck! Are you out there?" The old wooden chairs were empty. Damn! "Where the hell are you, Tuck?"

Rushing back inside, he jammed on his boots. One of

them felt funny; he pulled it off and shook it out. A slip of yellow paper—a credit card receipt, he realized—dropped out onto the wooden floor. He turned it over and read with difficulty the scribbled note Tucker had left him: "I started it. I'll finish it. Don't follow."

The hell I won't! Steve thought. He grabbed his car keys and headed for the front door. How long a start did Tuck have? Never mind; if he'd taken the road, it would be easy to catch him; he couldn't move fast in his condition. But what if he'd taken another route, through the swamp? Steve shuddered. Best not to think about that. Besides, Tuck had taken money; he wouldn't need money in the swamp.

He was glad now that Kate had persuaded him to keep the rental car and let her call a local taxi to drive her into Miami. Two days of rain had washed away most of the mud and grime; in contrast to the rickety cabins, it looked clean and strong and ready to go. It was only when he got close that he realized the rear right tire was completely flat.

Cursing loudly, and already sweating in the humid heat, he wrestled the spare out of the trunk, then began assembling the folding jack. From his hiding place just inside the line of cypress that bordered the creek, Tucker watched Steve for a few minutes. Then he turned and melted silently into the trees.

"But he has to see me!" Kate insisted. "It's urgent!"

"I'm sorry, Dr. Martin," the receptionist said. "He's in a creative review. We're never supposed to interrupt those meetings."

"Then let me talk to Dave Randazzo."

"He's in the same review. Look, maybe I could take a note into the conference room . . ."

But Kate had had enough. She was filthy and hungry, and she hadn't slept in days. Mac had asked her to warn him; well, here she was, and he would see her now. She headed down the hall toward the conference room, ignoring the receptionist's pleas to at least let her call Mac first.

Dave stood reading the copy for one of the many layouts he'd tacked up all around the room. He'd always hated creative reviews, but this one seemed better than most. Maybe it was because the whole agency was on an "up," thanks to the bailout by the anonymous investor. He looked at the happy faces around the long, pale table. Amazing, he thought, even Arthur's smiling. In his experience, account guys never smiled in creative reviews; probably part of their job description. He'd just gotten to the payoff, the big finish, when the door to the conference room burst open and Kate strode in. Damn! He'd have to start all over.

Mac stood up, his eyes blazing. "What are you doing here?" he demanded. "This is a closed meeting."

Kate sank into a vacant chair. "I have news about Genelife," she said. "You want everyone to hear it, or you want to clear the room?"

"You don't work for Randall Webber anymore," Mac said tightly. "Nolan fired you."

"That's right."

"And he's about to fire me, too. I understand Richard Day's the new agency of record. Or will be, any day now."

"Richard Day? What's he got to do with any of this?"

"Don't tell me you don't know!" Mac challenged. Kate shook her head. "Come on! You were the one who—" Suddenly he remembered the other four people in the room. "Look, would you people leave us alone for a minute? You, too, Dave." When the room had cleared, Mac went and shut the door, then turned back to Kate. "You were close to Day. Now he's getting the Genelife account. I figure you're responsible."

"That's a shitty thing to say," Kate told him hotly. "I don't give a damn about Day. And I don't know anything about Nolan switching agencies. But if it's true, you ought to thank your lucky stars!"

"What? What do you mean?"

"Genelife's a bomb. We were right about the side effects; they *are* higher than expected. That's because Nolan's been switching the drug that actually goes into the patches."

"My God!"

"It gets worse. There's a terrible side effect, one nobody knew about. After a number of years, eight, ten, we don't know for sure, you suddenly age. I mean, way beyond your years. I found Tucker in Florida . . . he's so old . . . I found the plants, too—" She heard herself rambling, and stopped short. "Mac, I can't talk anymore. I'm completely exhausted. All you really need to know is that you've got to resign the business right away."

"You're sure?"

"Jesus, Mac, weren't you listening? We're talking major fraud here! Not only that, people will be dying from this stuff! Get out while you can!"

Mac nodded vehemently. "I'll resign immediately. Thank you."

"And I'm counting on you to get us some media coverage. We have to warn people!"

"No problem. I'll set it up for tomorrow afternoon."

"Tomorrow?"

"Not soon enough?"

Kate thought for a moment. "With Butler contacting the FDA today, and your resignation statement this afternoon—you will announce it right away, won't you?" Mac nodded. "I think you'll have trouble holding off the press until tomorrow. But if you want to try ..."

"I do. A statement's one thing. A press conference ... well, I'd like to give us a chance to get organized, share our information first."

"Makes sense."

"Good. Let's get started." He flipped open a yellow pad and reached for a pencil.

"Mac, I'm so exhausted, I can barely speak. Can we do this tomorrow morning? Will there be time?"

"Sure, of course. Around nine?"

"I'll be here."

Mac hesitated, then reached for her hand. He looked embarrassed. "I guess I owe you an apology, Dr. Martin."

"Yes, you damn well do!"

"Well, I'm sorry. I really am. Victoria told me to trust you. I guess all the financial problems I've been having, keeping the agency afloat, well, they made me see enemies everywhere. I'm really sorry I doubted you."

"You're forgiven." She looked around at the layouts on the walls. "Are you going to be okay?"

"Yes, I think we're going to make it."

"I'm glad. Now I'd better go home and get some sleep." Kate levered herself up out of the chair and started for the door. Mac followed her.

"Can Victoria and I take you to dinner tonight?" he asked. "She's been worried about you."

"Thanks, but I plan to sleep through dinner, and possibly breakfast, too."

"Well, how about lunch before the news conference?" Kate nodded. "Good. And now I'd better write that resignation statement." He opened the door and they went out into the corridor. "I never thought I'd say this about a multimillion-dollar account," he said with a smile, "but I can't wait to get rid of the bugger." Suddenly a crafty look came into his eyes. "Look, would you have a problem if I didn't mention fraud in my resignation statement? If I sort of danced around it a little?"

"What? Why would you want to do that?"

"I have a personal score to settle with a mutual acquaintance of ours. And I've just thought of a brilliant way to do it."

"But why would you want to protect Michael Nolan?"

"That is not my intention, I assure you." They'd reached the bank of elevators, and Mac pushed the call button. "You go straight home and get some sleep," he said kindly. "Tomorrow's going to be one hell of a day."

He splashed through the knee-high water, heading toward the sun. "Atalpa!" he called out. But Atalpa didn't answer. "Steve! The river's flooding!" But Steve wasn't there, either. Had they both been washed away? Was he alone now?

His face was burning hot, and he splashed water on his head and neck as he pressed on. An anaconda came swimming toward him, and he scrambled out onto the bank to avoid it. Funny, he thought he remembered a much larger snake passing them in the flood. This one was thin and brown. Suddenly he felt confused and dizzy, and sat down on the grassy bank. What was he doing here? Then he remembered: he was searching for the tribal gathering place. He had to save the plants. No, that wasn't right. He had to destroy them. The tribe wouldn't like that, but he'd explain it to Kuna very carefully.

From his shirt pocket, he took a tangerine, complimenting himself on not having eaten all his food at once. Who knew when the tribe would leave another basket of fruit? He peeled it and ate it slowly, making it last. It was very refreshing. He got up and resettled himself under some trees a short distance away. The ground was damp and muddy, but at least there was shade.

He licked his fingers, tasting the sweetness of the tangerine and wishing for water. Within minutes, he was asleep.

"There! What's that?" Nolan yelled into the headset.

The helicopter pilot peered through the Plexiglas in the direction Nolan was pointing. "I don't see anything," he said. "Want me to go down a little more?"

"Yes . . . no, don't bother. I can see it now. It's nothing, a tree or something."

The pilot pulled up again. "Don't you think we should call the cops? A man lost out here in the swamp like this?"

Nolan shook his head. "We'll find him," he said. But he wasn't so sure. Three hours had passed since Delta Airlines had deposited him in Miami and the helicopter pilot, booked by Jenny in New York, picked him up. They'd flown to the greenhouse, the pilot marveling at the size of it, and had managed to set down, after some maneuvering, in the marshy field behind the glass structure.

"Nice place you've got here," the pilot had said laconically as Nolan had leapt out and waved away the armed security men.

They'd scoured the area, Beach told him, but found nothing. He'd apologized again and again for allowing Tucker to escape, but Nolan had had no time for either blame or punishment. "Keep looking!" he'd ordered, then jumped back into the aircraft to do the same from the air.

"Sorry, sir, but I need to refuel," the pilot now told Nolan through the headset. "I've only got about fifteen minutes of reserve." He banked away over the swamp, heading for the major road they'd crossed earlier. Alligator Alley. A stiff breeze had sprung up, and the copter bounced around in the rough air.

"Shit," Nolan said with feeling. It was nearly five o'clock, and the shadows were lengthening.

"Pardon?"

"I said 'sure.' You think you can remember this spot? So we can come right back here?"

"No problem. The Everglades is my backyard."

The damn fool's in the swamp, Steve thought angrily as he skidded the car to a stop beside the Randall Foundation's chain-link fence. He's out in the goddamn swamp.

He'd been driving back and forth, on this road and every

other, small or large, that skirted the swamp and marshland on which the compound had been built, but with no luck. Now he got out and slammed the door hard. There was no way he was going into the swamp after Tucker, not at five-thirty in the afternoon. Besides, which section of swamp, exactly? Where should he start? Sure, Tucker was trying to find his way back to the greenhouse, but the area was lousy with swampland and practically plaid with canals and creeks. Tucker could be anywhere by now.

Someone had put a new chain on the gate and locked it shut. Well, he still had his bolt cutter in the trunk. Soon he was heading down the narrow road toward the glass pyramid. If he couldn't stop Tucker along the way, perhaps he could head him off at the compound. If Tucker got that far.

The approach road was familiar to him by now, and he slowed as he entered the junglelike thicket of trees that led to the giant greenhouse. Ahead, he could see the light of the clearing filtering through the foliage. He stopped the car, pulling it over as far as he could. Then he got out and walked, staying well inside the tree line.

I should have tried to track him in the swamp, he berated himself. I shouldn't have spent all that time driving around. Maybe I would have found him. Well, it was too late for second-guessing. He had no choice now but to wait right where he was. Sooner or later, Tucker would show up. Unless he was already dead.

He settled himself against a tree from which he had a partial view of the clearing in front of him. The light was fading. Overhead, he heard the flutter of a helicopter.

Tucker was on the move again, refreshed by his sleep though still thirsty. He plodded through the sticky marsh, choosing his way carefully. He knew he was headed in the right direction, though he couldn't have said why he felt so sure.

His arms were scratched and bleeding; insect bites pocked his neck and face. He'd searched in vain for the low plant with the wide fleshy leaves, the one the Indians used to ward off certain biting insects, but hadn't been able to find it. This puzzled him greatly; he remembered it growing in profusion along the trail.

He stopped and sipped the water in the nearby creek;

no, it didn't taste right. If only it would rain, and he could drink the runoff from the leaves. Ah, that was water!

A great white heron lifted from the marsh and he stood and watched it with wonder; then a sudden stab of light made him shut his eyes. After a moment, he opened them cautiously and looked around. The light struck again, but this time he didn't flinch, only closed his eyes a little so he could locate its source. And there it was: a giant shining triangle floating above the trees. The setting sun, reflecting off its pinnacle, flashed brilliant gold and red.

Like a lighthouse, beckoning him home.

It was quite near, he realized. Just beyond those trees. He set off across the marsh at a run.

"There! There!" Nolan yelled. He grabbed the pilot's arm and the helicopter wobbled, then righted itself.

"You want to get us killed?" the pilot shouted over the intercom.

"I saw him!" Nolan shouted. "He went into those trees back there! Follow him! Hurry!" Yawing and bouncing, the helicopter turned back toward the line of trees that separated the compound from the surrounding swamp. "Lower!" Nolan shouted through his headset. "Get lower!"

"We'll go into the goddamn trees!" the pilot shouted back, pulling up. This guy was nuts.

"Where the fuck are you going?" Nolan demanded.

"If your friend went in there, he'll come out the other side. In the compound or whatever the fuck that place is. Anyway, he's safe now, so I'm heading back. It's getting late."

"You fly where I tell you to fly!" Nolan told him angrily. Then, seeing the pilot's stubborn frown, he softened his voice. "Look, this is important to me," he said. "Two hundred bucks, off the books. On top of the hourly fee."

The pilot shot him a sideways glance. "Okay. But keep your goddamn hand off my arm."

Nolan nodded. "We're all right on fuel?"

"We're fine. Nearly three-quarters full." He pushed the stick forward and the helicopter descended, hovering just above the treetops. "You see anything down there?"

The beat of the approaching helicopter was loud now. It bounced off the huge glass panels and echoed through the small clearing. Steve watched the men come running out, sidearms drawn. Bobby Beach, easy to recognize by his bulk, held a shotgun. They disappeared around the side of the massive structure, eyes on the sky, and Steve followed, crossing the tiny parking lot at a run and cutting across the bordering marsh at an angle.

And suddenly there it was, just above the trees, a huge metal insect that dipped and tilted in the wind. The noise was fierce, and Steve covered his ears. The guards had stopped just ahead, eyes up, and Steve slowed his pace. They were facing away from him at the moment, but it wouldn't do to get too close.

Then he gasped as a thin, white-haired man stumbled out of the trees and ran raggedly through the marsh grass. "Look out!" he cried, for the helicopter was suddenly descending fast, but the sound of the rotors drowned his warning.

"Down! Down!" Nolan screamed at the pilot who was struggling to steady the craft as it bucked and pitched in the updrafts.

The security men had seen Tucker too, and they started toward him, then paused. The helicopter was awfully close.

Tucker, who had seemed oblivious to the huge noisy machine hovering above him, now looked up with a bemused expression. Sorry, Father Jim, but I'm not ready to leave yet. I still have work to do. He waved at the helicopter and smiled an apology, but Father Jim didn't seem to understand, because he kept on coming.

Helpless, Steve watched the helicopter, no more than a hundred feet off the ground, herd Tucker toward the security men. "Go back!" he yelled to Tucker, although he knew his voice would never carry. He waved his arms above his head. "Get into the trees!" And suddenly it looked as if Tucker had understood, because he verged to the left. But one of the guards did the same, cutting off his retreat. The aircraft was lower now, bobbing and weaving as it pursued Tucker like an angry wasp.

Beach had his shotgun on his shoulder, attempting to fix the running figure in his sights. But Tucker changed direction again and headed toward the glass pyramid, glowing red in the setting sun. Beach fired and missed, and Steve shouted hoarsely and started to run. Tucker feinted to one side, then the other, and kept on running. He had reached the greenhouse and was pounding on the panes when Beach fired again; glass shattered and showered, and the helicopter wobbled upward.

"What the fuck is going on?" the pilot yelled. "I'm getting out of here!"

"No! We have to stop him!" Nolan yelled. The pilot began to bank away toward the trees, but Nolan clapped his hand over the pilot's and dragged the joystick back the other way. "Go back! Go back!" The copter banked hard, swinging over onto its side and sliding back toward the greenhouse at a sickening angle. As the white-faced pilot wrestled for control, Nolan grabbed his shoulder and shook him. "Get down there!" he yelled.

Below, Bobby fired again, and another section of the greenhouse dissolved in a shower of heavy glass. The pilot heard the loud pings on the rear rotor, felt it buckle, and knew he was a dead man.

The helicopter began to tumble. Like a wounded bird, it spun and fell, shearing through the greenhouse panels and bounding off the cross-struts before it exploded in a tumbling, spinning fireball that spread burning jet fuel across the vulnerable plants below.

For a moment, the men stood mesmerized, staring at the flames that leapt into the evening sky, the greasy black smoke roiling above the bent and ruined structure like an evil cloud. Then Bobby gave a hoarse cry and started running, not toward the burning helicopter but away toward the parking lot and his car. The other guards followed close behind him. If they recognized Steve, or even noticed him, they gave no sign.

Steve ran toward the crumpled figure lying on a bed of bloody glass. Tucker's shirt was red, his legs twisted behind him at an impossible angle. Steve knelt beside his friend, tears running down his cheeks. He felt in the torn chest for a pulse, but found none, expected none. Gently he cradled Tucker, so thin, so light, in his arms, and wept.

Chapter 36

"In other business news, Richard Day has announced the formation of a new advertising agency to take over all advertising and marketing for Randall Webber's Genelife account immediately."

Day turned up the volume of the car radio and smiled. He'd been glued to the news since waking at seven-fifteen, and hadn't yet tired of the sound of his own success.

"Mr. Day's announcement late last night follows closely on the heels of the MacAllister Agency's resignation of the account, which was made quite suddenly at midday yesterday via phone calls and faxed press releases to print and broadcast media around the country. It's unusual that an outgoing agency should be so eager to advertise its disassociation with a client's business, especially one as prestigious as Genelife. However, Mr. MacAllister refused to explain why he chose to publicize his agency's decision in this way."

Day smirked; MacAllister's reasoning seemed perfectly clear to him. Mac had guessed what was coming and decided to get the jump on Nolan. He must have figured it was better to resign the account than to get canned.

He swung into the fast lane, passed a van and two cars, and swerved back into the middle of the turnpike doing sixty-five. For a moment he wondered whether Nolan would be angry that he'd announced without asking permission. Then he shrugged. Nolan had said to wait until Mac was out of the picture. Well, Mac had taken himself out yesterday, and very publicly, too. Besides, the immediate announcement of Richard Day Advertising was actually in Randall Webber's best interests. It indicated that Nolan had anticipated the situation, and been prepared.

"When pressed, Mr. MacAllister cited creative differences as a major reason for the resignation. The agency has won numerous awards for its work on Genelife."

The story was generating far more coverage than he'd expected. But his announcement within hours of Mac's resignation was unusual, and the media smelled blood.

"MacAllister also mentioned that his agency's research department had turned up evidence of a higher incidence of side effects than expected, and he expressed worry about the implications. He is quoted as saying, 'We don't want to be associated with any product that might be harmful to the consumer.' MacAllister was one of the first major agencies to refuse to advertise cigarettes."

For a moment, Day felt a twinge of trepidation. Then he shrugged it off. Another of Mac's little ploys to save face, he decided. Nolan had explained to him that the figures were spurious. There was nothing wrong with Genelife. Hell, they had FDA approval, didn't they? Mac was a weenie.

"When asked to comment on MacAllister's statement, Day would say only that Michael Nolan, chairman of Randall Webber, had assured him Genelife was safe. Day characterized MacAllister's attitude as, quote, 'timidity in the face of advanced technology,' unquote."

And so it is, Day thought complacently.

"Michael Nolan was unavailable for comment. Coming up, a traffic and transit update . . ."

Good for Michael, Day thought, switching off the radio. He's too smart to get involved in a cat fight. The point is, I've got the business.

And the second mortgage and the office lease and everything I own in hock for the media buys . . .

But that would be all right now. The account was his. All he needed was the cash. And cash was precisely why he was on his way to Nolan's office at eleven-thirty this very beautiful day. Both Nolan and his secretary had been unavailable when Day had telephoned that morning, but he was determined not to be put off.

I've announced, he thought. I saved Nolan's ass. He's got to pay me.

It was five minutes short of noon when he strode into the atrium lobby. The receptionist was staring somberly at the top of her desk as he approached, and he had to rap on the marble countertop to get her attention. When she finally looked up, he noticed her red-rimmed eyes and stepped back smartly. The last thing he needed right now was a cold!

"Richard Day," he said briskly. "To see Michael Nolan." Her mouth opened in a startled O.

"Michael Nolan!" he repeated impatiently. Where did they find these women?

"Mr. Nolan's ... he's ..." the receptionist's voice quavered.

"In a meeting? Tell his secretary I'll wait!"

"No, no ... uh, Mr. Nolan's ... he's dead."

"What? He's what?" Day felt a cold stab of fear in his chest. "Are you sure? But I saw him yesterday!"

"He was in a helicopter crash. In Florida. They called this morning. It's so terrible!"

Nolan dead! Jesus! He felt the prickle of sweat in his armpits. What was his own position now? What should he do? He couldn't wait for Nolan's replacement to be chosen; he needed that money immediately!

"Do you want to talk to his secretary?" the receptionist asked. "You can use that phone over there ..."

"Yes, I—no. No." Don't panic! he told himself. Think! He paced to the sitting area and stood looking out into the parking lot. Genelife still needs an agency, he told himself. Mac's still out and I'm still in. Nothing's really changed except the signature on the check. But whose signature would it be? Who would step in and run the business until Nolan's successor had been chosen? Who should he be talking to, now?

Then he thought: Bettina Hollis. Of course.

He turned back to the receptionist with a lighter step. "Can you get me Omni in Chicago?" he asked.

"Omni?" she said vaguely.

"Your parent company! Omni!" he barked impatiently. God, what an airhead.

"Oh, Omni! I think we have a Watts line ..." She consulted a large red-covered manual. "Yes, here's the number." She looked up at him. "I'm really sorry. Everything's kind of upset today."

Richard nodded sympathetically. "I understand." Just dial the goddamn number!

"Who would you like to talk to at Omni?"

"Bettina Hollis."

The receptionist nodded. "I'll put it through to that phone over there on the coffee table," she told him. She consulted the manual again and began to dial.

"Jesus, Bettin—uh, Mrs. Hollis! Turn on the television!"

Bettina looked up and regarded her executive assistant with displeasure. "Another slip like that, William, and you'll be back in the trainee program at IBM," she said severely. "And straighten your jacket."

"But, Mrs. Hollis! They're talking about Genelife!"

"They're always talking about Genelife," she told him complacently. "That's why we have such a large public relations budget." But she went to the rosewood cabinet and swung back its doors. "What channel?"

"All of them. God, it's terrible—"

She heard the sound before the picture faded up, and the words sent a chill of fear through her. ". . . substituting a plant-derived enzyme for the FDA-approved synthetic . . ."

Three people, a woman and two men, sat facing the camera. She recognized Nick Butler, but who was the big blond? And that woman who was speaking, she knew she'd seen her before . . . Then her name was superimposed on the screen and Bettina thought: Of course, Kate Martin, the woman Nolan was planning to fire. Was this piece of slander her revenge?

"Call our attorneys!" she barked over her shoulder. "I want a meeting in here! Now!"

But as she watched, she quickly realized that this was not the stunt of a disgruntled employee. She staggered to a chair, horrified at the story of fraud and greed unfolding on the screen. She heard the legal staff enter the office behind her, but she didn't turn around. She couldn't. She was shaking. What had that prick gotten them into? What would she tell Tokyo? How could she save herself?

William appeared at her side with a glass of mineral water, but she grabbed it and hurled it across the room. It smashed against a wall. "Get me that bastard Nolan," she ordered. She paced between desk and window, snorting with fury, as William dialed the number. He spoke softly and listened. Then, ignoring her outstretched hand, he hung up the receiver.

"What the hell's the matter with you?" she turned on him. "I want to talk to that sonofabitch!"

But William shook his head. "Michael Nolan's dead," he said quietly. "His secretary got the call about half an hour ago."

"Dead? Let me talk to her! Call her back!"

"Please, Mrs. Hollis. She's crying ... everyone's upset ..."

"Nonsense. Nolan wasn't that lovable." An intake of breath behind her told her she'd shocked one of the attorneys. Probably the young one. Welcome to the real world, kid, she thought. She turned back to the screen. Butler was talking now. "What happened to him?" she asked William over her shoulder.

"A helicopter accident in Florida. They took him to a burn unit in Miami. He died this morning."

So Nolan was dead. Well, she couldn't be happier. Michael had really fucked them over. Defrauding the FDA! Defrauding *her*! Bettina's eyes were fixed on the television but her mind was churning. Damage control, she thought. What can I do? We'll pull the product, of course. Establish a fund to develop an antidote. Omni is innocent. I'm innocent. She remembered Nolan telling her about firing Martin and the ad agency. She'd suspected that bastard was up to something, but not anything like this! Should she have probed more deeply? It was easy to say yes now, after the fact. But Tokyo expected results, insisted on them, and Nolan had delivered. Whatever he was doing had been good for everybody's bottom line. Until now.

She stalked back to her desk and sank into the pale leather chair. None of this was her fault, dammit! But she knew Omni would blame her anyway; she was supposed to be Nolan's keeper. Shit! Well, maybe there was a way to twist the history of the project a little, invent a few conversations she and Michael had never had, produce copies of some back-dated memos. I probed and questioned, she thought. Again and again, I asked for clarifications, reassurances, and I received them. How could I know Nolan was lying to me? Her spirits began to rise a little. I'll put it all on Nolan. He's dead anyway.

She could hear the telephones ringing out in the corridor. Every line on her desk phone was alight and blinking. William dropped a sheaf of pink message slips on her desk but she waved him away. She'd need to think very carefully before she spoke to Tokyo or the press.

The company would take a terrific financial beating, of course. The lawsuits would go on for years. But her hands were clean. She'd find a way to survive.

She turned to the attorneys and began to speak, but William was back with more message slips. "I thought you understood—" she began angrily, but he leaned forward and spoke softly into her ear. "All right, all right. I'm sorry, gentlemen," she said to the attorneys. "It seems one of Randall Webber's would-be suppliers hasn't turned on his television this morning. No, don't leave," she added as she crossed the Chinese carpet to her Regency desk. "This will only take a moment. What line, William?"

"Three."

So Richard Day expected to be paid as agency of record, starting today . . . She reached for the phone, savoring the moment. Day had fronted a great deal of his own money, waiting for Nolan to dump MacAllister and award him the Genelife account. Well, Genelife was dead, and so was Day; he just didn't know enough to lie down. She recalled his smarmy innuendos at the cocktail party in Scottsdale, and smiled grimly; she was going to enjoy this. She stabbed one of the lighted buttons with a manicured forefinger. "Good morning, Mr. Day," she said pleasantly. "Are you anywhere near a television set?"

Chapter 37

"Nick Butler's just heard from Bettina," Kate reported as she hung up the gold-and-white telephone. "She's asked him to put together a research team, here in New York, to search for an antidote. He offered me a spot."

Steve's expression was consciously noncommittal. It's her decision, he thought.

"I told him 'thanks but no thanks,' " she continued, sinking down next to Steve on the plush velvet love seat. "I've had enough of the corporate world." She smiled as she saw Steve's face brighten. "I suggested they involve Chemstra. They have more experience with the drug than anyone else."

"Except Tucker," Steve said softly. "If only—"

Kate reached over and squeezed his hand.

"But wasn't Chemstra involved in the phony test results the FDA was given?" Mac asked.

Kate shook her head. "No, Chemstra's straight. Oh, their president may have kicked money back to Nolan, who set him up in business. But as far as everyone at Chemstra knew, Genelife contained the synthetic they'd made and tested."

Victoria sighed. "I keep thinking about what would have happened if you and Kate hadn't tracked down that poor Tucker Boone," she told Steve. "We still wouldn't know about that terrible side effect. People would still be using Genelife." She shuddered.

"I told you Tucker had been the victim of foul play!" Avram reminded Steve complacently. " 'Life follows art.' More cappuccino?"

Steve had flown up from Florida that morning with Tucker's body, then gone to comfort Marianne. He'd caught up with Kate at the end of the press conference, and suggested she and Mac flee the ringing phones and curiosity seekers who would surely descend upon them, and take refuge in Avram's town house. Victoria, who had accompanied Mac to the television studio, had come, too.

"I still feel a little guilty about not letting Omni know what was up, before we went public this afternoon," Mac said. "Seeing it on television is one helluva way to find out your company's been shot in the heart."

"I know," Kate agreed. "But we couldn't be sure how deep the thing went. What if Bettina Hollis had been involved?" She reached for a sugared cruller, hesitated, then thought what the hell. "And speaking of being shot in the heart," she said, "what about that little stunt you pulled with Richard Day?"

"Ah, your old flame," Mac said wickedly. Steve looked startled and Kate colored slightly. "I set him up beautifully, didn't I? Of course, I wasn't responsible for his losing all that money—he fronted a fortune, apparently, on the understanding that Randall Webber would assign Genelife to him once I was out of the picture. No, all I cost him were his reputation and credibility. Which he wouldn't have lost if he hadn't been so eager to one-up me."

"You egged him on. You taunted him."

"Not at all," Mac said blandly. "I issued a simple statement and answered a few questions. I did it rather well, I think. These crullers are delicious, Avram!"

"I'm glad you enjoy them," Avram answered graciously. "You must take some home with you."

"No, he mustn't," Victoria said. "He's developing quite a little paunch." She patted his stomach fondly.

"So. You are going back to being a doctor," Avram said to Kate. "And where will you practice your healing arts? I understand there is a great need of doctors in Boston." He winked conspiratorially at Steve, who raised his eyes to the ceiling and sighed.

"I'm not really sure," Kate told him. "I miss the excitement of the kind of medicine I used to practice. But emergency room doctors don't exactly open offices." She paused. "I could go back to New York General. Or another hospital somewhere," she added quickly, seeing Steve's face. "This last year has changed me a lot . . . I think I'd do a lot better, from a personal standpoint, than I did before."

"And you'll have Steve," Avram told her. "Right there beside you, loving and supportive and understanding . . ."

Kate and Victoria both laughed, but Steve flushed.

"Well, somebody has to say something!" Avram protested hotly. "Come on, nephew! Tell her how you feel!"

"She *knows* how I feel!" Steve looked over at Kate, and his heart jumped as he realized how deep his feelings went.

"Then tell her to come live with you in Boston!"

"She's a free agent." Steve said firmly, his eyes fixed on Kate's. "She makes her own decisions."

"Yes, of course," said Avram testily, "but you have to give her something to decide *about*! She can't read your mind!"

"Oh, I think she can," Steve said softly as Kate reached over and touched his cheek.

Thoroughly exasperated, Avram flung out his arms. "Romance!" he proclaimed. "It is dead!"

"Oh, I wouldn't be too sure," Victoria murmured as Steve wrapped Kate in his arms.

". . . so I thought you and Amzona would be the logical people to help us mount such an expedition," Bettina was saying. She twirled the phone cord nervously in her fingers. "Since you're already on the spot, so to speak. And we're family." Diplomacy was called for, she decided. Despite the fact that the Amzona Development Corporation was also owned by Omni, its president Brian Link was under no obligation to help her.

"Yes, I got yer fax, luv," Link said in the thick cockney accent she was having such trouble deciphering. A self-made millionaire, Link took great pleasure in flaunting his modest beginnings. "But wot about the plants in that green'ouse o' yours?"

Lord knows what his Portuguese is like, Bettina thought. "Ruined," she replied. "Much of the stock was burned or smoke damaged. The rest . . . well, we're talking about an isolated mini-environment, very sensitive. When the greenhouse itself was destroyed . . . Listen, you people have been getting a lot of bad press lately. Help us gather plants for our antidote research, and you'll suddenly be heroes." And so will I, she thought. A successful antidote program will put me back in favor with Omni.

"Okay, luv, I'll see wot we can do. These are the coordinates?"

"Yes, Dr. Butler retrieved them from Tucker Boone's

computer disk." She shuffled through the papers on her desk and retrieved the original of the roughly drawn map she'd faxed to Amzona along with her letter outlining the situation. "Do you think your men can find the place?"

"Hang on a minute, luv. Lorenzo's just come in. This is his bailiwick." Bettina tapped her fingers irritably on the table. Come on! she thought. Don't make a federal case out of this. Federal case; bad choice of metaphor.

"Listen, boyo," she heard Brian tell Lorenzo, "Omni needs 'elp with that Genelife debacle ... pickin' flowers or summat. No, I don't know where, but that there's 'er fax. 'Ave a butcher's and tell me wot you think." There was a crinkle of paper as the fax was handed over, then a pause while its contents were read and digested. At last Brian came back on the line. "Lorenzo runs the field operation, luv," he told her. "You best talk it over with 'im."

The phone was handed over before she could protest. "Mrs. Hollis? This is Lorenzo Delgado."

"How do you do, Mr. Delgado. As you know, we're caught in a ... situation here. Omni would be very grateful if you could—"

"I have read your letter and I would truly like to help. But I fear we have a problem."

"A problem? I certainly hope not. If it's money, I could arrange a substantial—"

"No, not money. It is the place."

"The place?"

"The location of which you write. The coordinates, they are accurate?"

"I believe so, yes. Why?"

"Well, that place ... I am very sorry, Mrs. Hollis. But we cannot take plants from that place."

"Don't be ridiculous!" Bettina replied firmly. "Surely you can arrange some protection from the local Indians!"

"It is not the Indians—"

"Superstition, then? I understand the plants are used in some sort of primitive ceremony. Is there some curse associated with the place? Are the men afraid? Is that it?"

"No, no! Please allow me to speak! We will not be able to send men to gather plants from that place, because that place no longer exists."

"What are you saying?" Bettina gasped.

"Amzona has been conducting logging operations in the

region for several years," he explained. "We have many teams. I have the work orders right here. We have been clearing that particular grid for the last week—"

"Well, stop them! Can't you stop them?"

"I'm afraid that would not be possible. The field office is some distance from the site, and we do not fly into the area at night. The earliest we could contact them would be tomorrow afternoon, and by then I'm quite certain—"

But Bettina Hollis was no longer listening. She stared unseeing at the glorious sunset outside her office window, and considered the bitter irony of what she had just learned.

EPILOGUE

Kuna led the remnants of his tiny tribe down to the river. Behind him, their land lay ravaged, dying. Ahead, two boats bobbed in the water, waiting to take them from their homeland.

Their possessions were few, but it had always been thus. Bows, a few arrows, and something new: a broken mirror carefully preserved. Suddenly a strange whine filled the air; they could hear trees crashing to the ground. Kuna's face was tight with pain, but he walked on.

At the end of the short procession came the shaman in his conical hat. He carried a sheaf of leaves bound with vines, cradling it as he would a child: tenderly, lovingly. Kuna, the last chief, stopped. He turned around and gestured. "Leave it here," he told the shaman. "We will have no need of that in our new life."

Sadly, slowly, reverently, the shaman laid down the bundle of leaves at the water's edge. Then he turned and followed the others to the waiting boats. They were large, strong boats. Never had he seen such boats.

Indians from the mission helped them in. Father Larry was there, too, smiling and nodding his head. How he had prayed for this day. Now everyone was on board. The boats moved out into the current.

Behind them, the bundle of leaves floated out onto the river. The current carried it along in the wake of the boats; the eddies pushed it from side to side. The shaman turned and watched.

The sheaf of leaves trailed the boats for a while, falling farther and farther behind. Then its vine wrappings snagged on a branch hanging low over the water. Half-submerged, the green bundle bobbed gently up and down against the bank.

The boats disappeared around a bend in the river.